Skald

The Branded Trilogy
Book 1

J.A. Guynn

Acknowledgements

Thank you to my wife for putting up with the weirdness that comes with living with a writer.

Thank you to Emily Armstrong for her efforts as a beta-reader, even when she growled at me. Emily, without your critique and suggestions, Skald would not be the same.

ISBN: 979-8-9856947-6-5

Library of Congress Control Number: 2022905838

Cover Design: 100covers.com

Editor: Charlie Knight at cknightwrites.com

Proofreader: Mark Schultz, the Hyper-Speller at www.wordrefiner.com

Publisher: 3220 Group, LLC. Alvin, TX

Publisher Note:

Chapter 1

Though my guards secured the area and Crum stood nearby, bow at the ready, Roi and I glanced over our shoulders as we created memorials. I clenched my jaw and wiped sweat away from my eyes. Fear of the raiders returning to finish their attack made it hard to keep my hand steady as I worked.

Four in total: a husband, two teenaged boys, and a young daughter. Making headstones was the least I could do for the poor woman they'd left behind.

I stood with my arm around the widow as my men lowered her family into the ground. *Family farms should be a source of happiness, not used as a graveyard.* We wept together as dirt flowed over them, sealing their bodies in the soil. The acrid smell of burnt wood mixed with the stench of dead livestock engraved itself in my memory the same way my finger dug into the stone, writing the family's names in the cool, dark, Hornblende burial markers.

"Do you have family to go to?" I asked her.

Her head bobbed once.

"My guards will travel with you to keep you safe."

She pulled me to her, hugging me tightly.

Four farms sacked. Twenty-eight graves in two weeks. This can't continue. I need the Thanes to return the warriors they ordered back to the capital.

Snapping fingers interrupted my thoughts.

• • • ● • ● • ● • •

I was back in my study, safe inside the gray stone walls and sitting at the table across from my mother.

"Fitzeirick, focus. This is important," she said, snapping her fingers once more.

I forced my concerns over Satra out of my thoughts and faked interest in the menu for my wedding feast. Every time I expressed my satisfaction, my mother found some little detail she insisted on changing. This time I tapped my foot and crossed my arms when she suggested switching the preserved pears for spiced, minced apples.

"Mother, it's food. Everyone will be happy to have a free meal."

She glared at me across the table and the candle in the alcove nearest her flared to life. "You're the son of Eirick, it's vital to make the right impression on your guests, especially the royals. They can't think the man governing Croy's newest skati is an uncultured commoner."

I'm only his son because he took you as a mistress.

"I doubt a single member of the Council of Thanes will travel this far east. You and I both know Jarl Eirickson won't bother to attend," I argued. "Since Father died, they couldn't care less about us. They'll send their least favorite hird, or even a squire, to represent them. I wouldn't be surprised if they tell the backstabbing schemers to stay awhile and spy on me."

"Nonsense. Your father made you a skald for a reason. Ruling over this territory is a stepping-stone to greater things. They have to come. Neither the councilmen nor your half-brother would ignore their traditional duties. Now, back to the topic at hand...I have a compromise."

I could almost taste the sugar in her voice. "What did you have in mind?

"We'll leave the menu as it is and move forward. The first dance."

"I don't dance."

My mother glanced toward the ceiling, then leaned forward and locked eyes with me. "You must dance with Aesa. You can't dishonor tradition and I won't allow you to insult her."

I shook my head. "I move with the grace of a lame draft horse. Aesa's the beautiful, graceful half of this couple. All eyes will be on her when she takes the floor. I might as well be invisible."

"If everyone's watching her, your clumsiness won't matter," she countered, smiling. "This is not open for debate. We have a month, more than enough time to teach you, and you will put an honest effort into the lessons. If I must, I'll have Roi escort you."

I tapped my fingers on the table, then pointed at her. "I do *not* dance."

She opened her mouth to respond, but jumped at the unexpected knock on the door. "I thought you set aside today to finish planning your wedding," she said, inking the quill.

I did, but I can't ignore my duties. Of course, I didn't dare say that to her.

"We will finish today. I don't know what your hurry is. There's no reason to rush. Aesa and I are both young and healthy. I'll make sure you have grandchildren to dote over. As a matter of fact, I plan to spend a lot of time working on that during our honeymoon."

The fire in her eyes told me I'd crossed a line.

"Roi knows to not disturb us unless absolutely necessary," I explained and turned to the door. "Come in."

Mother sighed.

My mentor stepped into the room. The creases in his forehead made a staircase to his bald scalp. *That expression never brings good news.*

He bowed. "Modir Sar'sa, I apologize for interrupting. Fitzeirick, the messenger returned with a sealed letter. He said you aren't going to like it."

How could they refuse my request for aid again?

I took the parchment, glanced over it, and read the official decision aloud. "As before, this is a regional dispute and not a concern of the Council of Thanes. Request denied."

My jaw clenched tight as my fist closed, wadding the message. I glared at it, wishing to be a firesyth, just once, so I could burn the Thane's refusal as it fell to the floor. Instead, I stomped on it and prepared to ground it into dust. "Fitzeirick," my mother barked.

"What?" I snapped back.

"Calm yourself. The floor's shaking."

It took a moment before I noticed the floor *was* trembling. I closed my eyes and took a deep breath to calm myself. "Can you blame me? The Thanes call these raids a regional dispute? The Satra nation sends soldiers into Croy, and the council doesn't consider it a deliberate act of war? What is wrong with —"

"Let me through! I must see the skald!"

Commotion in the hallway cut off my rant. A shiver ran down my back as Roi stepped out. He returned with a guard following him.

The guard coughed. "Beg pardon Skald Fitzeirick. Another raid from the south. A young man collapsed near the southern post. He's in bad shape, but managed to tell us about the raid on his family's farm yesterday evening. Men wearing blue and red, just like the last survivor described. He's the only one that got away. We sent for a herbalist, but it may be too late."

I looked at my mother and watched the color leave her face as I felt my cheeks grow warm. "The wedding plans can wait," I stated flatly. "I need to see to my people. Roi, get your sword and meet me at the stable."

Roi grabbed my shoulder. "Bad idea."

"Why?"

"Could be a trap. Why'd the raids stop after leaving one witness? Before the widow, nothing was left alive — not even crops went untouched. Now they let another escape. We have to consider the possibility Satran soldiers are lying in wait. If Satra captures or kills you, what happens to your skati? Too risky."

"I'll bring the guards from the southern post," I replied.

"And leave it unmanned?" Roi asked.

I threw up my hands. "I have to do something."

"I have a suggestion," Mother offered. "Go to the capital. Plead your case before the Council of Thanes in person."

"I should do something for the victims."

"If I may?" the guard said.

I nodded.

"I'll get three or four men to escort a couple of herbalists to the farm. If we find more survivors, we'll see to them. If not, we'll give them a proper burial."

I clenched my jaw for a second. "Hurry and take a stonesyth with a steady hand. The victims deserve proper headstones."

The guard hurried out, almost tripping himself.

I turned back to my mother. "You're right, I have to make the demand to the council myself. The raiders are slaughtering my people. I'll be back in five days, six at the most. Work with Aesa on the wedding plans. She'll be the centerpiece of the ceremony, after all. You two plan everything while I make sure I have a skati to be skald of. Roi, find Crum. Get the necessary supplies and meet me at the stable."

He nodded and hurried from the room, closing the door behind him.

Gathering the documents spread across the table, she looked at me and smiled. "I'm proud of you. Travel swift and safe."

Looking at the floor, I shook my head. "I'm not ready for this."

Mother cleared her throat. "Your father believed in you."

My head snapped up. I stared at her for a moment, slack-jawed. "How can you say he believed in me? Father left me on my own after making me a skald. He didn't even provide an advisor."

She pulled me into a hug and whispered in my ear, "He wanted you to be your own man. To govern without someone influencing your decisions. He thought it would make you a better leader and prepare you to sit on the Council of Thanes one day. I suspect Eirickson's hand in the trouble you're having."

I stepped back from her. "If he's behind this, what hope do I have? The Jarl can overrule the council."

She shook her head. "Why are you asking questions you already know the answer to? Don't be stone headed. Get the council on your side. Even as Jarl, I doubt Eirickson is bold enough to go against a unanimous decision in your favor."

"Assuming you're right, how do I secure their support?"

She smiled. "This is your first appearance before the council in some time, you must make the right impression. Dress like a proper Croian Skald." She paused and shook her finger at me. "And wear the family sword, not your hammer."

"I prefer my hammer when I have to fight."

The rest of the candles around the room burst into flame as she fixed me with a hard stare. For a heartbeat, they were brighter than the sunlight streaming through the windows.

She pursed her lips. "Fitzeirick, think. You're going to negotiate, not fight. If you go in looking for a fight, Eirickson will use that to turn the council against you. The sword represents your authority, Eirick's support. Make the right impression on the council and secure your skati. Keep your people safe."

She's right, as usual. I looked away from her for a moment, turned back, and nodded.

She grunted and strode out of the room, her short, brown hair bouncing with every step.

I considered what she said and packed my skaldic stole and the ornate sword. Looking at my hammer, I hesitated for a moment before packing it too. *Just in case.*

Making my way to the stable, I spared a moment to hope my mother calmed down before she got to Aesa's house. An argument between firesyths could end with burning buildings.

Quickly tacking my horse, I walked it out of the stable and squinted against the bright, midday sun. Crum stood on the other of his horse, his shaggy, brown hair more disheveled than usual.

"Good to see you, my friend," I called out.

He snorted and walked around his horse. His crumpled clothes looked slept in and I couldn't miss a chance to tease him. "I think you missed a belt loop or two."

He stomped over to me, putting us eye to eye. His bloodshot eyes confirmed my suspicion. "I want you to know I planned to sleep in today." He pointed his thumb over his shoulder. "Instead, this oaf rousted me. He told me about the letter and the attack. You know I hate the capital."

I heard Roi snicker.

"Sleeping in? It's nearly midday. More like sleeping it off, I'd guess. If you prefer, I'll send you to assist my mother and Aesa while they plan the wedding and festivities."

He shook his head and shivered. "No way I'm getting between those two. Aesa's the right woman for you, but she scares me and Sar'sa doesn't care for me at all."

Roi snorted and I didn't try to hide my smile.

"Aesa scares you because she's one of the few women around here immune to your advances, but you're wrong about my mother. She likes you well enough, but not your cavalier attitude toward growing up."

He rolled his eyes at me.

"And why do you hate the capital? You'll find plenty of young ladies you haven't charmed yet. Who knows? Maybe this trip will reward you with a fiancée of your own."

Crum sputtered as he walked back to his horse.

I worried Roi might pass out from choking back actual laughter.

After buckling my pack behind the saddle, I pulled a little strength from the ground to help me get mounted and shifted around until the saddle felt comfortable. *I need to ride more often.*

"Can we please get this trip underway?" Crum asked, settling into his saddle. "Where are we going to sleep tonight?"

Roi caught his breath and mounted his horse. "As long as we keep a good pace, we'll cross the river before needing to find someone to put us up for the night."

"Should I send a messenger ahead?" I asked.

Roi shook his head. "No messenger would arrive ahead of us."

"Lead the way," I said, and we spurred our horses into a comfortable trot.

He led us west through the small market square not far from my hall. Most of the merchants were busy, but a few noticed me and waved or bobbed their heads.

I smiled and waved back.

The guards at the western post snapped to attention as we passed.

We stuck to the well-worn path used by farmers and woodsmen to deliver their goods to the market in town. Smaller trails snaked away toward houses, farms, and shops. Except for a few farmers working their fields, we were the only people around. I breathed slowly and let some tension leave my shoulders.

"How will Eirickson react to your request to address the Thanes?" Crum asked.

I stared at him for a moment. *Mother has a point; he needs to grow up and pay attention.* "All Croian Skalds have the right to speak before the council and make requests. I expect him to allow me to present the facts. The Satran army *is* invading our country through my Skati."

Roi shook his head. "With all due respect, I don't think that's what he's asking."

"I know," I grumbled.

"How about this," Crum started, "when did you last speak with the Jarl?"

"At our father's funeral."

He gave a long whistle. "You didn't attend Brunor Jani's funeral?"

I looked at him. "I wasn't invited."

He nodded. "I'd heard only the Thanes attended the burial. Rumor has it Eirickson commanded her death. Some say he killed her himself."

Who starts such ridiculous rumors? "Please don't tell me you believe such nonsense. My half-brother and I may not see eye-to-eye, but it's not right for people to talk about our Jarl like that. Eirickson's got a cruel streak and a cold heart, but involvement in his own mother's death would be a new low. Crum, in the future, I want to know about rumors like that."

"Yes, my skald," he said, in a mocking tone, bowing in his saddle.

I pinched the bridge of my nose and sighed. "Roi, remind me why I told you to get Crum? I'm having trouble remembering why he's here."

"I didn't want to come in the first place," Crum argued.

Roi shook his head for a moment. "I'm sure it had something to do with his ability to get out of bad situations almost as easy as he gets into them."

"Ah, yes," I responded. "You are the voice of reason, Roi. Thanks for reminding me of the many benefits of having Crum in my company. He serves a purpose other than entertainment."

"Entertainment? Have you forgotten who all but saved your life when you fought Olver?" Crum asked.

"That would be Roi. Olver bested both of us."

"Fine, but I kept you from getting hurt when you decided it'd be a good idea to break a wild horse."

"Yes, you did. I fell on you when he bucked me off and then I had to carry you home with a broken leg," I drawled.

"Only because you wouldn't let me syth a brace."

"We were in the middle of a field with no wood in sight."

"Well...I guess you have a point, but who introduced you to your fiancée?" Crum demanded, his tone haughty and playful.

Roi barked out a laugh.

I grinned. "Thanks to one of your misguided attempts at romance."

Roi joined in. "And what a memorable meeting it was. She ran into you, knocked you out. She thought she'd killed you. Poor girl was white as fresh cotton, scared she'd end up imprisoned or worse. You woke and it was love at first sight. Ah, good times! Crum, it might be a good idea to quit while you are behind and save some face for once."

Crum snorted. "When you put it that way, why do you keep me around?"

"You and Roi will always have my back. The royal court is full of schemers and I know I can trust you two."

Crum grinned. "I do my best to keep the women from distracting you. It's a tough job, but someone's got to do it."

Roi groaned. "I'm sure Fitzeirick appreciates your hard work."

"The job is its own reward," he replied.

"At least I have Roi for a moral compass," I commented.

"A quality of all great men," Roi said.

"Great man," Crum scoffed.

"Of course, great men are never appreciated until they are gone," Roi replied.

As the friendly jabs continued, I suspected they were purposely trying to get my mind off the ugly business driving me to the capitol. *Of course, Crum never takes anything too serious.* That thought brought a smile to my face and I decided to let myself relax and try to enjoy the journey.

Our shadows grew long before I sent Crum ahead to find somewhere to rest. As he rode out of sight, Roi muttered, "I don't want to ride in the dark hoping to find Crum when he comes back."

"I agree. Let's pick up our pace a little, if nothing else to shorten his ride back."

We urged our horses to speed up and soon caught sight of Crum galloping toward us on a different horse.

"I found a farm not far from here. They made me take their horse so mine could rest. When the farmer heard you needed board, he insisted you spend the night in his bed. They're preparing a feast for you. I tried to talk them out of it. They wouldn't listen."

I sighed. "That isn't what I wanted. A warm, dry place to lay our heads after a modest meal would have been fine."

"I tried to convince them," Crum assured me. "I even insisted you'd slept in hay barns before, but that didn't matter to them."

Why must my title be such a burden? All I need is a simple meal and warm, safe place for the night. I shook my head and sighed heavily. "Fine, lead the way. What's the farmer's name? Maybe I can talk him into not giving up his own bed for the night."

"Arnfred. But I don't think you're going to change his mind."

Chapter 2

We pushed the horses to a faster pace and soon arrived at a modest farmhouse. Two young women stood waiting by the gate. They waved and called out, "Crum's back, Skald Fitzeirick's with him."

I shot a sideways glance at Crum as the horses slowed.

"Oh," he said, through a delighted smile. "Did I forget to mention Arnfred and Juliana have twin daughters? I'd like you to meet Tona and Maren."

I tried to tell them apart. Same long, thin, sandy blonde hair, light-brown eyes, and crooked grin. Even their simple, tan, cotton dresses matched. *Can't be older than sixteen.*

The girls curtsied when I dismounted.

"That's not necessary," I told them with a smile.

"Of course, it is," a weathered man said, walking toward us. "It's rare to see any nobles out this way, much less our skald." He bowed his head as he finished.

Roi dismounted and we unlashed our packs.

"My son will take care of your belongings. Tona, Maren, take Skald Fitzeirick and his men to the table." He looked back over this shoulder and yelled, "Thile, see to the horses and get their packs to the house."

The sisters took Crum's hands and led him down a well-worn path.

Roi followed, shaking his head and muttering, "I should have known. Of course, he'd find twins." I knew him well enough to hear the exasperation in his voice.

I paused, wanting to say something to our host in private.

A young man, Thile, most likely, with a sparse beard ran past Crum and the twins. He stood taller than the girls, was broader across the shoulders, and his forearms carried the thick muscle of a laborer. His plain, cotton shirt had several patches and his leather pants showed wear.

I offered Arnfred my hand. "This is all unnecessary. My friends and I only need a meal and a warm, dry place to sleep. Giving up your bed is too much. I didn't come here to be a burden."

Arnfred shook my hand and looked me in the eye. "I've heard of your modesty, but it wouldn't do for my house to spare anything for you. My wife, Juliana, raised a longer table out back to make sure we had room. I'd feel ashamed to give you less than our best."

I nodded. "We appreciate your generosity. It is my honor to eat with your family."

Arnfred walked with a slight limp as he led me behind his home. His dark, wrinkled skin told a story of many years working in the sun. Light-brown hair showed more than its fair share of gray. His clothes, like Thile's, looked worn, but cared for.

As we passed the house, he bowed again and waved me toward a stone table ringed with wooden chairs. Not far away a yearling cow hung over an open fire pit. The smell of roasting meat drifted across the yard, making my mouth water.

As I expected, Crum stayed near the twins trying to entertain them. An older woman, Juliana I assumed, kept a wary eye on him while chopping vegetables.

If I tried to work like that without watching the knife, I'd take off all my fingers.

She looked weathered, like her husband, but worked with confidence as she tended the meal.

Roi stood off to one side, watching for trouble...keeping an eye on Crum.

Crum saw me and stood before proclaiming, "Citizens of Croy, I present Skald Fitzeirick," then bowed with a flourish.

The twins copied him while Juliana curtsied. Arnfred and Thile dropped to one knee and bowed their heads. My cheeks warmed. "I appreciate your hospitality, but please, no more formality. Let us eat as friends."

Arnfred rose. "Skald Fitzeirick, we're not friends. You're the leader of this skati, ruler of the territory. You honor my family; please accept our respect. You've already met my son and daughters. This is my wife, Juliana."

The woman stood from her curtsy and walked toward me. When she got within arm's reach, she held out her hand and looked at the ground. Her long, blonde and gray hair spilled forward covering her face.

I took her hand. "Lady Juliana, thank you for the meal. I see where your daughters get their beauty."

As I released her hand, she murmured, "Thank you, skald," and returned to cooking.

"Smells like everything will be ready soon," Arnfred said. "Please take the head of the table."

I decided against arguing and sat. Crum and Roi took their places to my left and right. The family sat a respectful distance from us. "This is your house and your food, please sit with us," I urged them.

The twins moved first, jostling for position next to Crum. Their father cleared his throat and one of them gave up, opting to sit across the table from my best friend, next to Roi. Arnfred took the seat opposite mine and his son sat to his left, leaving the seat to the right for Juliana.

"Girls, perhaps we'd eat a little sooner if you two helped your mother," Arnfred suggested. They both apologized and left to help with the final preparations.

I looked at my companions. "How about you two help with the heavy lifting?"

They nodded and offered their assistance.

"My wife's a strong stonesyth, heavy lifting's not an issue," Arnfred said, with a thin smile.

"My friends should help. You are putting us up for the night," I replied.

The farmer nodded and watched Crum 'working' near the twins.

I hope he doesn't cause trouble.

After a short silence, Thile spoke, "Skald, Crum said you're going to ask the Council for troops to defend our borders. Do you think they'll send the help you need?"

His father shot him a look, but I waved, letting him know I didn't mind the question.

"Matters of the court can get complicated, often more than they should be. Without realizing it, the guards at the passage between Croy and Varia also deterred Satran attacks. For some reason, the Council of Thanes moved those forces elsewhere. I expected them to return the warriors as soon as they received word of the first incursion, but they didn't. After the most recent attacks, refusal is no longer acceptable."

Arnfred looked confused. "What's complicated about this? Croian people are in danger."

I nodded and tried to not sound frustrated. "I agree. They refuse to send the aid we need. Jarl Eirickson doesn't care for me which, I'm sure, isn't helping. It's a family matter."

"A family matter?" Juliana echoed, as she placed a platter of meat in the middle of the table.

I smiled at her and shook my head. "Let's not dwell on the shortcomings of my half-brother. Please, Arnfred, tell me about yourself and your family."

Everyone filled their plates. "Not much to tell. We've farmed for generations. My ancestors worked land around the capital before settling here. I took over part of the land after Juliana and I married. I'm not afraid of hard work, but my sything is weak. I can make straight lines in a field easy enough, move the dirt back over seed, and not much more. Juliana's the strong one."

She took his hand. "I do the hard, messy work, but the girls keep this place going. Tona and Maren, talented woodsyths on their own, are artists when they work together. Truth is our home would fall to the ground, if not for my daughters' attentions. Not to overlook the way they have with the crops and trees; this farm will never be as productive when they leave to start their own families."

The twins blushed.

"My wife tells the truth," Arnfred said, "but we can't overlook Thile's efforts. He can stonesyth a little. Has a nose for ore to be honest, and enough talent to increase his stamina. His strength is firesything. Taught himself how to heat the ore he finds and work it into tools. He made these plates along with the knives, forks, and spoons. I think he has a future as a blacksmith, if I could find a mentor."

Roi swallowed a forkful of beef and spoke up. "I know a couple of smith shops, about a full day's ride away, which could use a talented apprentice. He'd be gone from home for years, though. Are you and Juliana willing to let him go?"

Arnfred glanced at his son before looking his wife in the eyes. "We haven't talked about it."

I looked over the utensils, admiring the care put into making them. The boy had plenty of raw talent. "You need not decide right now, discuss it after we leave. If possible, we'll stop by on our way back and see if he's ready to take that step. If not, the offer still stands. When he's ready, send him to my hall. I will see he gets trained by the best in the skati," I promised, spearing a small potato.

Thile looked at me, his eyes opened wide. "Thank —" He coughed. "Thank you, skald. That's more than I could ever ask from you."

"Nonsense. I see the care you put into your work. You have potential, having a great mentor guiding you would make you even better." I took a bite and Roi smiled at me.

Arnfred moved to hold his wife as a tear welled in her eye.

"I am sorry if I misspoke. I meant no harm offering my aid," I said, trying to comfort our host.

Juliana looked at me, eyes shining. "Oh no, skald, you did nothing wrong...these are tears of joy. I never thought my son could gain such an honor. I feared his talent would go to waste here as we have little need for metalsmiths beyond simple tools and the like."

The twins smiled wide and spoke in unison. "And what of us?"

I saw Crum's jaw move as he prepared to say something. Everyone jumped when I clapped my hand on his shoulder. I stared at him and shook my head.

Roi snorted and took a bite of food.

What can I say to keep this from becoming uncomfortable?

I glanced from one sister to the other several times. "From what your father said earlier, you two are invaluable here. Your efforts help the whole family prosper. I have no

doubt you will both, in due time, find yourselves in love and starting your own families."
Unsure what to say next, I looked to Roi for help.

He shook his head slightly.

Fine time to not have any words of wisdom.

Tona and Maren whimpered before rushing into the house. Juliana's face went pale before she hurried after them.

Thile snickered as Arnfred sat slack-jawed.

I pressed my lips together tightly to steady my trembling chin. *Way to show this family how much I appreciate their hospitality.*

As I turned away from our host, Crum shoved my hand off his shoulder. "I wanted to say places like cities are bad for woodsyths like your daughters. Cities damage to the spirit of strong woodsyths. The stone and commotion dulls our connection to the materials we manipulate. Ask any woodsyth or herbalist who lives in a city, they'll tell you about the time and energy spent tending their gardens and green spaces, the strain they feel fighting against the rigid stone construction surrounding them. Arnfred, your daughters are special. Make sure they don't leave the farms and the forests. They will never enjoy the kind of life they have here in a city."

My slack-jawed expression mirrored our host's. *This can't be Crum; he never talks like that. Who is this insightful man and what has he done with my friend?*

Roi cocked his head and looked at Crum. "My friend, that's the most beautiful thing I've ever heard you say. I had no idea you were even capable —"

"I have many secrets," Crum replied, scowling, before sticking his tongue out at Roi.

I covered my face with my hands and closed my eyes, wanting to escape this uncomfortable situation. Trying to calm myself, I listened to the sounds accompanying the dimming daylight to clear my head. Did Arnfred and Juliana always have the fate of their children on their minds? It wasn't a topic my mother and I discussed over our meals. At least not until my father summoned me to the capital and burdened me with the title of skald.

Someone touched my arm and I flinched.

Roi whispered in my ear, "Juliana and her daughters have returned."

Uncovering my face, I blinked and held my breath for a moment, hoping to avoid further embarrassment.

Now, small lard candles lit table. The girls stood on either side of their father, with Juliana behind him. Again, Tona and Maren spoke together, "Skald Fitzeirick, Sir Crum, Sir Roi please accept our apology. We misunderstood you. We should not have taken offense and made such a spectacle."

I nodded and slowly released my breath. "I believe we're both guilty of misunderstanding. Please sit, I have a couple of things to say."

I paused, letting everyone get comfortable again.

"I've never counseled young men and women on what their future may hold. I make proclamations to large crowds, pass judgments, and declare punishments. Thile, if you and your family decide your talents lead you to work as a smith, Roi will put you in touch with the right people. Tona and Maren, I'm not sure living in a city is best for you. Considering your talents, Crum could offer better insight as to how it would affect you than I can. If you do find yourself moving that direction, I'll offer whatever help I can give. Now, let's finish this meal before it cools much more."

"No problem," Thile said, confidence clear in his voice. "Everyone step back."

Thile stood and glanced toward the still smoldering fire pit before looking over the food. Sparks streaked across his eyes. The fire flared and the air between the pit and table shimmered before visible waves of heat moved past him.

Watching him move heat through the air fascinated me so much I almost missed a slight tremor rippling through the ground.

Roi nodded when I glanced at him. *I didn't imagine it.* The farm boy pulled stamina from the ground while directing heat. I'd never seen such a thing.

He continued until the smell of hot food filled my nose, then closed his eyes and dropped his hands to his sides. The shimmer disappeared from the air. He took a deep breath and stretched his arms toward the sky as he exhaled and opened his eyes again.

"Be careful around the plates, they're hot," Thile warned. "I kept the heat from everything else. Mother, a pitcher of water. Please."

Juliana anticipated his request and had a jug ready. Thile quenched his thirst while we sat and resumed eating.

"Excuse my lack of manners, moving so much heat always leaves my throat dry. I will sleep well tonight," he commented, while placing the pitcher on the table and taking his seat.

I stared at Thile with new respect. *What could he do with better training? Mother never did anything like that.* My knife and fork were cool to the touch, but the plate gave off heat. I had more to learn about the abilities of strong firesyths.

After a drink, Arnfred asked, "Skald, we know of your engagement, but what about your companions. Roi. Crum. Do you have families?"

Roi closed his eyes, bowed his head for a moment, and drew a breath. Crum spoke first. "I must admit I'm envious of those with strong families, like you Arnfred. I did not grow up with such ties. I'm the youngest of three, born after my brother and sister left home to make their way in the world. Their house empty, my father and mother moved to the new eastern lands to live out the rest of their days. Then I came along; seemed mother's youthful vitality teas worked better than she thought. My father shunned me for being a new mouth to feed. Mother loved me, but ours was a broken house and I knew it would be best for me to strike out on my own, as soon as I could."

I'd heard that story so many times, it shouldn't affect me except I knew he wasn't exaggerating...every word was true. It made me appreciate my mother's love and guidance.

"That's...that is so sad," the twin sitting near Crum said.

"Do you...plan...to start a family?" the other girl asked.

Crum looked her in the eyes. "Maren, I may never be ready to marry. I don't know if I can provide the kind of life a proper woman deserves."

How does he tell them apart?

His answer seemed to upset her. I felt a growing concern our stay tonight would cause trouble.

Roi took a long drink and cleared his throat. "I could regale you with long and exciting tales of traveling with my father and mother. A story of hunting beasts for food and men for bounty, but that's not the man who sits before you.

"Jarl Eirick hired my parents to watch over a Varian woman living in the far eastern territory. This worked well for me because I had turned eighteen; I was ready to marry and start a family of my own. Little did I know I'd be a widower at twenty and helping my parents again after Fitzeirick was born. To be honest, it saved my life. Mentoring him helped me deal with the death of my wife and daughter. Once Crum started hanging around, keeping my charge out of trouble became more challenging."

It was always funny to hear Roi talk about me as a child. My earliest memory of him was the day we tested my talent. I was five or six.

• • • • • • • • • •

He led me well away from town to three older men, whose names I couldn't recall. The men sat near a fire and not far away was a rock and a block of wood.

"Each one has a treat," Roi said, "all you have to do is get it."

I walked directly to the stone and put my hand on it, like Roi taught me. Familiar, tingling energy in the stone flowed to my hand as I pushed my talent into it. I found a hollow and tore the rock open. It had sweetbread inside.

"Well done, stonesyth," one man said, smiling.

I devoured the small treat. "Is that all?"

He swept his hand toward the others. "Go see them."

Passing the fire, I smelled cooking meat.

"You must put the fire out," the man, nearest the fire said.

I stared at the flames for a moment, took a deep breath, and tried to blow them out.

He chuckled. "Good try, but you must use your talent."

I looked at him before reaching toward the flames. Heat washed over my hand, but I couldn't feel energy like I did in the stone. "I can't."

"You're not a firesyth. Try wood," he said.

When I reached for the block, the last man said, "Open it, with your talent, and enjoy what you find."

The wood had an interesting texture, not rough, but not smooth either. I tried to find energy in it, like with the stone, but felt nothing.

"Nothing?" he asked.

I shook my head.

"You're not a woodsyth."

At the time, I felt like a failure, but Roi helped me understand that was just how life worked.

• • • • • • • • • •

Someone nudged my shoulder.

"Juliana asked you a question," Crum said, tilting his head her direction.

I looked at her. "I'm sorry, I got lost in thought. What do you want to know?"

"I asked if Roi was your step-father."

"No," I replied. "My mother never married. He's my mentor and trusted advisor."

No one noticed Thile sleeping, until he started snoring.

I smiled. "I suppose that's a good sign it is time to get some sleep ourselves. I'd like to get an early start."

Arnfred nodded. "Juliana, get Thile to his bed. Daughters, take care of the rest of this food. Save what you can, feed the rest to the hogs. Then off to bed."

"Where are Roi and I sleeping?" Crum asked.

"I'm not picky," Roi said.

Arnfred looked sideways at him. "Tona and Maren can share a room for the night."

"Nonsense," I said. "I will *not* trouble your family any more than I must. Crum will share your bed with me or get his bedroll and sleep on the floor. Roi, I prefer you take up a post outside the girl's rooms."

Crum groaned before heading toward the stable. We waited for him to return, then followed Arnfred to the room where he and his wife slept.

"Did your daughters build the bed?" I asked.

He beamed. "Yes, they spent weeks gathering the right pieces. We replaced the straw earlier this season. I hope you find it to your liking."

"It looks to be almost as nice as my own, and a far sight better than I expected to sleep on. You have my gratitude. Could you please show Roi to a sturdy chair?"

The farmer shook his head. "I can't believe you wish him to sleep in such an uncomfortable position."

"I've slept in far worse, believe me. I don't mind and it gives me a chance to practice sleeping through court meetings," Roi said, a glimmer in his eye.

I chuckled. "Off to your post, my friend. Sleep well and keep the twins safe."

Roi closed the door behind him.

"You wound me with your lack of trust. Do you think I would move on those girls?" Crum asked.

"Sit," I said, pointing to the bed. "I trust you with my life. I know you're honorable, despite your never-ending pursuit of women. I did this to put our hosts at ease. This sleeping arrangement avoids unnecessary suspicion and uncomfortable accusations."

"I guess that's why you're a skald and I'm only associated with your court. You are *far* wiser than I. Sleep well."

"Sleep well, my brother," I replied.

I forgot something about Crum before creating the sleeping arrangements. He snored, like heavy cloth getting ripped in two. After a while, the rhythmic noise lulled me to sleep.

Chapter 3

I felt well rested when a knock on the door woke me. "Who's there?" I called out.

Crum didn't move.

Roi stepped into the room carrying our saddlebags. "Juliana's cooking breakfast, enough food to hold us to our next stop."

"These people are generous beyond measure. Such a pleasant change from the court life. I'll be right down."

Crum stayed asleep as I dressed.

Passing Roi, I grinned. "Please bring Crum to the table."

Roi smiled. "He'll join you soon."

While taking my seat, I heard Crum shout, "Where — what? Hey, I didn't — you oaf, put me down."

"No. Skald Fitzeirick ordered me to bring you to the table."

Roi carried him over his shoulder like a sack of grain. I didn't often notice how much bigger Roi was than Crum, but this sight gave a stark reminder. Roi stood head and shoulders above him. *And I'm about the same size as Crum; Roi could carry me much the same way.*

Crum continued yelling. "I'm not a child. Put me down now. If you don't, so help me —"

"You'll do what? You and Fitzeirick together can't best me," Roi teased, dropping him.

He landed hard on the floor. "Ow! You dolt, we have to ride all day today."

"And again tomorrow I expect," Roi added.

Juliana cleared her throat. "You two better behave yourselves. You may be grown men and guests, but I'll bring you both to heel, if need be."

Roi looked down.

Drooping his shoulders, Crum looked away and clasp his hands together behind him.

"Yes, mum," they answered in unison.

I couldn't help but chuckle.

Thile shuffled in at the end of the commotion and yawned. "Good morn all. Sorry for falling asleep at the table last night."

"Think nothing of it," I assured him, waving it off. "What you did...I saw it and still have trouble believing it happened."

Arnfred and the twins walked in. "We have some old saddlebags in the stable. We'll load them when you're ready to go."

"How can I repay your generosity? Gratitude doesn't seem like enough. Your family went beyond anything we expected," I told him sincerely.

"I suppose I could ask much. You insisted we met as friends. Would you take us in and feed us if we're ever near your hall? That's something a friend would do," Arnfred said.

"Of course. I'd be happy to put you and your family up for as long as you needed."

"Then we're even," Juliana said, placing food on the table.

"Agreed," I said.

One of the twins put a plate in front of me and the other loaded it with apple slices and strips of pork.

"Where will you sleep tonight?" Juliana asked.

I swallowed and opened my mouth to answer.

Roi tapped his foot against mine and gave a quick shake of his head.

Furrowing my brow, I looked at him.

"Although we haven't seen any Satran activity this far north," Roi began, "it's best if we keep our travel plans secret."

I relaxed and nodded.

"In any case, I hope you travel swift and safe. I've heard some places between here and the capital can be dangerous," Arnfred warned.

"I often talk my way out of trouble and, if my social graces fail, we have Roi. Brute force should triumph where good sense falls short," Crum said, chuckling.

Roi grunted in response and kept eating.

"Thank you, again, for your hospitality. I don't want to appear eager to leave, but it's important we get going. We have a long ride ahead of us."

"I understand," Arnfred said. "Thile, ready their horses."

Once we finished the meal, the rest of the family rose from the table with us. The twins stood last and bracketed Crum, shuffling their feet as he walked to his horse.

"Will you be back this way?" one of them asked.

"I hope so," he answered, while securing his bags and bedroll.

Roi and I strapped down our belongings and double-checked the bags. Thile had done a good job securing them.

We mounted up and I thanked the family once more.

They bid us good journey before we rode away.

Neither of my companions seemed eager to start the friendly banter we enjoyed yesterday. I used the silence to think about how best to sway the council. I had to find a way to show the seriousness of the situation while not appearing weak. The plight of my people should be enough, but none of the Thanes have visited my skati in so long. Maybe they've forgotten what we provide to the rest of the country.

While mulling over those thoughts, I remembered something Crum said before we left. "Why'd you give hope to those young women? I wouldn't mind visiting Arnfred and his family again, but we may not have the luxury on the trip back. I hope we'll be leading a warrior procession."

He shrugged. "What harm did it do? I *would* like to visit the family again. I've kept far worse company. Maybe this is a sign I'm maturing?"

"Anything's possible, Crum. You're always good for a surprise," Roi quipped.

"It's to my advantage to keep people guessing," Crum replied. "Speaking of which, are we really planning to ride to Skald Nikulas's hold today?"

"If possible," I said. "I'd hoped to get his opinion on a few things before facing the council."

"And how far to the inn Roi told us about?" Crum asked.

"It's a stone's throw from the entrance to the Scar," Roi said. "Why do you care?"

Crum pointed ahead of us. "Because those clouds are looking pretty ugly."

As he spoke, a cold wind hit us head on. My eyes followed his finger to a boiling mass of dark clouds rising over the swaying treetops. "He has a point. Let's get into the forest before that storm rolls over us. The trade path is well worn, but a hard-enough rain could still cause problems."

We pushed our horses to a near gallop. Large drops of rain fell as we reached the shelter of tall trees. The storm strengthened as we slowed to avoid exhausting our mounts, so early in the day. Soon the hammering downpour made it hard to hear each other, so we rode in silence until the path exited the line of trees.

The horses stopped when the blinding rain blew straight into our faces. I cursed myself for leaving in such a rush. I hadn't thought about getting caught in a storm. Sleeping on the wet ground was not my idea of a good time.

"You think we should wait this out?" I yelled.

"Not sure!" Roi replied, at the top of his voice. "Rain's too thick! Can't see the sky! Too loud to hear if any animals are leaving the area!"

"Can we at least ride back to get out of the spray?" Crum shouted, pointing into the forest.

We moved far enough to be out of the wind-driven water and dismounted.

"Crum, can you work some of the smaller trees into a passable shelter? Roi, gather firewood so we can at least stay warm. I'll tend the horses."

Crum stepped into the woods.

Roi rummaged through his pack to find his hand ax.

I gathered everyone's reins and followed Crum.

Roi fell behind as he stopped to gather dry limbs along the way. I sythed a few cairns to mark the path, in case he lost sight of us.

Crum found a stand of young trees and formed them into a solid wall against the wind with an effective roof over our heads in short order. About ten paces away, he worked more trees into a makeshift corral. Searching his saddlebags, he found his bow drill and went to work on a slab of wood pulled from an older tree. Smoke rose as Roi found us.

"Perfect timing," I said.

"Glad you marked the path. Tracking you in the rain while carrying a load of firewood is not my idea of fun," Roi said, dropping the wood. "Crum, I'll work the drill while you syth some of these limbs into kindling."

He nodded and they switched places. Once the smoke gave way to flame, Crum tossed small pieces of wood to Roi. We soon had our source of warmth.

Crum put his bow drill away and pulled out the parts of his flatbow and his quiver of arrows. He sythed the bow together and strung it with practiced ease.

"Hunting in this weather?" I asked.

He shook his head before nocking an arrow. "It's loud enough for someone or something to sneak up on us. Better safe than sorry."

"Roi," I said, "you lived around here, anything we should be wary of?"

"Saw signs of wild pigs while gathering wood, a sounder could do some damage."

"Predators in the area?"

"A few. Bears, but they aren't going to sneak up on us and we could handle one bear easy enough. Weather could drive a few mountain lions into the forest. One would have to be desperate to attack us, though. Still, I trust Crum's self-preservation instincts."

"I'll get my hammer. Want your sword, Roi?"

He shook his head. "Anything that shows up I should be able to handle with the ax."

"Suit yourself," I said. "Despite the storm, I'm enjoying the journey. It's nice to be out here with good traveling companions."

Crum flicked a clump of mud off his boot. "I could be in a nice, dry tavern, spending time with an admirer. Instead, I'm good travel company." He pointed at me. "I wouldn't do this for any other friend. Anyone else would have to pay."

"If I'm not mistaken, we're your only friends," Roi replied, smirking.

A loud snap interrupted the conversation. We looked for the source, but the constant roar of pouring rain made it hard to hear.

My heart pounded in my chest.

Cracking and snapping came from all around us. After a strong gust, a large branch crashed to the ground near our shelter.

Roi rubbed the back of his neck. "That was close."

Crum chuckled. "No kidding. I almost shot it. I hate to waste arrows."

Something stirred nearby. We all jumped, looking for the source of the new sound. The horses nickered and neighed as underbrush snapped. Something big was moving toward us, fast.

Crum drew his bow and Roi stood, ready for something to happen.

I gripped my hammer so tight my fingers tingled.

Several deer charged through the trees, running between the corral and our shelter. The horses crowded against the far side of the makeshift pen, kicking and nipping at each other.

Roi approached the corral, speaking trying to calm the horses.

"Be careful," Crum said.

"As bad as an injured horse would be, we can't treat you if you get hurt," I added.

"Relax," he replied, "I know what I'm doing."

A brown blur pounced toward my horse.

The horse reared and bucked, spoiling the attack.

Roi jumped back. Crum let fly an arrow as soon as the mountain lion hit the ground. It yowled and backed away.

His bowstring strummed two more times and the cat collapsed before it could get out of the corral.

Roi moved to put himself between the horses and the downed predator.

The injured cat swiped at him.

I focused on the area underneath the thrashing mountain lion and poured my will into the ground. A jagged hole opened. The animal fell to the bottom with a quiet thud, yowling when it hit. Reversing my efforts forced the crack closed. I felt the dying beast struggling against the dirt, but it didn't take long for it to stop moving.

"Took you long enough to do something," Roi called out, while trying to calm the horses.

"You know I have trouble working with loose ground."

"But I can't syth and keep the horses safe too," Roi replied.

"How am I supposed to get my arrows back?" Crum grumbled. "It takes time and effort to make those. I'll need one of you to make arrowheads for me."

"You let me know when you have shafts ready and I'll syth them out of whatever stone you want," I replied.

"Obsidian. I want Obsidian."

"Since you two have settled that," Roi drawled. "Try to be quiet. We've almost been crushed by a branch *and* fought off a mountain lion. Best be ready for what's next."

Crum nodded. "Any chance we're sitting in a dry stream bed?"

Roi nodded. "It's possible...why?"

He pointed into the forest. "Looks like the water's rising faster than I'd expect over there."

I turned and saw a small flow heading our way. "How far to the inn?"

"At a brisk pace, on a clear day, we could make it well before nightfall. Traveling in this weather, we'll be riding in the dark," Roi said.

"Guess I'll start looking for someplace to syth another quick shelter," Crum said.

"No," I said. "If we're going to move, I say we press on. It's no more dangerous to ride in the dark than to risk staying in the woods. And don't forget why we're making this trip. The lives of my people depend on me getting the warriors we need. As helpful as a visit with Nikulas may be, time is not on our side. We're staying at the inn."

"The mission *is* the most important thing," Roi agreed, moving dirt over the fire.

"I hope this inn has warm beds," Crum remarked, sything a section of the corral open to lead the horses out.

After putting my hammer away, I looked over my horse again to make sure Roi hadn't missed a serious injury. We mounted up and headed back to the trade path, into the wrath of the storm.

The closer we came to the edge of the forest, the harder the wind blew against us. The raindrops felt like small pebbles hitting our faces. We leaned forward, bracing against our horse's necks to avoid the stinging raindrops. The non-stop, howling wind made it impossible to hear each other. We rode nose to tail to keep from getting separated.

It seemed like forever before the rainfall tapered off. The wind kept blowing. It cut through our soaked clothes, biting to the bone.

"Roi," Crum called, through chattering teeth. "How much farther?"

Roi shivered as he looked around. "It's too dark. Can't tell where the mountains stand on the horizon with the cloud cover."

"Wait, we could ride right past this place?" Crum asked.

Roi shook his head. "I doubt we'll miss The Trader's Cup. It hosts a rowdy clientele, at least until the owner decides to go to bed. When Geri turns in for the night, everyone quiets down or leaves."

"Does he keep a regular bedtime?" I asked. "We may want to pick up our pace to avoid rousting him so we can get rooms."

"Best suggestion I've heard since we left the forest," Crum said and put his heels to his horse.

Roi and I followed his example.

We pushed the horses, and ourselves, to near-exhaustion before we noticed a light in the distance. As we got closer, we found people riding toward us.

"What's going on?" Roi asked an approaching man.

"Geri's gone to bed."

"No, he has *not*," Crum yelled and took off at a full gallop.

"Crum, stop!" Roi shouted and gave chase.

I shrugged at the confused man and set off after my companions.

Roi caught up to Crum, grabbed his reins, and stopped his horse.

Crum drew back his fist. Roi pushed him out of the saddle. He hit the ground with a thud, scrambled to his feet, and ran toward The Trader's Cup. Roi made a quick motion with his hand, raising a small amount of ground in Crum's path.

Crum tripped and fell, face first. Before he could get back up, Roi dismounted.

Mud slithered around Crum's legs, holding him down. "Let me go! I'm going to get us a room! I won't sleep on wet ground!"

"Crum, if you go beating on the door, Geri will get up, open the door, kill you, and go right back to bed," Roi replied.

"Kill me and go back to bed? What kind of place is this?" Crum demanded.

"Yes, Roi, I'd like to know too," I said.

"Someplace I can get us a room."

"But you said he'd kill Crum for beating on the door."

"Geri doesn't know Crum. Stay back and give me a moment."

As Roi walked away, I got off my horse, gathered up the other two, and pushed the mud off Crum. "Let's stay close," I suggested.

I felt Roi gather some strength before stepping on the porch. He banged on the door several times in a strange rhythm.

"I'm in bed," a gruff voice responded. "We're closed until morn."

"This is Roi, son of Rorec. I need beds for myself and two friends."

"If I get out of this bed, it'll be to cut out your tongue for lying. The man you claim to be hasn't been here in years. Go away!"

"My father saved your life, Geri. Is this how you treat his son when he asks for a room? You'd leave him outside, wet and cold?"

I heard someone stomping across the floor and feared for Roi's life. "You might want to get ready to fight," I whispered to Crum.

The gruff voice yelled from behind the door. "Final warning! If I open this door and you're not the man you say, you'll die where you stand!"

"Open it and find out!" Roi bellowed back.

My oldest friend didn't flinch when the door swung open.

A barrel-chested, grizzled, old man thrust a leaf-bladed sword straight at Roi's throat before looking him up and down. He lowered the blade. "You've grown, son of Rorec. I meant to put it between your eyes."

"Perhaps your age is catching up with you, Geri," Roi said, offering his hand. "It hasn't been that long."

They both laughed.

"Come in, friends of Roi," Geri called.

"Which way to the barn?" I asked.

"Einns," the innkeeper bellowed. "Drop the broom and get these horses to the barn. Bring their bags and set them by the fireplace."

A young boy ran past us and snatched the reins from my hands. I worried the horses would have trouble keeping up with him.

Geri led us to the table nearest the fireplace. The day's fire had burned down to glowing embers. He placed two logs on top of the coals and made a quick lifting motion. The fire flared bright enough to hurt my eyes.

"That'll get you warm and dry," he said. "I'll get Grima out of bed to fix you something hot to eat and drink. The first three rooms to the left upstairs are empty."

Roi nodded.

"Grima. We have late arrivals. Fix a pot of stew and keep hot tea coming."

A shrill voice answered. "I'm in bed already."

"If you want to keep a bed, you'll take care of my company."

Turning back to Roi, he asked, "Who is the son of Rorec traveling with these days?"

Roi pointed. "This is Crum, a silver-tongued devil and a good man to have at your side. Next to him...my liege, Fitzeirick, Skald of the far eastern skati."

Geri's face went pale. "Skald? You should've told me." He stood and bowed low. "Please, forgive my rudeness. I meant no offense."

"None taken. Please don't make a fuss over me. I apologize for disturbing you. Roi made it clear you valued your sleep."

Before he could answer, the young boy entered and dropped our packs nearby.

"Into the kitchen with you, help your mother. The sweeping can wait."

"Yes, sir," the boy responded, sounding exhausted.

Geri grinned at me. "I'm forever in debt to Roi's father. Two bandits had me cornered, set to kill me. He showed up and downed them both before either knew what happened. What's Rorec doing now?"

Roi shrugged. "Don't know. My parents went back on the road soon after I became Fitzeirick's mentor. Our paths haven't crossed."

"I see," Geri said. He rubbed his chin for a moment before looking at Crum. "I trust you'll keep your silver tongue away from Grima. She's working off a debt."

The boy interrupted the conversation with a large, steaming pitcher and set out four cups. He moved slow enough for me to notice his dark hair brushed the tops of his shoulders and see the fatigue in his large, brown eyes. I couldn't settle on his age, but he looked no older than ten or eleven. He yawned before turning back to the kitchen.

"Far be it from me to get into a man's business, but what about her husband?" Crum asked, filling the cups. "A decent man minds his own debts."

"You're right," Geri replied. "A decent man would. In this case, I never met the boy's father. Since you prefer to stay out of my business, that's all you need to know."

"We aren't here to get involved. I've got enough trouble of my own," I said, before Crum could speak again.

Geri nodded. "Trouble from Satra, so I hear. I take it you're headed to the capital."

I glanced at Crum. "I've heard news travels fast through the taverns."

Crum chuckled.

"I have to find out why the Council of Thanes took the warriors out of my skati and what it will take to get them back."

"I hear rumors about Varian raiding parties from the north. Jarl Eirickson is having trouble securing the border," Geri warned.

Roi and I looked at Crum.

He shrugged.

"But Varia borders my lands to the east. Why would they raid from the north? Is Skald Nikulas allowing them through this skati?" I asked.

By her name, I expected Grima to be an older woman. When she appeared, carrying a large pot, I guessed her age to be somewhere between mine and Roi's. Like her son, she had long, dark hair with the firelight showing a few lighter strands. It had the disheveled look of someone who tossed and turned in their sleep. She had the same round eyes too, sitting on top of dark bags. "Hot stew for the late guests. Do you need anything else, sir?" she asked, while her son placed bowls and spoons on the table.

Geri looked to each of us. Crum pointed to the pitcher.

"Another pitcher of tea, then off to bed with both of you," Geri said.

She dipped her head and they backed away before turning toward the kitchen.

Roi watched them until they left the room.

"Word is Varia found, or made, a passage through the northern peaks. Maybe they found a fault like the Scar and sythed it. If Eirick did it, why couldn't they?" Geri asked, shrugging.

I looked at Crum. "You heard anything about this?"

He shrugged. "What do you want from me? I don't frequent the trade taverns. I prefer to associate with the upper rungs of society. They're the ones with lonesome wives and adventurous daughters."

Geri looked at Roi while pointing at Crum. "You keep him away from my workers."

Roi gave Crum a toothy smile. "He'll conduct himself in an honorable manner, I promise."

I fought back a smile, remembering how he handled Crum in the farmer's house this morning.

After the last spoonful of stew, I yawned. "Geri, I hate to appear ungrateful, but we've had a rough day. I hear a bed calling my name. Crum, I think it best if you retire too. Roi, feel free to catch up with your friend."

Roi mumbled something I couldn't understand, but stood with me.

Geri stood and bowed. "Skald Fitzeirick, I hope you find the bed to your liking. Would you like someone to wake you for breakfast?"

"Anything beats sleeping on wet ground. Roi will wake me. I often wonder if he ever sleeps. Again, I apologize for rousting you from your bed."

"No, no, don't let my gruff nature trouble you. It's...well, if I let everyone know they can come and go as they please, I'd never get any rest."

"In that way, you're like a skald. People want your constant attention, regardless of how trivial the matter may be."

Roi coughed and glared at me.

Maybe trivial wasn't the right word.

Geri laughed. "Comparing me to a skald? Perhaps your companion isn't the only silver tongue here."

His rough laughter followed us up the stairs. When I closed the door, I couldn't hear anything outside. Shutters on the window blocked most of the moonlight. I felt my way to the bed.

It reminded me of the farmer's bed, and I didn't take long to drift into a comfortable sleep.

Chapter 4

Sudden pressure on my shoulder woke me.

Where am I? My stomach fluttered and in a half-asleep need to defend myself, I grabbed the hand and twisted.

"Ow," Roi cried out.

That brought me to my senses, and I let go. "Sorry."

"I hope you react more kindly to Aesa's touch," he muttered, rubbing his wrist. "Come down and eat. I've already settled with Geri. Einns has our horses ready and loaded."

"Are you sure it's safe to trust Geri? I mean, he could've slit your throat."

He patted my shoulder. "He's a good man, more than fair with most of his dealings. He just has strange ways."

I shrugged. "You know him better than I. Go ahead. I'll join you after I change."

Crum's voice carried above the din. I looked for him while descending the stairs, and found him seated at a table entertaining a group of women.

Glad Grima's not among them.

Several men glanced his direction while eating. Some seemed interested in his story, most looked jealous of the attention he commanded.

Roi was nowhere to be seen.

Sticking to the edges of the room, I got near the table as he struck it three times. Several of the women jumped and gasped.

After sneaking closer, I realized Crum was telling his version of yesterday's mountain lion attack. *No doubt he started working on the tale the moment after it happened.*

I waited in silence for him to finish and almost laughed when he said, "My skald owes me obsidian arrowheads for my heroic actions. He'll use stones originally meant to make breathtaking jewelry for his lovely bride to be. I'm the reason they met, by the way."

"How strange," I said, patting his shoulder. "It sounds like you're talking about the mountain lion attack yesterday, but I remember it differently. I recall a scrawny old cat, unable catch deer on the run. In fact, it couldn't even hurt a horse in a corral. But true, you did fire three arrows, and each hit the poor beast. But not a single one was a killing blow."

"Can I see the shaved spot under your ear?" a doe-eyed, young woman asked.

"Shaved spot?" I asked, squinting.

"From when the arrow passed," she said.

"Oh, I wasn't in the corral with the horses. I'm the one who put the poor, wounded beast out of its misery. Dispatched it by tearing a hole in the ground and burying it. Though I do owe him three obsidian arrowheads, but not as a reward. I broke his arrows when the dirt closed in on the cat."

Most of the seats around us emptied. Crum rubbed his chin as his eyes shifted back and forth, watching people leave. The girl stayed, staring at me. "You don't look like a skald."

I chuckled. "What's a skald supposed to look like?"

She looked me up and down several times. "I've never seen one, but I'd guess they look more...royal. With a crown and long robes and fancy shoes and...a sword. Yes, that's how a skald would look."

I held out my hand. "Skald Fitzeirick, of the far eastern skati. I do have a sword, but I'm not carrying it at the moment, and I only wear fancy clothes when I must."

She didn't take my hand. Instead, she stood and curtseyed. "And Roi's the one the arrow almost hit?"

We don't have time for this. I looked at her, pressing my lips together. "Miss...?"

She looked confused for a moment. "Oh, I'm Vass."

"Young Miss Vass," I said. "Consider this: Roi, a man at least a full head taller than me, stood near the corral while Crum, the man seated here, crouched near the ground. He let an arrow fly and struck the mountain lion which was also on the ground."

She stared at me.

"Do you know anything about the flight of arrows?"

She shook her head.

"In that case, please understand no arrow came near Roi's neck or any other part of his body."

She looked even more bewildered.

Hope my explanation sinks in. If not, it's Crum's problem. I sighed and turned my attention back to Crum. "Have you seen Roi? He woke me, but seems to have vanished."

He glanced over his shoulder. "Last I saw, he headed toward the kitchen with —"

A slap across his face interrupted his explanation. "You're a liar!" Vass screamed, and ran away.

The room erupted with laughter.

I wasn't expecting her to get violent. I looked toward the back of the inn and bit my lip to keep from laughing. "So...the kitchen, you say? I'll check there first."

The laughter continued as I left the great room.

I found Roi talking to Grima, tears running down her cheeks. "...he sent me here. It wasn't my fault. He's the troublemaker. He did this to me. It's not Einns' fault. He's a good boy, a hard worker. But I can't —"

She noticed me and gestured.

Roi turned, cheeks wet.

"Care to explain?" I asked.

He shook his head. "Not in here, not now. We need to eat and start for the capital."

I bobbed my head once. "Fine, but I expect an explanation."

"And you'll get one...later," he said, frowning. "Grima, would you please get food to our table?"

"Yes, of course," she replied, wiping her eyes.

I followed Roi out of the kitchen. He walked at a brisk pace until we reached the table. Crum was still rubbing his face, Vass' handprint a brilliant red against his cheek.

"Everything all right?" Crum asked.

Roi shook his head and Crum looked at me.

I shrugged. "Later."

He nodded and looked at Roi, waiting for him to question the hand mark on his face. The question didn't come before Grima put our loaded plates on the table. Crum shrugged and began eating.

Roi wolfed down his meal. "Have to talk to Geri. Don't wait for me. I'll catch up."
His tone told me it wasn't a request.

Concern appeared on Crum's face as Roi walked away.

I shook my head, telling him not to bother asking.

He waited until we were alone. "Do you know what he's doing?"

Guess the shake of my head wasn't clear enough. "No idea. I found him in the kitchen talking with Grima. Both were in tears. All I know is someone got her in some kind of trouble. I think Einns is part of it, but Roi wouldn't say anything when I asked."

"And he's letting us start for the Scar without him. When will he catch up?"

I shrugged. "Doesn't matter. We need to finish eating and get moving."

He nodded. "Get to the capital and get things settled. I'm ready to be back home."

• • • • • • • • • •

I looked toward the nearby mountains as we got close to the stables. The line of peaks reaching into the bright-blue sky made for a breathtaking sight. My eyes followed the range to a wide break, the opening to the Carved Scar. *Seems like forever since I've been this far west.*

As we rode, weaving past slow-moving carts, Crum rubbed his face occasionally, as if trying to ease the pain.

"That slap still bothering you? Should we find a herbalist?" I quipped.

"Ha. No, I've had much worse. But why'd you do that to me?" Crum asked, grinning.

"What? Point out the exaggerations in your tale?"

"I meant no harm," he said. "Everyone appreciates a good story. Why'd you have to talk to Vass like that?"

I cocked my head. "What do you mean? I was polite to her."

"You politely treated her like she was slow minded. She was nice and enjoying the story," he said, wagging his finger at me.

"Crum, my friend, she's easily confused at the least. As far as no harm, you weren't dealing with bored noblewomen. Those were traders, workers. For all you know, Vass was looking for a way out of a situation and you looked like *it*. Could be she has an overprotective father or boy who favors her. Either one might take offense to you playing her on."

"I did no such thing."

I pointed at him. "You don't think about how you act or how you say things. That's why Sar'sa says you haven't grown up. Consequences, your actions can have dire consequences. Keep that in mind."

"Speaking of...Roi?"

"Assuming Geri doesn't kill him, we'll find out when he's ready to tell us."

"I don't like it. It's not like him to keep secrets from you."

I nodded. *Maybe it's something from his past and nothing to worry about.*

The closer we got to the entrance of the Scar, the more crowded the road became, until we had to stop because people blocked the way. I asked the closest man, what was wrong.

"Storm caused a big rockslide. No one can pass."

"No stonesyths?" I asked.

"None strong enough."

"How far in?"

"From what I hear, near the midpoint."

I turned to Crum and caught sight of Roi, not far behind. "See if you can persuade people to let us through."

"You can count on me," Crum replied, and went to work making a path for Roi and me.

Wagons jammed in the sea of people slowed our progress a couple of times before we stopped at a field of debris ahead of the boulders, rocks, and thick mud blocking the pass.

Another delay. I must get to the capital.

Getting off my horse and walking up to the rubble, I could brush the top of a nearby boulder stretching my hand over my head. Weak pulses of energy from stonesyths on the other side made small tremors in the pile.

Roi yelled, "We're going to see if we can clear the way. Everyone over there, back away. I don't want anyone hurt by anything we knock loose."

I pointed at Crum. "Keep the crowd back in case something big falls from the walls."

"What about you?" he asked.

"*Someone* has to make this passable, and we're here," I replied. "It would help if you can talk a few of them into clearing loose rubble from the area."

He looked at me for a moment before nodding and walking back toward the crowd.

Roi put his hand on my shoulder. "Focus on the biggest boulder you find and force a crack open. I'll work with the rest."

He reached down into the sloppy mud before I closed my eyes and placed my hands on the pile. Searching for the ideal spot, where my energy didn't flow smoothly, I found a boulder to my right, not far from the canyon wall, with a long fracture near its surface.

I held my breath, focused on the fault line, then exhaled and pushed my will into the fracture. A sharp crack echoed as the fault gave way.

Roi forced wet dirt into the opening. He growled and the boulder split like a piece of chopped wood.

The pile shifted a little and cheers rose from the other side.

"Crum," I called over my shoulder. "Get water, lots of it. We'll need it by the time we've made this passable."

"Consider it done," he replied.

Roi said, "Again."

I reached into the pile and repeated the process.

As we worked, I felt smaller forces trying to help from the other side. Knowing we weren't working alone lifted my spirits.

Crum returned. "Water's on the way. Told them if they wanted to get through, they have to make sure you two stay quenched."

Someone pushed a water skin toward my face. I almost didn't open my mouth before water flowed out. As I swallowed, someone dumped water over my head.

"No more," I managed to choke out.

Roi coughed beside me.

Soon our effort dropped a small section low enough Roi could look over it. Cheers rose again.

He looked at me. "I'll push up on the left side and when you see movement, push whatever moves away from us as hard as you can."

I nodded and marveled at him; he wasn't breathing hard while I couldn't keep enough air in me to talk.

His power surged through the ground and I focused on the pile until nothing else existed. I didn't see the debris shift so much as felt it. Yelling and pushing hard, chunks of rock flew away from the pile.

Roi relaxed.

I fell to my knees and someone thrust a water skin at me.

"Rest," Roi said, before turning to the pile and yelling, "How many stonesyths on that side?"

"Seven," someone wheezed from the other side, "but two are too winded to continue."

"Fine. Do what you can to the pile against the wall. I'm going to work on this end. Be careful, I don't want anyone crushed."

They voiced their agreement.

Roi put his hands on a boulder. The ground shook as he poured energy into it. A loud buzzing started and grew steadily louder. Soon a chunk of stone dislodged and fell away. He moved his hands to another place on the rock. The noise never stopped, but mud muted the sound as Roi forced it into what was left of the boulder.

"Watch out!" Roi yelled, as more rock shifted away. A waist-high pile of debris stood at our end of the blockage.

"Be ready when I get back," Roi said, before clambering over the barrier.

Cheers rose behind me as my friend climbed over the rubble.

He returned with three men and two women. Covered in dirt and mud, they looked worse than I felt, but all wore smiles.

He held out his hand to help me to my feet. "I moved everyone farther back on the other side to be safe. I've got an idea. We can get enough debris out of the way for a wagon to pass through with one last big push. It's not perfect, but it gets people moving until the capital sends builders to clear the pass. I'll ripple the ground under the pile to help it move. These five will work with you to bind this part of the pile together and push it, like opening a big door. If this works, we're back underway. If not, foot traffic can pass and everyone else is stuck until we get a good night's sleep."

I stood, unsteady, and mumbled, "I vote we sleep now."

He smiled and shook his head. "A couple of hard pushes should do it. Ready?"

I closed my eyes, took several deep breaths, and nodded. As soon as I felt the weak energies flowing, I added my own.

Roi rippled the ground and the pile moved.

The crowd behind us yelled their support.

Grunts and growls echoed off the Scar's walls as the six of us pushed while the ground trembled under our feet until about half of the barrier moved out of the way. Like Roi said, it stood open like a big stone door.

We all fell to the ground, spent.

My eyes closed and I willed myself to breathe steady. *I may never move again.* I didn't expect a downpour of water. *All that work and now I'm going to drown.*

"Enough!" Crum's shout sounded muffled by the flood. "Back away, let them breathe."

I rested until I felt strong enough to sit up.

Crum sat next to me. "Good news. I found a group of traders headed back to the capital with room. You and Roi can rest as much as you need. I'll follow, leading your horses. We'll get in line as soon as you two are aboard."

My legs trembled when I tried to stand. "That'd be great news, if I had the strength to move."

He smiled and looked over his shoulder. "Men, get them loaded and get moving."

Some men hefted me in the back of a nearby wagon.

Someone cracked reins and called out, "Get up! Hee-yah! Let's go!"

Chapter 5

Crum's voice woke me. "Fitzeirick, we're here. Time to ready yourself to appear before the Thanes."

Opening my eyes, I yawned and looked around. The wagon wasn't moving, and the sky was growing dark. I sat up, wide awake, and tried to remember how late in the day the council would hear new business. *Was it nightfall or before? Doesn't matter, I must do this.*

"Where's my pack?" I asked. "I need my stole and sword."

"Right next to you. Roi got them after I woke him."

I yawned again and stretched, trying to convince my body to move. After a deep breath, I grabbed the long, gray robe and my ceremonial sword with its belt and crawled out of the wagon. I buckled the belt around my waist and clipped the scabbard in place. It took a couple of attempts to get it to fall alongside my leg. The heavy wool robe made an uncomfortable burden. I didn't wear it often and had to shrug my shoulders several times before it sat right. *Something's missing.* "Crum, bring me my hammer."

"No," Roi argued. "If it gets that heated in there, you've already lost."

I pursed my lips and shook my head. "If I didn't know better, I'd say you and Mother are conspiring against me."

He gave me a crooked smile and looked away.

"Crum, tie our horses nearby," I said, before shuffling to the front of the wagon to thank the drivers. "If you ever find yourself near my hall, please come see me. I'll make sure you are well cared for during your stay."

They voiced their gratitude and started the rest of their journey.

With the wagon out of the way, we started the short walk to the stairs. Roi took the lead while Crum fell into step behind.

At least there aren't many people around. I'm sure we make quite the spectacle.

The walk helped me get used to the heavy robe, but I worked up a sweat in the process. At the stairs, Roi and Crum hurried to the top and took one knee on either side, heads bowed.

Crum stood when I reached them. Roi stepped forward and opened the thick wooden door.

A guard stepped out. "State your business."

"Skald Fitzeirick, of the far eastern skati, has traveled two days to petition the Council of Thanes. By his authority, grant him entry," Crum said.

I smiled and gave a quick nod.

"The hour is late, hird. The council is no longer accepting petitions this day. Find lodging for the night and return on the morn."

I cleared my throat. "Perhaps you did not hear my man clearly. He spoke on a skald's behalf. The Thanes will hear me."

The guard stiffened. "It is the order of the Jarl. No new business starts so late in the day."

I glared at him. "That is not acceptable. I am half-brother to Jarl Eirickson. Jarl Eirick's blood flows in *my* veins. I will petition the Council of Thanes *now*!"

The guard returned my hard look.

"Is it wise to anger a skald?" I demanded, heat building in my cheeks.

"Better to face your wrath than the Jarl's."

"Let us in and I'll take whatever punishment my half-brother deems appropriate."

"You swear on your sword?"

"I do."

He stepped aside, bowed low, and fell in behind us.

Crum snickered.

I shivered at the sound of our steps echoing off the pristine, marble walls. It seemed to announce our presence to everyone in the building.

Two more guards stood at the door to the council room. They eyed us as we approached.

Our escort cleared his throat. "Skald Fitzeirick to appear before the council."

The guard to the left said, "Only the skald may enter. Hirds remain outside."

Roi and Crum stepped back. The guard nodded while the other pushed the door open and stepped inside. I heard the council's discussion taper off.

"A skald requests late entrance," he called out.

A voice I hadn't heard in a while replied, "The hour is passed for entrance. Escort him out."

This is more important than his silly rules. I stepped past the guard. "Jarl, I apologize for the interruption, but I must address the council today. The matter is of great importance to the people of the far-eastern skati."

Murmurs filled the room.

Eirickson spoke again, "Ah, Skald Fitzeirick. I should have known only you could have talked your way past the guard. Enter and we will hear this petition of 'great importance.'"

I bowed low before stepping further into the room.

A knot formed in my back when the door closed behind me with a dull thud.

My half-brother, seated on his ornate throne, crossed his arms and cleared his throat. "You've interrupted a vital discussion. Hurry to the table and let's get this over with."

My people depend on me. I took a calming breath and quickly approached the Thanes. Stopping near the seated councilmen, I placed a hand on the table to steady myself when my knees quivered. I turned to face Eirickson, but avoided looking at his icy, gray eyes, afraid he'd see how nervous I was. Instead, I focused on the faint scar that ran along his jawbone and across his chin. After bowing to him again, I turned to the council.

"I come asking the council to reconsider their decision to recall the warriors assigned to my skati. I've sent three messengers with the same petition I present now. The council must send warriors to secure the border with Satra. Without their protection, the Satran raid farms and kill Croian citizens. This cannot continue."

"Fitzeirick, your previous messengers returned to you intact did they not?" Eirickson asked.

"Yes."

"They delivered our response in a clear manner, correct? They informed you of the council's unanimous decision each time?"

I clenched my jaw for a moment before answering. *Don't let him get to you.*

"I do not recall if the messengers added that detail, but I fail to see —"

He cut me off. "And *that* is the problem. You fail to see. The council is not so short-sighted. The security of the capital is more important than your minor disagreement."

Stay calm. Eirickson is against you, but you can make the council see the need for soldiers at our border.

"The situation I face is no minor disagreement. Raiding savages are killing Croians, our citizens, *my* people," I replied, then turned to the council. "Satran barbarians easily cut down our defenseless farmers. Unprotected families can't stand against trained, fighting men. This is nothing short of an act of war, the start of an invasion. Of course, I agree the security of our capital is of the highest importance, but what is worse than the threat of Satra claiming Croian land?" I wiped sweat from my brow and felt my face turning red.

Eirickson sighed. "Questioning the judgment of the Thanes is not a sound strategy. Varia tests our border to the north and we have no men to spare. That is why you must take care of your region yourself. This is the fourth, and final, time we address this subject so long as the current council remains whole."

My heart pounded in my chest and my fists clenched tight, cracking the knuckles. "I see. How much longer must I dig graves and comfort widows?"

"Did you forget, or did Father not teach you? Appointment to the Council of Thanes is for life. Perhaps one is of age that their longevity is a concern, yet I expect the eldest should live many more years."

"Perhaps I should open a seat," I snapped, bitterly. Throwing my stole open and placing my hand on my sword, I reached into the stone floor for strength, but found nothing. The stone would not respond to me.

The men seated before me gasped. One stood and glared at me. "How dare you? You don't deserve the title you carry."

I cringed. *He got to me.*

"Enough!" Eirickson roared. "Fitzeirick, you *will* join me in my personal chamber...now." He rose, stomped to a door I hadn't noticed before and stepped inside.

I can't let my people down. I bowed deeply to the Thanes. "Please. I'm only trying to save Croian —"

"I said *now*!" my half-brother bellowed.

The seated Thanes stood as one and turned their backs to me.

I kept my head down and hurried to his chamber.

A smoldering fire behind his desk provided dim light. The wall opposite the desk featured a waterfall emptying into a small pool behind a single stone chair.

"Sit while I tend the fire."

I had no doubt it was a direct order.

Eirickson used a poker to move coals around then dropped three logs onto the coals. As he took his seat the fire grew bright.

He breathed heavily, nostrils flaring. "Did you actually think threatening violence would help you?"

I bowed my head again. "I apologize, Jarl. My actions were from desperation, not harmful intent."

"You moved toward the Thanes with your hand on your sword. If I'm not mistaken, you tried to pull strength from the floor. Is that not harmful intent?"

How did he know? I couldn't stop the gasp that escaped my lips as I looked toward the council chamber.

"How would heated debates ever reach an agreement where powerful syths could use their talents? If the room was not neutralized, it wouldn't last a week. Emotional outbursts alone would bring it to the ground. But that is not my concern right now."

"I agree," I pressed. "We need to stop the attacks on my people."

"No, that is *your* problem. My immediate priority is how to address your disrespect."

I kept my gaze down. "I, again, apologize for my outburst. I will gladly express my regret to the Thanes at their earliest possible convenience. Can we put that aside and secure my skati? Afterward, I will accept punishment willingly."

He shook his head, rose from his seat, and turned to the fire again. "Fitzeirick. Titled and landed bastard of father's favored, war-trophy whore." As he spoke, he prodded the blaze with the poker.

I fought the urge to stand. "My mother is not a whore. She loved our father."

Eirickson's laugh carried venom. "How can anyone be so ignorant? All things considered I wonder why he let you live. Regardless, this is the problem with common born receiving some authority. They simply do not understand the greater ramifications of their actions. They see no reason to honor long-standing traditions."

Before I could react, the chair flowed around me, binding my arms and legs.

"What is the meaning of this?" I cried out.

Eirickson turned. The look on his face reminded me of a predator, smiling before making a kill. "I mean for this to be a lesson you can never forget. Father's Varian, half-breed mistake will learn brash actions carry lasting consequences."

I looked from his face to the glowing poker in his hand. He carried a branding iron in the shape of an upside-down 'T'.

Before I could speak again, the stone chair slithered over the top of my head and my mouth before twisting my face to the right.

I pressed my will against the stone, but the chair would not respond.

"It's futile to struggle," he said, smirking, "but please fight if you feel it necessary."

The branding iron flared, changing from a dull red to nearly white, as Eirickson stalked me. My heartbeat pounded in my ears and sweat streamed down my chest. I tried to focus, to free myself, but the stone held.

He laughed. "Since it seems you were never schooled in the ways of the council, I'll brand you a traitor so, perhaps, you can find some tavern keep to take you in. Given your talent, someone could put you to work out of sight. Had I decided to mark you an exile, you'd have to live out your days in another land or risk death at the hand of decent, law-abiding citizens."

I didn't feel the hot iron touch my face. A moment later it felt like my left cheek burst into flame. I screamed. The sound of sizzling meat filled my ears. The smell of burning flesh assaulted my nose. Clenching my eyes tight against the pain, I screamed until my lungs were empty. The chair shook, but held fast throughout the ordeal.

Finally, the sizzling ended. "Yes, that will do," Eirickson practically purred. "Now I have corrected father's mistake. Half-breed bastards have no place among Croian royalty. No longer are you Skald Fitzeirick. Instead, you're Fitzeirick the marked traitor. I suppose it would be generous to help you numb the pain. Cold water is a good start toward treating a burn."

The chair rocked over backward and released me into the pool. I pressed against the bottom to get my head above the surface, to catch a breath.

The floor opened.

My chest tightened as I plummeted down a shaft. The watery contents of my stomach forced their way up my throat, spewing from my mouth as I fell. Grabbing in the fading light to catch anything and slow my fall, I bounced off unseen rocks randomly jutting from the walls.

The shaft emptied into open darkness and the water turned into a misty spray on its way to somewhere. My arms and legs flailed as I fell. It felt like forever before my back slammed into the ground, knocking the wind out of my chest.

I fought to breathe and understand what had happened as my consciousness faded.

Chapter 6

I woke moving...dragged by my arms. Absolute darkness greeted me when I opened my eyes. I thought I'd gone blind before realizing there was no light around me. The pain in my cheek overpowered any other aches. "R...R...Roi? Crum?" I croaked out, my throat dry and scratchy.

The movement stopped.

"I told you it wasn't dead," an unfamiliar feminine voice whispered.

"But if it does die, we're set for quite some time," a man's voice replied.

"What's Roicrum?" she asked. Her voice sounded young when she spoke up.

"I don't know," he said, gruffly. "Maybe it's Roicrum."

"Roicrum sounds like a terrible name for a...well...for anything," she replied.

It took a couple of raspy coughs to clear my throat. "I'm Skald Fitzeirick."

"Skald," the man said, thoughtfully. "Think I've heard that word before. Don't remember what it means though."

"How can you not — never mind. Where am I? Where are you taking me?"

"Where *is* it?" she asked. "It's right here and we're taking it somewhere else."

It? Somewhere else? What's happening? "Let me go," I blurted and pulled against their grip.

The dragging stopped. "Does it not want our help?" she asked.

I took a deep breath of stale air and fought against the confusion flooding my thoughts. *Remember who you are. Be polite.* "Thank you for the assistance, but I believe I can walk on my own. I don't want to be a burden."

"If it believes it, then maybe it can. I say it should try," the man said.

They released me. The water-soaked, heavy wool stole weighed on my arms, so they didn't move exactly the way I wanted. With some thrashing, I got free of the waterlogged garment.

I tried to stand, but wasn't sure which way was up. After several stumbling steps, I fell forward.

A hand grabbed my leg, and someone nudged their foot into my side.

"I guess it can't walk after all. Should we drag it away?" he asked.

"We could leave and try to find it later," she said.

"No. Others could come along and claim it," he said.

"I have a suggestion," I interrupted.

"Can it suggest better than it can walk?" he asked.

"Yes," I said.

"What's the suggestion?" he asked.

"You two help me stand and hold me so I can try to balance."

"Oh, no. That's a terrible suggestion," she argued. "It's much too heavy to pick up. That's why we're dragging it."

"No, I'm lighter now. I took off my stole."

"Ah, now we know why it's here. It's not the only thief here, so we won't hold that against it," he said.

"What makes you say I'm a thief?" I asked.

"It admitted it stole," she said. "Must have been something important to end up here."

"No, I didn't take anything. I meant I took off my heavy robe."

"It stole a heavy robe?" she asked.

"Must have been an important robe," he added.

"Can you forget about the *stole* and help me up?"

"So, it does want our help," he said.

"Yes, please help me stand."

There was a pause. "Since it asked so nice, especially after admitting to stealing an important robe, I think it deserves our help," the girl said.

I wanted to shake my head in disbelief, but feared it would cause more disorientation. With several grunts and groans, they lifted me by my arms. I wobbled at first, but stood with them on either side.

I closed my eyes and tried to ignore the dirty, musty stench assaulting my nose. "Now, let's walk. Slowly," I said.

They both moved forward. I almost fell again, but managed to catch myself while trying to match their pace.

"I think it can walk," she said.

"Where are we heading?" I asked.

"I thought it would tell us where it wanted to go," he said.

"I want to go to the exit."

"Never found one," he said.

"Where have you looked?" I asked.

"Everywhere I could get to safely," he said.

"Then there could be one you haven't found," I suggested, peering out into the pitch black.

"I don't know," he said.

"How can you not know?" I scratched my head. *There must be a way out.*

"Does it know how big this place is?" he asked.

"No," I replied, throwing my hands up, but trying to keep the agitation out of my voice.

"Neither do I, so I can't know if there's an exit I haven't found," he said.

My stomach quivered. I crossed my arms and forced the beginnings of doubt to the back of my mind.

"Since there's no exit, where else would you like to go?" she asked.

I sighed. "Where were you two headed when you found me?"

"We walk until we find someplace safe. We stay until it's not safe anymore and go somewhere else," he answered.

"Someplace safe. That sounds like a good idea until I recover. How far is it?"

"We won't know until we find it," she said.

Best to stop asking questions and let them take me there. "Lead the way."

We ran into walls, but kept moving for a while. Without warning, the man said, "Here. This place is safe."

"What do we do now?" I asked.

"We sleep," she said. "Though it was asleep when we found it. Maybe it's not tired."

"Do we lay down here?"

"Only the dead lay down. Sit," he said.

I sat, resting my back against the smooth wall, legs flat on the floor in front of me. My two new friends curled up against my sides. Instinctively I put my arms around them to protect them. They both felt thin, their bones easy to feel under rough skin. Their clothes felt like little more than tatters. None of that mattered; having someone with me was a comfort.

If I die, they'll most likely eat me. I bet that's what the man meant when he said they were set for a time if I died.

As I drifted off, I wondered where Roi and Crum were and what they were doing to find me. At the edge of sleep, the strange girl pulled tighter against me. I cried myself to sleep with Aesa filling my thoughts. *When will I get to hold her again?*

Chapter 7

I woke to something heavy sliding across my legs. Still groggy, I batted at the annoyance. "Go away, let me sleep," I mumbled.

Long, needle-sharp teeth sank into my forearm and pain shot up my arm. Jumping to my feet, I cried out and slapped at the creature.

"What is wrong with it?" the girl asked.

"Something's biting my arm and won't let go!" I yelled.

"A slither?" the man asked, his voice urgent. "Get away, slithers can kill."

Fully awake, I grabbed at the attacker. My hand closed around a thick, scaly tube. Pulling dug the teeth deeper into my arm, increasing the pain.

Remembering my ceremonial sword, I made a clumsy grab for the weapon and nearly dropped it after pulling the blade from its scabbard. The dull weapon represented my title and wasn't meant for combat, but I had to try something. I slashed downward, past my hand to avoid injuring myself.

The impact didn't make it let go, so I swung again. The creature bit harder. A shiver shook my body and I clenched my jaw against the pain. My heart pounded in my chest and short breaths hissed through my teeth as I stabbed at the attacker.

The rounded, dull point of the blade pushed into the animal, but it didn't let go. Its body writhed, wiggling my arm back and forth.

Screaming, I thrust again, and the sword sank deeper. Desperation took over and I stabbed until it stopped moving. Warmth spread through my chest bringing a burst of energy. "It's dead. How do I get it off my arm?"

"It is sure it killed a slither?" the man asked.

"I don't know if anyone can kill a slither with bare hands. Slithers are dangerous, deadly even," the girl said.

"Didn't use my hands, I used my ceremonial sword. Would you help me?"

"It has a sword? Steel? No one here has steel," he said.

I groaned and pressed my sword into the head of the animal, but nothing happened. *Maybe I can use the blade to pry its mouth open?* I slid the blade flat against my arm, up from my wrist. *Now I'm glad the edge isn't sharp.*

The steel pinched my skin against the snake's teeth. Pressing harder did nothing. I changed the angle and pushed the tip of the blade into the corner of the creature's mouth. As I pressed inward, a few teeth ripped free of my arm.

Pleased with this progress, I pressed harder until the blade pushed through the far side of the neck. Twisting the blade and lifting the hilt tore the snake's top teeth out of my arm, gouging small holes as they came free. This forced the bottom teeth deeper into my flesh.

Letting go of the hilt, I grabbed the now open mouth so it couldn't clamp back down. The teeth pricked my palm, but freedom was too close for scratches to bother me. I pushed the creature away while twisting my arm, yelling as the lower teeth tore out of my skin. *I'm free.* The feeling of warmth and energy flooded my body again.

"Did the slither finally kill it?" he asked.

"No, I don't think so," she replied. "It would have died during the fight if the slither was deadly."

While they discussed the probability of my death, I slid my sword into its scabbard and picked up the long, heavy-bodied animal. "Do you often run into snakes here?"

"Snakes?" they asked together.

"Uh, slithers. How long have you been down here?"

"Time doesn't move down here," the man said.

"Time moves everywhere."

"No sun, no moon, no stars, no time," the girl said, clapping her hands with the rhythm. "Will it share the slither with us?"

Does she know what those are or is she repeating a rhyme she heard somewhere?

"Yes, yes, please share," he said. "We helped it, didn't we?"

"Share the...Sir, you want to eat this snake?"

"A fine meal I'd think," he said. "But what did you call me?"

"Since I don't know your name, I called you Sir...out of respect."

He repeated the word a couple of times. "I might have called other men that before...before I was here."

"That would be proper," I said.

"No one calls me Sir. I don't deserve it," he said, "but I don't remember why."

"Would you mind if I call you Sir?" I asked. "At least until we learn your name."

"You can, if you want," he said.

"Did you forget about the slither?" the girl asked.

"Do you have a way to cook it?" I asked.

"Cook?" they asked.

"Hold it over a fire. Get the meat hot enough to sizzle." I said.

"Fire?" she asked. "Oh no, no fire here. Fire hurts our eyes, it's dangerous."

"Right," Sir agreed. "No fire here except..."

"A fire? Where?" I blurted out.

"No, it's not safe. I won't risk my life to go there," he said.

"Do you want to eat?" I asked.

"Yes," he said. "We helped, so feed us. It's only fair."

"I'll share if you tell me where the fire is. You don't have to go. You can stay safe here."

"I'd need more to eat than part of a slither before I'd risk going back there," Sir said.

"But this is a *big* slither. I'll even give you the largest part. Besides, what else do we have?"

"Hunt like the slither. I'm sure it got big and fat on squeakers. Find squeakers and you'll find more to eat," the girl said.

"Squeakers?"

"They squeak and you find them. They squeak loud when a slither finds them, but not for long," she said, then giggled.

"You mean rats?"

"Squeakers," she said, smacking her foot on the floor.

"If snakes and rats are down here, where do they come from?" I wondered aloud.

"Wherever they were before they got here," she said.

"Of course, makes *perfect* sense," I drawled.

"Glad we got that straight," Sir said, oblivious to my tone. "Can we eat now?"

"Fine, we'll eat. Any suggestions on how to eat raw snake?"

"It doesn't know how to eat?" the girl said.

"I do, but I've never eaten uncooked snake."

"Eat it the same as anything else, one bite at a time," Sir said. "But watch out for bones, they can poke you, and guts don't taste so good either."

"And don't eat the head," she said. "It can bite back."

"I'll do my best to remember your advice." I bit into the snake, tearing out a mouthful of scales, skin, and meat. After trying to chew scales and skin, I changed my technique to biting into the meat and pulling the skin off. The chewy flesh tasted like an odd mix of fish and wild bird. My stomach liked having food in it, but didn't like the raw meat.

"What do we do now?" I asked.

"We move. This place isn't safe anymore," Sir said.

"Lead me to the fire."

"Not yet," he said. "Have to wait, make sure others don't come looking first."

I pressed my lips together for a moment. "You said if I shared the meat, you'd take me to the fire."

"I will...when it's safe."

I took a deep breath and fought back a groan. "Lead the way to safety, please."

They took their places on either side of me and we started our odd, shuffling gait again. We ran into walls a few times, but kept moving. I couldn't tell how far we traveled before Sir said, "Here."

"We're safe here?"

"Yes, for now," Sir said.

"Would you tell me how you pick a safe place?"

"I feel it," he said.

I pushed my talent out into the surrounding area. We stood in a square hallway, too uniform to be natural. Four people could walk side-by-side with room to spare. Somewhere in the back of my mind, my unconscious had a deeper understanding of what I was doing. A grin forced its way onto my face while my thinking mind caught up. *I can see.*

I reached out with my talent again to make sure I felt the same thing. "I can see," I whispered.

"What?" the girl asked.

"I can see." I bounced on the balls of my feet and considered how this would help me escape.

"No one can see here, it's too dark." Sir said.

"Not with my eyes, I can see what's around us with my talent."

"Talent?" they asked, at the same time.

"My talent — sything. Everyone can manipulate material or energy, it's part of who you are. I do stone, others work wood or fire. You don't remember your talents?"

"W — wood, I think," the girl said. "From the things that grow...umm...up?"

"Yes, trees grow from the ground. They're wood. You're a woodsyth?"

"Maybe," she allowed, "but I haven't found a tree here so I can't be sure."

"Are you a woodsyth too, Sir?" I asked.

"Fire. I'm here because of fire," he said, softly.

"Because of... what did you do?"

"I don't remember. Fire touched me, my face. It burned me and I came here," he said. My cheek throbbed when he mentioned fire touching his face. "You were in a fire?"

"I — I don't remember what happened, except the burning," Sir said.

"Would you let me touch your face, where the burn happened?"

"Why?" he asked.

"My half-brother branded my face before he put me here. I want to see if you're marked the same way."

"Give me its hand," he said.

I touched the threadbare cloth on his bony chest. He grabbed my hand with rough, callused fingers and placed it on his face.

The scar interrupted his heavy beard. It started above the left side of his mouth, turned upward, across his cheek, and down as it approached his ear. I ran my fingers over it several times, fixing the shape in my mind. A sideways C.

"You're branded for cowardice. Do you know why?"

"No. All I remember is the burning," he said.

"At least we know a little more about each other," I said. "In the interest of learning more about our situation, may I ask what we're safe from?"

"Yes," the girl said.

I waited for more information. *Are they playing a game I don't know the rules for?* I sighed and asked again.

"We're safe from everything not here," she said. "Now, I've helped again. Can I ask it a question?"

I'm not even going to try to guess what she may ask. "Sure."

"It gave Sir a name. Does it know my name?"

"I don't, but I think it best to call you Mam if *you* don't know your name," I said.

"Hmmm...I don't know if I like Mam. What do you think, umm, Sir?"

"Is Mam better than what I call you?" he asked.

"You don't call me anything."

"Is Mam better than nothing?" I asked.

"Hmmm...I don't...yes, having a name is better than not having one. You may call me Mam."

"In case you've forgotten, my name's Fitzeirick."

"Fitzeirick. It has a long name," Mam said. "Feels funny when I say it."

"Then call it Fitz," Sir suggested.

No one has ever called me Fitz, but I can't think of a reason to argue with him.

"Maybe," Mam said, "but I'm not sure. How about Itfitz?"

That's worse than Fitz, but if it gets me out of here... "Call me what you'd like, I'm not going to be picky. We need to find a way out."

"There's no way out, we're always here. Others come from somewhere else, but none leave," Sir said.

"I don't believe we can't get out. If others come here, they have to get in from a passage. The snake...er, slither, got in here. It eats squeakers, which get in. The squeakers come here for some reason."

Mam laughed. "They come here because they don't want to stay where they were."

I shook my head and tried to forget her answer. "Sir, tell me about the fire you saw down here."

"I saw it once, when I was alone. The wall glowed, but the air wasn't hot. Fire should be hot. Oh, and fire smells...the fire on the wall didn't smell. It scared me, so I left and never went back."

"Fire's not safe. It can hurt you," Mam added.

"Mam, I'll do everything I can to keep you and Sir safe. Remember, I have steel."

"It may be gone," Sir said. "Fire doesn't last forever."

"Or the fire decided to go someplace else," Mam commented.

I'm getting nowhere. "What about water? Where do you get water?"

"We found Itfitz in a water place," she said.

"Do you mean there are more places for water?"

"Yes," Sir said. "But we run into others at different water places. Fitz was in a safe water place."

"You keep mentioning others. Are more people here?"

"No," she said. "The others are someplace else, not here."

I pinched the bridge of my nose. "Why did you take me from the safe water place?"

"To keep others from taking Itfitz," Mam replied.

"We thought Fitz might be dead. Didn't want Fitz to stay near the water if it was dead," Sir explained.

I almost dreaded the answer to my next question. "What were you going to do with me if I was dead?"

"Take what we could and leave the rest for others," he said.

I shivered and decided to not ask for details. "I could use a drink of water."

"Might not be safe now," she suggested.

"I'll keep you safe."

"Be happy to take you there," Sir said, after a big sigh. "But it's not going to help."

I pushed my talent into the stone as we walked. *I'm sure it's not natural, but nothing's perfect. Sooner or later I'll find a fault.*

By 'looking' ahead, I kept us from running into walls and pushed them to walk a little faster. Finally, I felt the passage open into a much larger area and smelled damp air. "I think we're getting close."

"How can you tell?" Sir asked.

"I feel a cavern ahead and smell water in the air. Let's drink and get some rest."

"We can drink here," Mam said, "but not rest. Others might come and make this place not safe."

My talent showed me where the stone got wet and I directed my friends toward it. While drinking water from my cupped hands, two thoughts came to mind. First, we were somewhere below the capital. Second, we didn't trip over my stole on the way back here. Had we taken a different tunnel or did someone or something take my heavy robe?

Mam interrupted my thoughts. "I think we need to move again."

"Sir, please lead us to a safe place to rest," I said.

A sneeze roared through the area. "Sorry, I got water up my nose," Sir explained. "I'm ready to go now."

I reached out with my talent to check our surroundings as we walked. The 'room' was large, but the damp air kept sound from echoing. At least a dozen tunnels lead away. I couldn't get an accurate count because water pooled in several places and blocked my power.

We exited into another square tunnel. I wondered why someone made them. Was this a dungeon? I'd never heard of such a thing before. Punishments for those who broke the law came swiftly; forcing someone to live out their life imprisoned was unheard of. *Yet Eirickson had no problem doing it to me.* The thought of pointless torture made my stomach burn, leaving a bitter taste in my mouth. *I need something to get me out of this bad mood.*

"Sir, you said you found the fire when you were alone. Where did you find Mam?" I asked.

"I found her huddled up, making sad sounds. Men fought to claim her," he said.

"Mam, do you remember anything from before you were here?"

"Has Itfitz forgotten? We were getting water before we were here."

I tried a different strategy. "Do you remember anything from before you found me?"

"Yes. I remember we weren't far from safe water when we heard noises. Loud noises. Yelling and a thump before the noises stopped. The noises scared us so we moved away to be safe. We wanted water and had to go back. Sir tripped over something as we crossed the room. He thought it was dead since it didn't move. I made him drag it to safety. I didn't think it was dead."

"You don't remember anything before that?" I asked.

She went quiet for a while before saying. "I think I'd like to sleep now."

It seemed like resting when you could was a good idea here. Sir agreed and led us somewhere safe to huddle together and sleep.

I wasn't sure how long I'd been asleep when something kicked my shin. Whatever struck me yelled and fell to the floor.

I jumped to my feet and drew my sword. "Someone's here. Stay on the floor, whoever you are."

"Not safe, not safe!" Mam screamed.

"Mam. Sir. Stay against the wall and be quiet," I whispered.

"We'll stay safe," Sir said.

"I won't stay on the floor," an angry male snarled. "You attacked me."

"We were sleeping here," I argued. "You kicked me. Stay down and let us leave in peace."

"I'll give you your peace once I get my hands on you, coward."

My earlier discovery came to mind and I pushed out my talent, finding where the angry man's feet pressed against the stone. I moved away. "How do you intend to fight me when you can't see me?"

"Keep talking. I'll find you."

I tracked his footsteps to make sure he followed me. "I don't understand how you tripping over me makes you feel wronged. After all, I was asleep. You woke me."

"Sounds like you keep moving away. Don't blame you for being scared of me. Let me find you, maybe I'll take it easy when I beat you down. Once I'm finished with you, I'll find your woman. She needs a better man."

He walked from wall to wall, angling across the tunnel. It must have worked well for him against people who couldn't see. It made him easy prey for me. I stayed silent, tracking his movement to figure out where to stand so he wouldn't find me.

"Where are you?" he bellowed, as he got closer.

I struck, swinging my sword hard toward where I guessed the back of his knee would be. The blow connected. His leg buckled and he fell screaming. As soon as the stone told me his hands were on the ground, I brought the pommel down toward his head. I struck him, but must have missed my mark because he bellowed again.

"What'd you hit me with? Doesn't matter. When I find you, I'll kill you and take it, too."

I stepped back. "I've already bested you. Go on and let this be over."

"Bested?" he yelled. "You don't best anyone down here. Only kill or be killed."

I put more distance between us as he spoke.

After standing, he shifted his weight from side to side before moving.

I took a moment to check where my friends were. The muscles in my chest grew tight as I planned my attack. *As much as I don't want to, I have to kill him. His death means our survival.*

"Last time I offer. Go away or this will be your grave," I warned.

He roared again and moved toward me, faster than before.

Crouching, I waited until his leg was within striking distance. After sucking a deep breath, I swung at his knee again. He screamed at the blow. His fist skimmed the side of my head. I stepped back, in case he took another swing, then thrust the sword toward his body. The blade pressed through his flesh, scraping bone as I pushed harder.

He recoiled from the wound, the violent movement threatening to yank the sword from my grip. It made a sickening, sucking sound as I pulled it from his body.

He fell and coughed. "What'd you do to me?" he bellowed.

I stayed quiet. My talent told me he lay where he fell, moaning and breathing heavy. He coughed again and spat. "I'll find you and make sure you suffer before you die." The downed man sucked in a wheezing breath.

A queasy feeling crept into my stomach.

Quietly stalking my injured opponent, I stopped a step away until I was sure he wasn't trying to get up. I stomped on his forehead to keep his head still.

He grabbed my leg. "What're you doing?"

My blood ran cold before I shoved my blade toward where I thought his neck would be. As it pushed through skin and muscle, his grip relaxed.

He made a couple of strange whistling gasps before the tunnel went silent.

I couldn't stop my legs from shaking. *Kill or be killed.*

I sat and breathed deep, swallowing until the nausea went away, before searching the dead man's body to see what I could find out about him. He felt thin, but in better condition than my two friends. His clothes were worn, but not threadbare. I used his shirt to wipe the blood from my sword and put the weapon away before returning to Sir and Mam.

As my footsteps got close, Sir called out, "Stay back!"

It was almost funny to hear him try to sound menacing. "Peace, Sir," I said. "It's Fitzeirick. He's dead. I'm fine."

"Take us to it," Mam said.

"Why?" I asked. "I told you he's dead. Don't you believe me?"

"It may have things we can use," Sir explained. "Dead, it doesn't need them. But we live."

I nodded and led them to the body.

"It feels big, tall...and it has a shirt," Mam said, excitedly. "Sir, can I have it?"

"It'll have blood on it," I warned her.

"A bloody shirt's better than none," she said.

"Fitz, help me lift it," Sir said.

The body weighed more than I expected. "Mam, hurry," I grunted.

The cloth bunched up against my arms and we dropped the body.

Mam giggled. "It's kind of itchy."

"Nothing on its feet," Sir commented. "It has pants."

"I bet they're too big," she mumbled.

"Even if they are, we can use them for something," he said. "Keeps others from getting them."

I shrugged. "If you want the pants, take them. What do we do with the body?"

"Leave it," she said. "The squeakers will clean it up and the slithers will hunt the squeakers. We can eat if we find them again."

Eat and get eaten seems almost the same as kill or be killed.

Sir grunted. "We should go. Others may come looking."

"Lead the way," I said, nodding.

I sythed to watch for surprises. The stone around us felt like nothing when I reached into it. The longer I searched, the stranger the dense, flawless material felt. Somehow, someone changed the natural stone as they made these square hallways. It reminded me of the floor in the council room.

We kept walking until, for reasons only known to Sir, we stopped at a safe place and sat to rest.

"Is everyone else here like the man I killed?"

"Violent, angry, and mean," Sir said. "Most are."

"We aren't like that," Mam noted.

"No, you're not. You two have helped me a lot."

"And Fitz has helped us in return," he said.

"Itfitz still hasn't said what it knows about me," she said.

I'm never going to get used to that name. "I tried. You don't seem to know much about yourself."

"I know I was a girl."

"How long ago were you a girl?" I asked.

"I was a girl before time stopped."

I sighed. "Time didn't stop. Without the sun, we can't tell what time it is."

"If we can't see time move, it's stopped," she argued.

"She's right," Sir agreed.

"I get the point, even if I don't believe it. Where were you a girl, before time stopped?"

"I don't remember the name of the other place. I remember the....um, trees. And blurry, tall rocks. Men were fighting."

"Blurry, tall rocks? What do you mean?" I asked, scratching my chin. *Stubble. Guess I've been down here a few days.*

"They were always far away, past the...the trees."

"Could be mountains," Sir offered, surprising me.

I nodded. "Far away tall rocks *could* be mountains. You said men were fighting. How many?"

"Many, many men. More than I could see, I think."

I closed my eyes and tried to imagine the scene. "Sounds like a battle. The last battle I know of happened before I was born. The Croian army drove Varia out of what became my skati. Are you Varian?"

Her foot smacked the floor. "Itfitz said I'm Mam. Is Itfitz trying to change my name now?"

"No. Your name's still Mam, but are you from Varia?"

"I don't remember. It doesn't sound like a word I know."

"How about Satra? Are you Satran?" I asked.

"I don't remember. I used to know I was me...now, I'm Mam." She sniffled a couple of times before sobbing.

I reached out to her and pulled her to me, trying to comfort the confused girl.

"You need to keep quiet," Sir said, gruffly. "Weak sounds can attract others. We should move."

I can't believe he spoke to her that way. "You can't blame her for being upset," I said. "There isn't much to be happy about down here."

"Weak noises like that can get us killed," Sir insisted.

I clenched my jaw. *Haven't I proven myself?* "I'll worry about that. Now, take me to the fire on the wall."

"I'll do my best to find it again," he said, stepping away from me.

As we walked, I tried to comfort the sobbing girl...woman. *If she was alive when Eirick drove the Varian out, how old is she?* At some point, she grew quiet and we continued to move in silence.

With no sense of time, we fell into a routine. Wake and move happened most often. I killed any creature we found so we could eat. Sometimes we made our way to water before moving or resting. I tried to keep count of how many times we slept. After a while, it didn't seem to matter.

We heard sounds of others, but I never picked out any large groups, two or three moving together at most. We avoided confrontation whenever possible.

When I had to fight, using my talent made them easy prey. Most wore threadbare clothes, at best. One carried three big squeakers. We ate well then. At first, I wondered why no one used their talent against me. Eventually, I decided it didn't matter. They were dead and we were alive.

Everything changed when I noticed a faint glow ahead of us. We turned a corner and a shining light stabbed my eyes before I could close them. Bright spots floated inside my eyelids while I waited for the pain to stop.

Chapter 8

We gasped and moved back to the comfort of dimmer light.

"The fire?" I asked.

"Yes," Sir said, voice trembling. "Now you've seen it and how it hurts. We should go, get far away from here."

No. I need to find out what I can. "You two can leave. I'm going to get a closer look."

Pushing my talent out, I found nothing pressing against the stone, but there was a slim line of warmth on the floor. Before turning the corner, I shifted my focus to the walls. My breath caught when my energy didn't flow smoothly down the right wall.

As I understood what I'd felt, my heart pounded in my chest. *A crack.* Sir had mistaken light coming through for a fire. I returned with the good news.

"Fitz has finally gone mad," he said, shaking his head. "The fire's right there, burning bright and hurting our eyes."

"I'm telling you, there's no fire. It's light shining through a crack in the wall."

"Madness," he said. "These tunnels are all smooth. No cracks, no holes."

"If I prove it to you, will you believe me?"

"I'd believe Itfitz," Mam said, putting her hands on her hips.

"If Fitz *can* prove it, I'll have to believe or I'd be the mad one," Sir said, nodding.

"Come with me and do as I say."

We walked together to the corner. A narrow line of light ran across the floor, from where I felt the crack, and stopped short of touching the left wall.

Sir and Mam shut their eyes tight against the glow.

"Wait here."

Shielding my eyes and pressing my back to the wall, I sidestepped to the crack.

"Look now."

"The fire's gone," Mam squealed.

"So it is," Sir said, rubbing his chin.

"I'm right. It's shining through a crack leading somewhere."

"Where?" she asked, looking around.

"Somewhere not here," I answered and chuckled. It felt good to give her a confusing answer for once. "I don't know yet. Could be a room on the other side of the wall with a fire or it could lead outside."

"What do we do now?" he asked.

"We go back around the corner and wait to see if the light goes away without someone blocking the crack," I explained.

Mam frowned. "Why?"

"If it goes away, maybe this crack opens to the outside. We'll rest nearby and I'll watch."

Mam and Sir drifted off to sleep. I studied them in the dim glow. They had much in common at first glance.

Both had long, matted hair. Their skin was caked with filth covered from head to foot. Sir's tangled beard reached the middle of his chest.

Their clothing told the same story of hard life as their hair. I already knew neither wore shoes. The oversized shirt hid Mam's body. Sir's shirt was almost gone, not much more than a collar with some shredded cloth. His loose-fitting pants were threadbare too, pant legs missing below his knees.

Excitement kept me awake, like a young child full of hope for the promise of what may come. I settled into a routine, counting to one hundred before looking.

All the movement and intense focus must have worn me out because Sir's yelling woke me. "It's gone, the fire's gone! Fitz was right!"

I didn't understand what he meant. "No fire here," I mumbled.

Mam giggled. "Right, the fire's gone. Itfitz said the fire might go away on its own. A good sign, right?"

My eyes flew open and I hurried to look around the corner. He was right, no light. I sythed and found the tunnel empty. *It must be nighttime.*

I jogged to the crack and placed my hands on either side of it. After several deep breaths, I pushed energy into the stone, trying to figure out what was going on inside the wall.

The edges feel like melted glass. Can't reach far enough to find the outside. Must be deep underground.

The opening ran nearly level with the floor for a couple of steps before turning upward. It felt like a natural flaw in the stone with several smaller faults splintering away from its rough walls. Still, there was the same unnatural feel of forced density and hardness. I sat down to rest.

"Mam, Sir, stay nearby. I need to gather my strength, see if I can work on this fault. If I can open it, we can get out of here. I have to concentrate for this, so I can't keep track of what's around us. We'll be safer staying together."

"What do we do if the fire comes back?" he asked.

"We'll move from here when the light gets too bright."

"Fine," he said. "Can Fitz really get us out of here?"

"I'm going to try," I promised and breathed deep to focus.

As soon as I felt ready, I stood and placed my hands on the right side of the crack searching for smaller faults to open. I found one deep in the wall, too far away for me to apply enough pressure.

I sighed, moved to the left, and found a good possibility. Not far past where the dead stone touched natural material, I felt a hole in the natural stone with a small opening facing the crack.

Be nice to have my hammer, my sword's useless for this. If I can get some of the natural stone, I'll make a tool to get us out.

I focused where the hole started and pushed to dislodge any loose material. To my surprise, the hole filled with rubble. I didn't think I'd pushed too hard, but any progress gave me hope.

Roi's recent advice about learning how to work with loose material suddenly came to mind. *My freedom depends on overcoming my weakness.* Sitting with my back to the wall, I breathed slowly and struggled to remember anything Roi tried to teach me. I couldn't recall the lessons. Shaking my head, I thought about what I could try.

I'd created debris from the surrounding rock. Compared to a large, solid rock the smaller stones were loose material, but each *was* a stone. Breaking the stones down into dirt left me with lots of tiny stones. *I can work stone, big or small.*

I stood, put my hands on the wall, and focused on pushing the loose debris out of the collapsed hole. When larger pieces were stuck, I smashed energy into them. The hard blows caused the wall to ring like a strange bell.

"What's that sound?" Sir asked.

"I'm breaking stone."

"It could make this place unsafe," he noted, sounding concerned.

Safe or not, it's going to get us out of these tunnels.

Mam hummed in tune with the ringing.

It took time, but I finally had a small pile of dirt at my feet. I sat to rest and catch my breath. Running my fingers through the material, I took a moment to admire my newfound ability and found comfort being in contact with natural stone again. Once my breathing slowed, I set to work forming a pick.

When the shape felt right, I scraped the point against the tunnel wall and ran my fingers over the area. I couldn't find a scratch. I focused on the point of the pick, added pressure, and forced the stone together making it denser and harder.

Again, I scratched the wall. This time it made an uncomfortable, scraping sound.

"What's that?" Mam asked.

"I think it's what's going to get us out of here," I answered, smiling.

The tool left a noticeable mark which meant the tip was hard enough. I concentrated and tried one more time to draw some strength from the tunnel. The dead stone gave me nothing. *I have to do this with my own strength.*

"Step away." I counted to five in my head and with a loud grunt, swung the hard, pointed stone toward the wall. Sparks flew and I heard a cracking noise.

"What happened?" Sir asked.

Running my fingers over the wall, I felt an irregular pattern of cracks in the surface. "It's going to take work, but I can break the wall. I can get us out."

"What will we do then?" Mam asked.

"Won't know until we figure out where we are," I said, running my finger over the pick's point. The impact blunted it, but I could fix the tool as often as needed, now that I knew what to do. I kept up a cycle of remaking the pick and striking the wall until a sizable piece of the unnatural stone fell to the floor. I felt exhausted and elated at the same time.

I yawned before shoving the pick into the crack. "I need to sleep."

"Good," Sir said. "I want to get away from here before others come looking."

"You always lead us to safety, Sir," I said.

It felt like we walked farther than ever, before he said, "Sleep here."

For the first time in however long I'd been down here, I fell asleep with a sense of hope.

I woke and told them, "I want to work for a while, but soon I'll need water."

The dim glow was comforting now. As we got close, I heard running water. A small stream trickled out of the crack. "Must be raining," I said. "Now we don't have to look for water. Come with me."

Sir sighed. "I haven't thought about rain in — seems like forever."

"No doubt this leads outside...somewhere," I said.

We sat and took turns drinking from our cupped hands. I spent a little time studying a piece of stone from the wall. The strange, green-black color made me feel uneasy for some reason. Its rounded edges and smooth surface reinforced the rock's unnatural quality. I'd hoped to make the piece work for me, but everything about this strange stone was wrong. I threw it down the hall and prepared to go back to work.

Placing my hand on the wall, I pushed my talent inside to find the best spot to strike. Feeling so many cracks made me hope for faster progress as I grabbed the pick. "Step away. I'm ready."

It took fewer strikes this time to break off another piece. The point still needed reforming after each hit, but it seemed to bite a little deeper now. The flow of water continued long after the light had gone. Stopping occasionally to splash water over my head kept me going. Soon the hole was big enough to step into. I reached deeper into the crack, but still couldn't touch natural stone.

"Time to sleep again, Sir. When we wake, I'll need something to eat."

"I wondered if Fitz had forgotten about eating," he said, leading the way to wherever he felt safest.

We woke and spent more time hunting than I would have liked. After killing a few squeakers, Sir led us back to the fault. This time, the light shined in eye-burning glory. *I can put up with the pain if that's what it takes to get out of here.* "I'm going to work now instead of waiting for darkness. My eyes will adjust."

I focused on my task, each blow getting us closer to the outside, closer to freedom. The hard, unnatural stone flaked and shattered easily once the surface was broken. Progress slowed when I had to make the opening wide enough to swing my pick after stepping out of the hallway. Work stopped when my pick wore to the point that I couldn't repair it without more natural material.

The wall rang even more out of tune when I repeated the process of creating dirt and moving it through the crack. I knew the odd sound made Sir uncomfortable, afraid it would attract unwanted attention. I hoped it frightened anyone who didn't know what I was doing. With luck, I'd reach the natural stone before I had to make a third pick.

The light grew steadily brighter as I worked. Having a solid sense of time passing carried a new kind of comfort. Before taking a break, I tried to feel how much farther away the natural stone sat. I almost yelled for joy when I found it was about one arm span away.

"I have good news," I announced.

"We're still in here so it can't be too good," Sir grumbled.

"Hush," Mam scolded him. "Itfitz thinks the news is good so it must be."

"I think I can reach natural stone soon."

"How will that help? We'll still be here," he said.

"I can pull strength and stamina from it and move it without a pick. Our freedom grows close."

"I'm afraid. You're making too much noise, attracting attention. I don't want this to get us killed," he said.

"You saved my life when you found me, Sir. How many times have I saved yours since?" I asked, sounding angrier than intended. *I shouldn't blame him. His fear has served him well so far.*

"Itfitz has fought and killed for us and is working hard to get us out of here. Be happy for now, please," Mam pled.

Sir snorted and walked a few paces away.

"When we get out, what's ItFitz going to do?" she asked.

"I'm going back to my skati. You two are welcome to join me."

"I think I'd like to...if I knew what a skati was."

"It's the territory I governed. I'm going to find my family and friends, and defend my people." I reached up to scratch my chin and felt hair, a respectable beard. *Barely had stubble on my face when I stood before the council.* My fingers brushed across the brand. It felt hard. *Have I been in here long enough for the burn to heal?* "I don't have any support from the council. But, maybe, I can convince some warriors to join my cause. Not sure how many will listen to me with this brand." My gut twisted as I considered that possibility. I took a calming breath. *I won't know until I escape.*

"Seems to me our only option is to follow Fitz," Sir said, walking back to us.

"Not your only option. You'll be free. Go wherever you want."

"Not sure I have anywhere to go. Here's the only place I know," he said.

"Decide later," Mam suggested.

He grunted.

I felt exhausted and excited and concerned. "Break's over," I said, before striking a hard blow. Maybe it was wishful thinking, but I felt like the pick dug deeper with every blow. As the light dimmed, I stretched my arm into it and my fingertips brushed natural stone.

That's it! We'll hunt and sleep underground one last time. My heart raced and I felt lightheaded. Next time I worked I'd be far enough in to use the stone for strength. *We are all but outside.* "Sir," I called out. "We hunt and rest. Things will be looking up afterward."

"Itfitz sounds happy," Mam said.

"I've had a brush with victory. We're much closer to being free."

I found a fair-sized slither and made short work of killing it. A larger one would've been ideal, but I didn't want to spend any more time hunting. *Escape is so close, almost in my grasp.* The excitement made it hard to relax, but I needed sleep.

· · · · ● · ● · · · ·

I woke and rushed us to the growing passage out of our prison. The light shined bright, but I didn't care. After every piece broke, I stretched into the fault for the natural stone. Finally, I placed my entire hand on rock. I took a few deep breaths and pulled in strength. It felt amazing! I stood ready to take on an entire army, to stand alone against a raging horde, confident of victory. I yelled out, not caring who heard me.

"What happened?" Sir yelled into the hole. "Is Fitz hurt?"

"My friend, I've never been better," I bellowed back.

Shaking with power, I focused on my pick and made the point harder than ever. I swung a mighty blow and shattered a man-sized crater in the hard, brittle stone. My pick broke, but I didn't mind. Replacing it was as easy as sything one from the natural stone in my reach.

Being able to draw strength from the ground made each blow hit like dozens of hammers at once. I set into a steady rhythm of gathering strength before slamming into the barrier. The only thing slowing me was clearing debris. Soon, I was through the dense tunnel wall and into natural stone. Now I could move material as I needed. I worked until thirst forced me to stop. Pushing energy into the stone, I felt where it ended. *The surface. We're so close.*

"Water," I announced, exiting the hole. "I need to drink and cool off. Rain would've been nice, but I guess beggars can't be choosers."

As we approached the watering cavern, I sensed small movements on the floor ahead of us and an odd odor floated in the air. "Something's here."

Sir and Mam stood still.

"What is it?" he whispered.

I tried to focus. After working with natural stone again, the dead tunnels felt horrible. "Squeakers, I think, but they're all huddled in the middle of the hallway. I can't pick out individuals."

"Squeakers stick to the walls unless they find food," Mam whispered.

"Smell that?" I asked.

I heard them inhale.

"Something rotting. Not a body, something different," Sir said.

"What should we do?" she asked.

"Stay back." I drew my sword and crept toward whatever was in the middle of the hall. My blade hit, making a sound between a splat and a thud, and several squeakers squealed in pain. More ran past me.

Mam shrieked.

I poked the thing with my sword. It penetrated with little resistance and no sound. I reached down to touch it and found it damp but firm. The texture felt familiar and after a moment feeling it, I realized it was my skaldic stole. I laughed and shook my head. "Unbelievable."

"What has Itfitz found?" she asked.

"My sto — robe. The one I wore when you two found me. Squeakers must have found it and made a nest. I killed a few so we can eat what should be our last meal down here."

"Itfitz didn't smell like that before," she said.

"I was soaking wet when you found me. The wool robe stayed damp after I took it off so it's rotting. That means —" My upper lip quivered. I touched the hard scar on my face. *No. Have I been here long enough for* — I didn't want to follow my thought to conclusion. I wanted to lay on the floor and wait for these thoughts to go away. *Stop. Be strong. Keep your wits. Quench your thirst and get out. Save Sir and Mam.*

"Fitz, what's it mean?" Sir pressed.

I groaned and forced myself to speak the truth. "It means I've been down here a long time. Wool takes time, months...many months, for rot to set in." The rotting stole made me wonder and fear what I would find once I was free.

"No sun, no moon, no stars, no time," Mam sang.

"I understand what you mean, Mam, but it's not true. You'll see when we get out. I promise."

I'd killed four, good-sized squeakers and several bare-skinned young ones. The young were too small to eat so we tossed them away from the cavern. We ate quickly and washed the meal down with plenty of water before heading back to the escape tunnel.

No light greeted us as we got close. I moved to the now gaping fault with a renewed sense of purpose. "You two stay nearby. When I break through at the top, I want to do some scouting. Once I know it's safe, I'll come get you."

"Good plan," Sir agreed.

It wasn't long before I smelled fresh air and almost cried. Hope swelled inside and drove me to work harder. When I stopped to catch my breath, I reached into the fault and felt nothing but air on the tips of my fingers.

I touched freedom.

Working through a blinding flow of joyous tears, I forced my body through the last of the fault, pushing dirt and stone out of my way by sheer will.

That was it. I stood outside.

Chapter 9

The moon's glow seemed like daylight compared to the complete darkness of the tunnels. A cool breeze carried the scent of pine to my nose. I shivered. *Excitement or have the seasons changed?*

I wanted to let loose a victory cry, but good sense prevailed, keeping me quiet to avoid discovery in case anyone was nearby.

Shading my eyes from the moonlight, I looked around to get my bearings. My tunnel opened on the side of a mountain, a few paces above the tree line. Looking behind me, I saw yellow light flickering in several windows beyond some foothills. Judging from the pattern of stars, I stood east of the capital.

Where should I go? Using my talent, I found straight ahead was a sheer drop into darkness. Pushing more energy into the ground showed safe routes north and northeast. *Now to get Sir and Mam.*

Walking back into the dungeon, I sythed steps in the natural stone floor to make it easier for my friends to walk up.

I stepped out and called them to me.

"I think others are coming this way," Sir said.

"You and Mam get in the tunnel. Walk carefully until you reach the steps, the climb will be easier then. At the top, don't walk away. You could fall off the cliff not far from the exit," I said, my hand on his shoulder, nudging him toward the hole. "I'll hold off anyone who comes before I make my way up."

"No," he said, pushing my hand away. "Fitz did the work. Take Mam and go up. I'll follow when I'm sure it's safe."

I pushed my sense into the floor and felt several footsteps. The group hadn't walked close enough for me to tell how many people headed our way. "It may be too many. Please go," I urged him. "I'll close the tunnel after we get out."

He pushed me. "Go now, get her to safety. I'll be fine...right behind you two."

I grunted in frustration, but wasn't going to argue. Taking Mam's hand, I moved her toward the gap in the wall.

She stepped up and tipped forward. "The floor's slippery."

I reached to steady her. "Let me help you to the steps."

She waited until I felt a few steps under my feet before saying, "I'm on the steps now. Can I make it all the way up?"

"I'm sure you can. Be careful and wait for us when you get out."

Near the bottom, I heard voices and stopped.

"Go away — leave...leave me be." Sir sounded terrified.

"What're you doing here old man? What's all this stuff on the floor?" The voice sounded cold and hard. I'd never heard it before in my time down here.

"I...I don't..." Sir stammered

"Don't lie to me. I'll crush your neck."

Jumping out of the passage, I crashed into someone. Luckily, I managed to get my feet back first, drew my sword, and thrust downward. A woman screamed when my attack connected.

I looked up and saw a tall, broad form holding Sir by the neck, high enough his feet couldn't touch the floor.

"Who are you?" the cold voice demanded.

"Fitzeirick. Let him go or die where you stand."

"We'll kill both of you," he growled.

Kill or be killed. I tried to sense how many people and where they stood. The dead stone masked the numbers as they closed around us.

"Go! Don't let them get out!" Sir shouted.

I heard him choke, then the crack of bones. Sir groaned before his limp body hit the floor with a sickening thud. I roared and whipped my sword back and forth in front of me, driving people away.

"Kill him," the cold voice ordered.

I jumped back into the escape passage and ran up. I didn't want to leave Sir's body to the others, but had no doubt they'd kill me before I could drag him out.

Shouts from the hallway told me they found the gaping hole in the wall. In my rush to get out, I tripped exiting the hole and fell into Mam.

She screamed and hit me.

"Stop. Peace. It's me — It's Fitz!" I yelled, grabbing her. "Others are coming. I've got to close the passage."

"But, Sir —"

"He's dead." Crawling back to the entrance, I shoved energy into the walls of the passage. Rage and sorrow helped me gather more strength from the ground and I let everything flood into my escape tunnel, collapsing most of its length and crushing everyone in it.

"Sir's dead?" she cried out.

Exhausted, I forced myself to stand and went to her. "He died covering our escape. I don't know who he was, but he wasn't a coward," I said, lifting her into a hug.

For a moment, she stood still, resting her head against my chest. We stood together for several heartbeats before she gasped and pushed against me. "Now the others will get us, kill us."

"No, I sealed the way out," I assured her. "Those dark tunnels can dine on everyone left inside, for all I care."

She squinted. "The light hurts my eyes."

"Shade them with your hand and follow me. We need to move, find shelter before sunrise."

She covered her eyes with her hand. "What happens at sunrise?"

"It'll be too bright for us to see. We need time for our eyes to adjust to daylight again."

"Where will we go if we can't see?"

I took her arm as we walked. "We'll sleep during the day. With a bit of luck, we'll find my friends or someone who knows where they are. I'll get you to a safe place. It's the least I can do to honor Sir."

I led us northeast, a heading I hoped would take us to The Trader's Cup. Using my talent, we followed the safest way I could find into the trees to block the bright moonlight and make it harder for anyone to see us.

I let go of her arm when I was sure she was steady. "We're shaded by the trees now. You can take your hands off your eyes."

She moved her hands and blinked as she looked at me. "Better."

"Stay near me. I'll keep you safe."

Keeping my talent pushed into the ground made it easy to avoid exposed roots hiding in the shadows. In the twilight before daybreak, I located a small deer bedded down and used the ground to hold it. I found a rock and sythed a sharp edge. After cutting the deer's throat, I skinned it with the stone knife and cut strips of meat for our meal.

"What's this?" Mam asked, after swallowing her first bite.

"Deer. I'm sure you've had it before."

"Maybe, but it tasted different."

"I'd guess it wasn't raw. I don't have tools to make a fire to cook it. A fire would hurt our eyes anyway. With all the raw slither and squeaker we've eaten, raw deer should be fine."

She nodded.

We ate our fill and looked for shelter. A downed tree was the best option I found. I created a depression in the ground beneath it and we sat down to sleep. I tried to lie down, but it didn't feel right. Mam sobbed softly as she drifted off, so I pulled her close to comfort her and help her feel safe.

Aesa filled my thoughts. *I'm out and alive...closer to holding my fiancée again.* A few tears rolled down my cheeks as I fell asleep.

It was dark when we woke.

Mam yelped after placing her hand on the tree to scoot out.

"What's wrong?" I asked.

"This thing, I...felt...something. It made me sad. It's dead," she said, shivering. She looked scared and confused.

"The tree? Can you tell me what you felt?"

"At first, I felt a strange twitch in my hand. I saw, in my head, how the thing...the tree, stood. It was tall and old. Bugs ate the part underground, cutting off its life." She had tears in her eyes.

"You're a woodsyth, no doubt," I said, trying to comfort her with a quick smile. "To me, it's only a fallen tree. I have a feeling you're going to have to learn how to control your talent all over again."

I took her by the hand and started walking.

After a few paces, she asked, "What does 'control my talent' mean?"

"We talked about this before. Everyone's born with their talent or talents. I guess if you go a long time without using yours, you forget about it and can't control it. Perhaps it would be best if you try to avoid touching wood until we find some help."

She let go of my hand. "Why? What harm can a twitch in my hand be?"

"Depending on your power, you could weaken the wood and cause a tree to fall or a wooden building to collapse. I wish Crum was here." *Assuming he's still alive.* I swallowed several times before the lump forming in my throat cleared.

"What's a Crum?"

"He. Crum's a close friend and a woodsyth. I suspect he'd help you."

"Where is he?"

I shrugged and looked toward our destination. "Don't know. I'm taking us someplace I might find him or someone who can help us find him."

"Sounds like a good idea."

"Glad you agree," I said, smiling. Pushing my talent ahead of us, I watched for obstacles and searched for a safe path. After walking a while, I sensed a low pass to the east. We hurried toward it, moving faster as the terrain smoothed. The sky grew brighter as we entered the pass.

"We need to find a shelter," I told her.

"Why? I thought ItFitz is taking me to Crum."

"We'll get there, in due time, but the sun will rise soon and blind us."

"Oh."

After a short search, I found a shallow cave not far to the south. Unfortunately, it wasn't tall enough for us to sit up so we lay down to get out of the sun. Neither of us slept well, but we stayed in the comfort of the shade until right before sunset.

"We need to get moving," I said.

"I'm thirsty," Mam said, after yawning.

"If I'm right, there's a river not too far away."

"That's where we should go," she decided.

The dim light wasn't painful, but my eyes still preferred darkness. *It's nice to be able to see where I'm going again.* We hadn't walked long before I heard frogs croaking and chirping in the distance.

"If we hurry, we can make the river with enough time to follow it north before we have to find shelter," I said.

"Which way?" Mam asked, glancing around.

I pointed toward the river and she took off running.

Her reaction caught me by surprise. I stood motionless for a moment before giving chase. When I caught her, I scooped her up from behind and carried her like a child.

She giggled.

Near the riverbank, I put her down and told her to wait until I knew the ground was solid enough to be safe. Not only was the bank safe, but a large patch of cattail grew along the river.

Mam watched me step into the warm, slow-moving water and pull several stalks. I sat down next to her and took a bite of the fibrous plant before handing her one. "Don't bite the dark part at the top, it's no good."

She nodded and bit into the stalk. "This isn't meat," she said, after swallowing.

"True, but it *is* food and we don't have to hunt it."

We ate our fill and quenched our thirst before following the river. "Why did you carry me?"

I shrugged. "It seemed like the thing to do, I guess. We were running, having fun. You laughed when I picked you up."

"Yes, I did."

"Why do you still call me Itfitz?" I asked. "We're out of the tunnels, why don't you use my name?"

She rubbed her hands down her arms. "Because the tunnels are still here."

A familiar feeling of frustration crept into my head. *It's not her fault; the tunnels made her this way.* I changed the subject instead of upsetting either of us further. "Can you swim?"

"What do you mean?"

"Move through water," I explained, moving my arms like I was swimming.

"I walked in the water in the tunnels sometimes."

"Not the same thing. The river's deeper than you are tall."

"But I touched the bottom of the river with my hand when we were drinking."

I nodded. "At the bank, the middle is much deeper."

She pointed at me. "You're taller than me, carry me across."

I shook my head. "I'll have to swim."

"Raise the bottom of the river."

I laughed and shook my head. "Water blocks a lot of my ability. I have trouble moving mud, wet dirt. Doubt I could push my power into the bottom of a river. Roi moves mud much better than I can, but I've never asked him if he can move anything under water."

"What's a Roi?"

"Another friend, like Crum, but he's older and bigger. He's a stonesyth, like me."

"Did he teach you how to use your talent?"

"Yes. Taught me almost everything I know about sything."

"And Crum will teach me?"

"I'm sure he'll do whatever he can, but we need to cross the river first."

"You'll think of something," she said, grinning.

I bowed low. "Thank you for your confidence in my abilities. I appreciate your trust."

She stared at me. "Why did you bend over?"

"Bowing is a show of respect," I told her.

"I think people have bowed around me before...before I was in the tunnels."

"Are you sure?"

"I think I'm sure," she replied, sounding less sure.

"Concentrate on what you feel right now. Did people bow around you or to you?"

She closed her eyes for a moment. "Umm...I think they bowed to others around me, not *to* me."

"It sounds like you were raised around royalty. Are you royalty or not? And, if so, where are you from?" I sighed heavily and rubbed the back of my neck. "So many things we don't know."

She shrugged and opened her eyes. "How do we find out?"

"Once we find my friends and get back to my skati, I'll put out a proclamation. Maybe representatives from Varia can identify you. If you're not Varian, you might be from Satra. I hope you aren't Satran."

"Why? What's wrong with being Satran?"

I sighed and told her about the raids and what Eirickson did to me. As I spoke, my speech to Crum about actions and consequences came to mind and I let loose a long, loud, belly laugh.

"What's so funny?" she asked, looking puzzled.

"Oh, I wasn't laughing at you. Something I'd said to Crum struck me as funny. My own words may have predicted my fate."

"Did you predict the mark on your face?"

I reached up to my left cheek. It hadn't hurt in a while. The brand had healed into a rough scar. "No. Being branded never crossed my mind."

"What does it mean?"

I shook my head. "It's not important now, but I'm sure it will come up in conversations soon enough. I need to figure out how to get you across the river. If you had control of your talent, you could fell a tree for a bridge. Of course, if you knew how to swim ..."

"A bridge or swim. Are those the only choices?"

I took a moment to think. "We could follow the river until it narrows and step across. Might take us back into the mountains, though. More walking than crossing here."

"I don't like how that sounds. Maybe when I see you swim, I'll remember. Like bowing reminded me of something before the tunnels."

"If nothing else, I'll teach you to float well enough to keep your head above water and pull you across," I said. "Still, I think we'll camp outside one more day before reaching The Trader's Cup."

"Lead the way."

We made it to the hills with plenty of time to find a depression, obscured by scrub brush, in the side of the hill. Mam curled up against me as we settled in.

We slept until twilight and then headed back to the river.

The frogs stopped croaking and splashed into the safety of the river as we got close.

"What was that?" Mam asked, startled.

"Frogs going for a swim to get away from us."

"Do you swim like a frog?"

I chuckled. "No, I don't swim that well. Now, watch me."

I backed into the river. "Lean down into the water and rotate your arms while kicking your legs like this," I said. After swimming a short distance, I stopped. "Remind you of anything?"

"Sorry. I don't think I've ever seen anyone swim."

"No problem, but now I have to ask. Do you trust me, Mam?"

"Itfitz, I've trusted you with my life since I met you and haven't been disappointed yet."

Except I had to leave Sir behind. A cold shiver shook me as I swam closer to the shore and stood. "Join me in the river, please. I'll teach you how to float so I can pull you across the river. Don't be afraid."

"Oh, it's warm," she said, stepping into the water.

"It is here, but toward the middle, it will be cooler. I need you to take a deep breath and hold it until I tell you to let it out."

Mam inhaled and closed her mouth with her cheeks puffed out.

I counted time in my head. "Let it out."

She exhaled before drawing several breaths. "Why did I do that?"

"It will help you float. Step out to me please."

The water was near the middle of my chest, almost to Mam's chin when she stopped. "I can't go any farther." She sounded at the edge of panic.

"Trust me?"

Her chin made little ripples in the water when she nodded.

"Turn around, take a deep breath, hold it, and fall over toward me. I'll catch you."

She did as instructed. I caught her and kept her head above water.

"I did it," she squealed and her body sank.

"Deep breath and hold it," I reminded her.

She inhaled.

"Relax. I'll swim and pull you along. Keep your legs together so I can kick."

I took a deep breath, lay back into the water, and kicked across the river. "You can stand and breathe now," I said. "We should eat a little and drink plenty of water. I'd like to reach the inn before daybreak."

"I'm cold now," she said, after we were on dry land.

"We're soaking wet and the night air has a bit of a chill. Walking will warm us and dry our clothes."

We stepped onto the porch of The Trader's Cup as the sky changed shades. I lifted my hand to knock on the door, but stopped when I remembered I had no idea when Geri would rise from his bed. *He might kill me if I wake him.*

"If it gets too bright, shade your eyes. We have to wait for the door to open."

As the sunlight grew steadily more uncomfortable, I wondered if Geri would ever wake.

Chapter 10

I have to get used to sunlight again. To distract myself from the wait, I opened my eyes a slit and counted to one hundred. Each time I finished counting, I opened them a little more. Somewhere around five hundred, the door opened.

"We don't serve your kind here, beggars. Be off with you before I make you leave."

At first glance, I thought it was Roi, but this man had brown hair and sounded Varian. I stood. "Please, let us in. We aren't beggars. I need to see Geri, he knows me."

"You both stink and wear beggar's clothes. Leave."

I told Mam to stay seated and raised my hands. "We're not here to cause trouble. I'm looking for some people and Geri may know where they are."

"Not doing what you're told *is* causing trouble," he said, shoving me off the porch.

After tripping and falling backward, I stood and drew my sword. "This blade is inscribed with my family line. It proves I'm no beggar. Get Geri, he'll tell you."

He laughed. "Beggar gets a child's training blade and thinks he's something special. Not only are you a beggar, you're touched with madness. For the third time, be gone. Don't make me beat you."

I frowned and slid my sword back into its scabbard. "Be reasonable. I've done nothing to you. All I ask is that you let me see Geri. We don't even have to go inside you could bring —"

He charged me.

Tracking his footsteps as soon as he stepped off the porch, I felt him sything and shifted to the right while pulling strength from the ground. My fist connected with his gut.

His body folded around my arm and he wheezed.

I let him drop to the ground and stood ready to hit him again if he started to rise.

Mam screamed.

"Stay your hand or I kill her," I heard a grumpy voice yell. "Slode, stay on the ground before you get beat to death."

I looked up and saw Geri standing behind Mam, his blade against her throat. She was stiff as a fence post, arms clenched across her chest and eyes squeezed shut.

"Geri, it's good to see you again. Please, let my friend go."

He squinted at me and tilted his head to the side before pulling the short sword away from her neck. "Skald Fitzeirick, is that you?"

"Doubt I'm still a skald, but yes, it's me," I answered, walking toward him. "Are Roi and Crum here?"

He frowned. "Come inside and...do you need to eat?"

"We'd appreciate a hot meal, yes. This is Mam. Mam, Geri, owner of The Trader's Cup."

Geri offered Mam his hand.

She shook it, but said nothing.

"Give her some time to get to know you, Geri. She's shy...for good reason."

He turned to me. "Please, excuse my earlier threat. It looked like Slode was in over his head. He's here to help with problem customers. Could be his size isn't the deterrent I hoped."

"Sorry it came to blows. He didn't believe me when I said knew you."

As we walked inside, Geri looked over his shoulder and yelled, "Dust yourself off and go help in the kitchen."

Mam clung to me as we entered the great room and didn't leave my side until I pulled out a chair for her.

"I'm looking for Crum and Roi," I said, sitting down.

"Crum checked in here last, oh, about three weeks ago. Roi...well, about a month after you went missing, he and Crum came here. He paid off Grima's debt, then left with her and Einns. Told Crum to stay behind and find you. Your silver-tongued friend's been searching most of nine months now."

I blinked. "Nine months? Are you sure?"

"Positive. Where have you been? I guess the brand on your face and the rags you're wearing are part of the story."

I nodded. "I'll explain soon enough, but if Crum's supposed to stay behind, where is he?"

"Lurking around Skald Nikulas' holdings, most likely. From what I know, he doesn't stay in one place long. A few months back, he told me he saw something he shouldn't have while looking for you. Best guess, he'll stop by here in the next week or two." He shrugged. "Never know for sure when he'll turn up."

"Do you know who's ruling my skati?"

Geri shook his head and sighed. "From what I understand...Satra."

"What?" For a moment, it felt like the room was going to spin around me. I thrust my finger toward Geri. "No. That can't be right." The room went quiet when my hand slapped the tabletop. "Tell me the truth!"

Mam jumped and whimpered.

"I haven't seen a trader from beyond the eastern woods in some time. Rumor is everyone who heads there is either captured or killed by Satran forces. They've conquered the far eastern territory."

Before I could say anything, a squat, older woman arrived with a tray of roasted meats. "Looked like you two could use a good meal," she said.

"Thank you, Luta," Geri said. "When you get a chance bring us boiled grains and keep coffee coming."

"Of course, sir."

"I miss Grima. She was much more pleasant," Geri muttered, after Luta walked out of sight.

Mam looked from the meat to Geri.

"Please miss, help yourself. You're so thin, I'm surprised you cast a shadow."

She responded with a weak smile before grabbing a handful of meat and eating like a starving animal.

Geri's eyes opened wide. "Not shy about eating. Where did you find her?"

I struggled to understand how Satra had conquered my lands and barely heard the question. "Are you sure my skati has fallen under Satran control?"

He nodded. "All indications point to that being the case. Now, about the brand...and this girl."

I rubbed my finger over the upside-down T and shivered. "Strange how the Council of Thanes let Satra invade, but I'm the one branded a traitor."

"Who did this to you?"

"Did I mention Jarl Eirickson doesn't like me?"

He rubbed his chin for a moment. "Hmm...don't recall hearing it before."

"My half-brother dislikes my Varian heritage. When I met with the Council of Thanes, I expressed my displeasure with their decision not to send aid to my skati while we were being attacked by Satra. Eirickson demanded he and I meet in private. There, he made clear his disdain for me and my mother. Bound me to a chair and branded me with a white-hot iron." I combed my fingers through my scraggly beard and muttered, "It seems I didn't escape soon enough."

Geri's eyes grew wide again as his jaw dropped. ""He held you captive in a chair all this time? How...how'd you get away?"

"I wasn't held in the chair long. He dumped me into a pitch-black maze of tunnels beneath the capital. I met Mam and another man, called him Sir. You could say they saved my life. I did everything I could to return their kindness and dug a way out."

I took a piece of meat and bit into it when Geri turned to Mam. The taste and texture of cooked meat took some getting used to.

"How long were you in those tunnels, miss?" Geri asked her.

She shook her head.

"She doesn't remember much," I answered after swallowing. "Doesn't trust people much either. Sir was a good person. The others were, at best, unsavory."

"Oh...oh my. I had no idea...none at all. I'm so sorry for what I did to you, Mam. Please, please forgive my earlier threat."

She nodded and kept eating.

"And this man, Sir, where is he?"

Mam whimpered.

I frowned. "He's dead. Sacrificed himself so we could escape."

Geri closed his eyes and shook his head.

Slode appeared, carrying a tray of steaming bowls and large mugs of coffee. He studied Mam for a moment before staring at me. "What'd you do to her?"

"Peace, my man," I said, raising my hands. "She's upset over what we've been through."

Geri motioned him away from the table after he put the tray in front of us. "How'd you survive?"

"We moved around a lot. Water wasn't too hard to find. Food was more of a problem. We had to catch squeakers or slithers...ate what we caught raw, no fire."

"Squeakers or slithers?" Geri asked.

I grinned. "Sorry, umm...rats and snakes."

Mam tugged on my sleeve and whispered, "I...I'd like to rest now."

"Geri, do you have a room she could use?"

He nodded and bellowed, "Luta, I need you...now."

She appeared in the passage from the kitchen and shuffled over to the table. "Yes, sir?" her old voice cracked.

"Take Mam to the room to the right of the stairs. See she's comfortable and get her some proper clothes."

Mam pulled my sleeve again. "Itfitz, come with me."

I looked at her for a moment and nodded before turning back to Geri.

"What did she call you?" he asked, eyebrows raised.

I patted Mam's hand. "I'll explain after she's settled."

"Take your time," he replied.

"Should I clean her first?" the woman asked, looking at Mam with a hint of disgust.

"She won't dirty the bed. She'll most likely rest sitting with her back to something solid. At worst you'll have to sweep the floor after we leave," I said.

Luta gave me a strange look before leading us to the room. "I'll be back with fresh clothes."

I walked with Mam into the room. "Find a corner and get comfortable."

She hesitated. "Will I be safe?"

I nodded. "This is a safe place. Rest."

She hurried to the corner farthest from the door, squeezed herself in, and looked at me one more time before closing her eyes. I waited until her breathing grew shallow before returning to the table.

Geri was rubbing his chin when I returned to the table. "Itfitz?" he questioned, grinning.

"The name she gave me in the tunnels," I said, shrugging. "At least she stopped calling me 'it'. I think part of her will always be stuck underground, but..." I paused and raised my hands. "She deserves a better life than she's had."

"I understand your concern for the girl, but don't forget to take care of yourself," Geri commented as I sat, "starting with a bath and a change of clothes."

I chuckled. "Truer words were never spoken. Afterward, I need figure out how to contact Roi or Crum."

"Unless I miss my guess, Crum's easier to find. The son of Rorec's on a mission."

"On a mission?" I asked, not trying to hide my confusion. "He wouldn't take on a mission while I'm missing."

"I think he put himself on this one. If I understood the look in his eyes, he's after blood for Grima's honor."

"I can't imagine what she said to make Roi leave without trying to find me. He's been there for me my whole life. I wouldn't be surprised if Crum took flight but Roi...he's been solid as long as I've known him."

Geri shrugged. "Perhaps there are things about him you don't know. His life was not always so easy."

"I've heard how rough it was when his wife and newborn daughter died. Still, he wouldn't leave Crum to search alone without good reason. Our paths will cross sooner or later, I have no doubt. You said Crum is most likely in Nikulas' territory?"

"Look in taverns around Nikulas' hall. Perhaps a visit with the skald himself is a good idea. Crum tends to attract attention. Some of Nikulas' guard may have dealt with him."

I nodded, thinking over what Geri had said about Roi, when he asked, "What about Mam? What do you intend to do with her?"

"I think it best if I keep her with me, at least a while longer. She can't remember much of her past, but has a fair grasp on what's going on around her. Don't know how long she was in those tunnels. I won't guess if she'll ever recover herself."

Geri nodded. "Tell me about the tunnels."

"They're under the capital, at least that's one way in, and filled with twists and turns. Eirickson dropped me down a passage in his private meeting room. The stone they're made from is...wrong."

"What do you mean?"

"It's not natural. Hard, dense, but when it breaks it's not sharp like obsidian. I couldn't syth it. It feels dead, no energy to speak of."

"Never heard of such a thing."

"Me either."

He shook his head several times and shivered. "Well, what can I do for you? You're welcome to stay, long as you need."

"A bath, a change of clothes, and a way to get to Nikulas would put me in your debt forever," I said, smiling.

He rubbed his chin again. "Bath and clothes are easy. I can spare a couple of horses, assuming you don't want to walk to Nikulas' hall."

"I don't know if Mam can ride."

He tapped a finger on his chin for a moment. "I'll find a wagon heading there."

"Thank you."

"Slode!" he bellowed. "Ready a bath and find Fitzeirick a change of clothes! Luta's in charge until I get back!"

I thought I heard a groan come from the kitchen.

"Feel free to use the room next to Mam's," Geri said.

"It's better for her if we share a room. I promised I'd keep her safe."

He gave me a hard look.

I smiled. "It's not what you think."

"I'll take your word for it," Geri said, then headed to the front door.

I sat, sipping coffee, until Slode let me know the bath was ready. I felt him staring at me as I left the common room.

Slipping into the tub of steaming water, my body wanted to jump out. The heat started a throbbing in the scar on my face as I fought the urge to get away from the burning sensation. I gripped the sides of the tub so tight my fingers ached. *Breathe, you're safe.* It took a while before I relaxed enough to scrub the filth off my body.

The short swim across the river had done little to clean me. When I started the bath, the water was clear, but quickly, muddy clouds floated through it. I sighed, pulled myself out of the cooling water, and dried with a large cloth from a nearby shelf.

Slode walked in carrying a bundle as I reached for my old clothes. "Best I could find on short notice. I'm sure these aren't up to the luxurious standards you're used to."

I bobbed my head. "After what I've been through, I don't think I'm going to enjoy any luxury for a while. I appreciate you doing this for me. I didn't wish you harm earlier."

He scowled at me.

I shook my head. "I gave you the opportunity to leave us be. You chose violence."

"Doing my job. If you need anything else, find Luta," he growled, before walking away.

I pulled on the simple cotton shirt and drawstring pants, then slid on my old boots. The shine of a silver mirror on the wall caught my eye. *Wonder how bad I look.*

Brushing the strands of damp hair out of my eyes, I stared at the face looking back at me. Pale, tight skin, and slightly sunken cheeks told the tale of missed meals. A bushy, misshapen mustache hid my upper lip and a wild beard covered my chin and neck. Shaggy hair threatened to cover my eyes again and brushed the tops of my shoulders. *The gray eyes look familiar, but the rest seem to belong to a hungry beggar.* Of course, I couldn't help but focus on the brand dominating the left side of my face. *No amount of hair's going to cover it.*

The rugged look suited me well enough, but hair dropping into my vision was an unnecessary distraction. I found a pair of small shears nearby and did a shaky job of trimming to keep it out of my eyes.

I wanted to get the bath ready for Mam before I woke her. Using a cart, I took the tub outside to dump the dirty water. On the way back, I realized I had no idea where to get more hot water so after placing the tub back over the coals, I looked for Luta and found her sitting at a small table, eating with Slode.

"Beg pardon, where would I get hot water to prepare a bath for Mam?"

Slode snorted.

Luta shot him a look that made him cower. "Fill the largest pot in the kitchen from the well out back. Heat it over the cooking fire. Should take three pots."

"Thank you," I said, with a shallow bow.

She smiled.

After trying to lift the first pot of water, I decided both she and Slode were stonesyths. I had to pull strength from the ground to move the load.

Huffing and puffing after hefting three pots, I headed to the room to check on Mam. She hadn't moved, still asleep in the far corner of the room.

"Mam," I called from the door.

She didn't respond.

I stepped into the room and called to her a little louder. Again, no response. I stood and looked at her.

Floating across the river hadn't washed off much. She looked like a beggar's child with filthy, matted, black hair. The large, ragged shirt made her look even smaller than she was. I shook my head and wondered if she'd ever be anything more than a lost, little girl.

"We need to move," I said, softly.

Her eyes shot open and she looked from side to side before opening her mouth to scream.

"Mam, it's me...Fitz. We're safe."

Her face changed in the blink of an eye from a look of terror to blissful relief. She looked me up and down. "It — you...Fitz. You're in different clothes...and clean. What happened to your hair?"

I smiled. "I trimmed it. Would you like to clean up and put on fresh clothes? Crossing the river didn't clean us much and I suspect you'll need time to scrub off everything caked on you."

"It's safe?"

"Yes. Come with me. I've got water heating for you."

We walked down to the private bathing room.

"Undress and soak in the tub for a while before you scrub off the dirt. I'll wait right outside. If you need me call out."

As I reached the door, she called, "The tub's too high. I can't pull myself up."

"I'll get Luta to help you."

"No, Fitz, I don't feel safe with her."

"It wouldn't be right for me to see you undressed. I mean, I'm not engaged to you. I'm sure Aesa would understand, but this would be difficult to explain to anyone who found us together in here."

"You can see in the dark." She argued.

"I can only do that with stone, this floor's wood."

"So. Close your eyes and walk to my voice. Sir and I did it all the time to get to you."

I thought about it for a moment and couldn't find a reason to disagree. *Aesa will understand helping a girl in need.*

"Guide me," I said, turning around.

"Walk straight, hold your hand out, and I'll guide you to me when you get close," she said.

I flinched when she grabbed my outstretched hand. The grit on her fingers scratched my clean skin.

"Pick me up."

I scooped her up like a child and almost wept when I noticed how light she was. She had to be moving through sheer willpower; I couldn't understand how she had any strength at all. *How did I miss how frail she felt when I carried her before?*

As I placed her into the tub, she squealed, "Hot, hot, hot."

"Shhh." I tried to calm her. "It'll be good for you. The water will cool some so lay back and enjoy it. If you can, move so your hair gets a good soaking. Should make it much easier to clean. I'm afraid Geri might run out of soap cakes before your hair's clean enough to comb, though. I'll wait outside. Call out if you need me."

"No," she yelled, panic in her voice. "Please stay...stay in the room. I can't stand to be alone while I'm awake. It's too much for me."

I wanted to explain why it wouldn't be proper for me to stay while she bathed. Before a word passed my lips, I stopped and thought about what it must be like for her. I'm the only person she knows, and I defended her honor and her life. *I'd never leave a child alone when they felt vulnerable and afraid.* "I'll sit nearby. You may not be able to see me, but I'll be here."

"Thank you, Fitz."

She splashed around, shifting in the tub as she cleaned her body. "Would you help me clean my back?"

I sighed and walked to the shelves stocked with bath supplies. After grabbing some soap and several washing cloths, I closed my eyes and walked back to the tub.

Before I opened my eyes, I heard Geri's voice. "Where's Fitzeirick?"

I looked toward the door. "Mam, it would be best if I meet with Geri in the hall. I'll be close by and you'll be safe, I swear."

"No. I need you in here."

I sighed. *She doesn't understand.* "Geri won't come in here while you're undressed. It's bad enough you have one man in your presence while you're bathing."

"If you must...but stay at the door. Please."

"I'll be right outside. You'll be fine."

I hurried out of the room and called out to Geri. "Back here, near the bathing rooms."

"Pardon me, I didn't mean to interrupt," he said, before looking me up and down.

"No interruption, I cleaned up earlier. Mam's in the tub."

"I see." He gave me another hard look.

I shook my head. "I told you it's nothing like that. She's afraid to be alone."

"You could've asked Luta to help."

"Mam doesn't trust her. She doesn't understand why I shouldn't stay with her while she washed."

"I run a clean place. If you two were promised, it wouldn't be so bad, but..." He paused and shook his head. "It wouldn't do for rumors —"

I raised my hands and interrupted him. "I know. It looks bad, I understand. Trust me, I won't tarnish the reputation of The Trader's Cup. You have my word."

He nodded. "I found a wagon team needing a couple of spare horses and bargained with the owner. I'll send you and Mam with three horses. He'll see you get to Nikulas' hall with all possible haste."

"Thank you." I smiled. "Don't know how I'll repay you. All I have left is my sword."

"The sword Eirick gave you?"

"Yes."

"I can't take that from you. To some, it would be the same as me claiming ownership of you and all you hold."

"To tell the truth, I may not hold anything. Will you take it as a partial payment —"

Mam interrupted. "Fitz, where are you?"

He raised his eyebrows. "It's Fitz now?"

I shrugged and half smiled. "She decided to change my nickname."

"Rumors will not do," he reminded me. "I do not allow improper relations in my place. If it were anyone else, I'd have already kicked you both out."

"If anyone speaks a rumor about Mam and me, tell them to ask me about the truth. I'll make sure they have a full understanding of the situation. Now, take my sword."

"I'll hold it, but I won't claim it. Go help the girl."

Mam stood in the tub, faced away from the door, to my relief. She was a disturbing sight. A large amount of dirt had washed off making it easier to see how underfed she was, her backbone visible along with her ribs. Seeing her in this condition, it amazed me she was alive. I wasn't sure I wanted to touch her, afraid it would break bones. If she'd washed her hair, it didn't do much good. It looked as filthy and matted as when I put her in the tub.

I dipped the soap and cloth into the cooling water and washed her back. She flinched and groaned before a shiver shot through her body. "Am I hurting you?"

"No, it's comforting. Please don't stop."

I scrubbed until it irritated her skin, but it still looked like she was dirty. The filth had stained her a strange gray color.

"I'm going to go get the fresh clothes from the room. Rinse off and wash your hair. If you don't get it clean, we'll never get it combed out. Do you need more hot water?"

"No, I'm fine. But please hurry back."

"I will."

I ran to the room and grabbed the bundle of clothes. When I turned to leave, Slode blocked the doorway.

"She your wife or promised?" he asked, glaring at me.

"No, I'm engaged to a woman named Aesa. I hope she's waiting for me somewhere."

"I thought as much. What you're doing is wrong."

I shook my head and looked him in the eyes. "I know how this looks, and in your boots, I'd agree with you. But I'm doing the right thing, taking care of her. You can't understand what she and I have been through. Mam doesn't remember much, hardly remembers herself. Only recently did she see me as a person and not simply another thing in her life. I'm saving her, as much from herself as from the rest of the world. I have no quarrel with you, so don't force me into a conflict. It won't end well for you."

To his credit, he didn't wither from my stare. "I'm doing my job. Geri hired me to deal with problem customers and you've looked like one since you showed up. I know what the brand on your face means...you're a traitor, lower than a commoner. Nothing I do to you will come with consequences. I'll act as I see fit."

I crossed my arms and stood tall. "I'm Geri's guest, so in here this mark means nothing. Do something and you *will* face consequences, regardless of what you think. Mam is waiting for these clothes. I suggest you move."

"Don't make me regret letting you stay," he muttered, as he left.

Don't make me regret letting you get off the ground. I glared at him before hurrying back to the bathing room. Mam stood shivering, outside the tub, green eyes darting back and forth. The effects of missing many meals were obvious. Her legs looked too skinny to hold her up. I knew she was a girl, but from the waist up, she could have been a thin, young boy. My heart grew heavy at the sight.

Her cleaner face resembled the Varian girls I'd grown up around. Teardrop shaped, narrow nose, high cheekbones, and slightly upturned corners of their eyes.

Strange, I didn't notice it before.

"Did you dry off?"

"Yes, but where have you been?"

"I'm sorry. Slode stopped me on my way out of your room. Here's your clothes. Did you try to clean your hair?"

"I tried, but it's all grown together. I can't pull it apart," she said, tugging at the matted mess.

"A comb would run away in fright if we tried to use it. I suppose we could...no, I don't think it's a good idea."

"What?"

"Cut it short, maybe all the way to the skin," I said.

"Would it help?"

"It would get rid of the matting...but I think it's a bad idea."

"Why? It's uncomfortable and scratches on my clean skin. I don't like it," she said.

"You'll look like a young boy until it grows back."

"But the dirt would be gone?"

"Yes, the dirt would be gone," I said.

"Cut it off."

"I'll find Geri and ask for shears while you dress."

"Stay with me while I dress," she demanded.

"For now, but you must learn to do things without me...and sooner instead of later." I shook my finger at her as I spoke.

"Why?"

"Because you put me in an uncomfortable position since I'm neither your husband nor your promised. I shouldn't be in your presence while you're dressing. This could cause problems for you, me, and Geri."

"But I trust you. I know you'll protect me from...from...from everything. I see no problem with this."

"Because you've forgotten social customs. Get dressed and we'll find Geri. I want to talk to him before we leave."

"I'm glad to be out of that itchy shirt. This feels much better," Mam said, after pulling the simple cotton dress over her head. "Where are we going?"

"To visit Skald Nikulas."

Chapter 11

I spotted Luta walking away from a table of customers when we entered the great room.

"Luta," I called out. "Where's Geri?"

She turned and looked at me. "He took Slode out to the stalls."

"Thank you," I said, and gave her a quick nod.

We walked to the stables and found Geri standing near three horses. He waved us over.

"I assume these are the horses we need to take with us," I said.

He nodded. "Yes. Not much for riding, but they'll pull."

"Oh, horses!" Mam exclaimed. "I think I remember horses."

Geri gave me a questioning look.

I shrugged and asked, "What do you remember about horses?"

"Hmm," she said, closing her eyes tightly before taking a deep breath. "A lot of them, people...no...men riding them in order." She ended her thought with a loud exhale.

"Men riding horses in order? What's does she mean?" he asked.

I shrugged again. "I'm sure it's something she saw before. Could I trouble you for a pair of shears?"

"Plan to tidy up before your trip north?" he asked, grinning.

"We're going to cut my hair off," Mam blurted out.

"What?" he exclaimed.

"It's still dirty and I want to get rid of everything from the tunnels."

"But you'll look like a young boy," he said.

"Fitz said the same thing. I'll look like someone else before looking like me again," she responded with a hint of a giggle.

Geri chuckled. "I don't have any shears handy, but I think we have a grooming knife in the stable. Give me a moment to find it."

She swayed from side to side, humming a strange tune, while we waited.

He returned with a curved knife. "Yes, this will do the job. Am I cutting —"

Slode approached, carrying a pack. "What are you doing?"

"She wants her hair cut off. It won't come clean," Geri explained.

Slode dropped the pack. "You'll do no such thing."

I looked at him. "Like he said, she wants this matted hair gone."

"She looks Varian. To cut a Varian woman's hair is to dishonor her...especially if a Croian's going to butcher it."

"Slode," I began, trying to be patient. "I appreciate your concern, but you don't know she's Varian. This is her wish and it *will* happen."

"No, it isn't," he said. "You're half-Varian, Fitzeirick. Would you let someone cut your mother's hair?"

"My mother wore her hair in several fashions, as I recall. Not once did she feel dishonored by having it cut. In fact, it made her happy."

"Then she carries the taint of Croy. I won't let you cut this girl's hair."

"Slode, you've bullied me all day. I've done nothing to deserve it. Insulting my mother is almost more than I'm willing to excuse, but I'd prefer to keep the peace. Please, leave the pack and go on your way," I said, glancing at Geri. "I meant to talk to you about this before we left, but it seems he's decided to show you himself."

Energy rushing through the ground told me Slode was sything. As I turned to face him, he shoved me away and reached for Mam.

"Keep your hands off her," I yelled. My body tensed and sweat flowed down my neck. *Slode should have left us alone.*

Mam squeaked when Geri grabbed her and spun around, putting his body between her and his servant.

I lunged at Slode, latched onto his arm, and yanked him away. He stumbled and fell to the ground. Instead of taking time to pull strength, I kicked him where my punch landed during our earlier fight. The blow cost him some breath, slowing his attempt to stand. I stomped on his hand, feeling the crunch of breaking bones. He howled and spat at me before rolling away.

He's weak and a coward. The weak don't survive.

I pulled in strength, jumped over him, then turned and kicked him in the back. Ribs cracked. He screamed, rolling onto his stomach. Pulling more strength from the ground, I drove my fist into the back of his neck before bending down to pick him up and hurt him more. *Someone has to teach him respect, might as well be me.*

Geri yelled, "Fitzeirick. Stop! He's dead. You broke his neck."

I glared at him, breathing heavy with fists clenched. *Who is he to tell me to stop? I offered Slode the chance to live. He wanted to fight. I'm alive. Mam's safe. That's what matters.* Then I remembered Geri was a good man and stepped back, dropping my arms.

Before I could apologize, Mam hurried to me. "Anything on it we can use?"

He stared at her, mouth open and eyes wide.

"His clothes are too big to be useful out here," I said.

He looked at me, expression unchanged.

"Would you like me to get rid of the body?" I asked.

He sputtered a couple of times before finally speaking. "What — what happened here?"

I crossed my arms and sighed. "He's pushed me since we arrived. I did everything I could to keep peace between us. He chose a different path and showed himself to be too weak to survive. Should I bury the body here or would you prefer I take it somewhere else?"

"I...I...bury him behind the stables. What am I going to tell Luta?"

Mam cleared her throat. "Tell her what Fitz said. Slode was big, but he didn't know how to fight."

His jaw dropped open again and it took him a moment to be able to speak. "When you're done, take the pack and those horses. Orest is waiting a short walk to the north. I think it best you don't come back for a while."

"I'm sorry this happened...I never meant for it to happen. I don't know why Slode held such a grudge, but I did what had to be done to protect Mam and myself. Thank you for your help. I *will* find a way to repay you. Mam, drag the pack to the horses and wait for me."

I carried the body a few paces past the stables. With a little effort, I opened a hole and dropped the body. After it hit bottom with a muffled thud, I closed the ground over him. Somewhere in the back of my mind, I knew I should feel sad, but this was Slode's fault. He chose to attack me, challenge me, and take Mam. I couldn't let that happen.

Mam stood, talking to the horses while holding their lead ropes. She stopped as soon as she saw me.

I took the pack and put a strap over my shoulder. "Did you see what's inside?"

"No, you killed it, you get your pick of what it left," she answered.

"That's not what happened here, Mam. Geri gave us the pack. Do you still want to cut your hair?"

"Yes, please."

I looked around for the grooming knife and remembered Geri had it. He made it clear I wasn't welcomed at The Trader's Cup, at least for a time, so chasing after him seemed like a bad idea. Setting the pack down, I searched it for anything useful.

A loaf of bread and some dried fruit sat on top. Spare changes of clothes took up the bulk of the pack, but at the bottom, I felt a handle. It was a large hunting knife in a leather sheath on a belt. I put the belt on, settled the knife on my left hip, and looked over the matted mess attached to Mam's head.

"Lift the hair from the back. I think it'll work best to cut from the bottom up."

She reached behind her head and lifted the tangled pile of dirty hair as high as she could.

The sharp knife made for quick work, but it was hard to control. I cut her scalp a few times, but she never flinched. By the time I finished, blood trickled from several small slices. I felt bad.

Still, she was free of the filthy burden. Her gray scalp matched the rest of her filth stained skin. The little hair left looked like black weeds mowed with a dull sickle.

She shook her head a couple of times. "Much better."

As we led the horses north, I thought about what had happened today. *I'm clean and well fed. Mam's happy. I don't know what Slode planned to do with her, but anyone else who tries to harm her will meet the same fate.*

It wasn't a long walk to find the wagons Geri told me about.

"I'm looking for Orest," I said, to the first man I saw. "I brought these horses in exchange for a ride to Skald Nikulas' hall."

He looked me up and down. "Leave the horses with me. Orest's driving the lead wagon."

We handed him the leads and hurried to the front of the caravan.

"Well met. Orest?" I called out, as we got close.

A heavyset man sitting on the wagon bench turned toward me. He looked older than Roi with leathery, wrinkled skin and graying hair. "Well met. What can I do for you?"

"Geri sent us."

He looked us both over. "He said a man and a girl..."

"I had my hair cut. I feel better now," Mam told him

Several expressions crossed Orest's face before he said anything. "You look like you lost a fight with a wildcat. You should wear a hat."

"I don't have one," she replied.

He nodded.

"Which wagon will we ride in and how soon do we leave?" I asked. "I have business to attend to when we arrive."

"I understand, Geri told me time was a concern. All new passengers ride in my wagon. The sooner you climb aboard the sooner we move out."

The wagon carried various bundles and baskets. A small area behind the bench had straw for padding. I took that to be our accommodations. After lifting Mam into the wagon, I handed the pack to her, and clambered in. "Ready," I called.

He nodded and yelled, "On the move!" The wagon lurched a couple of times before the horses fell into a steady pace.

Orest looked back at us as we settled in. "Syn, my dear wife, do you have a hat she can borrow?"

The lady sitting next to him rummaged through a sack between her feet and pulled out a black cap. It looked like it would be a tight fit on me. I felt sure it would engulf Mam's head. "Made this for my son. I think it'll be a bit big for such a little thing, but she's welcome to it."

Mam hesitated before taking it from her.

"Oh, but you are skin and bones," Syn said. "When's the last time you ate?"

"Earlier today," Mam said, with a big smile.

Syn turned to me. "Are you sure she's well? I don't want to bring any sickness with us."

"Thank you for your concern, but she's fine. We've had a hard go of it, as of late. Missed a few meals these past months."

"You're welcome," she said, with a slight smile. "Geri said you had business with Skald Nikulas. May I ask what kind of business?"

"Syn. He told us to leave these two to themselves. Their business is no concern of ours." Orest muttered. "Mind the mark on his face."

"Oh, oh...never mind," she stammered. "Please, excuse me."

"No harm done, my lady. I'm separated from my friends and Geri thinks the skald might know where one of them is. This mark's the result of a bad decision which led to an unfortunate misunderstanding. I'm still learning to carry its burden."

"I can't see with this hat on," Mam announced.

I turned to her. The cap fell almost to her nose. "Push it back to uncover your eyes."

She slid the front of the cap up and the back fell to the top of her shoulders. "Thank you, Fitz!"

Syn snickered.

As I tried to get comfortable and organize my thoughts, Mam hummed an odd tune that changed tempo at random. "Mam, can I ask you something?"

"I'm weaving this straw into a band to hold this cap in place," she said.

I glanced at her hands and she had a band about two fingers wide almost completed. "Did you remember how to do that?"

"No. I've known how to do this for a long time. I think all little girls learn it. I haven't had any straw until now."

Another mystery. "Why did you start calling me Fitz?"

She looked at me and grinned. "You washed off everything from the tunnels and changed out of your old clothes. You don't have any of the old you left. Neither of us does." As she explained, she placed the woven band on her head, pulling it to the top of her ears to hold the oversized cap in place.

I started to say something, but stopped to consider what she said. "Wish I understood your thoughts," I said, offhand.

"I feel the same way," she replied, frowning. Her face brightened after a moment. "Did I see bread in the pack?"

"Yes. Would you like some?"

She nodded. "Break off a piece, please."

I got enough for both of us to have a small snack.

Mam finished hers quickly. "I'm going to rest now."

I swallowed. "Sleep. I'll watch over you."

She backed into the corner of the wagon, curled her legs under her, and fell asleep.

I sat, alone with my thoughts, and tried to put a plan in order. First, find my friends. From what Geri said, Crum should be the easiest to find. Then what? *I want to find Aesa. With Satra controlling my skati, searching there would be near impossible. When I find her, will she still marry me, now that I'm branded a traitor?* I refused to believe she wouldn't.

How would she feel about Mam? *I'm sure Aesa will want to help her. Mam looks Varian, maybe my mother will know where she came from.* So many thoughts to organize and questions needing answers. I didn't realize I'd fallen asleep until someone shook me.

I grabbed the hand on my shoulder.

Orest yelled out. "Hey! Let me go!"

Surprised, I released his hand and looked around frantically for a moment. I noticed dimming daylight before I looked at him. "Sorry, you startled me. I meant you no harm."

"Strange way of showing it," he muttered, rubbing his hand. "We're here. Skald Nikulas' hall."

I nodded and looked at Mam, still asleep. "Mam, we need to move."

Her eyes flew open. "My name's not Mam."

"Do you remember your name?"

"No, but I remember it's not Mam."

"I never thought your real name was Mam. That's what we agreed to call you. We're at the skald's hall. Can we talk about this later?"

"Yes."

I jumped out of the wagon and motioned her to come to me.

She crawled across the straw and stood.

Helping her to the ground reminded me of how thin she was. *I almost hate to touch her; might hurt her by accident.*

"Mam, you should give the hat back. It's meant for someone else."

Orest laughed. "Keep it, please. You look so much better with it on. Syn's already making another for our son."

Mam gave a clumsy curtsy. "Thank you."

"Yes, thank you for everything. Do I owe you anything for the hat?" I asked.

Orest shook his head. "I got the better of Geri this time."

I reached for the pack and thought about what had happened before we left The Trader's Cup. *Geri's done so much for me, I'm afraid I already owe him more than I can repay.*

I took off the belt and knife and put them back in the pack. "Please, return this to Geri when you pass his way again. Once I rejoin with my friends, I shouldn't need it. Thank you again and travel well."

"And safe," Mam added.

Orest nodded and cracked the reins a couple of times to get his team moving.

I looked at Mam. "Are you ready to meet Skald Nikulas?"

"I must be," she said, smiling. "If I wasn't, I wouldn't be here."

"Stay near me," I advised, returning her smile. "I don't expect any problems, but it's been some time since last I saw him."

She nodded.

Chapter 12

We climbed the stairs to the entrance, where two guards stopped us.

"The skald is not expecting visitors this evening," one of them said.

"I kindly ask, let us in. We've traveled far and need to speak with Skald Nikulas. It is a matter of great importance," I said.

"What is important to a marked traitor is of no concern to a skald. Be gone before I am forced to remove you."

"Please," I pleaded. "I'm not trying to cause trouble. I need some information from your skald. In trade, I can tell him about Skald Fitzeirick."

"Everyone knows Skald Fitzeirick died during the Satran invasion. My skald isn't granting anyone an audience this evening. Leave."

Being told I was dead shocked me to silence.

Mam cleared her throat. "Kind guard, sir, do you mean to tell me it is customary for your skald to turn away travelers? Would such a wise leader refuse to spend a few moments of his precious time to meet with one in need of his assistance? Is it his desire to see good people, like ourselves, turned out like common beggars?"

The guard looked down on her. "Now, see here young man —"

Mam balled her fists, stepped toward him, and raised her voice. "I am *not* a young man. I am a woman of the Varian nation escorted by a good man of Croy. We have traveled, night and day, from the capital to speak with Skald Nikulas. I would ask you to stop insulting me and my capable companion and send word to your leader now."

The biggest mystery thus far.

Mam's tirade stunned the first guard so the second one spoke. "This is a diplomatic meeting?"

I feared Mam's façade would crumble and spoke before she could answer. "I hardly see what difference it makes now. He insulted my charge. Are you going to grant her request, or will she have to petition for redress?"

The first guard's face went pale.

The second guard stuttered. "No...no...a petition will not be necessary. Please follow me to the sitting room. I will fetch the skald."

I nodded and Mam curtsied while saying, "Thank you."

The first guard held the door for us, and we followed the more sensible man inside. "Please sit. I ask you to have a little patience. Skald Nikulas was not expecting visitors. It may take time to find him."

"Don't let our unexpected visit interrupt anything of importance. We'll wait as long as necessary," I said.

After his footsteps had gone silent, I looked at Mam. "How long have you known you were Varian? Is that something you recently remembered?"

"Slode said I was Varian. You mentioned I could be Varian. What's a Varian?"

I sighed and shook my head. "The people who live in Varia, the nation bordering Croy to the north and east. You look Varian, but it doesn't mean you are. Did you bluff the guards without understanding what you were saying?"

"I told the truth as I know it. He called me a young man. Several people said I looked like a young man, but I'm not. You are from Croy and said the tunnels were under the capital. You've never lied to me, so we must have been there. We traveled at night except for today. That's all true, isn't it?"

I rubbed my temples. "Yes, everything you said *is* true. I'm almost afraid to let you meet Crum. You may be better at twisting the truth than he is. If you're Varian, I'm willing to bet you're from their royal court. I've never met anyone more skilled at confusing people with the truth than royalty."

I stopped talking when footsteps echoed in the hall and motioned to Mam to be quiet.

Other than carrying a little more weight since I last saw him, Nikulas looked the same as I remembered. Maybe the wrinkles near the corners of his bright-brown eyes were a bit deeper. His thick, curly, straw-colored hair looked a little messy.

He wore comfortable-looking clothes, styled more Varian than Croian, dyed bright red and deep blue. "I'm sorry about the wait. I wasn't expecting a Varian...diplomat?"

I approached Nikulas with my hand extended. He stood slightly taller than me, but I could easily look him in the eye. "Thank you for taking time to meet with me. I need your help."

He took my offered hand with a strange look on his face. "Are you who I think you are?"

"If you think I'm Fitzeirick, yes. I'm searching for Crum and understand he may be near here."

"Sit. Word is you're dead and the Satran killed you. I need an explanation."

"First, introductions. Skald Nikulas, this is Mam. Mam, please present yourself to Skald Nikulas."

She bowed. "Pleasure to meet you, sir."

He inclined his head toward her. "Likewise, miss."

"Now, where should I start?" I asked.

"My guard said you came from the capital, but Jarl Eirickson sent word he expelled you for attacking the Thanes."

I thought about what he said before responding. "From a certain perspective, I did. Not my proudest moment. I was overzealous in expressing my disappointment toward the council when they refused to return warriors to defend my skati, so I offered to create an opening. Eirickson branded me a traitor and dropped me down a hole into tunnels below the capital. I was imprisoned for about nine months. I met Mam and a man, Sir. They'd been in the tunnels so long they didn't remember when they were free. I wouldn't have survived without them."

"Tunnels under the capital? I've never heard of such a thing. Why did he let you out?"

"I think Mam and I were the first to escape. Sir was killed before I got him out."

"You're fugitives? I can't house fugitives, especially not a branded traitor."

"I don't think Eirickson knows we're out. It's best, for me, he doesn't find out. I need to find Crum and return to my skati, to my mother and fiancé."

He shook his head. "You have nothing to go back to. It belongs to Satra. I haven't heard from your mother or Aesa, and Crum's on the run. He doesn't stay in one place for long. Rumor is he saw something in the capital he shouldn't have, though I don't know what. I've heard he comes around here from time to time, but..." He trailed off, shaking his head.

"Regardless, you can't stay here, in my hall. If word gets out a branded traitor is staying here, especially if someone figures out it's you, it could cause me no end of trouble. The best I can offer is to put you in contact with Varians I trust. They can get you out of Croy."

"Eirickson claimed Varia started attacking from a northern passage. The Council of Thanes pulled the warriors from my skati to defend the capital."

He gave me a confused look. "Varia isn't attacking. I have a great relationship with them. They asked me to talk to you about doing away with the guards at the eastern passage and opening trade. I assured them I'd ask you after your honeymoon."

"You're certain no one is attacking from the north?" I asked, brow furrowed.

"Absolutely," he insisted.

"Then why would Eirickson make such a claim?" I demanded, frowning and trying to keep my confusion from turning to anger.

Nikulas tilted his head slightly and scratched his ear. "I admit it sounds suspicious."

I nodded. "Regardless, I need to find Crum, especially if he's in trouble. It would be nice if Roi were here. Do you know where he might be?"

"Roi, hmm, I haven't heard his name in a while. Long before hearing the council stripped you of your title."

"All I know is he's on a mission. Can you get me out of here without exposing yourself? I'll do my best to avoid attention while searching for Crum."

"I can get you out unseen. What about Mam? I could put her up here. No one would look twice at a Varian in my hall."

She shook her head. "I stay with Fitz."

He nodded. "Please understand, I can't be associated with you. Regardless of the reason, you're marked a traitor and the repercussions could be —"

I held up my hand. "You know I understand your position and your obligations. If you see Crum, tell him I'm looking for him."

"If I have contact with him, I'll pass your message along."

"Then we part as friends. Thank you for taking the time to speak with me. Considering the false pretense, I appreciate your understanding. You can show us out now."

Nikulas smiled. "I have a secret passage out of this room. Tell the beggar where you want to go. He'll point you in the right direction."

"The beggar?"

"Not all guards wear uniforms." He pressed on a panel not far from where we sat. It popped inward and slid to the side, revealing a tunnel.

I stared into darkness. A cold chill crept down my back, my heart raced, and I licked a bead of sweat from my lip. "This isn't a trap, is it?"

"Not at all. This passageway goes on for about fifteen paces before a sharp right. Straight for another ten paces, then curves to the left while descending. It ends at a stone door. Pull it open. The exit's hidden behind scrub brush."

I took Mam's hand. "We'll be fine."

She squeezed my hand as we stepped into the passage. When the panel snapped back into place behind us, she gasped and started whimpering. I pushed my power out and found natural stone, which was a comfort.

The pathway was exactly as Nikulas described. The stone door opened with almost complete silence. Mam sucked in a deep breath as we pushed through the brush. We walked about two steps before a humpbacked man in rags shuffled up to us.

"Well met, travelers." He wheezed for a moment then coughed. "Have anything to spare for a fellow man that life left in such poor condition?"

"I take it you're Nikulas' watchman?" I whispered.

The beggar turned and looked around before standing straight.

Mam gasped.

"I am. Can I help you?" he asked, with a suddenly clear voice.

"We need food and shelter for the night, someplace where the gossip flows free would be ideal."

"I know the perfect place," he said, with a wide smile. "The Charming Raven Inn, where everyone who thinks they know something no one else knows goes to brag. The food's decent, the drink a little better, but the stories...ah, the stories. They challenge a wise man to believe them, but a cunning individual can pick out snippets of truth sprinkled about."

I nodded. "Sounds like as good a place to start our search as any. I don't see how Crum could avoid such a place for long."

"Did you say Crum?" he asked, eyes shifting back and forth.

"Yes, I'm looking for him."

"To be clear, we're talking about Crum from the conquered, far-eastern skati?"

"The same. Do you know where he is? The sooner I find him, the better."

"Why are you looking for him?" he asked, drawing his right hand up his sleeve. The movement was so subtle, I almost didn't notice.

I pushed my talent into the ground to track his feet. "I need to talk to him, to get some information, so I can decide where to go next."

The guard studied me for a few moments. "May I ask your name?"

"My name's none of your business."

"Ah, business...that's what it always comes down to, isn't it? You see, you have me at a disadvantage. You know I'm a guardsman, but all I know about you is you met with my skald and left under cover. You're branded a traitor, which raises questions. Why would a Croian traitor meet with a skald? Perhaps the traitor has turned hunter. Looking to collect a bounty and, maybe, clear his own name. Is that why you need to find Crum?"

I tilted my head and squinted. "What do you mean? Crum has a price on his head?"

I felt a slight shift in his weight as I spoke.

"You're asking more questions and not answering mine. Why are you stalling?" He looked around again.

"Relax. I'm no bounty hunter." I said, lifting my hands. "Crum's more than a friend. I've trusted him with my life. If you know where he is, tell me and I'll do everything I can to help him."

I felt him shift back to a more balanced position. His hand came out of his sleeve and he pushed it into a fold in one of the rags he wore. "If I find out you're lying to me, you won't live to claim the bounty."

"I swear on my life I'm telling the truth."

"Exactly," he said, offering me a slip of paper. "Follow these directions. Tell Ludin, the beggar sent you."

"This Ludin knows where Crum is?" I asked, taking the paper.

The guard hunched back over and shuffled away from us to take up a position in the shadows.

His instructions took us on a meandering route past several taverns and public houses. We stopped at a plain-looking building marked as a woodsyth shop. I knocked on the door and waited.

The door opened a crack. "Go away...we're closed for the night."

"Ludin?" I asked.

"Who told you he was here?"

"The beggar sent me to see Ludin."

"Were you followed?"

"As best I could tell, no."

The door swung open. "Inside...hurry."

We stepped in and the room went dark when the door closed behind us. I felt the strangest sensation, like the floor moved downward. I tried to reach out with my talent, but the floor was wooden. The movement stopped and I heard knocking in front of us.

Mam started making odd noises.

I don't need her to panic. A door opened in front of us as I reached back to comfort her, and light spilled into the alcove.

A voice from someone I couldn't see, said, "Welcome to those the beggar sent."

We stepped into a room with several tables placed randomly, away from the door. At first, I didn't see anyone.

A man walked out of the shadow near the edge of the room. "Choose a table and take a seat. Would you like something to drink?"

I took a moment to see if I recognized him.

Standing about my height with a slim build, he wore the simple clothes of a laborer. His eyes almost matched the long, brown hair hanging past his shoulders. A darker mustache hid his upper lip, distracting from his blunt nose.

"Are you Ludin?" I asked.

He shook his head. "No one named Ludin here."

"Why was I instructed to tell him the beggar sent me?"

"Lets us know it's safe to let you in," he said.

"What is this place?" I asked.

"Please, have a seat and a drink. Answers when the beggar arrives."

I led Mam to a table and sat where I could keep an eye on the door.

Again, our host asked if we would like something to drink.

I looked to Mam.

"Hot tea?"

"Ah, yes, excellent choice. And you, sir?"

I considered asking him what my choices were, but decided hot tea would do.

"Would it be a problem if I brought a pitcher and two cups?"

"Even better," I said.

He walked back into the shadows.

"Want to talk about your name while we wait?"

She smiled weakly. "I know it isn't Mam."

I leaned toward her and looked into her eyes. "Do you still want me to call you Mam?"

She nodded. "Only until I remember my name. Maybe it's a Varian name."

The man appeared with the tea and cups. "Would either of you like a sandwich while you wait? We have some wonderful roast mutton and the bread was baked this morning."

I poured the tea and looked at Mam. "I'd like one, yes, please," she said.

When he looked to me, I said, "Would it be too much to ask for two sandwiches each? As much as I hate to say it, we've both missed several meals lately. Such is life on the road if you know what I mean."

He patted my shoulder. "All too well. You eat what you can when you can. It's no trouble at all, plenty to go around." Again, he disappeared into shadow.

We drank the steaming tea in small sips, finishing our first cup as the man placed a tray with six large sandwiches on the table. "Like I said, more than enough."

I looked from the tray to Mam. Drool trickled from the corner of her mouth as she reached for a sandwich. I smiled, picked one up, and started eating.

We both finished our first round as the door opened.

The guard we met earlier, still dressed as a beggar, entered the room using his odd gait. As soon as the door closed, he stood upright and walked normally. He came straight to our table and sat with us.

"Thank you for ordering a spare for me and a guest. He should be joining us shortly." He pulled a wooden mug out from his clothes and poured it full of tea. "Ah, nice to have something to warm the bones, is it not? Though I'd have bet you were an ale man. Or maybe you'd have a taste for quality wine."

"I have questions," I replied, not interested in small talk.

"Be surprised if you didn't. But first, I told you I'd send you for food and drink...did I not? That should build some trust between us. I mean, this is no Charming Raven, but it *is* private and ideal for exchanging valuable information. In that sense, it's much better."

"Yes, you kept your word," I allowed. "Where are we exactly?"

He chewed and swallowed. "You're in a woodsyth shop. It's plainly marked on the door."

I took a dramatic look around the room as I chewed. "Oh, silly me. It's obvious when you point it out. I've been away so long I forgot woodsyth shops have food service and special guest seating in their hidden basement." I fixed a hard stare on him. "I've played your game, now, where are we?"

His manner turned serious. "Someplace safe. Thanks to information provided by Crum, and others, a growing movement has started against Jarl Eirickson."

My foot tapped on the floor as he spoke. I looked into my cup and sloshed the tea around. "What *are* you talking about?"

"I understand you don't trust me yet, or us, I suppose I should say, so we'll wait for another to show up. I'm certain you'll trust him."

"Crum? He's coming here?" I asked, looking around the room as my heartbeat thumped in my ears.

"Don't want to spoil the surprise," he answered, grinning.

"Does Skald Nikulas know of your involvement in this conspiracy?" I asked.

"No, and he needs to stay uninformed."

"How do you justify that?"

"It's my job to protect him and his interests. I take great pride in doing my job well. He can't give out information he doesn't know. If the Jarl catches wind of a movement against him, he'll order an investigation. Nikulas must be able to honestly answer, he knows nothing."

Mam looked at something behind me. Before I could turn, a hand clamped onto my shoulder.

Chapter 13

"You owe me three arrowheads...obsidian, in case you don't remember."

I jumped out of my chair, pulled Crum into a tight hug, and then stepped back to make sure it was him. Welling tears in my eyes made him look a little blurry.

He looked at me. "Something's different about you."

I nodded. "Eirickson. He —"

He put a finger to my lips. "Don't tell me, let me figure it out."

I pushed his hand away. "Are you serious?"

"Hush. You're distracting me."

I rolled my eyes and sighed.

He smiled. "First, you should find someone else to cut your hair. Whoever trimmed it last did a terrible job."

"My hair? That's what you noticed?"

"Only because you haven't worn it long in ages. However, the big change is the hair on your face. You've always been clean shaven. I suppose it makes a good disguise if you run into someone who doesn't know what you look like without it."

"Shaving hasn't been much of a concern, lately. You don't see anything else out of the ordinary?"

"Well, since you mentioned it, the brand on your cheek is new, but I figured you have a good explanation," he replied, with a crooked grin as tears welled in his eyes.

"We have a lot of catching up to do," I said.

He nodded. "Good thing we have food, drink, and plenty of time. Who's the young woman?"

Mam looked at me with concern evident on her face.

"Crum, this is Mam. We owe each other much. I'd ask you to direct your attentions away from her."

"I believe I've done my service to the cause," the guardsman said, after draining his mug. "My shift started early this morning. Unless one of you protests, I'll be off to bed now."

I held out my hand. "Thank you for everything you've done."

He shook it and headed for the door.

"Mam, sit next to me so I can look at Crum while we talk," I said.

"I'll be right back," Crum said, before walking toward the dark area our food and drink came from. He returned with another pitcher of tea, two more sandwiches, and a mug.

"Heard there's a price on your head. Sounds like an interesting story," I said.

He took a long drink. "You disappeared. Some say you're dead, yet I find you here, bearing the mark of a traitor. I'm certain your tale is more interesting than mine. What happened in the council room?"

"You don't know?"

"The Thanes talk to no one outside of themselves," he said.

I closed my eyes and steepled my fingers in front of my chin. "Eirickson controlled me like a puppet from the moment the door closed, I just didn't realize it. My emotions overran my judgement and the Thanes thought I was going to attack."

"Wait, you threatened the entire council?" he asked, wide eyed.

"All I did was set my hand on the hilt. I never drew it," I corrected.

"But you had to know that'd be considered a threat."

I sighed and looked Crum in the eye. "I needed to get their attention, make them take my request seriously."

He nodded and gestured for me to continue.

I told him how Eirickson trapped me in the chair, branded me, and dropped me into the tunnels.

He raised an eyebrow. "Tunnels under the capital?"

I frowned and gave him all the details. How I met Mam and Sir, the dead stone, fighting for survival, and eating raw meat.

Crum tore his second sandwich in half and placed the pieces in front of Mam and me. As our story unfolded, she sobbed next to me.

He kept quiet until I reached the point where Mam and I were out safely. "You...you killed people? With a dull sword no less?"

How dare he question me? "I defended myself, protected Mam and Sir. Would you have me do nothing and die or let them die?"

He held his hands up. "No, protecting others is exactly what I'd expect of you. It..." He shook his head. "It's not in your nature to talk so casually about taking a person's life. You often agonized over punishing a criminal. Now, you've killed who knows how many people, and it doesn't weigh on you?"

"You can't understand what I went through, what I did to live," I countered. "Life up here isn't the same as in those tunnels. The only law is 'kill or be killed.'"

Crum let out a low whistle. "This is a side I never knew you had."

"And *I* have Eirickson to thank for exposing it. I hope someday I'll be in a position to show him what he did to me."

"I know people who could help make it happen, but I'm not sure I like the idea. I'm not against someone taking down our budding tyrant, but the thought of you being the one to do it is disturbing."

"Tyrant?" I spat. "The Jarl exists to mediate between the Thanes. They hold the power."

Crum shook his head. "Not any more. Eirickson has the entire council bending to his will. He's running Croy as a dictator."

I tapped a finger on my chin for a moment. "How do you know?"

"Unlike the Thanes, guards get talkative after a few rounds. Spent a lot of time loosening them up while I was looking for you."

"I see. Is that why you have a price on your head?"

Crum looked at me for a long time. "You won't like what I'm about to tell you."

Mam flinched when I slapped my hands on the table. "My skati is no more, taken by the Satran army. I have no idea where my mother and Aesa are, if they're alive. I'm not sure you can tell me anything more unpleasant."

He nodded, but was still tense when he spoke. "Roi and I stayed outside the council room until the guards forced us to leave. Roi wanted to fight our way in, but I talked him out of it. After the second day, with no word from you, we knew something was wrong. We spent a month searching for you. Frustrated and getting nowhere, we headed to The Trader's Cup to be safe while planning our next move.

"The more Roi talked to Grima, the more he changed. It seemed like he got more upset after every conversation. He woke me early one morning and told me to keep searching for you. He had *that* look about him, the one you only see when —"

I interrupted him. "Geri told me he paid off her debt, left with her and her son."

He nodded. "Geri hired new help soon after they left."

"He's looking for a new hand now. I killed a man working for him before we came here."

"You killed Slode?" Crum asked, wide-eyed.

"Yes, and Geri all but ordered me to not come back. But what's that have to do with the price on your head?"

"Why did you kill Slode?"

"Later. Finish your story," I pressed.

He frowned and shook his head. "I had to leave the capital. While haunting every tavern, inn, and public room, I stumbled into a secret meeting. Eirickson sat at a table with some Satran men discussing various ways to divide Varia."

"*What?*" My heart beat so hard my fingers throbbed. I wanted to break something, hurt someone and looked around for a target.

Crum raised his hands. "Hey. Whoa. Take it easy. I'm just telling you what I heard. I know this is a lot to take in, and believe me, I'm beyond angry, but we're all friends here. Save your rage for Eirickson."

His face was hard to make out through the red haze clouding my vision. "So, my skati was a gift given to create an alliance? Eirickson told me the Varian made a northern passage and were testing the border near the capital. That's why the Council of Thanes pulled the warriors from my skati. Are you telling me he's conspiring with Satra?" I slammed my fist on the table.

Mam jumped and scooted her chair away.

"I hate to say it, but yes," he said, frowning before looking away.

Blood pounded in my ears. I buried my face in my hands and fought to keep from lashing out, hurting, my friends. "I'll...I will...kill...no, I will humiliate him before he dies. He branded me a traitor for trying to ensure the safety of my people and secure our border while he lets them take Croian lands. He'll lose everything before he draws his last breath...all by my hand." Spittle flew as I spoke.

"Fitzeirick, calm down...please," Crum urged softly. "You can't do this alone. I'm working with people, and we're making plans to stop this. Join our cause. You'll have to leave Croy to be safe until everything is in place. I'll get you to Varia, out of Eirickson's reach."

"Where's Roi?" I barked. "I could use him now."

He frowned. "If I knew, I'd tell you. When he left, he said something about making someone pay what they owe. I haven't seen him since nor have I run across anyone who says they've seen him."

I gazed at the table as if an answer might write itself in the wood. "If I agree to go to Varia, what awaits me?"

"At first, nothing. We're still early in making plans. Maybe Eirickson and Satra are too far ahead of us. I know I've sworn my life to you, and my oath still holds, but this is bigger than us. I know the kind of man you are...or were. Are you better or worse now? You know better than anyone what Eirickson can do, are you going to let him do this?"

"I told you, I'll kill him. As part of your group or lone assassin, I will end his life. He declared me a traitor, so I may as well show him he's right. One thing, though. I won't go to Varia alone. Mam comes with me."

She nodded.

Crum held his hand out to her. "If Fitzeirick trusts you, I trust you...without question. It'd be easy enough to get you into Varia. You could pass as Varian except for —"

"Filth stained her skin," I explained.

"You're sure?"

I nodded. "Her scalp is a little cleaner."

He squinted "Her scalp? What about her hair?"

I frowned. "Mam, take off the hat, please."

Crum gasped. "What happened?"

She gave a weak smile as she shook his offered hand. "Fitz cut it for me."

He looked to me. "Wait, you butchered a Varian woman's hair? I thought you two were...umm...friends? And why'd she call you Fitz? No one calls you that."

"She thinks Fitzeirick is too long," I told him, feeling a smile tug at my lips.

"Fitz and I *are* friends," she insisted.

Crum raised his eyebrows. "And you let him do this to you?"

"Asked him to," she said.

"Her hair was tangled, matted. It wouldn't come clean. Cutting it off was the only thing I could do," I said.

"But you didn't cut it, you slaughtered it...cut her scalp even. Fitzeirick, I hope my contacts in Varia aren't going to judge you too harshly for this."

"The first person who judged me for it is buried behind Geri's stable," I informed him.

"You killed Slode over this haircut?"

"I tried to keep peace between us, but he kept pushing. He disrespected me and tried to take Mam. He's dead because he wouldn't leave me to my business."

"You killed a man over disrespect. Do you hear yourself? Where's the understanding and merciful person I grew up with?" Crum asked, eyeing me like a stranger.

I leaned forward and glared at Crum. "He's dead," I said coldly. "Eirickson burned him to death with a branding iron and buried him in a dark prison of endless tunnels. That Fitzeirick wasn't strong enough to survive."

"But you found light which led you back out. It brought you back to the world. I hope that same spark can flash inside you. I think we'll need the other Fitzeirick to make right what Eirickson has done wrong," Crum said, after blinking several times.

"Then find Aesa or my mother," I growled, throwing my hands in the air. "At the very least, find proof they're alive."

"I'd like nothing more," he whispered.

Mam cleared her throat. "You two are talking about the future, but don't ignore now. Are we safe here or should we move?"

Crum looked confused. "Is she always..."

I smiled. "Aware of the present? Yes, here and now is what she knows best. In some ways, I find it refreshing. Now to her question...are we safe here?"

"I was going to ask if she's always so blunt. We're safe here, but I'll have to find us someplace to sleep. I already have people working on passage to Varia. Do you have a problem traveling at night?"

"We prefer it," I said.

"Mam, can you ride a horse?" Crum asked.

"I don't remember," she answered.

He looked at me. "Is she joking?"

I shook my head. "When she talks about remembering something, she's being serious."

"I'll get us a place to rest for the night and locate a horse to practice with. Even if she can't ride now, I think I can teach her enough to make the trip on a seasoned horse. Mam, would you like to learn to ride a horse?"

She looked at him with a blank stare for so long, I started wondering if something was wrong with her. Finally, she focused on his face. "If I already know how to ride a horse, but can't remember, would I still be learning how to ride?"

The look on his face told me he had no idea how to respond.

"Mam," I began, "if you remember riding, once you get on a horse, you won't have to learn. You'll only need to practice a little to get comfortable."

She pursed her lips for a moment. "I think that makes sense. Hopefully, I'll remember something."

Crum shook his head, said, "Wait here until I get back," and walked back into the shadows.

Mam and I started eating again. He brought us another pitcher of tea before leaving the room. I thanked him through a mouth full of mutton. We finished our tea and sandwiches as he returned.

"Mam you should put your cap back on. We need to go. I found us a safe place for the night."

She pulled the cap over her head. "I'm blind again."

I sighed and moved it to uncover her eyes. "Use your band to hold it."

"Of course, that's why I made it."

Crum looked at me and whispered, "Are you sure you two are not..."

"No," I cut him off. "We aren't."

He grinned. "If I didn't know better I'd guess you were. You'll fool a lot of people with that act. Maybe we can use it to our advantage."

"We'll worry about it tomorrow. I think we could all use some sleep tonight," I said.

He nodded and we followed him into the night. Mam grabbed the back of my shirt as I used my talent to keep track of Crum and check for anyone nearby.

He avoided large, open spaces and led us through alleys I never would've noticed. I kept telling him we were alone, but he didn't seem to believe me.

Finally, we walked next to an old house. He knocked twice near a window and waited. A curtain drew back, exposing a lantern. He gave some sort of signal with his hand. The lantern winked off and on. A second light appeared for a moment before the curtain closed.

"What was —" I started to ask.

Crum raised his hand and shook his head before leading us past the house to a rundown-looking barn.

"Follow me," he said, continuing to the back of the building. "Climb the ladder to the loft and feel around for the opening in the haystack. That's our room for the night. Plenty of room for us to stretch out, assuming you don't mind all three of us sleeping together."

"Will I have a corner?" Mam asked.

"Why do you need a corner?" he asked.

"They're safer," she replied.

"We both prefer to sleep sitting. Survival habit from the tunnels," I explained.

"Sitting?"

"Only the dead lay down," she said.

"Guess that makes sense," he muttered, scratching his head. "I'll let you have your choice of four corners."

"Good," she replied. "What's a ladder?"

I don't think Crum could've kept from laughing if his life depended on it. Once he caught his breath, he asked, "How can you not know what a ladder is?"

"I don't remember hearing that word before," she said.

"Fitzeirick, you still know what a ladder is...right?" he asked.

"Yes, I know what a ladder is. Mam, it's wood planks running across a narrow opening. You climb them one at a time until you reach the top."

She gasped. "Wood planks? Should I touch them?"

Crum blurted out, "Should you touch them? Let me guess, you remembered wood is bad for you or something even more preposterous."

Before I could explain, she spoke. "Fitz says I'm a woodsyth, but I don't remember anything about it. He told me to not touch wood because I could damage something on accident."

"Oh...yes, that could be a problem. How do you propose we get her up the ladder?"

"Mam, I think you'll be fine. Focus on your hands and feet and not on what you're touching. Let me go first so I can help you at the top," I said. "Crum will be right behind you, right?"

"Yes...yes. Of course. Sure...I will. We'll be fine," he said.

I climbed the ladder and waited for Mam.

She chanted, "hand, hand, foot, foot" during her slow climb.

Crum surprised me by not screaming in frustration.

"That was fun." Mam smiled wide as I helped her into the loft.

"Glad you enjoyed yourself," he muttered.

I chuckled while searching for the hidden opening and guided Mam inside once I found it. She fell asleep soon after curling into her chosen corner.

"Are you sure about her?" he whispered.

"What do you mean?"

"I think she may be insane."

"Don't take it upon yourself to judge her," I chided him. "Everything I went through in the tunnels, she dealt with longer. The fact she survived to make it out is amazing enough to be unbelievable."

"I hear what you're saying, but the things she doesn't know or remember... How long was she in those tunnels?"

I shrugged. "To her, time didn't pass. It's easy to lose track in constant darkness."

"Any idea how old she is?"

"No," I confessed. "Her mind can be childlike. Having missed eating so much, she's skin and bones, built more like a young boy. Outside of finding someone who knew her before, we may never know her age."

He yawned. "I guess we'll figure it out as we can. Let's get some sleep, focus on horses in the morning."

"Good idea, my friend. You have no idea how good it is to see you."

• • • • • ● • ● • • •

Mam woke first. I don't know how much longer I would've slept if her odd humming hadn't disturbed me. After blinking the sleep from my eyes, I noticed she was weaving straw. "What are you making?" I asked, after yawning.

"Wrist things...I think."

"You mean bracelets?" I asked.

Her hands stayed busy while she repeated the word. "Yes, I think that's right. Are they shiny?"

"Gold or silver bracelets would be shiny. Do you remember gold and silver?"

She scratched her head. "Gold...it's yellow like this straw, but shines. Silver's not white, but shines unless it's old. Right?"

I nodded. "Sounds like you remember them. Any idea why?"

"No, but is it important?"

"Knowing about gold and silver could be important," Crum mumbled.

"Thank you, Crum," she said, turning back to her weaving.

He shook his head. "You two wait here. I'll see about breakfast."

"Roast meat," she blurted out.

"Most likely not, sorry. I'd be ready for boiled grains if I were you," Crum replied, leaving the hidden room.

"Boiled grains are good, too," she mumbled.

Crum's head soon reappeared. "Breakfast is ready. Let's go eat."

Mam dropped her work. "Hand, hand, foot, foot again?"

"Yes. Let Crum go first so he can wait for you at the bottom."

I helped her onto the ladder and watched as she made her way down, chanting softly.

Despite my haste in descending, Crum and Mam were already seated at one end of a long stone table by the time I got there. *This table wasn't here when we came in last night.*

Two people I didn't recognize sat at the other end. Open pots of boiled grains sat in the middle of the table with a bowl in front of each chair. Crum, being the gentleman, served Mam before preparing a bowl for himself.

"Thanks for waiting for me," I said.

"Eat when food's available," Mam said, after swallowing.

"Can't argue with that."

"This is good," Mam remarked, as she emptied her bowl. "Can I have more?"

Crum nodded and served her another bowl full.

"Reminds me of the boiled grains my mother made when I was young," I said.

"They're cooked using the Varian method, more spiced than sweet."

"Do you think I like it so much because I'm Varian?" Mam asked.

Crum shot her a look. "Are you saying you know you're Varian?"

"Slode said I was Varian, both of you say I look Varian, and it seems I like Varian food."

I shook my head. "Mam, none of it means you're Varian. Looking Varian and liking Varian food doesn't make you from the country of Varia. My mother's Varian, and served me some Varian dishes, but I'm from Croy."

She nodded as I spoke. "So, what does that make me?"

"Along with so many other things about you, that remains hidden, dear little Mam," Crum said, with a sly smile. "Now, eat your fill. I know a place not far from here with horses."

She dropped her spoon. "I'm ready now!"

"Mam, these people have given us a place to sleep and fed us. It wouldn't be proper to leave food uneaten," I told her quietly.

"Yes, you're right. I'm sorry," she said, in the childlike manner that appeared without warning.

We finished our food in relative silence and Crum led us out of the barn.

The sun was well up in the sky, shining brightly.

"I thought we'd be traveling at night," I said.

"When we leave Croy, we will be. For now, we're three friends out to see about horses."

"But the price..." I questioned.

"Not to worry, all the gossip has me headed south."

"Are the horses south of here?" Mam asked.

He chuckled. "No, we're heading northeast. It's not far."

Chapter 14

Mam bounced as she walked, following Crum like a puppy chasing its new master. It didn't take long for her to start humming her strange tune.

He glanced back at me.

I shrugged and shook my head.

Her humming seemed to make the time pass faster. I knew we were close when I heard a loud whinny.

"Was that a horse?" she asked, her eyes open wide.

"Yes," Crum said. "And it sounds happy or excited."

"Maybe because I'm happy and excited?"

"More likely because someone's feeding them," he replied.

"Can we ride them while they eat?"

I couldn't help but laugh.

Crum chuckled for a moment before answering. "No. A wagon team can eat on the move, but a riding horse needs to have its attention focused on the rider."

"Oh," she said, sounding dejected.

"It won't take long," I said, trying to keep her spirits up. Since we'd escaped, I always felt better when I thought she was happy.

"Good," she replied, before humming again.

Soon, we got our first look at the stables, a large wooden building about twice as long as it was wide with a walkway down the middle. "Stay with me," Crum said, as we walked inside.

The scent of fresh hay mingling with the musky smell of horses almost covered the pungent odor of manure. Those smells combined with the neighs and snorts reminded me of my stable. A lump formed in my throat as I thought about leaving my home nearly a year ago.

Crum jogged down the aisle, pausing every so often to look around. Finally, he spotted a tall man grooming a sleek, black horse. The man had thick arms, broad shoulders, and sun-darkened skin. "Vekel, I need to teach someone to ride. Have you got a horse I can use?"

"Should I put this on your tab or you going to pay me?" he said, with a laugh. "First-time rider?"

Crum nodded. "This young lady."

Vekel looked her up and down several times. "You sure that's a young lady?"

Mam glared at him and I reached to her shoulder to calm her.

Vekel raised his hands and smiled. "My but you are a slight one. Still, you should be fine on Andale. He's even tempered, well trained. Go to the second stall from the end, the left side. Big bay horse, but don't let his size scare you, he's gentle. Walk him out the back. Crum, you know where I store the tack."

"I *will* pay you back!" Crum yelled, as we headed farther into the building.

Mam started running and almost beat him to the stall.

I picked up my pace to keep up with them.

"What's a bay horse?" she asked, as they reached the gate.

"See the big, dark-brown horse?"

"Yes."

"That color's called bay. If he were lighter he'd be chestnut."

"Do I climb onto him?" she asked.

"No. We have to put the tack on him...the saddle, and a bridle with reins so you can control his head."

"How long will it take?" she asked.

"Not long. Let me get a lead rope on him."

She stepped back as he opened the gate. I saw her shiver when Andale walked past. I wasn't sure if it was fear or excitement. Maybe both. I told her to stay to the side of the horse in case he got startled and kicked.

Crum led the large animal to a small, wooden shack and tied him to a post. "Mam, stand next to him, maybe pet his neck. Fitzeirick, would you help me gather tack?"

"Of course," I said, following him. An overwhelming smell of leather and oils greeted us.

He closed the door. "What if she can't ride?"

I shrugged. "We'll find another way to travel. Walk there if we must."

"You're willing to walk from here to deep inside Varia?"

I nodded. "Over the past ten months, I've walked more than in the rest of my life. Walking to Varia doesn't seem like much of a challenge."

He shook his head and sighed. "Bring the big saddle and let's hope this works out better than it should."

When we walked out, Mam had her cheek against the horse, humming and petting his neck. She looked at home with the animal.

"Do you remember being around horses?" I asked.

"Maybe. He feels so gentle. It felt right to pet him. He feels safe to me," she said.

"That's a good sign," Crum said, smiling as he fit the bridle and strapped on the saddle.

Andale's patience impressed me as he stood still while Crum worked.

Crum checked everything over one last time and turned to Mam. "Do you remember anything about mounting a horse?"

Mam stood for a few moments studying the saddle. "Am I supposed to climb the strap hanging down?"

"Not exactly," Crum said. "It's called a stirrup, and you put your foot in it. I'll mount him to show you."

"Sounds like a good idea," she replied.

"Watch. It isn't hard," he said, placing his left foot in the stirrup. He brought his right leg over the horse's back and settled into the saddle. "Like that."

Mam giggled, which made me smile. "I think I can do that. But how do you get down?"

"Provided you don't fall off," he began with a grin, "I'll show you the safest way to dismount." Using slow, exaggerated movements, he took both feet out of the stirrups, lay down on the horse, swung his right leg back over, and slid to the ground.

"Yes, I see how it works. Let me try," she said.

"First, put your left foot in the stirrup," he guided her.

She leaned awkwardly, lifted her leg, and fell over backward.

"Oh!" he exclaimed, helping her to her feet. "You have to stay balanced. Horse riding is all about balance. Let me help."

He bent over and put his hands on her waist to steady her as she tried to mount Andale. As slight as she was, he all but threw her onto the horse. Still, she was sitting in the saddle.

"Something doesn't feel right." Her face scrunched up as she looked around.

"He's a big horse," I said. "The wide saddle may feel uncomfortable. Do you want to get down?"

"No," she said, twisting and fidgeting.

"I can hold the reins and get Andale to move a few steps, if you feel ready," Crum suggested.

"Yes," she said, with some hesitation, still trying to settle. "I think I'm ready."

The big horse moved at Crum's command, plodding forward. They walked about ten steps before Mam screamed, "No, no, no...this isn't right at all! None of this is right! Stop! I'm doing this wrong!"

I ran to her side and begged her to come down. She jumped into my arms with a look of frustration, and maybe anger, in her eyes.

"What's wrong?" I asked.

"Did you remember something?" Crum pressed.

She nodded and asked me to put her down.

After her feet hit the ground, she looked at Andale. "He's beautiful, but he's not my horse."

"You have a horse?" I asked.

"Yes. A whole stable. I think. White, every one. So white they almost shine. Like they're polished. And the saddle...it's all wrong."

Crum shrugged when I looked at him.

"What's wrong with the saddle?" I asked.

"The proper way for a woman to ride is sitting sideways with both legs on one side."

"I hate to say this, but I have no idea what you're talking about," I said. "Crum? Any idea?"

"I don't think I've ever heard of such a thing either," he admitted. "Give me the lead rope and head back to the stable. Wait for me to get this tack off Andale so I can put him back in his run. Then we'll talk to Vekel."

Mam and I waited at the gate to Andale's stall.

"Want to talk about it?" I asked.

"How can I talk about something I don't understand? I remembered something. I should be happy. Instead, I have more unanswered questions. I think I like horses, but I couldn't enjoy riding. My memories told me it was wrong." She started crying.

I put my arm around her and whispered, "You looked happy riding. Maybe Vekel will have some ideas about what you remembered."

She sniffled and wiped her eyes as Crum passed us and yelled for Vekel.

From somewhere ahead of us the big man bellowed, "Is everything alright? Did she get hurt?"

I turned Mam toward his voice. We walked quickly enough to catch up with Crum and spotted Vekel running down the walkway.

"Calm yourself," Crum called out. "Everyone's fine. Dear little Mam had a memory about riding. We're hoping you could answer some questions."

The hefty man slowed to a fast, walking pace. When he got close, he asked, "What did you remember?"

"A proper woman rides with both legs on the same side of the horse. Also, I should be riding a white horse."

"Have you ever heard of anything like that?" Crum asked. "How does the rider keep from falling off?"

Vekel waved at him. "I want to hear more about the white horse."

"A whole stable of white horses. They shine in the sun, like they're polished." She closed her eyes for a moment. "They lifted their legs high in the air when they walked."

Vekel scratched his chin for a moment. "I have good news, bad news, and worse news. I know exactly what kind of horse you're talking about: the Varian Parade. Bred to be especially white and walk with a distinctive gait. Some believe they can't run. No one has seen a Varian Parade horse since Croy drove the Varian out of the far eastern territory. However, that's not the worst part. This young woman may be a big problem for you, if you plan to head into Varia with her."

How dare he call her a problem? "What do you mean?" I demanded.

"If she's ridden Varian Parades, she's Varian royalty. Even the royal horse trainers didn't ride them. They worked them with a royal family member riding. Anyone else caught on one...put to death on the spot."

I shivered. *Is she related to the Varian royal family?* As I struggled to gather my thoughts, Crum spoke. "If dear little Mam was Varian royalty, we'd know. Someone would be looking for her. I'm more concerned with the strange way of riding she described."

Among my troubled thoughts about Mam's possible lineage, I noticed Crum had called her 'dear little Mam' a few times recently. The strange thing was, it sounded respectful. Almost with adoration. *I need to keep an eye on him. He wouldn't hurt her on purpose, but he doesn't know how delicate she is.*

"She means riding sidesaddle," Vekel said. "That style fell out of favor in Croy many years ago, when I was but a boy. However, the Varian royal women were still riding sidesaddle until fifteen or twenty years ago. It takes a special saddle and —"

"And you have no idea where we could find one," Crum interrupted.

Vekel looked at me. "Does he always speak before he thinks?"

"Sounds like the Crum I know," I laughed.

Vekel chuckled. "I have a sidesaddle, but it'll need attention and won't fit Andale. Crum, come with me to the tack shed. Mam, would you go wait at the last stall on the left? You'll find a gray mare with white spots. Her name's Aspeit. She won't be as calm as Andale, but I think you can ride her."

She let out a slight chirp, grabbed my hand, and all but dragged me to the end of the stable. The horse Vekel described paced in her run and trotted in when we reached the gate. She greeted us with a loud neigh and a powerful snort.

Mam didn't flinch. Instead, she grabbed the horse's nose. I expected the mare to pull away, but she stood still while Mam examined her teeth.

"Why'd you do that?" I asked.

"I've seen people do it before. You can tell things about a horse from their teeth. Aspeit has good teeth, so she's well cared for. I expect I can trust her, even if she's not white."

"Mam," Crum called, "I need you in here."

She glanced at me before running to the shed.

For a moment, I thought Aspeit expected me to explain what happened. I decided to ignore the possibility the horse was asking me a question and headed to the tack shed.

A chorus of coughs and sniffles greeted me when I stepped inside. I heard Mam say, "Not exactly like I remember, but it might be close enough."

"Take it outside and set it on a post so we can get a better look at it," Vekel said.

I heard the distinctive grunt of Crum lifting something heavy and moved out of the way. He carried a saddle with two horns and only one stirrup. It made a chorus of creaking sounds while he balanced it on the post.

Vekel and Mam came out, coughing and sneezing, and walked over to the strange saddle. The big man patted it and dust flew. "Yes, it'll need some attention. Crum, since you're the one causing all this trouble, you get to do the work. Get a pot of pure tallow and another of tallow and beeswax from the shed while I get a fire going. Grab plenty of cloths, this leather's old and thirsty."

Vekel showed some amount of firesyth talent by quickly starting a small fire. Crum placed the clay pots on the fire. Their solid contents turned to liquid as I watched.

Vekel nodded. "Show Mam how to clean the saddle with tallow and beeswax. Then use pure tallow to quench the old leather's thirst. Mam, you can help if you want...or simply watch and learn."

Crum groaned and went to work. Mam picked up cloths and followed his example. Soon all the dust was gone and, after a lot of rubbing, the saddle looked almost new.

Vekel's eyes were shiny. "Never thought that hidden treasure would get used again. I can't believe it looks this good with so little work."

"Little work?" Crum snarled. "I'm not sure my arms will ever feel right again. I haven't been this sore in ages."

"You haven't worked so hard in ages," I quipped. "Mam isn't complaining."

When I said her name, she looked at me with a wide smile. "When can we put this on Aspeit?"

"As soon as it's dry to the touch," Vekel answered. "I'll go get her and we'll get a bridle on her now, unless you think you can handle her by yourself."

Mam ran back into the stables. I heard her calling out to the horse. Soon she returned with a lead rope on the horse's neck, exactly like Crum had done with Andale.

"You're a quick student," Crum said.

Her smile widened, eyes sparkling at the praise.

Vekel helped her fit the bridle and she bounced in place until he pronounced the saddle ready for use. When Crum lifted it, I noticed the creaking sounds were almost gone. Again, he took his time getting the saddle in place and adjusted for the horse's comfort.

Vekel watched with a critical eye. "Crum, you do that well. Mam are you ready?"

"Yes," she squealed, mounting the horse like she'd been doing it her whole life. Her left foot stayed in the stirrup while her right leg rested on top of the second horn. It was easy to see how comfortable she looked in the saddle. "Much better. This feels right."

"Varian royalty," Vekel whispered to me.

I didn't respond, but a quiver ran through my stomach. *We don't know that for sure. He could be wrong.*

"You want me to lead her for a few steps to be sure?" Crum asked.

"No. Give me the reins."

He looked to me.

I shrugged. "You heard her."

"Please be careful little dear," he said.

She made a clicking sound and pushed her heel into the horse's side. Aspeit walked and Mam giggled.

The happy sound lifted some weight off my shoulders. I couldn't help but smile. *One less thing to worry about.*

"Can you walk her to the fence and back?" Vekel asked.

She nodded and guided the horse as he asked. When she got back, she asked, "Does she go faster?"

Crum and Vekel both looked at me.

Again, I shrugged. "Looks like she knows what she's doing. Vekel, does Aspeit go faster?"

He chuckled. "Yes, she'll go faster. Get her walking and heel her a couple more times. She should trot for you."

"To the fence and back?" she asked.

Crum nodded.

She directed the horse to trot. At first, the faster gait bounced Mam around, but soon she fell into a rhythm and flowed along at a good pace.

"She can ride," Vekel said.

"Yes...yes, she can," Crum agreed, with something sounding like admiration. "Vekel and I need to talk business."

"Faster?" Mam called out, before she reached us.

"Oh, yes. Aspeit's a runner," Vekel responded. "Get on the trot and poke her good, she'll skip the canter and go right to gallop."

Mam turned the horse without skipping a beat, let out a shriek, and kicked her left heel into Aspeit's flank. The mare whinnied and took off like an arrow loosed from a bow.

Mam leaned forward as they sped toward the fence. With a feral scream, she prodded the horse into jumping the barrier and kept going at full speed.

My jaw dropped at the sight.

Vekel and Crum looked at each other. The stable owner looked panicked, and Crum's face lost all color. Without a word, they ran to the stable.

I'd better watch where she goes.

Chapter 15

Vekel flew past me on a black blur of a horse while Crum passed on the other side, riding Andale.

I pointed. "She headed into the forest."

Though I saw clouds moving, it felt like time stood still.

The trio eventually emerged from the dense stand of trees. The men flanked her with Crum holding Aspeit's reins. Mam's big, bright smile was easy to see, even from a distance.

I heard Crum yelling at her while she nodded in response. "...ever do that again. You could've been hurt or worse. Now, we have three, worn-out horses. There's more to riding horses than running around. You have to care for them. Your first lesson is how to bathe and groom these fine animals, and you will do it to Vekel's approval."

His continued verbal lashing was soon masked by Vekel's laughter.

"Leave some hide on the little thing," he chided. "You're only angry she rides better than you. Handled Aspeit like a seasoned trainer, she did. I'd consider offering you a job if I thought you'd take it, Mam."

Crum stopped yelling, but his face was bright red.

"Give me back the reins, so I can jump back over," Mam said.

"Over my grave will I let you jump again."

"How do you propose we get her and Aspeit to the other side of the fence?" Vekel asked.

"You hold her reins. I'll get down and syth the fence down so we can cross."

"You make sure the fence is sound when you raise it," Vekel said.

When Crum dismounted Andale, I noticed both men had ridden after Mam bareback. I couldn't remember the last time I'd seen Crum ride without a saddle. Staying in control at a gallop was an impressive feat.

Crum had the fence down with little effort.

"You didn't have to yell at her, Crum," I said, once Mam and Vekel were out of earshot.

After putting the fence back in place, he double-checked his work. "We need to avoid attention as much as possible. An injury means a trip to a herbalist. Any decent healer would raise questions about her general condition...unnecessary attention."

"I understand, but it looked like she knew what she was doing."

"She could've gotten lost. We'd spend precious time looking for her. You said you wouldn't go to Varia without her, so how long would we have searched, Fitzeirick? Would you have ever given up?"

I shook my head and shrugged. "I promised to keep her safe. You haven't made such a promise, have you?"

"She means something to you, so she means something to me, too."

I grinned. "About time you admit it. How long were you going to wait to tell me?"

"Tell you what?"

"I'm glad I got Mam out of the tunnels alive. I like to see her happy. I wonder who she was before, but she isn't a substitute for Aesa. You're talking like you're ready to take on responsibility. Sar'sa might even say you're starting to mature." I chuckled. "When did Mam start meaning something to you?"

"I didn't...I would never...you think I meant you were using her to take the place of Aesa?"

"Crum, you're avoiding the question," I countered. "What do you feel for 'dear little Mam'?"

He crossed his arms, looked away from me, and kicked at the dirt. "It's...see...you know...I'm not sure." He blushed as he stammered. "I mean...we have no idea how old she is."

I grinned and put my hand on his shoulder. "We'll talk when you're ready, but think about what Vekel said about sidesaddle riding. Mam may have been cast into those tunnels more than fifteen years ago. If she's our age, she would've been no older than ten."

"Oh," he muttered. "Oh...oh no, that couldn't..." He scratched his head for a moment and squinted. "Who would do such a thing to a child?"

"Eirickson," I growled, my grin bending into a frown. "While you ponder that, I want you to consider something else. If she's royalty, what happens if someone in Varia recognizes her?"

He closed his eyes and shook his head. "We'll cross that bridge if we must, but avoid it given the chance."

"Life has a strange way of putting one on a bridge before they realize they've stepped on it."

He frowned and nodded. "Let's go check on her."

As we got close to the wash rack, I heard Vekel barking orders and Mam laughing. We looked at each other and picked up our pace. When we arrived, Mam and Vekel were soaked. Her cap was on the ground and three stable boys were working on the horses.

"What is going on here?" Crum bellowed.

Mam yelped and hid behind Vekel.

"Now see here —" Vekel said.

"No," Crum interrupted. "She's supposed to learn a lesson. Why are both of you wet and neither of you bathing horses?"

"I can explain," Mam said, her head bowed as she stepped out from behind her living shield. "I wasn't getting Andale wet enough. Vekel dumped a bucket over my head to point out how much water I should have used. My cap fell over my eyes and I couldn't see so I dumped a bucket on Vekel by accident. He yanked the cap off my head, saw my hair and said, 'If a Varian woman can't take better care of her hair, she has no business grooming a horse.' He's forbidden me from grooming any of his horses."

I couldn't help myself and laughed.

Crum sputtered, unable to form words.

Vekel laughed, grabbed a full bucket, and dumped it on Crum.

Mam burst into laughter.

Crum didn't laugh with us. Instead, he balled his hand into a fist and drew it back.

I grabbed his arm and drew a little extra strength from the stone floor. "Hey," I warned him. "We're all friends here. Vekel didn't harm you and, well, it *was* funny." I started laughing again and lost all my strength.

He twisted out of my grip and walked away.

Vekel made a shooing motion toward him. "He'll get over it. Pride heals quick enough."

I looked sideways at him. "How long have you known Crum?"

"Long enough to know he's a good man. I should go apologize."

"Stay, give him a little time alone." I glanced at Mam and made sure Vekel noticed. "He has a few things on his mind."

"I see." He grinned and looked back to Mam. "Care to tell me the story behind this haircut? She insisted you were involved."

I paused, unsure of what Mam told him, before explaining I'd rescued her from a bad situation and her hair was so matted the only real choice was to cut it off. "Judging by the result, it seems I'd never make it as a groomer."

"Yes, I agree...you're no groomer. I'll find her a proper fitting riding cap. Now, I do believe Crum and I have business to discuss. Don't worry about me; he knows I can break him in half."

I looked him up and down. "I believe you could. Take it easy on him, though. He's dealing with lots of new thoughts. I'd almost say my 'brother' is growing up."

Vekel laughed as he walked past. "I don't believe it's possible for him to grow up."

Mam, dripping wet, shivered.

"How about we walk back to the fire and get you dried out?" I suggested.

"Sounds like a good idea," she said, smiling.

The fire was down to embers, so I went back to the stables and grabbed a couple of handfuls of hay. The hay burned quickly, but gave me time to find some sticks to rebuild the fire. Soon, I had a respectable fire and Mam stood near it waiting for the water to leave her clothes.

"It seems like you've had a good day," I said.

She smiled. "It felt great to ride again, but I think I made Crum angry. Does he hate me now?"

"No, I'm almost certain he doesn't hate you. He's angry, but maybe more at himself."

"Why?"

"His life is more complicated now, and he has a lot to think about. Some of it's my fault. If I hadn't ended up in the tunnels, he wouldn't be in so much trouble. At least not the same kind of trouble."

"Oh," she sighed. "Is that why we're going to Varia?"

"I'd say it's the main reason. Varia's safer for me. If I stay in Croy, someone will see me, and word will get to Eirickson."

"What's Varia hold for me?"

I looked at her, searching her face for a hint of what she felt. My quest came up empty. "Like so much about you, it's a mystery until some new piece gets uncovered. You know, you impressed Vekel."

"Riding felt wonderful. I haven't felt so good since I saw the night sky for the first time after getting out of the tunnels. And this time the feeling wasn't buried under the burden of guilt for Sir's death."

I pulled her to me for a tight hug. It didn't matter my clothes would get a little damp. *His sacrifice gave us a bond that, for better or worse, will never go away.* "I know exactly what you mean."

"When do I get a hug?" Crum asked, as he got close to us.

I looked him over. He seemed to be whole and unscathed, so I assumed he'd worked his differences out with Vekel. I let go of Mam, stepped to Crum, and embraced him in a bear hug.

"Not from you," he quietly grunted, in my ear.

I chuckled and let him go.

"Did you say anything to her?" he whispered.

"No. Not for me to do or for you to do right now. What did you and Vekel work out?"

"Mam gets the saddle to keep, no charge," he said.

"And horses for us?" I asked.

"Mam gets Aspeit, you ride Andale, and I take Sinar, Andale's last son. My smooth talking made a deal, but he expects payment when we win," he said.

"What do you mean?"

"When we return, I have to deliver two saddlebags of Varian gold."

I pressed my lips together for a moment. "Once I'm running Croy, I'll make sure he's repaid."

Crum smiled and nodded. "I need you and Mam to stay here. There are a few things I need to get. It's easier to avoid unwanted attention if I'm alone. I'll be back before sunset. We'll head toward a big forest northeast of here. I figure it's safest to use the woods as cover until we reach the Varian border. From there, we head to a tavern near the mountains. Assuming the messenger doesn't get held up, someone will be expecting us."

"Messenger?" I asked.

"I talked over a few options with some people before I came back for you two last night. We're heading to the nearest safe place in Varia that will also put you close to people with money and influence."

"Sounds like a solid plan. Which, given how things have gone lately, makes me a little nervous," I confessed, smiling.

"You're right to feel that way," he said, laughing. "If Vekel needs anything, help as best you can. Otherwise, stay out of the way."

"It does sound like a good plan," Mam said. "What will Varia be like?"

"I don't know," I replied. "Never been there myself. My mother's Varian, but she lived in the land conquered by Eirick. She hasn't been to the northern part of Varia or, if she has, she never talked about it."

"Are the people nice?" she asked.

"The Varian I grew up around were. They took care of each other and hardly knew a stranger. Where we're going, people may act different when they find out who I am."

"What difference would it make who you are?"

"My father took land from Varia and, when I was old enough, put me in control of it. I wouldn't blame them for being angry. I understand what it means to have something you cherish taken from you."

"We both do." She turned back to the fire and stared into it.

I put my arm around her. "I fear you've lost much more than I."

We weren't alone with our thoughts long before Vekel walked up. "I believe I owe her a cap. Young lady, would you come with me?"

I nodded to her and watched them walk to the shed.

"Fits like it's made for you," I heard Vekel say. "No, no...take it. I insist. Go show Fitzeirick."

She wore a short, leather cap with a stiff brim, wide enough to shade her ears and forehead.

"Seems to me you couldn't ask for a better fit," I said.

She giggled and blushed. "Thank you. Vekel told me to wear it until my hair grows out some and then give it to a cute boy."

"I'm not sure it fits with Varian tradition, but we'll keep it in mind," I replied.

"Fitzeirick, I think we should talk," Vekel said, as he got closer. "Walk with me."

"Mam, do you feel comfortable tending the fire for a little while?" I asked.

"Put a couple of sticks on top, right?"

"Yes. Be careful when you drop them."

"I will."

He led me about halfway into the stable and then turned to me. "I'm not going to guess who that girl is, and I don't want to know where you found her, but my gut tells me she's important. I'd advise you to take good care of her."

I crossed my arms. "Have been from the moment she and I met. Not to get into your business, but is she the reason you asked for Varian gold?"

He shook his head. "I've traveled with men like Crum before. They tend to land on their feet wherever they go. I'm not always so lucky so I want a piece of it this time."

I stared at him for a while, unsure if I believed him. "Why do I feel like there's something you're not telling me?"

He offered me his hand. "Honestly, I'm on your side. That's it."

I eyed his hand. *Crum's no fool. If he trusts Vekel, why shouldn't I?* "I think I'm going to need all the people I can get on my side," I said, smiling before shaking his hand.

He smiled back. "Thank you. No need for bad blood between us. You seem like a good man."

I smiled and replied, "As do you. I'd better check on Mam. She tends to get overwhelmed if left alone for long."

He nodded. "Go see to her, I have work to do."

I jogged back to the fire and didn't see Mam. I looked left and right, but saw no hint of her. My heart raced as I called out her name, but got no response.

She's gone.

Chapter 16

I didn't walk past her leaving the stables. Where is she? I wasn't gone long. No one can simply vanish. My frantic search began after yelling for her once more.

The tack shed was empty.

I've lost her...I failed her. Beads of sweat trickled down my forehead. My heart pounded in my chest and ears. I couldn't stop my eyes from darting back and forth long enough to focus. "Mam!"

Panic isn't helping. I covered my face with my hands and forced myself to take deep breaths. Pushing my fear into the ground, I noticed a trail of footprints leading behind the shed to a stand of trees. The dense roots blocked my search past that point.

I ran to the edge of the trees and drew a breath to yell her name again as she appeared from behind a tree carrying several branches.

My body trembled. "Where have you been?"

She jumped. "The fire's getting low. I ran out of sticks and went to get more."

I grabbed her shoulders. "Why didn't you answer when I called?"

She shrugged. "I didn't hear you. Did you need me?"

Pointing back toward the fire, I said, "I told you to stay at the fire. I didn't know where you were. When you didn't answer I thought you'd been taken." I looked at the branches cradled in her arms. "Where did you get those?"

"I pulled them from the trees," she said, smiling.

I squinted at her. "Pulled them?"

"I grabbed the branch, felt how it's attached to the tree, and told the branch to let go of the tree." Her expression changed as she explained. "Oh, I wasn't supposed to touch wood...and the sticks are wood."

"Did you tell the trees anything?"

"No, only the branches."

"May I see one?"

She nodded.

I grabbed the one on top. The end where it grew from the tree was smoother than any axe could have cut it. *I wish Crum was here.* "You did fine, but try to remember: don't touch wood until we get someone to work with you. You could've knocked over a whole tree and crushed the tack shed."

Her eyes opened wide and she dropped all the branches. "I...I...oh, no...I never thought about it."

"Good. If you had, it might have happened," I said, gathering the wood.

We tended the fire, mostly to pass the time waiting for Crum. The fresh branches crackled and popped as they burned. She jumped at every unexpected sound.

"Why's the fire so noisy?"

"Those branches are full of sap. When they get hot, the sap boils, forcing its way out with a loud crack."

"How do you get rid of sap so the fire's quiet?"

"Gather the wood and leave it lying in the sun to dry...it takes a while," I said. "Maybe an experienced woodsyth can push the sap out faster, but I've never seen it done."

"Does Crum know how?"

"He might."

"Would he teach me?" she asked.

"I have a feeling he'd like nothing more. When the time is right."

"How do I know when the time's right?" she asked.

"You may need to remember more or maybe Crum has to wait for the time to be right, too. We'll talk to him about it when we have a chance," I assured her with a smile.

She nodded as if she understood. The look on her face told me different. "Do you think I'm a Varian royal?"

"Several things you've remembered make us think you may be. From what Vekel said, it wouldn't surprise me."

"Should I tell someone when we get into Varia?"

"I think it'd be best to keep it to ourselves. It could be troubling for people to hear a stranger claim relation to the Varian royal family. If you remember more, we could request an audience with the royals. We have to be careful, though. If they start asking questions you can't answer, they may accuse us of trying to trick them. That could be bad for us."

"How bad?" she asked, voice dropping with fear.

I shrugged. "I know nothing about Varian punishment, but they could imprison us or force us to leave the country. If we're forced out of Varia, where do we go? Satra is *not* an option."

"Imprisoned?" Her face went pale. "Do you think they have tunnels too?"

"I don't know. I never knew Croy had such a thing until Eirickson dropped me in them. I hope no one else is so vile as to build such a place, but it's possible."

"I think I'll keep my secret to myself," she decided.

A chorus of horse hooves hitting the ground inside the stable interrupted our conversation. "I guess we need to get ready to leave."

"You two, take Aspeit and Andale to finish drying near the fire." Vekel directed his stable boys. "Don't saddle them before they dry."

Crum sat bareback on Sinar with three sets of bulging saddlebags draped across the horse's back. When he dismounted, I noticed the pack on his back. He took it off and handed it to me. "Clothes for each of us on top. Enough food and drink for two days of travel. Change in the tack shed. Vekel, see to the rest of your work and I'll fit the horses after they dry. We'll be out of your way soon."

"What's in the saddle bags?" I asked.

"One has my stuff. The other two have bedrolls and other necessities to get us through the next few days," he said.

Vekel took the lead ropes from the boys and handed them to Mam. He looked at me. "May the way be smooth, and don't forget your obligations."

Crum was about to say something, but I cut him off. "Thank you for your generosity. I'll see you're rewarded."

Crum glared at me, but held his tongue until we were inside the shed. "What was that about?"

Won't hurt him to squirm a little. "He and I reached an agreement."

His jaw dropped open. "I thought you were against the idea of indentured servants."

It took some effort to keep from smiling. "Never said I wasn't. I agreed you'd hold up your end of the bargain, and I'd help in any way I could. We need to put this matter to rest, there's a bigger concern. Mam."

"What about her?" he asked, looking worried.

"A couple of things, and I'm not sure which is more important."

He pulled clothes out of the pack and handed them to me. "Pick the one you think I can help with most. Unless you don't think you can talk and change clothes at the same time."

I crossed my arms, cocked my head to the side, and squinted at him. "At least I don't see a way you could make this one any worse. She used her talent a while ago, and it sounds like she did it by instinct."

Crum's face lost some color. "What happened? Is she hurt? Did she damage anything?"

"She's fine, nothing was damaged. She pulled branches off trees to feed the fire."

He looked at me for a long moment before saying anything. "What do you mean?"

"She said she touched the branches, felt where they attached to the trees, and told them to let go. The ends were smoother than the sharpest axe cut."

"She did it by instinct? Are you sure?"

"Had to be," I answered. "I've talked to her about this before. She doesn't remember being tested or trained. You didn't see how disturbed she was when she touched a rotten tree."

"As soon as I can, I'll work with her. Between this and how easily she weaves straw, I think she has a lot of potential."

"It seems the weaving is a childhood memory she never lost," I commented.

He nodded. "What's your other concern?"

"Her possible ties to the Varian royal family," I said.

"Do you believe she's royalty?"

I nodded. "It's a real possibility. I told her it'd be best for her to keep it to herself when we get to Varia. She said she'd try."

He nodded, but didn't say anything as he changed.

The only time he's quiet is when he's deep in thought.

After pulling his shirt on, he said, "We trust her to keep it secret and deal with the royalty problem should it come up."

"I agree. Are we leaving our old clothes here?"

"I'll put them in the pack when we're done."

I left the shed wearing a mottled, dark, gray-and-black woven shirt and matching pants. Crum's outfit matched mine, but looked tailored to him.

"Mam, go change your clothes," I said.

"I'm holding the horses."

"I'll take care of them while you change," I said.

"When you're done, I'll get the tack. I hope someone brings the saddle for Aspeit soon," Crum said.

Before she closed the door, she asked, "Do I get a new hat?"

Crum looked at her. "No, little one, I'm afraid not. But I like the one you have now."

"Thank you," she replied, smiling. "I should keep wearing it?"

We answered yes in unison and she hurried into the tack shed.

Crum finished securing his saddle as a stable boy brought Mam's special saddle. "Would you like me to get her ready?" he asked.

"Make sure everything is right," Crum ordered.

"Of course, sir. Vekel would accept nothing less," he responded, and set to his task.

Mam's new clothes hung limply off her thin frame. Her leather cap almost matched the outfit.

Crum looked her over and nodded his approval before heading into the shed.

"Mam, maybe one day you'll fit in those clothes," I said.

"I don't remember being any size other than this one."

"Knowing what you've lived through, I believe you," I said.

"Will we have plenty to eat on the trip?"

I chuckled. "I'm sure Crum packed enough food for six of us."

She laughed. "Can he not count?"

I let out a long, loud, belly laugh.

She jumped and the horses snorted.

"He can count fine. He prefers to eat like each meal is the one keeping him from starving to death."

"He's spent time in someplace like the tunnels?" she asked.

"Umm...no. That's not — I should've said he likes to eat big meals as often as he can."

She smiled and nodded.

Crum exited the tack shed with the pack on his back, reins hanging over one shoulder, and carrying a saddle. He walked to Andale, fit the saddle in place, and secured his reins before getting the other two horses outfitted. "Front bags are mine. I'll move Mam's to Aspeit. Fitzeirick, you get the last set of bags. Oh, be sure to look in yours...I have a surprise for you."

I waited until he was out of the way and grabbed my saddlebags. One bag was heavier than the other. After securing the bags behind the saddle, I reached into the heavy one. My hand brushed against a piece of stone. I pushed a little energy into it and found a familiar rectangular block of granite. The hair on my arm stood as I pulled out the gray stone.

My hammer! My stomach quivered. The wooden handle felt exactly as I remembered. I slipped the leather thong over my wrist, gripped the handle, and took a few swings. I thought I might cry as I choked out my thanks. "You kept it all this time?"

He nodded. "Of course. It was a little trouble to keep finding suitable hiding places when I moved, but I knew you'd want it. Keep looking," he said, with a sly grin.

I reached inside the bag and felt around. I found a thin, leather strap and pulled it out, but I had no idea what it was.

"A sling for it, so it's always within reach," he explained.

I arranged the strap across my chest with the pouch on my left hip. The sling held the hammer well enough to keep it in place while riding. "Again, thank you," I said. "I feel like this trip's already a success."

He smiled and said, "You're most welcome."

"Did I get anything?" Mam asked.

His eyes flew open and he looked at me in a panic. "Umm...sorry dear, I didn't think you'd need anything else. I do have something for us to work with before we bed down, though."

"Oh," she said. "You *did* think of me after all."

He looked relieved. "Yes, I did. Do you know anything about fighting?"

"I know to stay out of the way."

"Good enough," I said. "Shall we be on our way?"

"I packed a riding cloak in each of our bags. If it starts to rain, put the cloak on. The weaver made them to shed water. Also, if we see anyone coming, put the cloak on so the hoods hide our faces. Mount up. I'll lead. Mam, you stay between me and Fitzeirick."

She settled on Aspeit before Crum's foot was in a stirrup. It took me two hops to get on Andale.

A sliver of sun showed over the horizon as he led us through the stand of trees behind the tack shed. He pushed Sinar into a trot when we reached the edge of a prairie. The full moon gave enough light to follow my fellow travelers into the great sea of tall grass. The stalks brushed my knees.

I felt nervous traveling in the dark without being able to feel the ground and watch for unseen threats. *No telling what's in the shadows, waiting for the right moment to attack.* We kept a steady pace and reached the edge of a forest without incident, despite my fears.

Crum waved for us to ride next to him. "We're close to Satran controlled land. I'm told they patrol deep in the forest during the day, but usually stay out at night. When we get into the trees, we'll have to dismount and walk. I plan to move us north by northeast until we find somewhere thick enough to hide our camp. Fitzeirick, watch for anything moving."

I nodded. "Lead on."

We entered the forest, turned north and walked several horse lengths before he brought us to a stop. "Dismount here and keep a tight grip on the reins. We don't need to lose a horse in this brush," Crum directed. He turned to Mam. "Stay in the middle, but first can you get a roll for each of us out of my pack? Oh, and hand out the wineskins, but go easy on the drink. It has to last."

"I thought you'd forgotten what it felt like to be hungry," she said, approaching him.

"Wine?" I asked.

"Only strong enough to keep the water from spoiling," he replied.

"Remember, I haven't had anything stronger than tea in almost a year. And I don't know if Mam's ever had wine," I said.

"I am sure we'll be fine," he said.

I didn't feel reassured.

She handed me a roll the size of my two fists together.

"What's this?" I asked.

"Bread baked around boiled meat," he said, before taking a big bite.

Mam followed his example, but coughed.

"Smaller bites, dear little Mam," Crum advised. "And maybe take a drink to moisten the roll. Goes down easier that way."

She nodded and drank some of the watered-down wine. Her lips puckered and she squeezed her eyes tight.

I couldn't help but chuckle before taking a bite, chewing as we walked.

The clumps of trees made it hard for me to pick out details from the ground around us. Watching for activity near us through the roots was challenging. I slowed to maintain my focus. Our meandering path stopped at some dense undergrowth. Crum put his hand on my shoulder when I turned east.

"Wait," he whispered, before touching the nearest tree. He closed his eyes and took several deep breaths. "I can open a path through this. Mam, take my horse and follow Fitzeirick. I'll come in behind you soon."

I gave him a questioning look.

"Don't worry," he said. "I found a clearing. Follow the path."

I nodded and turned to wait for the brush to move.

He took a deep breath and the growth moved aside. After several twists and turns, I stepped into a clearing. The trees around it blocked sunlight, so only the hardiest of grasses grew.

I pushed my talent into the ground and found a patch of stone near the surface. I tried to track Crum, but dense roots blinded me at the edge of the clearing. I heard the occasional creak and crackle of wood moving, and hoped it was Crum coming to join us.

Mam stood near me, shivering and humming.

"Go tie the horses to those low branches," I whispered. I hoped giving her something to do would calm her.

"The branches are wood, right?" she asked, with a quivering voice.

"Yes," I replied. "Don't tell the branches to do anything and you shouldn't cause any problems. I need you to do this for me."

"I'll do my best."

I wasn't watching her, focused instead on the sounds which seemed to get closer. I licked my lips. The memory of a charging mountain lion flashed through my mind, and I grabbed my hammer tightly. Its weight comforted me.

Something pressed against my back. I jumped away, raising my hammer to strike as I turned.

Chapter 17

Mam stood frozen near the spot I'd leapt from.

When I saw her, I let go of the hammer mid-swing. It tumbled over her head and struck a tree on the other side of the clearing with a solid thunk.

Birds woke and flew away, making an incredible racket. The noise rousted more birds, adding their frightened calls to the commotion. The sudden sound startled the horses and they cried out.

Mam fell to the ground and curled into a ball.

I tried to ignore the strange, mewing noises coming from her, as I searched for my hammer while still watching for the real threat.

"What happened to being quiet? You two have awoken the entire forest."

I punched the intruder in the face. He yelped and dropped to the ground.

Having addressed that threat, I resumed looking for my hammer. It seemed like an eternity passed before I found it and returned to defend my friends.

Crum rose to a knee. "You do realize you're protecting us from you, right?" He held his hand over his face, and his voice sounded muffled.

"What?" I asked, watching the edges of the clearing.

"Put your hammer away before you kill one of us and go settle the horses. I'll see if I can calm Mam back into being a person," he said, in the funny voice.

"Wait. When did you get here and why do you sound strange?"

"I got here before you punched me in the nose. I'm talking like this because you *punched me in the nose*. Go settle the horses."

"Are you sure I punched you?" I asked, still confused.

"Does your right hand hurt?" He sounded frustrated.

I looked at my hand and felt some throbbing. "A little."

"Because you punched me! Now, see to the horses!" he shouted.

The horses nickered and snorted as I approached. I spoke their names softly, trying to sound soothing. Andale kicked at me a couple of times when I got too close for his comfort. I backed away and moved to where he could see me. That seemed to do the job, and soon I had them settled.

I walked back toward Crum. He held Mam, talking to her. She'd finally stopped making the strange noise.

"Stalking us for another go?" he asked.

"I...I'm sorry. I heard noises in the underbrush. Mam got nervous so I gave her a task, then forgot about her. When she touched me, I thought it was an attack. I panicked and almost hit her with my hammer and...I guess you know the rest."

He looked at me, still holding his nose. "I'm aware you panicked for no good reason. And because of it, we can't risk making a fire without worrying about attracting attention."

He turned his attention back to Mam. "Little one, you're safe. No one's going to hurt you."

"Are you sure we're safe?" she asked, in a weak, little voice.

He glared at me again. "Yes. Fitzeirick got startled, lost his mind a little, but we're all fine now. Would you like to eat?"

I smiled when her cap bobbed up and down. *Good thinking Crum, using food to distract her.* The smile hid the nausea threatening to empty my stomach. *If I can't keep my wits about me now, how am I going to beat Eirickson? He's already outmaneuvered me once...*

Crum grabbed my arm and led me close to the edge of the clearing. "I wanted to test her woodsything before we went to sleep. Now, she's so skittish, I'll never be able to get her to focus. What happened to you?"

I blinked several times before shaking my head. "I have no excuse. All that time watching for threats while we moved through the tunnels and the woods set my mind on kill or be killed. I couldn't feel anything past the edge of the clearing, so I pulled my talent back out of the ground. Mam touched me and I thought something was attacking us."

"Kill or be killed?" he repeated. "You've never been like that before. You've always been steady, thinking things through."

"That's how I survived in the tunnels for all those months."

"You're outside, free now. I need you to remember that. If things go well in Varia, people will look to you for leadership. With luck, you'll lead Croy, the entire nation. You can't have 'kill or be killed' on your mind. If you keep thinking like that, you will fail. *We* will fail. Eirickson will carry out his plans with Satra, and Varia *will* fall. That's certain. Can you guess how long until a stronger Satra decides to conquer the rest of Croy?"

I crouched down and pressed my fingers into the dirt, looking for comfort from the ground. *He's right. I have to get myself back under control. Nine bad months can't define the rest of my life.* A shiver racked my body when I looked up at Crum. "No, but what if things don't go well in Varia?"

He looked at me for a long time. "I...well, honestly, I hadn't considered that. Should that come to pass, kill or be killed will be the law of the land for a while, I suppose."

"Trust me, you don't want that to happen."

"Fitz," Mam called out.

We hurried back to her.

"Yes?"

She looked at me. Her chin trembled, voice wavering as she spoke. "Why'd you try to hit me before? Did I do something wrong?"

Crum huffed and looked away.

I shook my head. "You did exactly what I asked. If I said you scared me, would you understand?"

"Why would I scare you?"

I sat next to her and put my arm around her. "Well...I, umm...I wasn't scared of you exactly. I, uhh...I didn't expect you to come up behind me. When you touched me, I thought you were an attacker."

"Like the others in the tunnels?"

"Yes, like them," I said, nodding.

"But they were mean, and you've always told me you'd keep me safe."

I frowned. "I thought I was keeping us all safe, but I made a mistake and almost hurt you. I'm sorry, Mam."

"Did you hit Crum?"

"Yes."

"Why?" she asked.

"Another mistake. I wasn't expecting him."

"Is he always going to talk funny now?"

I smiled weakly. "No, it will go away given some time."

"I'm sleepy. No corners," she said, glancing around the clearing.

Her ability to skip from subject to subject amazed me.

Crum turned to her. "You're right, no corners at all. Give me and Fitzeirick a little time to see what we can do." He pointed to an area opposite the horses. "I think I can arrange some brush into something close to a corner. Could you move some dirt into a low wall?"

"I have a better idea. There's a stone slab right below the surface. I'll make a corner near some bushes and you cover it with soft branches so she's comfortable."

"Sounds good," he agreed.

I moved to the edge of the clearing and stabbed my fingers into the dirt. Concentrating on the picture of a corner, I pushed my will into the ground and raised a wall about waist high. A second wall joined it, making a tight corner for her to snuggle into.

"Well done," Crum said. "My turn." He reached over the stone and grabbed a branch. Several leafy bushes slithered over, making their way to the ground.

"Now you have a safe corner to sleep in," he announced proudly.

She smiled and moved to wedge herself into it.

Crum walked to Aspeit and took Mam's riding cloak out of a saddle bag. He jogged over and covered her. "This'll keep you warm. Sleep well, dear little Mam."

She yawned and quickly fell into the slow, steady, rhythmic breathing of slumber.

"We should get some sleep ourselves," he said.

I found a large tree to sit against so I could sleep.

• • • • •• • •• • • ••

Something tapping on my hand woke me. I looked around. The sun was high enough to light the clearing.

Crum sat next to me with his hand over his mouth. His black and blue nose stood out against his lightly tanned skin.

I nodded and kept quiet.

He touched his ear.

I closed my eyes to focus on sounds.

It wasn't long until I heard a voice, but I couldn't make out any words. Then I heard sticks breaking somewhere outside the clearing. The sounds were hard to locate through the thick underbrush.

He tapped my hand again.

I opened my eyes.

He held up three fingers, then added a fourth.

I nodded.

He pointed toward where we entered the clearing and swept his hand back and forth.

I grabbed my hammer and crept forward, softening the ground as I moved to mask my footsteps.

Near the edge, I heard the voice again. "The tracks stop right here. Horses and at least two sets of footprints. And you said night patrol was scared."

"No," another voice replied, "I said they got spooked by birds."

I jumped when one of the horses stomped the ground and snorted.

Someone yelled. "That was a horse. It's around here."

I looked toward the horses.

Crum stood near Sinar, looking aggravated while he put his bow together. Once he was ready, he motioned for me to move and stay low.

I took two side steps and crouched as someone hacked at the underbrush.

The noise startled the horses. They added neighs, whinnies, and snorts to the sound of blades chopping wood.

"That's more than one horse. Go! Push through this!" someone shouted.

Mam woke. "What's wrong with the horses?"

"Did you hear that?" another voice asked.

Crum moved toward her when he saw her eyes open wide.

The chopping stopped, replaced by the sound of branches and saplings cracking. The tops of the shorter scrub and trees swayed as the group pushed its way toward us.

Crum reached Mam as someone burst into the clearing.

The dark-headed man wore Satran armor. His mottled, gray skin left no doubt.

I yelled and he turned toward me.

Crum's bow thrummed as the soldier swung his sword. He bellowed, dropping the weapon when the arrow punched through his forearm.

I lunged, knocking him into two more soldiers. A fourth crashed through the bushes behind me.

Something struck the back of my head and my vision blurred. Mam screamed when I fell to the ground, and a boot struck me hard in the side. I pulled some strength from the ground to push myself up, but the next kick hit my chest and I felt some ribs crack. I grunted and rolled away from the attack.

Twice more, Crum's bow thrummed.

Yells followed shortly after, but I could make out four blurry forms still standing.

"The horses and the young one are worth taking," one of them said.

I was on my hands and knees when another kick plunged into my stomach. I lost my breath and fell flat again. "Stay down!" someone shouted.

A blurry leg stepped toward me. I swung my hammer wildly toward it and connected. The blow shattered bone. The soldier screamed. As he fell, he thrust his sword toward my head.

I moved too slow to avoid the strike completely. A stinging line burned its way along the left side of my scalp as the blade slid on my skull. My blurred vision turned into a red haze.

I've got to get up.

I yelled, pushed myself up onto my knees, and turned toward the downed soldier. The yell continued as my hammer slammed down where I expected his head to be. The impact crushed it, making a sickening sound.

I sucked in a breath and bellowed a challenge. Crum's bow thrummed again.

The soldier standing farthest from me dropped to one knee. A second shot followed and felled the injured man.

I pulled in more strength and charged the nearest Satran. Lifting him off the ground and slamming him down, I landed with all my weight on him. Pain stabbed across my chest. His breath escaped with a loud 'whuff'.

I sat astride him, pounding his chest and head with my hammer.

Without warning, everything went black.

• • • • • • • • • • •

I woke, flat on my back, to dim light. My head and chest ached. Pain shot through me when I moved. All I could do was groan and lay still.

I heard, "Shhh."

A woman's voice said, "Relax. You're not dead."

"He's awake?" a man asked.

"Yes," she answered.

My blurred vision filled with Crum's face.

"Can you see me?"

"Ye...oh." My head hurt when I tried to talk.

"I'll take that as a yes," he said, grinning. "Mam, do you have the horses ready?"

"Yes, but how —"

He cut her off. "You let me worry about how. We can't stay here."

"Wha...ow." The pain interrupted again.

"No time to explain. I need you to pull some strength and get on a horse. We have to move."

I can't see out of my left eye. I reached up, touched my face, and felt cloth. A bandage. That was a slight relief. I tried to concentrate and use my talent, but it made my head pound harder.

"I...ugh...I can't." The pain was too much.

Crum stood over me. "If you don't get up, Satran patrols will find us again. They'll kill us this time. Are you going to let that happen?"

I couldn't shake my head or talk, so I did what I had to do. Forcing myself to focus, to ignore the pain, I pulled strength from the ground. The effort covered me in sweat, stinging the wound on my scalp. *Exactly what I don't need, a new pain.*

Finally, I felt a slow trickle of strength enter my body. It hurt to move. Bone ground against bone in my chest as I sat up. The world spun around me.

"I'll help you to your feet," he said, grabbing my right arm.

He pulled as I tried to stand, but muscles stretched across my chest and I screamed.

"Push!" Crum barked. "Your life depends on it. All our lives depend on you getting on a horse. Mam will die, if you don't move *now*."

Clenching my teeth and grunting, I forced myself to my stand. I wobbled and nearly fell, but he kept me upright.

"Lean on me. I'll get you Andale," he said.

I put too much weight on him, and he nearly buckled.

It took more effort than it should have, but I finally balanced enough to walk. Every step jarred my body. My head throbbed, my chest burned with pain. Tears flowed as bright spots floated in front of my eyes.

"You can pass out once you're on horseback," Crum grunted.

I lost track of time. All that mattered was moving forward.

• • • • • • • • • • •

I didn't remember getting to Andale, or getting into the saddle, but jarring movements told me I was riding.

"Is he still out?" someone asked.

"He hasn't moved in quite a while," a woman answered.

My head pounded, so I decided I was still alive. I opened my eyes to darkness. Coarse hair rubbed my face. I guessed I was lying forward on a horse. "Where...ow." It still hurt to talk.

"Fitzeirick, are you back with us? Wait, don't answer," a man said.

Crum's face came into view. "We're at an inn, and they've sent for a herbalist. She's highly recommended. I'll help you down and walk you in. Mam, let them know we're coming."

Chapter 18

Crum took my feet out of the stirrups. "You're already leaning forward, so bring your leg over. I'll help you down."

I wasn't sure my leg would move and felt less confident he could catch me as I fell. Still, a bed would be more comfortable than where I was. With some effort, my leg moved, but my chest protested the entire time. The jolt from hitting the ground brought even more pain.

I couldn't help but gasp, causing more aches and throbbing in my head. At least the world had stopped spinning and I could walk by myself.

"Take it slow, no hurry," he said. "When you get inside, we'll take the hallway on the right to the second door on the right."

I wobbled and grabbed his shoulder. "Stick close."

Mam greeted me when I walked into the room. "Lay down. The herbalist should be here soon."

I groaned as I eased onto the bed and was almost asleep when an odd combination of smells, fragrant flowers trying to overpower hot, onion soup assaulted my nose.

Mam coughed.

Crum groaned. "Hope that's not the herbalist."

As the smell grew stronger, I watched the door.

A squat woman with wild hair in various shades of brown waddled into the room, carrying a large, black, leather bag. "Give me room so I can work," she said.

Her voice reminded me of jagged rocks rubbing together.

"We'll leave," Crum said.

"You don't have to go, but stay out of my way."

She set the bag on the floor. "What happened to you?"

"Ambushed by Satran soldiers in the —" Crum started to say.

"Didn't ask you," the herbalist barked, whipping her head around to look at him. She turned back to me. "You tell me."

"Hurts my head to talk," I moaned.

"Choose your words with care."

I pointed to where I felt the bones crack. "Kicked in the chest."

"Horse?"

"Soldier."

"Why is your head bandaged?"

"Sword."

"Someone stopped the bleeding, kept you alive. What about this scar on your face?"

"Misunderstanding."

"I see. At least it healed well. Any other injuries?"

I squinted. "Don't remember."

"You took a blow to the back of your head," Crum offered.

The herbalist shook her head. "Some people can't stay quiet. First, I'll see about your chest."

I tried to sit up to take off my shirt, but she pressed her hand against my shoulder. "Lay still."

I relaxed and closed my eyes as she rummaged through the bag.

Before I could react, she slit my shirt, bottom to top. The blade shaved a few hairs from my chin as it passed my face. My eyes flew open in time to catch the glint of candlelight off the knife.

"Hey!" Crum yelled. "What are you trying to do? You almost slit his throat!"

I could tell he'd stepped closer as he spoke.

The herbalist turned to face him, still holding the knife. "Told you to leave me room to work. Stay back. I know what I'm doing. I won't harm him."

She turned back to me and peeled the shirt off the left side of my chest.

When I tried to look at the damage, she thumped me on the nose. "No moving. Lay still."

Muttering something I couldn't understand, she took her time looking at my chest before poking me.

I cried out in pain.

She nodded and rummaged through the bag again before poking my chest again. When I yelled, she pushed a thick piece of leather into my mouth. "Bite. The yelling hurts my ears."

It tasted strange, sort of musty. I tried to spit it out, but she held it in place.

"Bite!" she barked.

I heard Mam whimper.

"Now, I can work." The herbalist pushed and rubbed on my chest. It seemed like she worked for hours. "Broken ribs, nothing too serious. Drink lots of milk and they'll heal fine. Now, for your head."

Using the knife again, she cut the cloth tied around my head. "Long, deep wound. I'll have to sew it shut or it'll never heal. Keep biting." Another search through the bag and she revealed a slender, curved needle and black thread. "I need a chair."

Someone dragged a chair across the floor. The herbalist scooted it closer and heaved her ample body onto the seat. "Sorry you're not drunk. This will hurt. No need to apologize if you pass out."

I felt the needle pierce the skin on the top of my head and scrape against my skull before exiting the other side of the wound. As I came to terms with the new pain, the thread slid through. In a strange way, it almost tickled compared to the rest of the torture.

An unexpected flash of pain erupted when she pulled the thread tight to close the wound. If not for the leather, I would've either screamed myself hoarse or bitten through my own tongue, maybe both.

She developed a rhythm of discomfort. In, scrape, out, slide, tug, and repeat. I tried to focus on anything except the sewing. Finally, she reached for the knife again, cut the thread, and tied it with another tug.

"Done, and you stayed awake...I'm impressed. Keep biting. This will sting," she said, before smearing something thick and smelly on the wound.

She was right, it stings.

"That'll help it heal faster. Don't wash your hair; once it's hardened and fallen out on its own, you can remove the thread."

She turned away from me. "You. Lift him."

Crum stood over me. His face had lost all its natural color, making his discolored nose look even worse. He leaned close to my ear and whispered, "I'm sorry."

"Hold him up so I can examine the rest of his head."

He put his hands under my shoulders and lifted with a grunt.

I did my best to help him, but any pressure on my left arm caused my chest to hurt worse. With a little effort, and a lot of discomfort, I was sitting.

The herbalist poked several places on the back of my head and neck. Several times she started what almost felt like a massage before poking me again.

At least it doesn't make my head hurt worse.

"Set him down," she said, sliding off the chair.

After my head hit the pillow, the herbalist took the leather out of my mouth.

She dug through her bag then handed something to Crum. "This'll help with the bump on his head. Make a tea from these leaves, twice a day for three days. He drinks it hot. Don't add anything; it must be pure to work."

He nodded.

She looked at me. "It won't taste good, but you must drink it all."

"Hot and he drinks it all. Got it," Crum said. "Thank you."

"Be glad I know where I can sell those Satran swords. Doubt you could afford this treatment otherwise. Want me to look at your nose?"

He sputtered for a moment. "No...no, not necessary. Thanks for the kind offer, though."

"I bid you all a good evening. He must rest. Leave him in bed until he's strong enough to get up by himself."

I turned to watch her waddle back out of the room.

"Mam," Crum said. "Find some milk and tell Hendri we need hot water for tea."

She left in a hurry.

"Want me to get you something to eat?" he asked me.

"No," I muttered.

I heard footsteps as someone entered the room.

"I have a mug of fresh milk. Kettle's on to boil."

"You're going to have to sit to drink. I'll help you," he said. "Mam, can you hold the mug and help him drink from it?"

"I'll do my best."

He lifted me by my shoulders again, and I clenched my teeth against the pain.

She pressed the mug against my lips, wetting them with milk. I opened my mouth and a small amount of warm, thick liquid flowed in, soothing my sore throat.

In her eagerness to help, she tilted the mug too far and half the milk spilled onto my chest. She gasped. "Oh no, something's wrong. Fitz can't drink milk."

Crum chuckled and almost dropped me. "I think you tried to get him to drink it too fast. Next time, don't tilt the mug so much. Please get a cloth to clean him."

"I'm doing my best to help," she murmured.

"She means well," Crum commented, lowering me.

I grunted a response.

She ran back into the room. "I have a cloth and the water's ready."

"Clean up the milk. I'll make the tea."

Bounding to the side of the bed, she dried my chest, scrubbing hard.

"Easy, easy," I hissed.

She jumped back. "What's wrong?"

"You're pushing too hard. It hurt."

"Oh, I'm sorry. Do you still want me to help?"

"Yes, but try to be gentle. Please."

"I'll do my best," she said, dabbing the cloth into the milk.

She was still cleaning the mess when a pungent odor assaulted my nose.

Crum entered the room and the warning about how bad the tea would taste echoed in my ears. "This stuff better help," he said, "because it smells terrible."

I grunted.

Mam dropped the cloth on the floor and took the large cup from him.

"Time to sit again," he said.

Once I was back in position, she touched the cup to my lips. The steam rising from the tea burned the inside of my nose.

I opened my mouth and hot liquid poured in. My tongue told me I was drinking rancid mud, and it took all my willpower to not spit it out. *Is this cup ever going to empty?*

I looked at Mam as he lowered me. She looked proud, not a single drop spilled this time. *It's nice to see her happy.*

Crum handed her the mug and cup. "Take these back to the kitchen and thank them for their help." As she hurried through the door, he looked at me. "Hungry?"

The milk and tea fought over which would be the first to come up when I got sick. Food was the last thing on my mind. I tried to shake my head, but it hurt too much, so instead I blurted out, "No."

"Suit yourself. I'll eat with Mam."

I waved at him and closed my eyes. I didn't remember falling asleep. When I woke, the room was bright with sunlight.

"I'll go get milk," Mam said, when she saw me stir.

I heard her open the door and say, "He's awake."

Crum walked in and handed me a piece of bread and a small hunk of cheese. "Eat this before she gets back."

My stomach growled at the sight of food. I tried pushing myself up, but my chest protested. "Help me up."

He lifted me and I braced against the wall enough to sit on my own.

"Looks like you're getting better already," he said, handing me the simple meal.

I swallowed the last bite before Mam entered with a mug of milk.

"So nice to see you sitting. Think you can drink this by yourself?"

I held out my hand for the mug. "I'll try." The weight of the full mug surprised me, but I managed to drink it without spilling any.

"Mam, did you ask them to boil water for tea?" Crum asked.

"Oh...no. I forgot."

"I think it can wait a few minutes," I said.

"Want to try a chair?" he asked, grinning.

"No. I'm fine here."

"Keep an eye on him, I'll go get the tea started," he said.

I groaned at the thought of drinking that stuff again.

"What's it like to sleep lying down?" Mam asked.

"It didn't feel strange to wake lying down. Are you still sleeping sitting up?"

She nodded. "I slept against your bed last night, in case you needed anything."

"Where'd Crum sleep?"

"Right outside so no one would bother you," she answered.

I took her hand and squeezed it. "Thank you for seeing to me."

"You've done nothing less for me since I met you," she said, smiling.

Before I could say anything else, I caught a whiff of the tea. The odor filled the room when Crum walked in. "Do you have any idea what I'm drinking?"

He shook his head. "I didn't bother to ask. To be honest, she scared me."

"I thought she was going to kill you," Mam added.

I wanted to laugh, but was afraid it would hurt. "We survived an attack by four soldiers, one scary herbalist shouldn't be a concern. That reminds me, how did I get knocked out?"

"Mam," Crum said.

"What?" she asked.

He snickered. "I wasn't calling your name. I was answering his question."

"My turn," I said. "What?"

"You were busy smashing the one you tackled when the last soldier standing came at you. Mam jumped to her feet, yanked a good-sized branch off a tree, and charged with a respectable yell. She got a great swing and hit you right in the back of the head. When you slumped forward, she dropped the club and froze. That stunned the solder and gave me a clear shot to put him down," he explained.

She turned to me, tears forming in her eyes. "Fitz, I'm so sorry. I wanted to help." Without warning, she dove and wrapped her arms around me.

It hurt.

I choked back a scream before patting her on the back.

"Can you forgive me?" she pled. "I could've killed you."

"I lived," I grunted. "Did you mean to hit me?"

"Of course not," she said.

"It was an accident...and one made trying to defend me. Did you do your best?"

"I tried," she said.

"What else could I do, but forgive you...except, maybe, ask you not to defend me again."

She laughed a little.

"Now, please get off. I still hurt."

She jumped back, apologizing again.

"I forgive you."

Crum tapped his finger against his chin and smiled. "This would make a great tale for telling over drinks. Perhaps I should set it to music instead. An ode to misplaced, good intentions."

I glared at him. "You aren't helping right now."

He smiled wider. "Are you ready to get out of bed, great warrior? I have contacts to track down."

I lifted my left arm to stretch a little and my chest told me it was a bad idea. "No. I think I need, at least, another day to rest."

"I understand. Rest," he agreed. "I'll need to find a messenger. Dear little Mam, would you care to join me? While we're out, you can pick out a new shirt for Fitzeirick."

"Seems it's the least I could do to make up for my mistake," she said, through sniffles.

"Send more milk on your way out," I said.

She smiled. "I'll ask someone to bring some."

I nodded off shortly after they left.

A young boy, carrying a mug almost overflowing with milk, woke me. "Here, sir."

I blinked a couple of times and took it from him. "If you stay a moment, you can take the empty mug back."

He nodded and stood still, staring.

I drank the milk and handed the mug back to him.

"What happened to you?"

"Got in a fight. I won. You wouldn't like to see the losers," I said, smiling.

The boy's eyes opened wide as he backed away.

The door flew open, slamming into the wall. Crum ran into the room and almost knocked the startled boy to the floor.

"We have to move."

Chapter 19

"Why?"

"Someone spotted Satran soldiers in the woods last night. I'd bet anything they're looking for us."

My mouth went dry as my heartbeat sped up, threatening to make my head hurt worse. "You know I can't ride in this condition."

"If you can walk, we can get to a safe place."

Looking past him, I asked, "Where's Mam?"

"Hidden for now. She attracted some attention while we were out. Stares and whispers from older people for the most part, but it made me nervous."

"Hidden where?"

"Don't worry, she's safe. We need to get moving. It's bold of Satra to send soldiers this far north. If they don't meet any resistance, I expect a group will make their way into town soon, maybe tomorrow, and start asking questions. We *don't* want to be here."

I knew how a worried Crum looked, and his expression was worse than that.

"Fine, help me up and...a shirt?"

"Mam has it. I grabbed your riding cloak."

I held out my hand.

He took it, braced himself, and leveraged me to my feet.

Moving my left arm to put on the cloak was its own special torture, but I was ready to go. "I'm steady enough to walk. Don't ask me to run."

He ushered me out the back door.

"Where are we going?" I asked.

"Short hike into the foothills to a hidden cabin."

"Hike? I'm barely able to walk and you want me to hike?"

"You're a stonesyth. Pull strength from the ground, force yourself...or risk capture."

I didn't want to consider what Satra would do to me. I drew enough strength to do what I had to do. *I'll pay for this later.*

The sun had started its downward plunge when we reached the cabin. Crum took several wrong paths before we arrived. I accused him of getting lost.

He mumbled something about taking those paths on purpose to confuse anyone trying to track us.

The cabin wasn't much more than four walls and a roof. A thick layer of dust covered everything. The fireplace looked choked with cobwebs. *This may be the worst idea he's ever had.* There was no time for complaining, though.

"I need to lie down," I admitted.

"And here I was hoping you'd syth all this dirt out," he said.

"I'm in no shape —"

He put his hand on my shoulder. "I know. I was joking. Wait outside, I'll clean up."

I groaned and found a large tree to lean against while waiting for Crum's extraordinary cleaning abilities to appear. Sleeping on the floor, or even in the dirt, didn't bother me. Suffocating on dust while I slumbered was a concern.

I'd become comfortable enough to nod off when Crum announced the cabin was ready.

By ready, he meant the dust sat in a large pile in the middle of the room.

I touched the pile and pushed enough energy into it to bind it together. "Now you can take it outside. Where can I lie down?"

He pointed to the far-right corner of the room. "Two bedrolls ready for you."

Muttering my thanks, I lay down and didn't realize I was asleep until a pungent odor shocked me awake. Looking around, I noticed the fire was lit.

"Time for your tea," Mam said.

"Milk?" I grunted.

"We didn't bring any," she said. "I have a new shirt for you, though, and we brought some pork sandwiches and cheese. Drink your tea first."

"Where's Crum?"

"Outside, getting firewood."

I pushed myself up. The tea tasted just as bad as the first two cups.

This time, she laughed at the look on my face. "Would you sit at the table with me?"

My body ached, but if I'd walked from the inn to here, I could walk from the corner to the table.

She walked next to me and pulled out a chair.

"My shirt?" I asked.

She hurried to the pile of saddlebags near the door, pulled a shirt out, and brought it to me. The bright-green cloth showed a Varian influence, even if the cut didn't. Their taste for loose-fitting, airy clothes never felt right to me. "Thank you. I'd prefer heavier, more tailored clothes, but you made a good choice." My chest argued with the decision to put the shirt on, but I felt more civilized wearing it.

"Eat now. When Crum gets back, I need to talk to both of you."

I looked at her and blinked a couple of times. "What's wrong?"

She shook her head and handed me a sandwich before taking a bite of hers.

I didn't realize how hungry I was and ate so fast I had to check my fingers for bite marks.

She giggled and offered me a large chunk of cheese.

"He lives," Crum quipped, carrying a load of firewood when he waltzed back in.

"Seems I do," I said, between tangy bites.

"He's had tea and we've eaten," she said. "Sit."

He dropped the firewood next to the fireplace and came to the table. "Yes, dear little Mam."

She handed him a sandwich. "I noticed something today. Older people were looking at me. Some of them pointed and whispered among themselves. It made me uncomfortable, like they knew something about me...something I should know."

"Mam, many things make you stand out," I told her.

"I look the same as I've always looked," she said.

"Not exactly what I meant," I said. "Have you noticed all the women wear their hair long or braided?"

"The herbalist didn't," she replied.

Crum chuckled. "She may be a special case."

I choked back my own laugh to save my chest. "Most Varian women take pride in their hair. They never cut it and wouldn't hide it under a hat. You look Varian, but wear a hat. That could be the cause of your unwelcome attention."

"Also, you're starting to fill out, but you're still thin enough to look unhealthy," Crum added. "You tend to walk looking down. You need to carry yourself with more confidence. People may think you're a mistreated servant or escaped slave."

She tilted her head, furrowing her brow. "I'm not sure I understand."

"The easiest thing to change is walking with your eyes up, not looking at the ground. Change your posture, square your shoulders. You'll look comfortable and confident," Crum said.

"That doesn't help," she argued.

"Watch." He stood and took on an exaggerated, submissive posture; head down, chin almost touching his chest. He rolled his shoulders so far forward he resembled a hunchback. He shuffled along, often scuffing his shoes on the floor. After about ten steps he stopped. "Keep that in mind and look at the difference this makes."

Straightening his back, he puffed out his chest and held his head so high he almost had to look down his nose to see where he was going. His walk took on a slight bounce with long, confident strides. He was so intent on watching Mam's reaction, he almost walked into the wall.

She giggled.

"If you were out on the town with a man one evening, which would you want with you?" he asked.

I raised an eyebrow at the question.

She sat silent for some time, tilting her head from side to side. "Neither."

A look of shock raced across his face. The only thing keeping me from laughing was the threat of pain.

"What? Why?" he blurted out.

"The first man moved so slow he'd starve to death before he got anywhere to eat. And the second man looked like he only respected himself. He thought everyone else was beneath him, not worthy of his attention. He was so focused on whether others were looking at him, he didn't pay attention to where he's going. How can he keep anyone safe if he doesn't watch where he's going?" she said.

"Good points. How about this?"

My friend took on his normal posture, casual and confident with a hint of wariness. He took his typical smooth steps, occasionally glancing to each side. He stopped right in front of her. "Well?"

"Him," she exclaimed.

"Why?" I asked.

"He looks comfortable, relaxed. He looks safe."

Crum smiled wide. "And that's how you need to look, dear little Mam. Creatures that look and act like prey are often preyed upon. I hate to say it, but more often than not, you look like prey. I think that's why people noticed you while we were out today."

"I'll try to keep it in mind."

"Crum," I said. "I noticed the saddlebags, where are the horses?"

"Hendri agreed to keep them. He'll cover for us if anyone asks about them."

"You trust him?" I asked.

He shrugged. "Didn't have much choice."

I frowned. *He's right, but it seems risky.* "So, what's the plan?"

"We hide here until you're well enough to ride or we're forced to move again."

I nodded.

He turned to Mam and smiled. "Interested in working with your talent?"

She looked at me. "Is it safe?"

"I'm sure he won't have you to do anything dangerous," I said. "It's past time to try. Might boost your confidence or trigger a memory."

A faint smile appeared on her face. "Yes, I'd like to."

Crum hurried to the saddlebags and returned with some straw, a couple of green vines, and some dry sticks. He placed the straw on the table in front of her. "Do you mind if I touch your arm while you weave this?"

"Why?"

"To feel the energy moving as you work."

"Can you do that?" she asked.

"A woodsyth should be able to feel another woodsyth's energy," he said.

"Go ahead," she said, and started weaving several strands of straw.

After placing his hand on her shoulder, he immediately furrowed his brow. He moved his hand down her arm, touching different spots for a few heartbeats before moving. His stress was more evident when he got to her wrist. I finally saw a hint of relief as his fingers brushed hers.

"Interesting," he commented. "Do you always concentrate the energy in your fingers?"

She stopped. "I don't understand what you're asking."

"You don't notice your fingers growing warm when you weave?" he asked.

She shook her head.

"Interesting," he said again. "Would it bother you if I touched the straw while you work?"

"No. Should I weave some more?"

He nodded and touched the straw, well away from where she worked. The furrowed brow returned. Sliding his fingers as close as he could without interfering, he said, "You have amazing control."

She stopped again. "What do you mean?"

"You're using only enough energy to bind the fibers and keep it contained in the spot you're working. I can't feel any extra energy pushed into the rest of the straw. I've never seen another woodsyth do anything like it," he explained.

"I still don't understand."

"It'll be easier to show you. Put your hand near my shoulder." He took a handful of straw and twisted it into something like a small rope.

She yanked her hand away. "I felt a tingle and your arm's hot."

"The tingle is the energy flowing through my arms. I don't work well with more flexible fibers, so I use extra energy, making my arms hot. You concentrate energy in your fingers and they barely warmed. Touch the straw."

She brushed a finger against it. "It's warm."

He nodded. "Once I push energy into it, I don't bother to contain it."

"What's this mean?" I asked.

"Don't know yet. I want to test a few other things. Mam, ready to try something else?"

"If it will help," she said.

He handed her the vines. "Do something with those, but don't weave them like the straw."

She held one of the thin vines by the end and let the others drop to the table. It hung in front of her face for a while before she wiggled it back and forth. The pliable vine moved in a serpentine manner. She wrapped it around her finger and unrolled it before studying it from several angles.

Finally, she pinched the vine and drew it through her other thumb and forefinger. It flattened, like a ribbon, and she tied it in a neat bow.

"Do it again while I touch your hand."

She grabbed another vine.

He touched the back of the hand holding the vine and moved his fingers as she worked, stopping at her wrist before she finished flattening it.

"You used more energy. I felt it until I got to your wrist. Can you tie it while I touch you?"

"I'll try," she said.

He couldn't keep good contact with her as she worked, but I heard him whisper, "only her fingers again."

"Would you like me to do another one?"

"No," he said. "Do something with the sticks. Pull one apart without snapping it. When you try, I want to touch both of your arms."

Taking a stick, she waited for him to get his hands in position.

He put one hand on her right wrist and the other near her left elbow.

She held it sideways in front of her eyes.

His hands moved along her arms, settling near the middle of each forearm as the stick split.

I noticed a faint puff of smoke.

"What was that?" she exclaimed.

"Crum, have you ever seen that before?" I asked.

"Not that I remember," he replied.

"Is it normal?" she asked.

"Well...I'm no expert, but I *am* a pretty good woodsyth. I'm not sure anything I've seen you do is normal."

"What do you mean?" I asked, gruffly.

He shot me a look. "Calm yourself, it wasn't an insult. I think she has an easier time with grasses and vines. She put more energy into breaking the stick, but I didn't expect smoke. The puff means she should've set the tree on fire when she pulled the club and knocked you out."

"Oh," I said, rubbing my chin. "Can a woodsyth start a fire that way?"

He shrugged. "Never thought about it until now."

"I didn't pull the branch like that," she said.

"What do you mean? You didn't break the limb from the tree?" he asked.

She shook her head. "I found where the branch attached to the tree and told it to let go, like when I gathered branches for the fire at the stables."

"That *is* what she told me before," I said, nodding.

"Hmm...let me try something." He took a piece of the broken stick from her and held it against an unbroken one.

I watched the fibers creep together.

He handed it to her. "Take it apart like you took the branches off trees."

She held the new 'branch' in one hand and the unbroken stick in the other. She pursed her lips and stared at the joint, but after a few moments said, "I can't."

"Why not?" he asked.

"You forced them together. The spot won't respond to me."

"Interesting. Can you put the other piece onto the unbroken stick?" he asked.

"I'll try." She looked the whole stick over and pressed the piece against her chosen spot. She closed her eyes for a moment. "They won't go together."

"Why not?" he asked.

"The pieces don't belong together."

"You have to force them together," he said.

"I can't."

"I did it; you should be able to."

"It would make the stick feel not right. I can't force it together. It has to feel right."

He grunted and rubbed his chin. "Could you put the two pieces back together, since they belong together?"

"Yes."

"You are sure?" I asked.

"They'll want to be together." She held the 'branch' near the joint Crum made and touched the ends of the split stick together. Faster than I could blink, the fibers worked themselves together. Once joined, bark formed at the joint. "See," she said, smiling.

"May I?" he asked.

Mam handed him the stick.

Closing his eyes, he slid his fingers along the rejoined stick. After a moment, he opened them and shook his head. "I can't even find where they rejoined. The grain of the wood flows smooth, like nothing happened. The fibers show no interruption at all. This is amazing work. Who taught you how to do this?"

She shrugged.

He took her hand. "We'll figure this out."

She smiled and yawned.

"You've done a lot of sything and you're out of practice," I said. "Go rest."

She stood and looked unsteady, so Crum moved next to her. "Where do you want to sleep?"

She pointed to the corner near my bedrolls.

He chuckled. "I should've known."

Helping her to the corner, he waited until she went to sleep before returning to the table.

I studied his face. "What's on your mind?"

He let out a long breath. "A lot. Her, the fight, your injuries...everything. We're behind schedule. When do you think you'll be comfortable riding?"

"In a day or two, at a walking pace. Any faster and I'd say I am down at least a week, likely longer. Speaking of injuries, how does the wound on my head look?"

"Can't tell. It's still covered by the muck the herbalist put on it."

I frowned. "Where are we going?"

"My contact's waiting at a tavern. I meant for us to ride straight through, but you got hurt."

"How long will they wait?" I asked.

"I don't know. I've sent word, so they know we're delayed," he said. "You do understand getting everything together to overthrow Eirickson will take time, right?"

"Only if we do it your way," I replied, smiling. "I'll kill him myself, no matter what."

He shook his head. "I have no doubt you'll die trying. You can't do this alone. We may not be able to do this at all. The longer we take, the longer Eirickson has to get organized. If we wait long enough, the Satran army will make a real push into Varia and take away all our options. He wins."

I glared at him. The thought of Eirickson winning made me stick to my stomach. Even worse, I knew what he said was true. "Then we ride tomorrow. I'll heal later."

"Not trying to push you," he assured me. "Just making sure you understand the situation."

"I do understand," I said, rubbing my brand, "all too well. How long will we ride?"

"At a walk? Two days, if all goes well."
I nodded. "Bring enough supplies for four days. I'm going to sleep."
He fed the fire as I made my way to bed.
The door closed as I lay down.

Chapter 20

"Fitz... Fitz..."

I groaned and rubbed my eyes. "Yes, Mam, what's wrong?"

"Wrong? Nothing. Crum told me to wake you and make sure you ate something and drank milk, before you had the tea. He's busy with the horses."

She wore a loose, bright, red-and-yellow dress. On her thin frame, the Varian clothing made her look like a young girl after a successful raid on her mother's wardrobe.

For the first time since leaving the inn, my head wasn't throbbing, but the pain in my chest remained as I pushed myself to my feet. "What did he bring to eat?"

"Those wonderful rolls with meat in them. Two for you."

As I walked to the table, she put a kettle on the coals.

I managed to finish my meal, and the cup of milk, before she poured my tea. "Last cup."

"Good thing," I said. "Not sure I could take any more of this nasty concoction."

"Does it taste as bad as it smells?"

"Worse."

She shivered and scrunched her face. "I'm sorry you've had to drink it."

"That makes two of us."

Crum walked into the cabin. "What are you two making?"

"Nothing," she answered, looking confused.

"I'd like to make sure I don't have to drink any more of this wretched tea," I said, with a chuckle. It hurt to laugh.

"We'll try to avoid such dire consequences in the future," he said, smiling as he grabbed the last saddlebag.

"Are we ready to leave?" I asked.

"Almost. Rest a little longer," he said.

"Do you need any help?" she asked.

He shook his head. "After I've secured the bags, I'll make sure we aren't leaving anything we might need, then we'll go."

"I'll join you anyway. It's nice to be outside," she said.

I smiled as they walked out together. She was adapting well to life outside the tunnels, but had a long way to go as far as her memories coming back. *If I didn't trust Crum so much, I'd worry about her.*

The idea of a relationship developing between them brought Aesa to mind. *I hate not knowing if she is alive and safe. I have to hang on to hope.*

Those thoughts threatened to sour my mood before Mam bounced into the cabin and announced it was time to leave.

Crum followed her in. "You two mount up. I'll gather the bedrolls."

I wasn't sure her feet hit the ground after she turned and ran back out. He barely managed to avoid being knocked to the floor.

I took my time walking out the door.

Mam was settled on Aspeit when I got outside. "You take too long."

"Ribs don't heal overnight. I'm pushing myself as it is." I drew strength as soon as my feet touched the ground. I wasn't sure I could afford more than one attempt to get in the saddle. *Doesn't matter, I have to do it.* My preparation paid off and I mounted Andale with a single hop.

Crum exited the cabin as I got settled.

"Glad you didn't need any help," he said, securing my bedrolls.

"Trip isn't over yet," I grumbled.

Mam giggled. "Not over? It hasn't begun."

"And it won't if we don't get moving," Crum said, mounting Sinar.

With a click of his tongue, he nudged the horse into a walk. "Mam, follow me. Fitzeirick, take the rear."

"It'd be nice if we could stick to smooth ground," I yelled.

He didn't say anything and picked up the pace a little.

I shook my head and held my left arm tight against my chest, supporting my ribs.

Crum looked more wary than normal. Between my injuries and not knowing the best route to take through the hills I couldn't blame him.

Mam entertained herself humming her odd tunes.

All I had were my pains and thoughts I didn't want to deal with. The more I ignored them, the more self-doubt crept in. *Crum thinks I can lead an army against Eirickson. What if I can't? What if the group he's working with rejects me?* I followed a downward slope toward despair until he called out, "Good place to stop and eat."

We were in a flat, almost large enough to hold a small town, surrounded by hills.

"I'll eat in the saddle," I said.

"Good idea. I'll bring your food to you," he replied.

"Where are we going?" I asked, as he handed me a sandwich and waterskin.

Mam sat near us.

Crum took a big bite and chewed for a while. "Big tavern near the mountains. I expect it will be our base of operations for a while. You'll need to spend time establishing a reputation."

"Doing what?" I asked.

"Crowd control."

"Excuse me?"

"It'll give people around the area a chance to know you, prove yourself a little."

"And what will you and Mam do while I'm watching tavern goers?" I asked, frowning.

"Depends, Mam can you cook?"

"Not that I remember."

"You're too thin to be a server," he mused. "Maybe people would believe you're an escaped slave. Is that a story you'd be comfortable with?"

"What's a slave?"

He sighed. "Someone, often captured in battle, forced into being a laborer or servant. Their only hope for freedom is to escape, otherwise they die a captive."

"I was captive in the tunnels and escaped. Was I a slave?" she asked.

"We weren't slaves, we were prisoners," I said.

"But you can use the experience to make people think you were a slave," he said. "If anyone asks, tell them you felt trapped in a dark place with no way out. It was so bad you don't remember anything until you escaped."

"I think I can do that," she said, with a crooked smile.

"Good," he said. "We can make this work. Let's finish eating and get moving again. We'll have to find a place to sleep tonight. If we make good progress tomorrow, we'll be at the tavern before nightfall."

"Mam, remember what we told you about being confident?" I said.

"Yes," she said, smiling.

"Forget it. If you're going to act like an escaped slave, you need to keep your head down. No confidence at all. If you can even act a little more afraid or jumpy, that'll help. Whatever you do, avoid looking people in the eye. A slave would never look someone in the eye," I said.

"Right," Crum agreed. "Some masters aren't nice. Slaves have no confidence, don't want to stand out at all. Standing out draws attention and attention can lead to beatings or worse."

"I'll do my best," she said, but it sounded like she doubted herself.

"Remember how you felt in the tunnels?" I asked.

She shivered and hugged herself. "Don't think I'll ever forget."

"Remember those feelings when you are out among people. They'll make a good slave cover," Crum said.

She looked at me with somber eyes and nodded.

I felt sorry for her. If she got the same reaction from others, she'd pass as an escaped slave.

"A horse ride should cheer you up. We need to get moving," Crum said.

She bounced to Aspeit. She'd never convince anyone she was a slave on the run if they saw her near horses.

"I still have questions about your plan," I said.

Crum led at a brisk walking pace. "What do you want to know?"

"First, how long am I supposed to work in this place?"

"Don't know. Figure a couple of months, at least."

"Are you insane?" I asked.

"That your second question? Doesn't matter, the answer's no, I'm not insane."

"Not so sure I believe you," I muttered. "What makes you think I'm going to watch over drunken crowds at some tavern for any length of time?"

"You need time for your chest to heal. I need time to make solid contacts in Varia and show people you'll do what's necessary when the time is right. Also, your work will provide us a place to stay and might help some people in the process. The man I grew up with always wanted to help people. It's what made him an admired skald."

I thought about what he said. All valid reasons, but I wasn't sure about the last one. *Am I still that man?* Keeping my thoughts to myself, I simply said, "I see."

Mam started humming.

I decided to let her contentment set the tone for the ride.

A stiff wind blew from the north, carrying the distinct smell of rain.

"Not a good sign," Crum yelled. "We need to pick up the pace."

I pulled my left arm tighter to my chest and bellowed, "Go."

We pushed our mounts into a trot and Mam squealed. Grinding my teeth, I did my best to absorb the impacts. Daylight dimmed as large, angry, green-black clouds boiled higher into the sky. Crum looked from side to side. "This could get ugly soon. We need shelter."

Hills surrounded us, no shelter in sight. Lightning lit the roiling mass of clouds. A short time later thunder rolled along the ground.

He pointed. "Turn west, try to skirt the edge!"

Lightning flashed again. This time the thunder hit a little sooner.

"Take us to the tallest hill you see. Shelter on the south side while I still have time to keep us dry," I yelled.

He pushed Sinar into a gallop. Mam let loose a loud cry and took off after him. I groaned and dug my heels into Andale's side. He whinnied and sped up, but it was clear he wasn't bred for speed. It took everything he had to keep pace with the faster horses.

We stopped at the base of a good-sized hill. Crum dismounted and ran back to me. "Are you sure you can do this?" he yelled, over the wind.

After sliding to the ground, I looked him in the eye and spoke through clenched teeth. "I'm open to any other option you have."

He looked around one more time and shook his head.

"Hold the horses. Keep them calm," I said, before pressing my hand against the hill. About an arm span under the surface, I found a boulder, but it wasn't big enough to make a shelter by itself. I'd have to go farther into the hill to get us out of the storm. If the wind shifted, we'd get soaked. *The horses have to fend for themselves.*

I closed my eyes and started breathing deeply, broken ribs protesting in agony. My chest throbbed with every heartbeat. I moved the dirt to make a narrow opening, wide enough to squeeze through sideways.

Thunder roared twice; the second time shook the ground.

I took it as a challenge. Pushing my way into the opening, I set my hand on the stone. The pain from having my chest pressed against the dirt was an unwelcome surprise. Forcing energy through the rock, I found several small cracks. I took a deep breath, held it for three heartbeats, and released it with a roar. At the same time, I drew strength from around me and smashed it into the little faults. The ground shook as the boulder split.

"Starting to get wet out here," Crum yelled.

"Working as fast as I can," I bellowed.

It took longer than I wanted to get through the boulder and to the dirt behind it. Precious minutes were spent making the stone stronger. Now, I could move enough dirt to get us out of the weather.

My vision blurred from moving so much energy, but I wasn't finished. After several deep breaths, I screamed, pouring everything I had into moving the mass.

• • • ●•● ● • •

The room smelled earthy.

My bed was cool and uncomfortable, but my body ached. I feared it would hurt to move my eyelids.

"You're sure he's breathing?" I heard a man ask.

"I'm sure. I've checked every time you ask," a woman's voice answered.

"Can you tell if he hit his head?"

"It's too dark to see. I don't feel any blood. Some of the herbalist stuff on his head is gone."

I knew the voices, but wasn't awake enough to remember names.

"Should I poke him again?" he asked.

"Did it work last time?"

Something pressed into my injured chest.

"Ouch!" I cried out and grabbed an arm.

"He's awake. I think he's going to break my arm."

"Fitz, let him go," she said.

"Not my name," I growled.

"Fitzeirick, this isn't funny," he snapped.

I released him and recalled who I was traveling with. "Where are we? Why's it so dark?"

"You don't remember?" Mam asked, sounding concerned.

"He must have hit his head," Crum said. "You sythed this shelter in the hill to get us out of the storm."

"Storm?" A gust of wind howled outside our shelter.

"We were riding. A storm blew in. Any of this sound familiar?"

"Maybe," I answered. "When did this happen?"

"Sky's dark, can't tell where the sun is. We've been in here a while," he said.

"No sun, no moon, no stars, no time," she added.

That I remember. "Feels like I died," I groaned.

"We were outside, waiting for you to finish, when I heard you scream. By the time I got in here, you were on the floor," he said.

"Guess I found my limit. Food?"

"The bread's damp. Here," he said, pressing a roll into my hand.

"No fire?"

"No wood, no fire," she answered.

"No room either," he added.

"Looks like we eat and sleep," I said.

"We didn't want to sleep until we knew you would wake," he said.

"I hope the horses are all right," she said, voice quivering a little.

"I'm sure they'll be fine," I said, after swallowing my last bite. "Wake me when it's light out."

• • • • ● • ● • • •

I felt something tapping my leg. "It's still wet, but the sun's up," Crum said.

I yawned and started to stretch. The yawn turned into a groan. "You may have to drag me out of here. I hurt everywhere."

"Expected you'd be sore," he said, laughing. "You pushed yourself pretty hard."

"Seems to be the case. Where's Mam?"

"Trying to find our horses. Hers stuck around throughout the storm."

I rubbed my temples. "You let the girl who can't remember her real name go riding through these hills alone?"

"When you put it that way it sounds like a bad idea," he quipped.

"I thought you had feelings for her."

"Well...yes...you could say I've taken a liking to her."

"But you let her ride off?" I confirmed.

He shrugged. "I can't ride in her weird saddle and we need the horses. What else was I going to do?"

"Still don't like it," I grumbled.

"Stay here, rest. I'll climb the hill, see if I can spot anything."

"Best idea I've heard since you woke me," I said. "I'll be out once I feel like I can move."

He walked out laughing.

I took a deep breath and forced myself to stand. Every move hurt. Grinding my teeth against the pain, I walked, stiff-legged, out onto the rain-soaked ground. Thick clouds made it hard to tell how late it the day it was. "Do you see her?"

"No, but I think I know which way she went. There's a trail of fresh hoof prints heading northeast, toward a forest."

"Why didn't we head for the forest?"

"Didn't know it was there," he said.

"So, we walk to the forest?"

"I can't carry all the saddlebags that far and if Mam comes back a different way, we'll lose her," he said, as he came down.

"Then we stay and hope she returns?"

"Well, if she doesn't come back, we won't have horses," he said.

"What if she finds her way back without our horses?" I asked. "We still don't have horses and we walk."

"It's a long walk, but we can strap all the bags to Aspeit," he said. "Can you locate her through the ground?"

"Even with dry ground I couldn't sense all the way to the forest."

"Seems I'm not much of a leader," he muttered. "What do you think we should do?"

I shrugged. "I know one thing we shouldn't do."

"What?"

I glared at him. "Split up."

He looked at his feet. "I agree."

"We stay here for now. She survived in the tunnels before Sir found her, surviving out here shouldn't pose much of a problem. The question is can she find the horses and find her way back?"

"How long do we wait?" he asked.

"Until morning."

"And then?"

"Grab what supplies we can carry and start walking," I said.

He nodded. "I was afraid you'd say that."

"Don't suppose you packed anything to use for a fire."

"No. Didn't expect us to need one," he admitted.

"Even after I told you to pack for four day's travel."

"I thought you were joking."

I shook my head "I wish you'd have taken me seriously."

"I'm sorry." He frowned. "This is the farthest I've been from a town, tavern, or inn since we left for the capital. Haven't had to plan for the worst often enough I guess."

"You're nothing if not optimistic. Right now, that may be better than seeing me as a leader," I said.

"What do you mean? I'll always look to you as a leader. Can't think of anyone else I'd trust to make the kind of decisions you'll need to make."

"I don't think you understand," I said. "I'm not the same man you traveled with before. He died in the tunnels."

"We'll see," he said. "When the time's right, I'm sure the Fitzeirick I've always known will show himself."

"Maybe. But this Fitzeirick is going to get something to eat," I said, shuffling back into the hill.

Chapter 21

After taking my second bite, I heard a muffled yell. I swallowed and walked back outside. "What is it?"

"I see Mam," Crum said.

"What makes you so sure?"

"Who else would be galloping this way leading two horses?"

"Good point," I said, and went back to eating.

Soon, I heard hooves slapping the wet ground and Mam screaming, "I found them, Crum! I found the horses!"

The rhythm of the hoofbeats slowed before she appeared from behind a nearby hill. The horses looked exhausted, but it seemed they'd made it through the storm no worse for wear.

"Good to see you again, Mam," I said.

She gave me a wide smile. "I'm glad I found these two."

"You did fine, dear little Mam," Crum called out, rushing from his perch.

"Going by how they look, we're staying here another night," I commented.

"I'll look them over after they rest awhile. I'd prefer to camp in the woods," he said. "Fitzeirick, keep an eye on the horses while Mam and I eat."

I watched the animals munch on the wet grass. My knowledge of horse care amounted to making sure they eat, had no open wounds, and moved well. They'd galloped here, which meant they were sound. Other than a few minor scrapes, I saw no visible injuries. Our mounts seemed fine, but worn out. Crum was right, we'd make camp in the forest. I noted the bedrolls, while soaked through and through, were still secured.

"...and they were right together in the forest. It took me longer to find my way back than it did to find them, I think," Mam said, walking out of the shelter.

"We're glad you made it back safe. Finding Sinar and Andale is all the better for us," Crum replied.

When they came into view, he had all three saddlebags over his shoulders. I hadn't realized how strong he'd become.

"I'll need help getting on Andale."

"Let me get the bags settled and then I'll help you."

I pulled strength from the ground while waiting for him. The effort made me hurt even more, but I couldn't get in the saddle without using my talent, even with help. The only upside was I could no longer pick out the pain of my injured ribs from the rest of my aches.

Crum secured the bags to Andale and knelt on one knee next to me. "Use my leg as a step."

It took several attempts, and many moans and groans, but I finally settled on Andale. Crum mounted Sinar and we were off at a slow pace for the forest.

"No hurry, but I want to make the forest before nightfall," he said. "It isn't easy setting up camp in the dark."

The short trip went smoothly, and we arrived with plenty of sunlight.

"Fitzeirick, stay mounted until I get ties ready for the horses," Crum said, after we stopped. "Dear little Mam, I'm going to need your help. Ready to work with your talent again?"

"I can try. Do you think I can do it?"

"Of course, I do," he reassured her. "Pull three branches, about as big around as your wrist, and bring them to me."

She worked fast and returned with her bounty.

"Can you bend them?" he asked.

She tried to flex one, but, despite all her grunts, nothing happened.

He smiled. "Not with your arm strength, with your talent. Syth them into an arch."

"Oh!" she exclaimed, and focused on the branches. Soon all three bent into near-perfect arches. "Is this good?"

"Perfect."

She smiled at the praise.

"Can you attach those to trees at about waist level?"

She chewed her bottom lip for a moment before pressing one against a tree. Furrowing her brow, she took a deep breath and stared at the spot where the branch touched the trunk, but soon looked at the ground. "It doesn't belong here."

He patted her on the back. "You tried. I wasn't expecting you to do it. You need to practice forcing wood together. Or maybe you can't force things together. Everyone has limits. But thank you for trying. I'll take care of it."

He took the bent branches from her and quickly attached one. "Tie Aspeit's reins to the arch, she can move back and forth as she needs. I'll get the other two in place."

She nodded and went to get her horse.

He placed the other tie-outs and walked over to me. "Ready to get back on the ground?"

I'd have fallen if he hadn't steadied me as my boots hit the dirt.

After securing her horse, Mam turned toward us, smiling. "Anything else?"

"Gather some firewood while I lay out the bedrolls. They'll never dry if we don't get a fire going," Crum said.

She skipped away, humming one of her odd songs.

"It's good to see her happy," I commented, "but was it a good idea to send her after wood alone?"

Crum nodded while he made sure our horses couldn't get loose. "She's good at pulling branches. Worst she could do out here is fell a tree. Not much of a concern as long as she doesn't crush herself. Remember what happened last time we camped in the woods?"

"All too well. Is that why you tied the horses that way?"

"No, the trees are too far apart to make a quick corral. Also, I wanted her to practice. Never seen a woodsyth work the way she does."

"Any idea why her talent's so different?"

He shook his head. "Everyone syths different ways. It's either their personal limits or how they're taught. I have a feeling her uniqueness is a combination of training and forgetting. One thing I do know is we need to figure out whether we need a shelter."

"I don't have the strength to make one."

"I know. I'm guessing you haven't worked that hard in a long time."

"Not since getting out of those tunnels, but a lot that was simple brute force."

He looked around. "I don't feel any wind. I think we'll be fine."

I nodded.

He searched his saddlebags and pulled out his bow drill. "Well, this isn't good."

"What?"

"The string's soaked and the drill stick's too wet to do any good. I need a fire to dry them."

"So, no fire tonight?"

"Let me think," he mused, clearing a circle for the fire.

Mam returned carrying several branches. "Is this good?" she asked, dropping them. The poor girl looked winded.

"Never need an axe when you travel with a woodsyth," I said, chuckling.

She smiled at me.

"Those'd be perfect if they were dry *and* we had a way to start a fire," Crum muttered. "Can you push the sap out of them?"

"I don't know how."

He stared at her for a moment and then snapped his fingers. "Remember flattening the vine?"

"Yes."

"Pushing out sap is almost the same, except you don't flatten the wood. Watch." He grabbed a branch and took several breaths. Holding the small end in one hand, he ran his other hand along it, making slight squeezing motions. A large amount of sticky sap flowed freely. "Now, you try."

She chose a small branch, copied his movements, and produced a trickle. She frowned.

"Good try," he assured her. "Push more energy through the squeezing hand. Let me show you again." He took another branch and looked at it for a moment. "Do you remember where you got this?"

She gave him a questioning look. "Why?"

"Don't you know what this is?"

"It's a branch I pulled from a tree."

"This came from a maple tree. We're in for a treat," he answered, with a big grin.

"Oh!" I exclaimed, simple joy bringing a skip to my heart. "I haven't had maple water in a long time."

"maple water?" she asked.

"You don't know about maple water?" He gaped at her and then smiled. "Open your mouth and stick out your tongue."

She looked like a baby bird waiting for a meal.

Holding the end of the maple branch close to her mouth, he squeezed a few drops of runny sap onto her tongue.

"It's sweet," She squealed, and her eyes opened wide. "Can I have more?"

He nodded. "Open up."

"Is all sap sweet?" she asked, after swallowing.

"No, only a few trees make sweet sap. maple's the most common. After we get a fire going, I want to find the maples here."

The two woodsyths pushed sap out of all the branches that weren't maple. Crum made sure to set those aside, four in total. Mam looked worn out after they finished.

"Is this too much for you?" he asked.

"It's making me tired."

He grabbed a maple limb. "This will help."

She swallowed some of the sap.

"Wait a few minutes, you'll feel better."

He looked at me. "Can you empty a waterskin? I want to store the rest of this."

I walked to Andale and grabbed mine. After taking a long drink, I poured the rest on the ground and made my way back to Crum.

"Hold it steady," he said, and emptied the maple limbs into it. The skin felt about a third full of sweet sap.

"Now...how are we going to start a fire?" he wondered aloud, tapping a finger on his chin. A smile slowly spread across his face and he looked at Mam. "How are you feeling?"

"Still a little tired, why?"

"You and I may be able to start the fire together."

"How?" I asked. "You're both woodsyths, you don't start fires without tools. Most firesyths can't make fire from nothing."

"I know, but I have an idea," he said. "Mam, remember the tiny puff of smoke when you split the twig in the cabin?"

"Yes."

"Do you remember what you did, how you made it happen?" he asked.

"I told the stick to split, but it didn't have enough life to do it on its own."

"So, you pushed energy into it, correct?"

She nodded.

He grabbed the biggest branch she'd gathered and placed it in the middle of the cleared circle. "You push energy into this branch to break it, like the twig. I'm going to try to keep it from breaking. If we force enough energy into the same spot, I think it'll start burning. Can you do this with me?"

She looked at me and I nodded, encouraging her with a smile.

"I...I can...try."

"That's all I ask," he promised, grinning. "You do a better job of focusing your energy, I'm sloppy. I think it'll work best if you hold the branch near the ends. I'll sit on the opposite side and grab onto the wood near the center."

She moved into position, closed her eyes, and breathed deeply. Finally, she nodded, opened her eyes, and stared at the branch.

He wrapped his hands around it and clenched his jaw.

I heard strange, muted, crackling sounds.

Mam let out one of her feral screams. Crum responded with a grunt, like he'd taken a punch in the gut.

She slumped forward, limp.

Dropping the branch, he shoved her away as it burst into flame.

He was pale and shaking. "See to her," he muttered before laying back himself.

"Out, but breathing. I think she's lost color, but I can't tell for sure. She's sweating rivers down her forehead, but cold to the touch. Rest. I'll work the fire and keep an eye on her."

"Good," he moaned.

At least he's conscious.

My aches slowed the process of breaking sticks from the forced-dry branches to feed the fire. Fortunately, Crum sat up before I had to break the limbs themselves. He looked at the fire before turning his attention to Mam. "She's still out?"

"Yes, but the sweating has stopped. Are you up to breaking some of these branches? I don't think the fire is ready for a whole one."

"Let me have some maple water and then I'll take care of it. Go get another waterskin. She'll be thirsty when she wakes."

I tossed the waterskin to him and he took a long draw from it.

We both groaned as we stood and set to our tasks.

He grumbled while sything the branches into smaller pieces, but soon had a nice fire going.

Mam breathed deeper, but didn't move.

"I underestimated her strength," he said, staring at her. "At the same time, I think I pushed her too hard."

"That's an understatement."

He shook his head. "Her talent's stronger than mine. She can move a lot more energy than I can. I felt it. The scary part is she's using raw talent. With training and practice, I think she could start a fire all by herself."

"Maybe she has both fire and wood sything?"

"I've never heard of anyone who could work wood and fire. Wood and stone, sure. Those people make great builders. Fire and stone syths work ores into metals. But fire and wood are opposing talents. Fire destroys and wood creates, wood builds...wood exists."

"You have a better grasp on the subject. I only break rocks," I said, smiling.

"I went about the fire all wrong," he admitted. "I should've had both of us try to force the wood together. Removing all the sap didn't help either. The heat could've boiled it in the wood, making a sort of pitch which would've burned easier."

"Sounds like you've got this worked out."

"It's strange what runs through your head while trying to not pass out," he said, grinning.

I watched him wet his finger with maple water. "What are you doing?"

"Going to smear this on her lips and see if she reacts."

"Worth a try, I suppose," I said, shrugging.

I put a piece of wood on the fire as he touched Mam's lips.

"Ouch," he cried out, yanking his hand away from her face.

"What happened?"

"She bit me."

I was about to say something when she moaned, "More."

It hurt to laugh.

He placed the opening of the waterskin close to her mouth and let more sweet sap trickle out. She took on the baby bird pose again and swallowed twice before opening her eyes.

"What happened?" she asked, while moving to sit.

"Crum worked you too hard," I said.

"But we did manage to make a fire," he added.

"Did someone give me something to eat?"

I chuckled. "No, but you did bite his finger."

"I'm sorry. Why was your finger in my mouth?"

"To wake you by wetting your lips with maple water," he answered.

"I dreamed someone was giving me sweets," she said, frowning.

"You remember sweets?" I asked.

"Not exactly...except that they're something to eat."

"So long as you remember my fingers aren't something to eat," Crum joked, grinning.

"Don't put them in my mouth when I'm not awake."

He nodded. "Fair enough."

After staring at the fire for a while, he asked me to get some food.

"Why me?"

"Because you're the least exhausted of the three of us and a good skald always thinks of his people," he said, smiling.

I glared at him. "But I'm no longer a skald, good or otherwise."

"But you're still a good person and an even better friend."

Not so sure about that, but I'm trying. "I suppose we should eat," I grumbled, carefully getting to my feet.

"It sure will be nice when we get to our destination. A hot meal and a bath would make a big difference right now," he said, before biting into his roll.

"Sounds nice, but I want to find someone to take these threads out of my scalp. They're starting to itch."

Mam took a drink of water before asking, "Where are we going?"

"We're heading to the Stone Roof, the largest tavern in the area," he said.

"In Swinter?" she asked.

Crum and I looked at each other.

"How'd you know?" he asked.

"I'm not sure. I remember the name. I think I've been there before, maybe to visit someone. Wonder if I've seen the tavern."

"Crum, what do you know about Swinter?" I asked.

"It serves as a getaway for the wealthy and powerful of Varia. It's not your typical Varian city since it grew around a tavern instead of a market square or farms. Stone Roof is the only tavern in the town."

"Not that I don't trust you, but how will we raise an army there?" I asked.

"We won't. We're going to make contacts with people who will introduce us to those who can help raise an army in Varia. But aren't you curious why dear little Mam remembers Swinter?"

I nodded and looked to her. "What do you remember about Swinter?"

She furrowed her brow before turning to stare at the fire. After a few moments, she closed her eyes and shook her head. "I remember the name. I think I remember visiting, staying a while, maybe with someone...a family member. I'm not sure."

"Crum, by chance does any Varian royalty visit or live in Swinter?" I asked.

"Live there? I don't know. Visit? That's what it's known for."

I clapped my hands together and nodded. "Vekel's right. She has to be Varian royalty. It's the only thing that makes any sense."

"How do you explain a young Varian royal getting dropped into a Croian prison no one knows exists?" he asked.

I shook my head. "Why else would she remember those special horses and this town? Do commoners live in Swinter?"

"Tavern workers and servants, I would think," he said.

"Mam, do you remember anything else?" I asked. "The family...was it yours?"

She sighed heavily. "I don't remember."

Crum put his arm around her. "No need to get upset, we're just trying to figure things out."

She nodded and nuzzled her face into his shirt.

His eyes opened wide and he looked at me for an answer, but I shrugged and shook my head. The helpless look on his face remained while rubbing her back. I felt sorry for him. He had no idea how to deal with an emotional woman.

It seemed like an eternity passed before she moved away from him. She sniffed a couple of times. "Where am I going to sleep?"

"Pick a tree near the fire. We'll keep you safe."

She mumbled her thanks between sniffles and moved to the closest tree.

I made sure she saw me move close before she closed her eyes. Once she started breathing slow and steady, I motioned for Crum to sit near me.

"You have a lot to learn about women," I said.

"Happy, pleased, even angry I can handle. I don't know what she was just now, but I'm not sure I liked it."

"You did fine for the most part, but some words of encouragement would've helped."

"Maybe I don't want to learn."

"If you want a relationship you'll have to learn to deal with upset and worse." I patted him on the shoulder. "Relationships aren't only about the good times and being happy. Anyone can stay around when people are happy. Staying with them when they're unhappy, supporting them through the bad times...that makes a relationship."

He looked at me for a while with an expression I couldn't read. "You talk like we're putting down roots tomorrow. She looks to you for comfort and security, not me. Are you sure she isn't taking Aesa's place at your side?"

A chill gripped my heart when Crum said her name. "I'm not looking for a new partner. If I haven't found Aesa by the time Eirickson draws his last breath, she becomes my top priority. I'll tear apart the entire Satran nation to find her. Besides, you're the one who has a cute nickname for Mam."

He looked surprised. "What do you mean?"

"Dear little Mam," I teased. "Did you think I hadn't noticed?"

He grinned. "I do call her that when it feels right."

"It feels right to you, but have you asked her how she feels?"

He crossed his arms and glared at me. "How about when she calls you Fitz? How does *that* feel?"

I chuckled and shook my head. "You have to admit my name is a bit of a mouthful."

"True, but no one else calls you Fitz. Aesa never called you Fitz. I'm one your closest friends and I've never even considered it. Mam calls you Fitz, and you accept it as normal?"

I grinned. "Mam and normal often don't belong in the same sentence."

"She *is* one of the more unique individuals I've ever come across," he said, laughing. "Maybe that's why I find her attractive...she isn't the typical girl. You've given me a lot to think about. I need to sleep on it."

I nodded. "Find a spot where you can get comfortable. I'll tend the fire a little longer. Sleep well, my friend."

He yawned and moved a little closer to Mam.

I stared at the fire, as if I might find answers to my problems there. The flames danced and sparks flew when some burning branches shifted, but the fire brought no enlightenment. Chuckling at the idea fire was going to tell me anything, I decided I was too tired to ponder much of anything and piled enough wood on the fire to keep it burning until morning.

Chapter 22

I woke alone. Looking for a sign of my companions, I noticed someone had tended the fire recently and the horses were still secured. They had walked wherever they went.

Relieved, I changed my focus to breakfast and rummaged through his saddlebags. Hard biscuits and strips of dried meat were all we had left. *If we don't make it to Stone Roof today, we have to find supplies somewhere.* I choked down the dry meal and looked for a waterskin. All four were gone.

I pushed my talent into the ground to locate either of them, tree roots made it difficult for me to pick out much of anything. Thirst made me consider searching for my friends when I heard Crum talking.

"...good idea you had. I wish I'd have thought of it."

"It wasn't so different from what you wanted to do," she replied.

"But it never occurred to me to try it that way. Guess I should expect surprises from you."

"*You* do things the way *you* learned. I don't have that luxury. It's the first time I'd ever tried anything like that. I like how it worked out."

"What are you two talking about?" I yelled.

"How Mam harvested four skins worth of maple water," he replied.

"It's not hard, is it?" I asked.

"Hold on, I'll explain when we get to you," he said.

Mam walked into camp wearing a smile so big I thought her face was glowing.

"What's so special?" I asked.

"When I harvest maple sap, I find a stick about the size of my thumb, hollow it out, and force it into the tree," he said.

"I've done the same with a stone."

"Right. She opened the bark, formed it so the sap poured right into the skins, and pushed it back into place when we finished. Made perfect sense once I saw her do it."

"And it didn't hurt the tree," she added.

"I'm glad you could learn something, Crum," I said. "Now, I need to wet my throat after eating biscuits and dried meat."

"Oh, yeah." He tossed a bulging waterskin to me.

It took two mouthfuls of the watery, sweet sap to make me feel like I hadn't swallowed a handful of sand.

"How far to Swinter?" I asked.

"If we get moving, we should arrive before dinner," he said. "We've eaten. I'll put away the bedrolls and then we're ready to go."

I moved so fast getting in the saddle, I beat Mam as she got onto Aspeit. The thought of a warm meal helped me ignore my tender ribs as I settled onto Andale.

"Seems you're feeling better," Crum commented.

"Not sure I about better," I said, "but the chance for a bath and a hot meal helps get me moving."

We rode out of the forest into a large, grassy plain with an unobstructed view of mountains in the distance. Crum stopped and motioned us to come beside him. He pointed toward one of the taller peaks. "Swinter's near the bottom of that mountain. We should be able to ride straight to it."

"The sooner the better," I said.

"Why the hurry?" Mam asked.

"I want to get these threads out of my scalp, a hot bath, and a hot meal."

"I'll try to put off any serious meetings until afterward," he said.

• • • • ● • ● • • •

A guard wearing shiny, leather armor stepped out of a small building near the path. He eyed us for a moment. "You don't look like you belong here."

Crum nodded. "We've ridden from Croy. We have business at Stone Roof."

"Hmm." He rubbed his chin and fixed his gaze on Mam.

She looked away.

He frowned, looking hard at me. "For all I know, you're Croian bandits...or worse."

"I assure you, my good and observant man, we're not bandits. We helped this young woman escape Satran slavers," Crum said.

"You expect me to believe such a tale?" he asked.

"If the story were not true, anyone would see right through it. I could not hope to deceive a perceptive individual, like you, with a preposterous tale. Would you agree, Fitz?"

Good idea using my nickname. I looked sideways at him and nodded.

"I think I should hear from her lips how she came to be a captive of Satra."

With perfect timing, Mam started crying.

"Kind sir," Crum said. "Hers is a terrible burden. The horror those savages inflicted still weighs on her. Even though we've befriended her during the long journey of escape, she will not tell us. I'm no expert in these matters, but it could be she may never speak of it."

"True," I chimed in. "Some believe speaking of horrific events invites them to happen again. I think she avoids telling her tale to stave off such a possibility."

"Maybe," the guard replied. "It doesn't explain why she rides on such an odd saddle."

Crum smiled and nodded. "As you said yourself, it is odd. A stable-keep felt sympathy for her plight, but would only part with his oldest, most unkempt saddles. We had no funds for higher quality tack. He did take pity on us and allowed us to clean it before putting it on a horse."

Crum is doing himself proud.

The guard continued scratching at his chin and fell into a blank stare before focusing his gaze on me. "If you're telling the truth, why are you branded a traitor and have stitches in your head?"

I ran a finger along the scar on my face. "The mark is the result of an unfortunate misunderstanding. As for the threads, four Satran soldiers found us hiding in the woods. I fought through broken ribs and blows to the head defending this Varian maiden. Without the attention of a skilled, and somewhat charitable, herbalist, I could have died. She took pity on our situation when she heard what we were doing. As it was, we almost couldn't afford her fee."

"I've heard of rumors of Satran incursions from the south. The stitching looks like the work of a well-trained herbalist. In that case, thank you for rescuing one of my fellow citizens. Stay on this road. You can't miss the tavern."

Crum bowed low in his saddle and I dipped my head.

"Thank you, sir," Crum said.

He returned the bow and motioned for us to continue on our way.

As we rode into town, I looked around and noticed the homes. Some were modest, wooden construction while others were large with artistic stonework. Often one style butted against the other. The people moving about wore varied styles of clothing, a reflection of the buildings.

Finally, we reached our destination, a huge stone building. It took the space of at least four typical houses, looked tall enough to have at least three floors, and was a hive of activity.

Crum jerked his head to the side and led us toward the back of the building. We dismounted and secured our horses to nearby posts before walking to the back door. He pounded on it and stepped back.

Shortly it swung open and an older-looking man stuck his head out. "Can I help you?"

Crum cleared his throat. "Yes, sir, you may. Please let Jahon know his appointment has finally arrived. We brought a gift to show our appreciation for his patience."

The man nodded and closed the door.

"A gift?" I asked.

"Get the skins."

I hurried to the horses and grabbed the bulging waterskins. The door opened as I made it back.

"Come with me please," someone said.

Crum stepped in, Mam followed, and I brought up the rear.

A young man led us through the large kitchen to a staircase. He never broke stride as he climbed the stairs only stopping at the top to knock on a door.

It opened without a sound and we stepped into a cramped vestibule.

"Wait here."

I could only see a small part of the next room. His footsteps made a faint echo. I pushed my talent into the floor to get a feel for what we were walking into. I wasn't expecting to find it was more wood than stone. It felt like the room was large and almost empty. I suspected the wooden core hid some details from me.

"Yes, yes...bring them to me," a voice bellowed.

I looked at Crum.

He shook his head and pinched his lips between his forefinger and thumb.

I nodded as the young man appeared in the opening.

"Follow me."

My suspicion proved correct; the room was large, but not empty. An arrangement of tables and chairs sat around a much larger table in the center. Clean white cloth covered each table. *A dining hall, it would seem.*

Our guide stopped near an open door and motioned for us to go inside.

A man, built like a bear, stood behind a large, ornate, wooden desk. "Crum, it's good to finally meet you," his deep voice boomed.

Mam moved behind me.

"I feared you wouldn't make it before I had to leave town. Please, introduce your friends. And I understand you brought me something."

Crum stepped toward the huge man and held out his hand. "Jahon, I'm glad we made it. This is all...impressive. I mean, I'd heard of Stone Roof, but to see it for myself? It is magnificent."

Jahon took Crum's hand. Really, his hand enveloped Crum's. "Thank you for the compliments. Now, your friends?"

Crum stepped back and inclined his head toward me. "This is Fitzeirick...half-brother to Eirickson and, until recently, skald of the far eastern skati of Croy. Fitzeirick, Jahon, owner of Stone Roof and master of all that entails."

I placed the skins on the floor, stepped forward, and held out my hand. He had a firm grip, but not to the point of being uncomfortable. His hand felt rough, like a working man's.

"Fitzeirick, I hope it will be my pleasure to make your acquaintance. I understand the territory you ran now belongs to the accursed Satra. If you are the man I'm told you are, I believe we can help each other."

"I must admit, you have me at a disadvantage, sir," I responded. "While I despise Satra, I know nothing about you or your goals. I hope you don't take it as a slight if I withhold my enthusiasm until I get to know you better."

He squeezed my hand a little tighter and let loose an unbelievably loud, belly laugh. "A wise man indeed," he said, letting me go. "And who is hiding behind you?"

Crum put his arm around her protectively and moved her into his view. "It is my pleasure to introduce you to Mam. Until recently, she was a captive of Croy." He nudged her toward Jahon and whispered, "Take off your hat."

She stepped forward, removed the riding hat, and bowed.

"No need for such formality, little one, we are all friends here...or should be," Jahon said. "Please, look at me."

She stood straight and lifted her eyes.

"You look like..." He shook his head, disbelief coloring his features. "Who are you? Why are you traveling with these men?"

"Fitz named me Mam when we met. They've both defended my life and cared for me. Who else would I travel with?"

He looked from me to Crum. "She was never mentioned before. Why?"

Crum looked at me.

I cleared my throat. "I suspect you don't know everything about me either. Is that going to be a problem?"

"I mean no disrespect," Jahon replied.

"Before things get too serious," Crum said, "Fitzeirick, please give Jahon our gift."

I placed the skins on the desk.

Jahon eyed them, lifted one, and rolled it from one hand to the other. "And what is this?"

Crum smiled. "maple water, harvested fresh this morning."

His eyes opened wide and he smiled before taking a long draw from a skin. "Wonderful!" he exclaimed. "Thank you for the gift." He set the skin on the desk and bellowed, "Boy!"

The young man who led us to his office appeared in the door. "Yes, sir?"

"Take these skins to the brew master. Tell him I expect mapled ale with dinner."

He ran across the room, hefted the heavy skins off the desk, and exited...slower than he came in.

"Would it be possible to discuss concerns and situations over dinner?" Crum asked.

"Excellent idea," Jahon agreed.

"Do you happen to have any place we could bathe before we eat?" I asked. "And I would love to get these threads removed from my scalp."

"I can accommodate your needs and will be glad to send for someone to see to your stitches. Do you need fresh clothes?"

"As you see fit," Crum said.

"Please, sit. Get comfortable while you wait," Jahon said, stepping out from behind the desk. He was an imposing individual.

The plush chairs were a welcome luxury compared to being on horseback.

Crum spoke first when we were alone. "He seems overly concerned about Mam for some reason."

"What do you know about him?" I asked.

"The people I've been working with trust him. I know he's respected, has a reputation for taking care of business. His contacts should be good for us."

"Anyone his size is respected or at least feared," I noted.

"He *is* big," Mam added.

"What kind of contacts?" I pressed.

"People with money, power, and other useful resources. People who understand someone must remove Eirickson and deal with Satra," Crum replied, his voice serious.

"What if his concern with Mam gets in the way?"

"I'll get her away from here and leave you to negotiate with him," he said, turning to Mam. "Would that be a problem?"

She looked from me to Crum several times. "Where would you take me?"

"I'll find someplace safe."

"When would Fitz join us?"

"It could take some time," I said.

"I'd have to think about it. Do I have to answer now?"

"No," I said, "but don't take too long thinking about it. You could have to leave on short notice."

She nodded and started humming.

"Well, it's nice to have nothing settled at all," Crum drawled.

I held up my hand at the echo of footsteps approaching.

Jahon returned, followed by two women. One carried a small pouch.

"Elvra, show Mam to her bath in the basement. Ulka, I need you to remove the stitches from Fitzeirick's head before escorting him and Crum to bathe."

"Basement?" Mam asked.

Jahon gave her a strange look.

"It's a room underground," Crum said.

She cringed and shook her head. "Underground? No. I won't go underground without Fitz. He's the only one who could get me out."

Jahon looked at me.

"Long story. She can come with me after Ulka takes the thread out," I said.

"At some point, I want an explanation," Jahon said, his tone leaving no room for argument. "Elvra, please show Crum to his bath."

I nodded. "I'll be glad to explain...later."

Mam watched Crum leave the room.

"Are you ready for me to remove those stitches?" Ulka asked.

"More than."

"Hold still," she said, reaching into the pouch.

I felt the cold sting of metal touch my scalp. In one quick motion, she sliced through the silk thread.

"You'll feel a little tugging. It may tickle. Feel free to giggle," she said.

When the thread slid out of my skin, it felt more like an itch I couldn't scratch than a tickle. *At least I don't have a needle scraping against my skull again.* I fought the urge to twitch, as the itching sensation grew stronger.

"Done," she said, stepping back. "The area may be a little tender for a day or so. Try not to scratch it. It left a pretty scar. Some women think a few scars make a man more attractive." She winked at me before turning and walking out of the room.

I walked over to Mam. "Are you ready for a bath?"

She looked at me and smiled. "Like at The Trader's Cup?"

I smiled back at her. "Yes, except here it's in the basement."

"Only if you go with me."

"If Jahon will lead the way, I'll be happy to," I said holding out my hand for her.

She took it and then looked at Jahon. "You can take us to the basement now."

He bristled. "Little one, you do know who's in charge here, correct?"

She nodded. "You own the building."

"She can be a little direct," I interjected. "It's her way. Doesn't mean anything by it."

"If I didn't know for a fact the princess isn't in Swinter right now, I'd think she's Stina trying to trick me. She looks exactly like her."

"Princess Stina?" I asked.

"Last living daughter of King Ander and Queen Ines."

Mam sucked in a quick breath.

"What about their other children?" I asked.

"Only one other. A daughter they lost escaping the battle with Croy."

"Lost? As in she died?" I asked.

He shook his head. "No one knows what happened to her. She vanished."

"What was her name?" I asked.

"Jesca," he replied.

"Jesca?" Mam gasped and gripped my hand tightly. "That...it's...my...my name. My name's Jesca."

Chapter 23

"What!" Jahon shouted. "How dare you disrespect —"

Maybe she misunderstood him. I sucked in a quick breath and held up my hand, interrupting him. "Mam, are you sure? Are you certain you're Jesca?"

Tears streamed down her cheeks. "I knew my name wasn't Mam. I couldn't remember my name on my own. When he said that name, it rang true. I have no doubt, I'm Jesca."

His face reddened as he moved toward her.

I stepped between them. "Jahon, trust me, she does *not* lie. I'm not sure she knows how to lie. She's gone through something you'll never understand. It damaged her. She doesn't remember much of her past, but when she does, the memories are always true. If she says she's Jesca, I believe her and won't let anyone harm her."

He looked at me. "What makes you so certain?"

"Because I experienced a few months of what she'd been through much longer."

"Where did you find her?"

As I talked about the tunnels, she turned away and hummed one of her songs.

He interrupted me. "Little one, where'd you learn that?"

She looked at him, eyes red from crying. "I've known it my whole life. Someone used to sing me songs. I don't remember the words."

"Do you remember who sang them?" he asked.

"A woman, I think. She had white hair."

I saw him relax. "I take it the song is important?"

"It's an old lullaby, used by nannies taking care of royal children."

"Please don't take this as an insult, but how would you know?" I asked.

"Suffice it to say my grandmothers were court nannies." He pointed at her. "She may be Jesca. We need to get her clean. What happened to her hair?"

"Fitz cut it," she said.

"What?" he roared.

"I asked him to. It was uncomfortable. He did it to spare me more misery."

"It was necessary. Her hair was bound together with filth after living so long in the tunnels. It wouldn't come clean," I explained.

He sighed. "This could complicate matters. Fitzeirick, you might have to appear before the court, maybe face punishment."

"Punishment?" I shouted. "I saved her life, protected her. Why should I face —"

He lifted his hand. "Honor and tradition. Still, your actions far outweigh any reason for punishing you. Also, if she is Jesca, you've brought the king's daughter back from the dead. It's likely you'll be able to name your reward."

"I doubt he can give me what I want."

Jahon tilted his head. "You could have a title, wealth, power. Anything, short of the crown, is yours for the asking."

"Mam — er, Jesca, may get reunited with her family which makes me happy, more than you can understand." I shook my head. "But it's not what *I* want. I want to find my mother, my fiancée. And Eirickson must pay for what he's done."

He nodded. "King Ander could be more helpful than you realize. Let's get you two clean and get her into more appropriate attire. We'll discuss this further over dinner. I have some decisions to make."

"Lead the way," I said, offering Mam my hand.

As we walked, I asked her, "Do I call you Mam or Jesca?"

"Can I still call you Fitz?"

"Always."

"Then you can still call me Mam."

"What about Crum?"

"He should call me Jesca," she answered, grinning.

"Are you going to get upset with him if he calls you Mam?"

"Of course not. It's the only name he knows me by."

"Don't you think it will cause some confusion?" I asked.

"I expect it will," she replied and giggled.

Jahon stopped in front of a large, wooden door. "Wait here."

I nodded. After he stepped inside, I said, "You know I won't be in the room with you, but you are safe here."

She nodded. "You've kept me safe for as long as I've known you."

As a few people exited, Jahon called for us.

I led Mam into a long hallway, with several doors on each side.

"My lady, the first door on the right is for you. The two ladies waiting inside are the best I have. They will tend to your every need," he assured her. "Fitzeirick, go to the last door on the right. You'll find everything you need to clean yourself. Someone will deliver fresh clothes soon."

"She gets servants and I have to take care of myself?" I said, grinning.

He laughed. "I could drop you in a watering trough."

I chuckled and said, "Doubt either of us would like that," before walking to the bathing room.

A large, metal tub sat on a stone platform in the middle of the room. Within arm's reach stood a wooden table with various soaps and cloths. The air felt surprisingly warm, so I pushed some energy into the floor to find the source. The platform was a fireplace used to heat the water.

I undressed and settled into the soothing bath. Holding my breath, I sank under the water. The warmth caused an odd burning sensation in the scar on my face. The fresh scar on my scalp tingled. I tolerated those small discomforts, until I had to take a breath. *As relaxing as this is, dinner and meetings are waiting. Time to get clean.*

While rinsing for the last time, the door opened. A man set fresh clothes on the floor and then closed the door. They were colored in the traditional Varian style, brilliant purple and bright red. I laughed, thinking about Crum dressed in Varian clothes.

I dried myself and dressed. The free-flowing clothing was well made and comfortable, but I preferred tighter-fitting Croian clothes.

Looking around as I left the room, Jahon was nowhere to be seen. Crum stood near the door at the end of the hall, looking uncomfortable in his dark-blue and bright-green outfit.

He saw me and shook his head.

"You don't know the half of it," I said, walking toward him.

"Not to sound ungrateful, but I don't like Varian clothes. How can anyone fight dressed like this?" he said.

"Not all Varian are fighters."

"Where's Mam?"

A crooked smile crept across my face. "Still bathing, I guess."

He squinted. "I know that look. You're hiding something. What do you know that I don't?"

"Wait for dinner."

"Why? What happens at dinner?" he asked.

The door behind us opened before I could answer.

Jahon said, "Gentlemen. If you would please come with me."

"But what about —" Crum started to ask.

"She'll join us when she's ready," he said.

Crum looked at me for an answer.

I nodded toward Jahon.

Our host led us to a table in the room outside his office. "Sit with me. We can discuss some business while waiting for our most esteemed guest."

Crum gave me a questioning look as we took our seats.

I shook my head.

"I understand you'd like to establish a reputation in Varia," Jahon said.

Pointing at Crum, I said, "Some think it's necessary to gather the resources I need."

"In light of...recent developments, I've sent messengers out on my fastest horses. The necessity of your reputation will hinge on the answers they bring back."

Before I could respond, Crum spoke. "What does everyone know that I don't?"

"Patience." I couldn't stop the smile as it returned. "Jahon," I continued, "what are we doing while we wait for your messengers to return?"

"It's in my best interests to keep you here until word comes back. I have rooms on the third floor for special guests. You can make yourselves at home."

Crum sighed. "More often than not, I'm the one who knows secrets and chooses who gets to know what and when. Now, something's happened and I don't know anything. This is annoying."

"Have a little —" I couldn't finish because Mam walked into the room and took my breath away.

Her skin was clean. Truly clean. The filth from the tunnels was gone, revealing a creamy white complexion. Her face glowed and she smiled with her head held high, green eyes shining. Dressed in the finest, gold-hued silk wrap I'd ever seen, she looked so nice it almost kept one from noticing her butchered hair.

Crum looked at Jahon. "What have you done? This isn't going to work. She's supposed to be an escaped slave on the run from Satra. She looks like royalty. This will never work."

Jahon and I stood, and bowed.

"Crum, I would like you to meet Jesca," I announced, motioning to Mam.

"Eldest daughter of King Ander and Queen Ines," Jahon added.

He laughed. "Even worse. Everyone knows Jesca's dead. I've heard Varian bards pour out their hearts singing about the tragic and mysterious loss of their young princess."

Mam sauntered to Crum.

When he looked at her, she raised her hand and patted him firmly on the cheek. "I *am* Jesca, eldest daughter of the King and Queen of Varia. You will show proper respect."

He leapt from his chair. "Is this a joke? No one is going to believe this. What is going on?"

Jahon placed his huge hand on Crum's shoulder and pushed him back into the chair. "I think it would be best if you stay seated for this."

I nodded and took my seat.

"First, Princess Jesca, would you do us the honor of joining us?" Jahon asked.

"Of course," she said, and giggled.

"Crum," I said. "It seems Vekel was right. She's Varian royalty. It's almost certain I'll stand before the king and queen to explain everything. I may even face punishment."

"No," he interjected. "I won't allow anyone to punish you for anything related to Mam —"

"Jesca," she corrected.

"Jesca," he repeated, frowning. "Fitzeirick, you *saved* her."

"My friend, I appreciate your loyalty, but you have to let this run its course. I'm willing to do whatever's necessary."

She cleared her throat. "If it's accepted I'm Jesca, you have my word, no harm will come to Fitz."

"Dear little Mam," Crum breathed.

"Jesca," she corrected, again.

He groaned. "Dear little Jesca, I understand you *think* you can keep Fitzeirick safe, but should the king and queen decide to punish him, their word is law. It isn't questioned, nor defied, by someone claiming to be their long-lost daughter. That's not how this works."

Jahon chuckled. "Crum, have you so little faith in those you associate with?"

"What do you mean?"

"Why do you think I sent more than one messenger? If all I wanted was to alert the throne to someone claiming to be Jesca, I'd only need to send one man. I've sent several messengers to various locations. I'm placing pieces and planning moves. It will take time. Relax, enjoy yourself, and prepare for a celebration, the likes of which you've never seen."

Crum looked from Jahon to me and back. "You think everything will come out in our favor?"

"I can't be certain, but I believe this will be a boon to Fitzeirick," he said. "After all, how often does someone bring a lost princess back to her loving parents?"

Crum looked at him for a long time before he gave a pained smile and nodded his head. "Good point. Let's eat."

Jahon clapped his hands twice and bellowed, "Drinks."

Two servers rushed into the room. One carried four cups, the other a large pitcher. They placed cups in front of us, poured them full of an amber-colored liquid, and left the pitcher on the table before hurrying from the room.

Jahon took a long drink. "Ah, fresh mapled ale, courtesy of my new friends. Thank you."

I raised my cup. "To new friends and the future, whatever wonders it may hold."

Crum responded with "Here, here," and Mam giggled.

"This tastes wonderful," she said.

"My compliments to your brewer," Crum said. "This may be the finest mapled ale I've ever had the pleasure of drinking."

I looked at him and shook my head. "I'm willing to believe this is the only mapled ale you've ever had the pleasure of drinking."

"True," he admitted. "But it doesn't make what I said false." He frowned and looked at me, "Fitzeirick, why do you insist on ruining my moments?"

I laughed. "Because you make it so easy."

Jahon was unsuccessful in choking back his laughter.

Mam chuckled, too.

We emptied the pitcher and Jahon clapped again. A fresh pitcher took its place as servers placed plates and utensils for each of us and trays of food on the serving table.

As soon as they were gone, Jahon said, "If you go to bed hungry, it's your fault."

I tapped Crum's foot and twitched my head toward Mam.

He nodded. "Mam, err, Jesca…would you like me to fill your plate?"

She looked at him for a moment and smiled. "Yes, thank you. How thoughtful of you, Crum."

He stood and bowed before taking her plate.

She giggled. "You don't have to bow to me, Crum."

"I wanted to show proper respect," he quipped, with a grin.

Jahon and I snickered, while she shook her head.

The amount of food was overwhelming with a variety of meats and vegetables, making up the meal, each prepared using the spicy seasonings preferred by the Varian. The wonderful aroma of so many hot dishes assaulted my nose.

"This seems like too much food," Mam commented.

"Don't concern yourself, m'lady," Jahon said. "Guests get first choice. Whatever's left goes to tavern customers and my employees."

"How nice of you," she said.

"I'm glad you approve, Your Highness."

Crum placed the plate in front of Mam. "Isn't it a bit soon to address her as royalty?"

"Wouldn't it be better to treat her as such until we know for sure?" Jahon asked. "A happy commoner doesn't cause problems, but a royal who feels disrespected…let's just say, some are not so tolerant."

Crum rubbed his cheek where Jesca had cupped it. "I see your point and find myself in agreement."

"Jahon, what do we have to look forward to in the coming days?" I asked.

"I must leave in the morning. As much as I'd like to get to know you three, I have business I cannot put it off any longer. Consider my tavern your home. All I ask is you not cause trouble here."

"I can't make any promises," Crum said. "Trouble seems to find me no matter where I hide."

"Will we be eating here in the morning?" I asked, shaking my head at Crum.

"In the common room," Jahon said.

"What about going outside?" Mam asked.

Crum nodded. "Yes, I'd like to see the fine town of Swinter myself."

Jahon smiled. "Of course, explore as you will. We don't have a great market district like the trading towns, but there are shops to browse, wares to haggle over."

"If she's going out, she should wear something to attract less attention," I noted.

"There's more modest clothing in your rooms," Jahon said.

"More Varian styled clothes?" Crum grumbled.

"Not the finery you wear now," Jahon said. "More common clothes, suited for working if you're so inclined."

"That should do," Crum said, as he rose to get more food.

"I'd like to see the city after breakfast," Mam said.

"I believe Crum would do a fine job escorting you," I said. "But it might not be wise for him to call you Jesca before the king and queen determine you are their eldest."

"But I'm clean now, nothing from the tunnels remains. I am who I am," she said.

Jahon cleared his throat. "He's right. Declaring yourself Jesca in public could raise unneeded attention and complicate your stay in Swinter, maybe the entire country."

Crum took her hand. "I've known you as Mam since we met. May I please call you Mam, a little longer?"

She looked at each of us in turn, stopping at Crum and smiling. "It's true you've known Mam longer than Jesca. I see no reason to cause complications. I'll be happy no matter what you call me. Keep calling me Mam...for now."

Jahon sighed his relief. "Glad we have it settled, at least for now. Fitzeirick, do you plan to join them?"

"Not tomorrow. I'd prefer to stay here to rest and relax. My ribs could use a break, and I'd like to spend time with your patrons."

Crum chuckled. "You are a man of the people."

Jahon smiled. "Getting to know people is a good way to get to know the land. Many of my customers aren't commoners, but you're familiar with the ways of courts. You'll be fine."

I nodded. "I think I'm ready to turn in for the evening. The ale's making me sleepy."

Jahon clapped his hands twice and a servant rushed into the room. "Please, take Fitzeirick to his room."

The man bobbed his head, but otherwise didn't move until I stood. He held his hand out. "Nice to meet you, sir. Follow me, please."

He led me up the staircase, opening the door at the top without breaking stride.

We walked into a hallway that went around the perimeter of the tavern. Large windows in the outside wall gave a view of the surrounding area. The inside wall had doors spaced at near even intervals. I followed him around the corner.

We stopped at the last door before the next corner. "Are you a firesyth?" he asked.

"No, stonesyth."

"Wait here," he said, before walking in. After a moment he announced, "Your room is ready, sir. May I ask if either of your traveling companions are firesyths?"

"They are not."

"Thank you, sir. I'll prepare their rooms now."

"May I ask how many guests stay here now?"

"I am not allowed to answer."

I nodded and thanked him before closing the door.

Several candles lit the room and a lantern sat on a small table near the large bed. A larger table sat in the middle of the room with enough chairs for a small meeting. A large, wooden armoire covered most of one wall.

I found my saddlebags in the bottom of the armoire and several suits of clothes on shelves inside. Searching through the bags, I located my hammer and placed it on the small table next to the lantern before blowing out the candles, shuttering the lantern, and crawling into bed.

Chapter 24

A knock on the door interrupted my sleep.

I woke and looked around the dim room. "One moment," I said, before tumbling out of bed.

Sunlight assaulted my eyes when I opened the door.

"Beg pardon, sir," a young boy said. "Your friends insisted I not disturb you unless you were going to miss breakfast."

Yawning, I rubbed my eyes. "My friends?"

"The esteemed Mister Crum and Miss Mam, sir."

That woke me up. "Esteemed Mister Crum? How much did he pay you to say that?"

"Pay me, sir? Nothing except compliments and entertainment. He held the whole tavern in thrall with his tales this morning. I can't believe the laughter and cheers didn't wake you."

I'm surprised I slept so long, and on a soft bed. "Must have needed the rest," I muttered. "Are they still eating?"

He shook his head. "They finished their meals and left. Crum asked me to tell you to not expect them until the afternoon, at the earliest."

I nodded. "And breakfast is over soon?"

"Yes, sir."

"Please run down to the kitchen and ask them to hold a plate for me."

He nodded and ran off.

I closed the door and shook my head, thinking about Crum's antics. Shuffling back to the lantern, I used it to light a few candles. Searching through the armoire, I chose the simplest clothes I could find, hoping to go unnoticed. Dyed a light brown, they were looser fitting than I preferred, but who was I to complain. I blew out the flames and hurried down the stairs. On the way, my stomach reminded me it was time to eat.

As I stepped into the common room, someone called my name loud enough to hear above the din of conversation. My young helper stood at a table near the corner of the room, waving his hand. Two plates greeted me. One piled with glazed, sweet rolls, and another with at least a dozen sausages, each one as thick as two fingers.

"Thank you, young man," I said, sitting. "I asked for one plate. This is too much."

"That's what I told them, sir. The kitchen staff gave me this."

"Sit. Eat with me."

"Oh, sir, we don't dine with customers," he said, eyes cast down.

"Where do you eat?"

"Grab what I can from the kitchen, when I can."

"By whose rule?"

He shrugged. "No one's rule, sir. That's how it's done,"

I nodded. "Guess things are different in Varia. One more question. Do you take requests from customers?"

"Jahon says to do whatever I can to make guests happy."

"I hate to eat alone. It would make me, the customer, happy if you eat with me." I smiled.

He looked over his shoulder.

I nudged a chair out. "Relax. Sit. Eat."

After another quick glance, he sat, but made no move to pick up any food.

"What are you waiting for?" I asked.

"Wouldn't be right to eat before you."

I grabbed a roll and took a bite.

As soon as it hit my mouth, he stuffed a sausage into his and chewed like a starving man. We ate in silence until I noticed he took longer reaching for his next bite.

"What's your name?" I asked.

"Sten," he blurted, before grabbing a sweet roll.

"It's nice to meet you, Sten, I'm Fitzeirick."

He nodded, mouth full of sugary bread.

"How old are you?" I asked.

He swallowed. "Close to eleven," he said, with a smile.

"Do your mother and father work for Jahon?"

"No. They're in the scarlet tower."

"Where?"

"It's a prison."

I furrowed my brow. "Do you know why?"

He nodded. "Got caught stealing again."

"I see. How'd you come to work here?"

"Jahon takes pity on kids like me. Puts us to work. Gives us a chance many won't."

"Sounds like he's a good man," I said.

"More than fair," he agreed. "Can I ask you something?"

"Can't think of a reason why not."

"The scar on your face. What's it mean?"

I touched the brand. "I'm branded a traitor."

"Oh," he said, suddenly looking uncomfortable.

"I'm not, though. My half-brother and I had a serious misunderstanding," I said, trying to put him at ease.

His expression didn't change. "I can't eat any more — should get back to work."

"Of course. I do appreciate you keeping me company. I've had my fill as well. Please send someone to collect what's left."

"That's one of my jobs."

I chuckled. "Best get to work then."

He cleared the table with well-practiced efficiency. "Anything else for you, sir?"

"Yes, I'd like a drink. What's good?"

"This early in the day, our most popular cup's an Apple Clever."

"Have one brought to me at your convenience. I'm in no hurry."

On his way to the kitchen, he stopped at the long stone bar taking up the right side of the room. Pointing my direction, he spoke with a middle-aged man. The man nodded and picked up a wooden pitcher.

I distracted myself by watching people come and go. The clientele reminded me of the people who hung around the fringes of Croian courts. They dressed to stand out from commoners, but didn't carry the attitude of a courtier. *So many people here trying to catch favor and better their lot.*

Sten returned to my table with the pitcher and a cup. As I took a drink, I spotted a man, about my age, who seemed to be playing Crum's game. I kept drinking and watched him work.

He was far enough away, I couldn't hear what he said, but his body language was easy to read. After 'accidentally' bumping into a nicely dressed, young lady, he started to apologize. Part of the way into the apology, he changed his expression and acted like he knew her. Soon, he'd convinced her they had met before. She invited him to sit at the table with her party. Before long, she laughed at his stories and looked entertained. My entertainment ended when they left.

I'd finished the pitcher without realizing it and looked around the room for a server. Sten made his way to my table. "Lunch soon. Do you want to eat early or late?"

"I'll wait awhile to eat. Could I have some water or tea now?"

"Weak or strong tea?"

"A nice, strong tea."

"I will be right back, sir," he said, returning quickly with a pitcher of tea.

I continued to watch people come and go while sipping my drink. Groups of men and women sat around tables while individuals took seats at the bar. The sea of bright-colored outfits made it difficult to pick out the wealthy from the hopeful.

Sten surprised me with another pitcher of tea and a plate of food.

"Lunch already?" I asked.

He shrugged. "You can wait, but I figured you'd wanna eat before we get busy."

"Good idea. Thank you again."

I turned my attention to the large rolls holding stacks of meat on the plate in front of me. The smell of the stewed vegetables from the bowl next to it almost overpowered the aroma of the spiced goat. I took it as a personal challenge to eat everything, but left a fair amount when I had my fill. No servants were in sight, so I made my way to the bar.

"Can I help ya?" a young woman asked, as I approached.

"Do you know where Sten is?"

"Right now? I'd guess he's either up ta no good, scampering about the kitchen, or working in the stables. Why?"

"I wanted him to take the food from my table, and maybe recommend someplace to take a short walk outside to settle my meal."

"I'll get someone ta take care of your table. Far as a walk, what are ya looking for?"

"Some quiet. A chance to relax."

"Orchard's usually quiet about now. Behind the building, off ta the left toward the sounds and smells of horses. Keep going about fifty paces or so past the stables. Ya can't miss it."

"Sounds perfect. Thank you."

I followed her directions and soon found myself surrounded by apple and pear trees. Listening to the different bird songs and calls, I couldn't pick out a single species.

I listened to my own private concert while walking to stretch my muscles and relax my mind. Despite trying to focus on what I needed to do in Swinter, my mind drifted to people I hadn't seen in a long time.

Aesa and Roi were both missed, for different reasons, as was my mother. Thinking of her made me wonder when she last was in Varia. I briefly thought about Nikulas, if the aid he'd given me caused him difficulties. It could cost him his title, or worse.

That sobering thought ended my contemplation and I noticed shadows growing longer. I headed back to the Stone Roof, hoping to get a table and meet with Mam and Crum. The idea of her having a good day brightened my mood a little.

A wall of mingled conversations greeted me when I entered the common room. Glancing around, my eyes settled on a large man, dressed in dark clothes and standing in a dim corner. His eyes darted back and forth, never stopping in one spot for long.

I didn't see my friends and worked through the crowd between me and the table I'd used before. Making good progress, I managed to avoid bumping into anyone until someone tripped and fell into me.

Stumbling sideways, I jostled a patron standing at the bar.

They spilled their drink on another customer.

The doused man stood and roared, "Someone's going to pay for that."

Though his voice was vaguely familiar, I didn't recognize him until he turned toward me. "Olver," I said. "It's been years. How have you been?"

He studied me before laughing. "Fitzeirick, the over-privileged half breed. I can't believe it's you." Pointing at my cheek, he said, "Went and got yourself branded. Does it come with a price on your head? The Council of Thanes should pay well for proof a traitor's dead and Jarl Eirickson would owe me another favor."

Why would Eirickson owe him anything? I shook my head. "I'm not the man you knew when we were younger. Let me replace your drinks and we'll both go about our business. No reason to fight over an honest accident."

"Sounds like you need a coward's brand too," he said, raising his fist.

I saw movement over his shoulder. The big man I'd seen before pushed through the crowd toward us.

"Don't do something you're going to regret," I said. Energy flowed through the floor. Olver drew back his fist, smashing his elbow into the man's nose.

When he turned to see who he'd hit. I rushed forward, dropped my shoulder, and knocked him over. We fell on top of the guard.

Someone slammed a bar stool into my back as I tried to get to my feet.

Olver threw me off, and I landed in a heap at the feet of one of his friends who lifted me off the floor in a tight, bear hug.

My childhood nemesis stood, kicked the guard in the head a couple of times, and turned his attention back to me. He swung his fist, but I managed to move enough for the blow to glance down the side of my head. His friend took most of the hit and loosened his grip. I slid down and sythed strength as soon as my feet touched the floor.

My blood burned. Sweat beaded on my neck. Pain I'd been ignoring shot across my chest as I turned, putting my captor between me and Olver. With a grunt, I shoved my captor into Olver. They fell to the floor together.

Another stool broke over my back. Flashes of light raced across my vision and everything went blurry. *I have to end this.*

I grabbed a piece of the chair and swung it at whoever hit me.

He tried to stop it. Instead, his hand bent backward. He screamed. I punched him across his jaw, snapping his head back.

He collapsed.

Rage took over as I advanced on Olver and his friend, still trying to untangle themselves. I kicked his friend hard enough to lift him off Olver. He landed on the downed guard. Olver sprang toward me. The impact carried us into a table. It toppled and we fell to the floor. He sat on top of me, grabbed my hair, and slammed the right side of my face into the floor.

I swung the chair leg into his back. He bellowed in pain and smashed my head into the floor again. I hit him again and the chair leg broke, leaving a jagged piece in my grip. When he lifted my head again, I stabbed him with the stake.

He screamed and rolled off me.

Ignoring my throbbing head, I forced myself to stand up. My right eye was swelling shut, but I picked up another chair leg and searched for Olver. As I looked around, I noticed a few people hiding as best they could. One or two stuck their heads out to see if it was safe to leave.

I heard a yell behind me and saw Olver cowering under a large table, bleeding and shaking, holding the jagged piece of wood in his hand.

I growled and strode toward the table, stopping only to kick it over. Before he could say anything, I swung the chair leg and hit him in the head. *Kill or be killed.*

He fell over without making another sound.

My heart pounded in my chest and thumped in my ears. Spittle flew as I roared, challenging anyone who dared to come at me. The swelling around my eye forced me to turn in circles to watch for anyone coming toward me. Before my eye shut completely, I thought I saw a shadow move across the floor.

Turning to look for movement, something yanked my right arm.

I pulled away and took a swing. A dark figure crossed in front of me.

Spinning around, I tried to keep my open eye on it, but it moved too fast. Something hit my right ankle. Pain shot up my leg. I jumped back and looked down to see the shadow moving away from me.

Lunging toward the fleeing attacker, something struck my wrist. My hand went numb, and I couldn't hold onto the chair leg.

Another strike followed, this time on my left ankle. Before I could react, my leg buckled to a blow on the back of my right knee.

I lashed out and grabbed something silky.

"Almost. Keep trying," a woman's voice called out.

I glanced at the slick, black fabric in my hand, threw it to the floor, and bellowed, "Who are you?" as I stood.

"No answers until we're done dancing," she responded, sounding happy.

"Dancing?" I yelled. "What are you talking —"

As I spoke, the shadow woman put her hands on my shoulders and vaulted over my head from behind. When her feet hit the floor, she spun around and lunged toward me.

Surprise froze me in place. All I could do was brace for the impact.

She wrapped her arms around my neck and her legs around my waist and kissed me...hard.

I ground my teeth, snarled, and turned my head to break the kiss before grabbing her in a bear hug to squeeze the life out of her.

She laughed and said, "Not yet," then slapped my ears.

I flinched and let go.

She pushed off, into a backflip. When she landed, she drew a sword with her right hand, holding the scabbard in her left.

"I think you're holding back on me," she said, slapping my ankle with the flat of her blade.

The pain caused me to hop back. *I need a weapon. I'm no match for a blade with my bare hands.* Looking down, using my one open eye, I searched for something to use against her.

She lunged forward and smacked the side of my knee with her scabbard. "Keep your eyes on me," she said, laughing as she rolled outside my reach.

I decided it was better to keep my eye on this crazy woman and gave up looking for a weapon. She laughed again and said, "Good," then sprang toward me.

"Have you lost your —"

She slapped the flat of her blade across my lips.

"Shut up and dance with me!" she shouted, laughing again, as she landed and smacked my ankle with her scabbard.

I dove toward her. She tried to sidestep my attack. But I grabbed her left wrist. With a squeal, she slapped the back of my hand with the flat of her sword.

I didn't let go.

She jumped over me, pulling my arm across my back. Pain shot out from my shoulder, but I refused to let go. I heard her laughing as I tried to free myself.

Something hit the back of my neck and everything went black.

Chapter 25

I woke, hurting all over. My throbbing head rested on a firm, silky surface and my hands and feet were bound. Everything looked blurry, but I figured out my head was on the woman in black's lap.

Her finger traced the scar on my face. "Good, you're finally awake. You have some people here to see you."

"Where am I? Why am I tied up? Why is my head in your lap?"

"So many questions," she said, with a laugh. "I'm holding your head to make sure you were breathing and keep you comfortable. We're still at the Stone Roof, for now. You're under my protection, but I had to secure you because you're dangerous."

"I'm not dangerous. I was attacked," I argued. "Who are you? Why are you here?"

"Tindra," she said, with a predatory smile. "I'm investigating a rumor. Never expected my investigation to come with so much excitement."

"Rumor?"

"Word of a branded Croian arriving in Swinter created some interest in the capital. I'm here to find out what I can. To my surprise, I found him brawling in the Stone Roof."

"It was a misunderstanding," I said, for what felt like the millionth time.

"The brand or the brawl?"

"Both."

"You have some explaining to do," she said.

"Can it wait until my head stops throbbing?"

She laughed. "No reason to explain anything to me. My mission is delivering you to the capital."

"And my friends?"

"The fast talker and the strange young woman? They may come...if they wish."

"Can I talk to them first?"

"Don't see why not," she agreed. "Lay here, don't move."

"Tied like this? I'm not sure I can move much anyway." She lowered my head to the floor, chuckling as she walked away.

"Fitzeirick, what happened in here?" Crum yelled.

"Big fight!" I yelled back, aggravating my headache.

"Who won?" he asked, as he got closer. "Why are you tied up?"

"Tindra, but she cheated. Came in fresh at the end."

"Tindra?" he repeated.

"Woman, wearing black, the one who let you in. She tied me up because I'm 'dangerous.'"

He whistled. "I'd lose a few fights to her too, I'm afraid, but I wouldn't let her put me in ropes...at least not until we got to know each other better."

I tried to laugh. My head hurt too much. "I didn't *let* her tie me up. She knocked me out. She's fast, fights dirty. Distracted me with a kiss."

He laughed. "She kissed you *and* knocked you out."

"Told you, she's a dirty fighter."

He laughed harder.

"Would you focus? I'm in trouble here," I exclaimed.

He nodded, said, "It's —", and giggled.

"Crum," I growled.

"Sorry. I know I shouldn't laugh, but you've been knocked out by three women now."

"Listen to me. Someone in the Varian capital sent her to check out a rumor about a branded man arriving in Swinter. Sound familiar?"

"Hmm..." he said, rubbing his chin and smiling. "I may have run across him once or twice recently."

"Are you going to take this seriously?"

"Of course, I am, but you have to admit it is kind of funny."

"I don't find it funny at all. People in the Varian capital are looking for me. Where's Mam?"

"Waiting outside." He knelt next to me. "I was coming back with good news."

I groaned. "What?"

"We ran into Grima and Einns."

"Are you sure?"

He nodded. "She asked if we'd seen Roi yet."

"Roi's in Swinter?"

"Been here about a month. Caught word the man he's been after visits Swinter often." He smiled. "He's looking for Olver."

"Oh, you mean him?" I said, looking toward the still body of my childhood nemesis. He followed my stare. "Umm...that's a lot of blood. His? Is he dead?"

"I stabbed him with a broken chair leg and bashed his head with another. He hasn't moved since I hit him."

Tindra walked over. "He's dead. I checked after securing you."

"Why is Roi looking for Olver?" I asked.

"Grima said he left her with Geri to settle a debt. She told Roi before we left Trader's Cup for the capital. He knew he couldn't do anything about it until later. It seems your disappearance made him decide to free her and hunt Olver. Why'd you kill him?"

"An honest accident. I bumped into someone, a drink spilled on Olver, and he wouldn't back down. I gave him plenty of opportunity," I said. "Tindra, how long do you plan to keep me bound?"

"Until I can arrange your safe passage out of here," she replied.

"Let me get my hammer from my room and I'll see to my own safety."

"How do I know you won't kill me and flee?" she asked.

"I'm guessing you don't know he's a stonesyth," Crum said. "Considering he's lying on a stone floor, how long do you think rope will hold him?"

"I've already knocked him out once."

"We were going to the capital sooner or later," I said.

"Why?" she asked.

"None of your business. Crum, my hammer's in my room."

"Don't do anything until I get back," he said.

"Tindra, since I'm under your protection, any plans to get me to a herbalist? I'm sure I need some attention," I said.

"I'll make sure you make it to the capital alive. He called you Fitzeirick. You're the dead Croian Skald?"

"I am."

She sat and moved my head back into her lap. "Why are you in Varia?"

"To make contacts, establish my reputation...Crum's idea. I need to raise an army to kill Eirickson," I said, spitting out my half-brother's name, "and take Croy back."

She made a strange, purring sound. "Bad blood in the family certainly gets passions flowing. Let me guess...he stole your woman, took your holdings?"

I wanted to shake my head, but was afraid it would hurt too much. "No, he let Satra invade...aided them, or so I hear. He sat back and allowed the slaughter of Croian people, my people. And he branded me a traitor when I challenged the Thanes to do something."

"Sounds like there's more to the story."

"I'll tell the rest to the Varian king. All you need to know is the longer Eirickson lives, the greater threat Varia may face."

"You must have hidden your hammer well. Your friend, Crum, was it? He's taking his time to return."

I looked at her, my eye still not focusing well. She had dark hair, honey-colored skin, and intense, amber eyes. "It's not right for you to keep my head in your lap. I'm promised to someone."

She smiled. "I figured an attractive, powerful man would be used to such treatment. Is your promise to the strange one outside? I assume her name is Mam."

"No. My promised is a Croian woman named Aesa."

"Yet you traveled all this way without her? Where's your bride-to-be?"

Crum answered for me. "He doesn't know, no one does. Best guess, she was in his skati when Satra invaded."

I turned toward his voice. He looked bulkier than I remembered.

"Why are you carrying saddlebags?" Tindra asked.

"It seems one way or another we're leaving."

I've waited long enough. Pulling some strength from the stone beneath me, I broke the rope around my arms, and untied my legs.

Tindra rolled away from me and drew her sword. "What do you think you're doing?"

I stood up, swayed a little, and shrugged. "Looked like he needed help carrying those."

Crum walked to my side and handed me the strap for my hammer. "You are such a benevolent leader, ever willing and able to overlook your own pains to help people."

I fastened the hammer's holder in place and settled the weapon at my hip. The familiar weight felt comforting. "We, my friends and I, will leave for the capital after a herbalist looks me over. You plan to stop us?"

Crum tapped my shoulder. "We should find Roi. He needs to know you're alive and Olver's dead."

I nodded, ignoring the pain in my neck, and took two steps toward Tindra.

She held her sword at the ready. I pushed it aside. "Are we going to fight again or are you going to help? I mean, I am your mission after all."

Crum laughed.

She sputtered. "There's a herbalist I know well. Shop's at the edge of town." She put her sword away and hurried out the door.

"Are all Varian women insane?" I asked.

"Haven't spent quality time with enough of them to be certain," Crum replied. "You sure she's Varian?"

"She works for the throne, why would they use someone who wasn't native?"

He shrugged. "I don't know, but her hair is cut short."

"To the fire with her hair!" I shouted. "I've had it with hearing about Varian women's hair."

"I happen to like long hair," he teased.

We exited to an unexpected scene.

Mam stood, red-faced, screaming at two men. Tindra saw us and yelled, "Get over here."

Crum dropped the saddlebags and ran. I moved as fast as I could, despite protests from my knees and ankles. Mam hugged Crum tight when he reached her. *Mam's safe, good. Crum will take care of her if I have to fight again. Better that way, one less thing to worry about.*

As I got close, I placed my hand on my hammer. "Back away from her."

The guards took a step back.

Tindra glared at me. "I'm in charge here."

"Not when it comes to her," I countered.

"Shhh," Crum said, trying to calm her. "We're here and we're fine, or at least I am. Fitzeirick's a little beat up."

At the mention of my name, she pushed away from him and looked at me. "What happened?"

"I got in a fight."

"Where did your eye go?"

Tindra snorted.

"It's swollen shut," I said. "It'll be back in a few days, maybe sooner if I can get to a herbalist."

"I told you, I'd get you help before we leave," Tindra said.

"Crum, leave Mam with me. Take Tindra, and these guards and get our horses ready."

"I think you've forgotten who's in charge here," Tindra snapped.

"How do you expect us to get to the capital?" I asked.

"I'll get a wagon and secure you in the back. Your friends can ride alongside."

"Secure me?" I shouted. "I thought I was the one kicked in the head. You think I'm going to be bound again?" My hand went to my hammer on its own. I slid my feet apart, ready for anything. *I don't want to do this...not sure I can, but I'm going down easy.*

"You're unknown and dangerous. You can't expect to appear before the royal court a free man."

I took a deep breath, drew my hammer, and pulled strength from the ground. "We better settle this now."

She stepped back. "What are you doing?"

"Making sure no one *ever* takes me captive again."

The two guards pulled clubs from their belts and moved toward me; I could feel them sything strength as they walked.

Crum cleared his throat. "You two don't want to do this. Fitzeirick's a nice person, but charge in like this and you won't like the outcome."

Tindra glanced at him. "Are you threatening members of the Swinter guard?"

"Consider it a friendly warning," he said, smiling.

The guards looked at each other. One shrugged, the other nodded, and they moved apart. I couldn't see the one to my right. The one to my left took another step toward me.

"Take Mam to the stables. She doesn't need to see this," I said, tracking their footsteps.

The guard to my right advanced faster. I softened the ground where he would most likely step next and his foot sank to about the middle of his calf. Immediately, I hardened the ground to hold him and charged when his will pushed against mine.

"Enough!" Tindra screamed.

I looked at her, but didn't let release the guard's leg.

"Why are you being so difficult?" she asked.

I glared at her. "You offered me protection. I did *not* agree to be a prisoner. I may be your mission, but I *don't* answer to you."

"Let him go," she said, calmly. "We'll do it your way."

I pointed to the guard on my left. "Take him, help my friends. I'll hold the other one until they get back with our horses. We don't leave for the capital until I at least get word to Roi. I'd prefer to talk to him face to face, if at all possible."

"Who's Roi?" she asked.

"No one of your concern," I said. "My friends and our horses, the sooner the better."

Tindra and the free guard hurried toward the stables and I walked closer to my captive. "You'll break your leg if you don't quit struggling."

"How'd you know where I was?" he asked. "No way you saw me."

"When's the last time you had to fight to survive?"

"Never. Swinter's pretty peaceful."

"Not long ago I would've answered the same way about where I came from. Lately, survival depends on me protecting myself and my friends. Live that way long enough, you learn some tricks. Things best kept secret."

"Understood. The young woman...Mam. She looks like Princess Stina."

I shrugged. "Can't speak to the resemblance. I've never met the princess."

"Ahh," he replied. "You could say I know her well. I'm usually on escort duty for her when she's in Swinter. Mam could be her sister. At first, I thought she *was* Stina. I asked her how she got here without anyone knowing and why she cut her hair off. She went crazy when I mentioned her hair."

I nodded. "Her hair has been a touchy subject for a while now. A man died over it."

The guard chuckled and shook his head. "Women can be that way, I suppose, but she doesn't look like she has it in her to kill someone."

"*I* killed him," I informed him, smiling.

"That," he stammered, "that I believe. I trust you're a man of your word."

"Of course. What would make you think otherwise?"

"The brand on your face says something about your character," he said. "I want to get out of this alive."

"I expect you will...unless you mention the brand again. I do have a question."

He looked at his leg. "Seems I'm not going anywhere."

"What do you know about Tindra?"

He cocked his head for a moment. "She's a spion for the crown, gathers information and fixes problems the king and queen want swept under the rug. Nasty work."

"Can I take her at her word?"

"Trust a spion to do their job or die trying, but professional liar is one of their qualities."

"Makes sense. Assuming you're telling the truth."

"Considering the position I'm in, it's in my best interest to be honest."

"Wise answer," I said, releasing his leg. "Go to the stables and hurry them along. I'm tired of waiting."

He looked at me in surprise. "I'll make sure to express your growing eagerness to be on your way."

• • • ● • ● • ● • • •

"For the last time, ask Fitzeirick!" Crum shouted, as they passed the corner of the tavern.

"Ask me what?"

"I have questions and he won't answer me," Tindra said, Andale's reins in hand.

"He told you where to get your answers. Where are the guards?"

"I sent them inside to check for any wounded, take care of the body, and cleanup. They weren't needed in the stables."

I nodded. "Your questions?"

She glanced toward the setting sun. "It's getting late in the day. Where are we staying?"

"I'd guess we're no longer welcome at Stone Roof," I mused. "Where have you been staying?"

"Somewhere you can't," Tindra said.

"We're accustomed to sleeping outdoors, if necessary."

"No."

"Then, where are we staying?" I asked, grinning.

She sighed. "I'll find us a place for the evening, after we get you looked at."

I nodded. "Anything else you want to know?"

"The rest can wait."

"Where's your horse?" I asked.

She smiled. "I'll ride with you."

Crum laughed.

"Why should I let you on my horse?"

"I stay close to my targets. If you get away, it damages my credibility."

I groaned while pulling myself onto Andale. Offering my hand to help her mount the big animal, I groaned louder as she used me for leverage.

"Don't make me regret this," I said. "Where's the herbalist?"

"Follow the street to the east. We'll turn north before we leave town."

We hadn't ridden long before Mam started humming.

"I was wrong," Tindra whispered. "Some questions can't wait."

"Ask."

"Mam. She's Varian?"

"We think so."

"Where did you meet her?"

"It's a longer story than I care to tell right now. I suspect you'll hear it when I speak to the king and queen."

"You know why she rides the old way?"

"It's comfortable for her and she does it well. Watched her jump a fence at a full gallop."

"Sidesaddle riding fell out of favor long ago."

"Not for her."

"Last question, I think. Do you know the tune she's humming?"

"There are several she entertains herself with. I think she finds them calming."

"But what are they?"

I lied, "Don't know. Why do you care?"

"She could pass for Princess Stina."

I chuckled. "You're the third person to mention her strong resemblance to Stina. Maybe I should meet the princess and see for myself. By the way, when are we turning north?"

"Turn north on the next street and follow your nose. You'll smell Hampus' house long before you see it."

Vivid memories of the horrible tea came to mind. "I'm not looking forward to this," I muttered.

"Bad experience with herbalists?" she asked, running a finger along the scar on my scalp. "Looks like one of them did a good job for you recently. It left a nice scar."

The touch of her finger sent tingles along my spine. "Don't do that," I growled. "The treatment was almost as bad as the injury."

"No reason to be so touchy. Not all herbalists use the same methods."

I started to say something when I caught the faintest whiff of something spicy. It smelled so good it almost made my mouth water.

Tindra drew in a deep breath. "Hampus and his wife must be brewing something special. I'd guess they've already heard about the brawl."

The increasingly stronger scent led to a modest, by Swinter standards, stone house.

Tindra dismounted and walked to the door.

It opened before she knocked.

Chapter 26

"Should I guess why you're here?" a raspy voice asked, behind the door.

I waved Crum over to me. "Take Mam and find Grima. If possible, bring Roi here. If not, leave word for him about Olver, and let him know we're headed to the capital."

Tindra stepped back from the door and motioned to me.

I dismounted Andale and tied his reins to a nearby bush. Riding made my joints ache and my muscles stiffer, so walking was its own punishment.

"Where are they going?" she asked, as I approached.

"Sent them on an errand."

She sighed. "Let's get you taken care of."

My nose and throat burned as we walked into the house. Entering the common room caused my left eye to water. I sneezed and followed the watery image of Tindra.

"Get a hold of yourself," she said. "Varian spices aren't that bad."

"Not to eat, but unpleasant to breathe," I said, sneezing again.

She laughed. "Sit."

"I'm so glad I'm entertaining you this evening," I said, feeling my way to a chair.

"And yet the evening hasn't even begun," she replied.

A blurry blob shuffled into the room. The raspy voice asked, "What happened to you, young man?"

"I won one fight, lost another."

"Let me look closer, my eyes aren't as good as they used to be."

"Mine are worse since I walked in here," I commented.

"Yes, yes...my wife is cooking a wonder for dinner," he said, smacking his lips.

"You're Hampus, I assume?"

"I am."

"What can you do to help him?" Tindra asked. "We need to be on our way."

"Good work takes time," he said, before poking at the right side of my face. "What happened?"

"An old enemy bashed my head into the floor a few times. After I took care of that problem, Tindra decided to beat me about the knees and ankles before knocking me out."

"No open wounds?" he asked.

"Not this time."

The blur nodded. "Wait here."

He shuffled out and returned quicker than I thought possible. "Take these."

"These what," I said. "I can't see anything with my eye watering this much."

Tindra laughed again.

"Hold out your hands." He placed a weighty cloth bag in my right hand and a small clay pot in my left.

"Eat three peppers from the bag with every meal to help with the pain and swelling. Rub some of the oil from the pot on the right side of your face, at least once a day, until the swelling goes away."

"Sounds easy enough," I said, placing the pot on the chair between my legs. I reached into the bag and pulled out three peppers about the size and shape of a finger. "Eat these?"

"Stems and all," he said.

"But it will burn," I countered, warily.

"The burn means it's working," he said, chuckling.

"Don't tell me the man I faced earlier can't take a little heat," Tindra teased.

I growled at her and tossed all three in my mouth. The burn started on my tongue with the first bite. It spread quickly to the roof of my mouth before reaching my gums and lips. My watering eye turned into a tiny waterfall as I swallowed.

Heat flowed down my throat, into my stomach. I had no way of knowing if the rest of my body still hurt because my mind focused on the smoldering fire in my belly.

"We should dry you off before putting on the oil," Tindra said.

"Why?" I wheezed.

"You're sweating like you've worked a field all day and your eye's running like a river. Hampus, a cloth please."

Blinded more than ever, I couldn't see where he produced the cloth from, but he came prepared.

She wiped my face and pressed the cloth over my left eye. "Hold this here."

The oil felt slick before warming my swollen cheek. The longer she rubbed, the hotter it grew.

"What is that?" I asked.

"My own blend of pepper oils," Hampus said.

"How long does it burn?"

"Don't know. The skin goes numb before the burning stops," he said.

"I think all herbalists are trained torturers," I muttered.

"Hampus supplies concoctions to fit many needs," Tindra said.

Taking the cloth away from my left eye allowed me to see again.

Hampus was an old man with dark, leathery skin wearing rough clothes resembling a dark-green feed sack. A blossom of silvery-white hair, like dandelion fluff, covered his head. He stood hunched over, but didn't seem to need a walking stick.

"How much do I owe you, sir?" I asked.

He shook his head. "Tindra brought you. The crown will pay me in due time."

"You heal everyone she brings at no cost?"

"Didn't say I healed everyone."

"Concoctions for many needs," she repeated.

I wanted to know more, but someone knocked on the front door.

Hampus and Tindra looked at each other. She shrugged after he shook his head.

"I guess I'll get the door," I said.

"No. Sit. Rest a little longer," Tindra said, before leaving the room.

"Do you work with her often?" I asked quietly.

"I don't discuss my work with others."

"Fitzeirick, your friends are back!" Tindra yelled.

"I'm going to see if my wife has dinner ready." He waved to me and shuffled out of the room.

I made my way to the front door, making sure to take the bag of peppers and pot of oil. "Crum," I called out, as I got close to the door. "Did you find Grima?"

"Even better," a familiar voice replied. "He found Roi."

I ran past Tindra, almost knocking her over.

He stood next to Sinar, and I noticed Crum fidgeting on Aspeit.

A warmth flowed through my body. I blinked a couple of times, making sure it was Roi, before grabbing his shoulder. I had to make sure he really was there...and my legs weren't as steady. "We need to talk."

"Yes, it seems we have much to catch up on — especially the scar," Roi said. "Where are you staying?"

I glanced over my shoulder. "Tindra doesn't want me to get away from her, so she's supposed to find us rooms for the night."

"You're staying with me," he stated.

"I don't think so," Tindra said, stopping beside me.

I flicked my hand at her. "Roi can best me and Crum together, you're outnumbered here. If you want to keep an eye on me, you'll have to come along. Do you have room for us?" I asked him.

"For you, I'll make room," he said, pulling me into a tight hug. I grunted. He let me go and gave me a strange look.

"It's been a long day, I hurt all over," I explained.

"Does this have anything to do with you heading to the Varian capital?"

"Yes, but it'd be best if we're sitting for me to tell you everything."

He nodded. "Follow me."

I stored my treatments in a saddlebag, pulled myself onto Andale, and looked at Tindra.

"I didn't agree to this," she said.

"Either come with me or hope you find me again before I get to the capital."

"For all I know, you're conspiring with your friends to hold me for nefarious intent," she said.

"I think you're more familiar with holding people for nefarious reasons than I am."

She chuckled. "Going by what I know, you're right. Help me up."

• • • • • • • • •

The sun sank below the horizon, as we arrived at Roi's home on the far, northern edge of town. *Leave it to Roi to have a house carved into a hill.*

"How deep into the hill does it go?" I asked.

"As far as I need," he replied, smiling.

He opened the door and stepped aside to allow me in first. Crum followed, but Roi stopped Tindra.

"I don't know you," he said, gruffly.

She held out her hand. "Can't say I know you either. I'm Tindra. I work for the royal family."

His hand engulfed hers. "I'm Roi. That's all you need to know."

She nodded and he let her go.

Crum walked into a dim hallway to the left of the generous entryway and I pushed some energy into the floor to figure out the layout of the house. Two sets of feet were on the floor in the room Crum walked toward. I felt the pressure of the chair legs where someone sat.

Roi closed the door and asked us to follow him.

I nodded and Tindra stayed close to me.

"Where's Einns?" I asked, as we walked.

"Asleep. Why do you ask?"

"I found the women, but I couldn't feel him anywhere."

"What do you mean?"

"New habit. When I get someplace I'm not familiar with I start searching for pressure points on the ground or stone floor. I can track people even if I can't see them. Crum's sitting on the floor near someone. I'd guess Mam."

Roi laughed and shook his head.

"It's not the only trick I learned. Taught myself how to work dirt back into stone," I told him, smiling.

He clapped his hand on my back. "After all these years, it finally sunk in. How many times did I try to explain it?"

"Desperate times."

We entered a large room, round with a domed ceiling. Several alcoves held candles, lighting the room. Grima sat on a well-cushioned chair, facing the door. Her expression brightened when she saw me before I read concern on her face.

"Fitzeirick, you look...I mean, I've seen you looking better," she said, blushing.

"What, this?" I quipped, pointing at the swollen side of my face. "Herbalist gave me something to make the swelling go down faster."

"I'm pretty sure she meant your hair and the brand," Roi said, smiling. He pointed to a comfortable looking bench. "Sit and tell us the story."

Grima stood to let Roi have the chair, then she settled into his lap.

That's a new development.

Tindra stuck near me as I sat.

"Could I get a drink to cool the burning in my mouth and throat?" I asked.

"I bet we could all use some drinks," Roi said.

"Fitzeirick, would you like milk or water?" Grima asked.

"Milk," I answered. "Tell me where it is and I'll go get it."

"I'm not going to let our guest serve himself," she argued, waving me off. "Mam, would you mind helping?"

"Not at all."

"Guess you'd like to know why I left Crum alone to look for you," Roi said.

I nodded. "The thought *has* crossed my mind once or twice."

"I have no justifiable reason for abandoning you. When we realized something dire had happened, we snooped around the capital until Eirickson's personal guard started harassing us. We went to Geri's to discuss our options without having to watch our backs. We had no idea if you were alive. I saw Grima, and everything I'd ever felt for Sysia came crashing down on me. I couldn't save my wife, I couldn't save you, but I *could* save her.

"Right then, it's all I could think to do — save *someone*. During our first visit, she told me Olver was responsible for her situation. He delivered her to pay off someone's debt. Geri wouldn't tell me who, and Grima's too ashamed to talk about it. I'd already planned to take her and Einns back to your skati when we returned from the capital. With you gone and the future in doubt, I decided to hunt Olver."

"He's dead," I said.

He nodded. "Crum told me. It felt good to be on the move with 'my family' again and teach Einns things my father taught me. Grima was happy to be out from under her burden so she stayed with me. At first, I tried operating out of Nikulas' skati, but Eirickson's men kept track of me with ease. After three of them accosted me looking for Crum, I decided Varia would be safer. After I knew Grima and Einns were out of Eirickson's reach, I did nothing but hunt Olver."

I saw tears and he paused.

It must be bad.

"His trail led back to your skati. Dodging Satran patrols, I made my way in. There's no gentle way to say this. Your house, the grounds, everything...gone, leveled. I found out Modir Sar'sa gave her life protecting Aesa. Survivors told me your mother stood fast, yelling her defiance and holding a wall of fire. She fell to arrows and burned to ash."

My mother's dead. Of course, she died protecting people. From what Geri had said, I'd feared the worst, but didn't want to believe it. Knowing was almost a relief. Hearing she died honorably made me proud. "Is Aesa —" The question caught on a lump in my throat.

Tindra put her arm around me.

I shrugged her off and scowled. "I don't need your pity," I grumbled.

She squinted and slid away.

"Alive? I don't know for sure. Accounts vary. Most said she got out, but some insisted she went back for Sar'sa. I know this much: if she's alive, she hides well. I never found evidence of her in Croy. It's better for her to be dead than captured by the Satran savages. They are not kind to prisoners, especially women."

Mam and Grima walked in as Roi finished his story. Grima hurried to me and held out a large cup. "I'm so sorry for what's happened."

I took the cup and nodded. The thick milk brought some relief as it flowed down my throat.

Mam finished handing out cups and came back to me. "What can I do for you?"

"Give him space," Tindra said.

My chest grew tight. *Does this woman never learn?* I glared at her with my open eye. "Do not *ever* tell her what to do."

Crum was at Mam's side in an instant. "Tindra, I'd suggest you take your own advice and give Fitzeirick his space."

I shook my head again. "She doesn't know, but she'll learn soon enough."

Mam whispered, "I'm here if you need me."

Crum patted me on the shoulder before returning to his spot on the floor.

Emotions flooded my mind. A jumble of anger, fear, sadness, and shame twisted together with pride, happiness, and hope. I put my head in my hands and trying to sort it all out. Everyone jumped when I let loose the roar of frustration.

Tindra moved away from me.

"Eirickson!" I yelled. "He let this happen! He made this happen! He'll pay! I'll make sure he loses everything before I see him dead by my own hands!" It took me a moment to look beyond my rage and notice the room shaking from my outburst.

"Calm yourself," Roi warned, softly. "Don't bring the room down on us."

I closed my eyes, rested my head in my hands, and forced myself to take deep breaths. Tears came. I felt an odd comfort when Tindra moved near again.

"Does Roi know about the tunnels?" Mam asked.

"I'd like to hear about them, when Fitzeirick's ready," Roi said.

Mam sat at my feet, hugged my leg, and hummed one of her songs.

I couldn't help but grin at her attempt to cheer me up. Patting her head, I whispered, "Thank you, Mam. That's what I needed."

She looked at me with tear-filled eyes and smiled.

I drew in a deep breath, held it for a time, and let it out with a loud whoosh before telling the story. Mam clung tightly to me as I spoke.

Tindra drew a hissing breath as I explained the savagery necessary to survive.

At one point, Grima left the room in tears.

I told everything except Mam's secret. *Not in front of Tindra.*

When I finished, Roi wore an expression I couldn't read. After studying his face for a few seconds, I decided he had trouble believing what he'd heard.

He shook his head. "You were trapped for most of a year."

I nodded.

He looked at Mam. "How long ago were you locked away?"

"I don't remember," she answered.

"Everything we've found out says it was a long time," I said.

"I can't even start to understand how evil Eirickson must be to do something like this," Roi said. "I've seen cruelty from one man to another, and I've done some things I'm not proud of, but never could I consider being so heartless."

"Then you understand why he must die," I stated.

"I do, but I hate what you'll have to become to do it," he replied.

Grima returned carrying a tray with sandwiches and salads. "I assume everyone's hungry," she said. "It's not much, but it's the best I could do on such short notice."

"Don't apologize," I said. "We're the unexpected guests. We had no intention of ruining your evening."

"Nonsense," Roi said. "You could never ruin our evening. A gathering of friends, especially long-lost friends, is cause for a celebration. True, some the conversation is unpleasant, but at least we're together. Crum, lift the mood, regale us with an entertaining story."

Mam patted my knee and returned to her chair while Grima handed out food.

Crum stood, cleared his throat, and started a tale.

Tindra tapped me on the shoulder. "I know a little about treating injuries. Massaging your face will help the swelling go down sooner."

I half-heartedly rubbed my face, but couldn't stop thinking about my mother and Aesa.

"You're not doing it right," she whispered. "Let me."

I was too overwhelmed to protest when she started rubbing my face.

Roi noticed and stared as Crum continued his story.

"Roi doesn't like you," I told her.

"Is that a problem?"

"It could be."

"I'll burn that bridge after I cross it."

"... all I could do was stand in shadows, still as an ancient oak on a windless night, until the guards ran by. Believe me, it was hard to keep from laughing as they moved along with no idea where I was. It wasn't long afterward I heard rumors about a haunted alleyway. That's how I'm responsible for some people believing in ghosts," he said, and bowed to applause and laughter.

I remembered how good it felt to hear Mam laugh. The thought made me smile wide and gave me an idea. "Mam, tell them how you talked your way into Skald Nikulas' hall."

She looked at me and her eyes opened wide before she shook her head and blushed.

"Oh, please tell it. You did such a good job. I was impressed," I pressed.

"What will they think of me?"

I chuckled. "They'll consider you a smart, resourceful woman."

She turned to the rest of the room. "Will you?"

"Dear little Mam, I already find you amazing," Crum confessed.

Roi choked back a laugh. "Please, Mam, I'd enjoy hearing your story."

Looking at me again, she smiled and started by stomping her foot, to show how she got the guard's attention. To my surprise, she gave me credit for stepping in when she ran out of things to say to the guard.

When she finished, Crum stood. "Outstanding performance. Take a bow."

Mam curtsied and laughed.

We all clapped and laughed with her, except Tindra.

She cleared her throat. "I have a question."

I turned to look at her, as Mam answered, "Yes?"

"Do you know you're Varian?"

"Quite a few people have told me I look Varian. I've found I prefer Varian cooking. Varian clothes are comfortable if a bit bright in color. But I don't remember where I'm from."

"I only ask because you look almost identical to someone I know...but I'm certain you aren't her. This troubles me."

"I'm sorry," Mam replied, frowning as she sat. "I don't mean to cause trouble."

Crum took a step toward Tindra, but I raised my hand to stop him. "Mam, I think you misunderstood. You aren't causing trouble. Your resemblance to Tindra's friend makes her wonder where you're from."

Mam cocked her head and looked at me for a moment. Crum stepped back and sat on the floor next to her.

I yawned. "Roi, do you have room enough for us to sleep here?"

"We'll make do. The men can sleep in here and the women sleep in our bed."

"Mam, is it going to be a problem for you?" I asked.

"Will I have a place to sit if I can't sleep lying down?"

"Are you not well?" Tindra asked.

She shook her head. "It's a habit from our time in the tunnels."

"Do you need a chair?" Grima asked.

"No, the floor is fine."

"I'll get a spare blanket for you."

Tindra looked from me to Roi. "I'm surprised you'd trust a stranger to sleep in your house."

"Should I secure you to a post outside?" Roi asked.

"I assure you it won't be necessary," she said. "In my line of work trust doesn't come so easy. Like I said, it's a surprise."

"Crum, would you get our saddlebags?" I asked.

"Of course. Anyone care to help?"

Roi and Tindra both offered to help at the same time.

"It's rare to get so many volunteers," he said, laughing.

Grima followed them with a tray full of cups.

"Are you sure you're going to be alright?" I asked Mam.

"Grima seems nice enough. Tindra's strange, though."

"I believe you and Grima will get along well. I'll agree with your opinion of Tindra. I don't know how much I trust her."

"Why'd you let her touch you? Especially on the face?"

My stomach churned and I shrugged. "She's trying to help me heal...and...it felt nice. I'm not going to lie." My shoulders drooped. "Part of me liked it. No one's touched me like that in a while."

"Because you miss —"

"Aesa, yes. In a way, having Tindra near me reminds me how much I miss her. I wish I knew if she's alive or..."

She moved to sit next to me. "I know what it's like to lose everyone and have someone find me. First Sir, then you and, maybe, Crum. Sir kept me alive and safe, you rescued me. Crum, I don't know. He means something to me, but I'm not sure I know what."

I took her hand. "You mean something to him too, but he's not sure what it means yet either. Give him time and, maybe more importantly, give yourself time to figure it all out."

She smiled. "Is that how you feel about Tindra?"

"No. It's nothing like you and Crum. I met her today and she beat me up. She might be a valuable ally when I speak with the Varian royal court or she could be a terrible hindrance. Have you wondered why the crown would send someone looking for me?"

She shook her head.

"Of course not." I smiled. "You don't think like most people. No doubt, the time in the tunnels damaged you, but also gave you an amazing amount of clarity. Your only concerns are immediate. Do you ever think about the future?"

"I'd like to eat tomorrow, and a bath would be nice."

"Anything else?" I asked.

"Nothing else seems important right now."

"That's what I mean," I said, smiling. "The here and now are where you exist with no concern for the future. It's a luxury many, myself included, can't or don't afford themselves. One day, you may find you're forced to worry about the future, but I hope it doesn't come for you soon."

She hugged me. "Thank you. Do you know where Grima is?"

I focused on my talent for a moment. "Several people are coming this way. I bet she's with them."

"Good. I don't know the way to the bedroom."

Roi, Tindra, and Crum, wearing saddle bags, followed Grima into the room.

Mam walked to Tindra. "My bags, please."

"I'm more than happy to carry them for you," she said.

"We're going to the same room," Grima said.

"True," Mam responded. "Thank you for helping."

Crum turned and bowed. "We'll see you ladies in the morning...you too, Tindra."

Roi and I laughed. Grima gasped.

"I'll remember that, smooth talker," Tindra warned, somewhat playfully.

Roi placed my bags at my feet and Crum dropped his near the chair Mam used.

"What was that about Crum?" I asked.

"A barb to keep her from getting too comfortable. Believe me, she can give at least as good as she gets."

"You know her?" I asked.

He shook his head. "Any information I have about Varian spies is rumor or warnings from people who claim to have crossed one."

"Odd," Roi said. "I haven't heard anything about them, and I've been in Varia tracking Olver for a while."

"You and I tend to travel in different circles," Crum said.

"Good point. What have you heard?"

"They work for the crown, but some take outside jobs. Their skills command high prices and more often than not, their work tends to get messy."

"Does this mean she's going to be a problem?" I asked.

Crum shrugged. "Depends on who sent her and why. A casual curiosity from the crown is no worry for us. However, if someone, say Eirickson, got wind you're free and in Varia and hired her...she's a real problem."

Roi laughed for a moment. "She does seem focused on you, Fitzeirick."

"Are you saying I should've noticed something going on?" I asked, half grinning.

"I can understand your distraction. Crawling into your lap and caressing your face is an excellent way to get on your good side," Roi teased.

"She didn't get into my lap," I said, in protest. "Speaking of which, are you and Grima..."

"Married?" Roi said. "Short of having an official agreement, yes we are."

I pulled him into a tight hug. "Congratulations. I wish you all the happiness you could hope for. How does Einns feel about it?"

"He seems happy. If nothing else, I've taught him how to survive on his own if he has to," Roi said, with pride.

"Being a father agrees with you," I said.

"Being happy agrees with him and being asleep would agree with me," Crum commented.

Roi and I yawned at his suggestion.

"You two get comfortable, I'll snuff the candles. Sleep well my friends," Roi said.

Chapter 27

Crashing onto the floor snapped me awake. I fought to free myself from the blanket. My head throbbed, throat burned, and I hurt all over, like I'd been fighting for hours.

Roi and Crum stood over me, holding candles.

"Fitzeirick, calm down. You're safe," Roi called, softly.

"What happened?" I asked.

"Do you know where you are?" Crum asked.

I sat up and looked around. "Roi's home."

"Having a nightmare best I could tell," Crum said.

"Water?" Roi asked.

I nodded and he hurried out of the room.

Crum sat next to me and put his arm around my shoulders. "Remember, we're here with you. You're safe."

I grunted my appreciation. It seemed like it took forever for Roi to get back. The water felt good on the way down. I held the mug up for more, and he smiled and handed me another cup.

"After your grunts woke us, it looked like you were fighting for your life," Crum said.

"Want to talk about it?" Roi asked.

I took a deep breath and tried to remember. "It's all blurred flashes of fighting, wrestling. Noises...laughter, screams, crying. I can't make sense of the jumbled mess."

Crum frowned. "Do you think Tindra's attentions are making you doubt your feelings for Aesa?"

I glared at him. "My love for her hasn't wavered, not once."

He raised his hands and shrugged.

"Your thoughts, Roi?" I asked.

He cocked his head. "I'm no expert on the matter, but dreams don't always make sense. You just learned your mother's dead. It would surprise me if you weren't disturbed by that knowledge. Not knowing Aesa's fate, combined with Tindra's apparent interest in you, might bother you more than you know. How long since you've been the object of a woman's attention?"

"Most of a year."

"That'd be enough to conflict any man's feelings," Crum commented.

Roi shook his head. "Some of us are more stable than others."

I sighed. "Help me off the floor and let's get back to sleep."

"It's nearly morning; I expect Einns to stir shortly. Soon after he rises, he'll start cooking, but he doesn't know we have guests. I'll wake him and let him know," Roi said.

"He doesn't have to cook for us," I said.

"He loves it. He'll own a bakery, or something, when he's of age," he said, and left the room.

Crum opened and closed his mouth, several times, before shaking his head.

"Whatever you have to say spit it out. You know you can tell me anything," I said.

"Keep Tindra at arm's length."

"What makes you think I'd do anything else?" I asked, nodding.

"You let her get too close last night." He pointed at me. "Never forget she's good at her job. She has many ways to get information. Toying with emotions isn't a problem for her."

I think the dandelion's calling the thistle a weed. "Are you telling me you've never played with women's emotions?"

"Not with malicious intent," he said.

I crossed my arms and pursed my lips. "I doubt intent matters to the victim."

He frowned. "All I'm saying is watch yourself. I think you have some conflicting feelings toward her."

"Until I *know* Aesa's dead, I'm holding out hope."

"From what I've heard, if Satra has her, she's better off dead," he said.

"Probably," I replied, looking away from him.

"Good news," Roi announced, entering the room. "Einns will start cooking soon. When I woke the ladies, Grima suggested we go to the hot spring baths before we eat."

"Where?" Crum and I asked.

"Nice fellow owns a bathhouse fed by a natural hot spring. His great, great grandfather discovered it, built up the business, and managed to keep it under his family's control. Most of the water's in a public pool, but there are some private rooms. I helped him collect some debts, so I have a standing invitation. Bring a change of clothes."

"Why?" I asked.

Roi chuckled. "Marcus' number one rule. No one is allowed in the water wearing clothes. He believes it's bad for the water. One thing for certain, you'll want to be in clean clothes after getting out."

"Women don't have a problem with this arrangement? I mean, it goes against Croian custom," I said.

"You're not in Croy," Roi said, smiling. "Varians aren't as strict in their societal interactions. Men and women together in public baths is normal here. Grima loves it. We go at least once a week."

"This should be interesting," Crum said, grinning.

I shook my finger at him. "You'll behave yourself and act with honor."

"And I'll make sure of it," Roi added. "Meet me outside when you're ready."

Crum and I grabbed fresh clothes from our saddlebags and headed outside.

"Tindra didn't have a change of clothes" Crum said. "Wonder what she's going to do."

"I'll wear clothes Grima gave me," Tindra said, sneaking in from behind me. I flinched and stepped away from the unexpected voice.

Everyone snickered.

"That's nice of her," I said.

"We're close enough in size. I'm leaving my silks in exchange."

"Such a shame," Crum commented.

"Why?" she asked.

"Because you look stunning in them," he replied, smiling.

"I make everything I wear look good," she said, through a toothy grin.

Grima handed Roi his clothes as we left the house.

I smelled bread baking as the breeze shifted. Roi inhaled and smiled. "Einns is an artist when it comes to cooking."

"He cooks so much better now than when we worked for Geri," Grima added.

"Freedom is a wonderful thing," I said.

"Yes, it is," Mam agreed, before humming as we walked.

Roi glanced back at her.

I shrugged and shook my head. "If someone doesn't stop Eirickson and Satra, no one will be free for long."

"I've seen the destruction first hand," Roi said, putting his hand on my shoulder. "Stay focused on what's right. I'd hate for you to lose yourself, while saving everyone else."

"I've missed your wisdom," I said. "I'll do my best."

Tindra occasionally glanced around. No one paid us undue attention, as far as I noticed, but maybe she knew something I didn't. Crum seemed focused on Mam.

If he's not worried, I'm not worried.

We stopped in front of a building so plain it all but blended into the surrounding structures. Roi knocked on the door and waited.

It swung inward and a soft voice invited us inside.

A tall, thin man greeted Roi and Grima by name when we stepped inside. "And you have friends with you, wonderful."

I couldn't tell how old he was. His clean-shaven face made me think young, but his bald head said old man. The youthful spark in his light-gray eyes and lack of wrinkles convinced me that he was around my age.

"Marcus," Roi began, "this is my longtime friend, Fitzeirick, and another good friend, Crum. Mam's traveling with them. We recently met Tindra."

He looked at me and gasped. "What happened to you?"

I smiled. "A spilled beer and an old misunderstanding got my face smashed into a floor yesterday."

"Oh."

His eyes skipped Crum as he turned his attention to the two women. He looked at Tindra and his happy expression immediately changed, looking like he'd bitten into something rotten. "You, I know, at least by reputation."

Tindra smiled and nodded. "It's all true."

Focusing on Mam, he said, "I don't believe we've met, but you look —"

"She has one of those looks," I said. "Everyone thinks they know her or she looks like someone familiar."

He snapped his fingers. "Stina. You could be her sister."

"You're not the first to notice," Mam said, bowing her head.

Roi cleared his throat. "Marcus, we'd like to use a private pool."

"Oh, yes. Of course. I do have a favor to ask."

"What can I do for you?"

"Please ask Einns to bring more of those spicy, sweet loaves. They are fantastic. Everyone asks for them."

"I'm sure he'd love to make some for you," Grima said. "How many do you want?"

"Oh, whatever he can spare when he has time. My needs are modest."

"I'll let him know how much you appreciate his work," Roi said.

"Your guests know the rules?"

Roi nodded. "I let them know."

"Thank you. It would be impossible to keep this place clean if everyone did their washing here. Enjoy your soak."

Roi led us through a concealed passage to a plain, wooden door. It swung inward with a soft, creaking sound into a well-lit room. The warm air smelled salty. A narrow, stone walkway down the right side of the room gave access to a large pool. Near the door, a shelf held cloths to dry ourselves. A second set of shelves sat empty not far away.

"Put your fresh clothes on the empty shelves, get undressed, and head in," Roi said, closing the door.

Grima had her change of clothes stored and undressed as soon as the door closed. She was in the water before Roi reached the shelves.

He chased after her as soon as he undressed.

I stored my clean clothes and crossed my arms. *They seem comfortable but ...*

Crum looked at the rest of us and shrugged. "Guess he wasn't joking." He shed his clothes and stepped into the pool.

"Feels like a giant bathing tub," he said, moving into deeper water.

Tindra undressed and sauntered into the pool without hesitation. She may have been the same size as Grima, but she was in much better shape. Her clothes hid several scars showing the violent side of her work. *She's still nice to look at.* Crum's advice echoed in my head...*keep her at arm's length.*

Mam looked from the water to me, blinking several times. "Fitz, do I have to swim?"

"It's deep enough to swim in the middle," Roi said. "If you'd rather sit and soak, use the seats along the walls."

"Sounds like you won't have to swim," I replied.

Her eyes lit up.

"Dear little Mam, you don't know how to swim?" Crum asked.

She shook her head. "Fitz tried to teach me."

He smiled, moved into shallower water, and held out his hand. "Maybe you need a better teacher."

She smiled back and undressed.

Crum sucked in a hissing breath.

She looked better than the first time I'd seen her undressed, thanks to eating more and better meals. Still, the years of imprisonment had damaged her body.

She waded into the water and took his offered hand. They walked together until the water touched her neck.

I'm the only one still dressed.

Crum looked ready to say something. I reached for the bottom of my shirt and paused. My left eye twitched. "Sorry, I can't. This doesn't feel right. Maybe, if Aesa were here."

"Fitzeirick," Roi said. "We're all friends here." He glanced toward Tindra and shrugged. "Most of us are anyway. This happens all over Varia. We're not doing anything wrong."

I shook my head. "I hear what you're saying, but I was raised to be an example of Croian society. People looked to me as the standard. If I ignore my way of life now, how am I any better than Eirickson? I'm not judging any of you, only doing what feels right for me. Enjoy yourselves. I'll wait for you outside so we can eat together when you're done." I grabbed my clothes and headed for the door.

"I didn't think this would bother you," Crum called.

"We've always seen things differently," I replied and left.

Marcus eyed me as I walked out of the hallway. "Something wrong?"

"No, I just...I don't feel right in there. It's the way I was raised."

He gave me a slight smile and nodded. "If you're not used to the Varian way of life, it can be a little overwhelming. I hope you don't think poorly of me."

I returned his smile. "Not at all. Roi speaks well of you, and that means you're good. Looks like you run a nice place, but I'm not ready for it. I'm going to wait outside."

He bobbed his head and hurried down another hallway.

I walked a short distance from the bathhouse and sat on the ground, holding the clean clothes in my lap. The same doubts I felt the day I left home crept into my mind. *What am I doing here? I failed the people in my skati, how can I do any better for all of Croy?*

• • • • • • • • • •

Tindra sat next to me, wet hair shiny in the morning light. "I wanted to talk with you."

"What do we have to talk about?"

"There are several things to discuss before we reach the capital."

"I know what you are, how you work. I'll talk to you as much as you want, but I will *not* be manipulated."

"I can't believe you expect such behavior from me," she said. "I should take offense."

"I notice you didn't say you took offense, only you should. Which means you aren't offended at all."

"A wise leader notices such details," she said.

"And that sounds like manipulation."

"I can compliment you without ulterior motives."

"If you insist," I said. "What's on your mind?"

"Lots of things, but you only want to talk. What are your plans if you can't get the resources to overthrow your half-brother?"

"Die trying."

She laughed. "All or nothing. I like a man with deep conviction."

"It doesn't matter what you like. Why did the crown send you?"

"What will you do if Aesa's dead?" she asked.

"None of your business," I said, pointing at her. "You didn't answer my question."

"What if I told you I could help you?"

"I thought you were here to deliver me," I said.

"I am, in a manner of speaking, by proposing a union with you."

"What kind of union?" I asked, frowning.

"We knew you disappeared around the time Satra conquered your territory. Most believed you died fighting the invasion, but Crum's search got our attention. Word reached the capital that he'd entered Swinter with someone who could be you. I came to confirm the rumor. If I found you, my task was working toward a union between us...one which benefits Varia and you."

"They sent you to marry me?"

She nodded.

I stared at her, trying to figure out if she expected me to believe her. "Some kind of agreement or treaty is one thing, but marriage? I can't believe the Varian crown would sanction a marriage."

She shrugged. "People marry for worse reasons all the time. Also, I'm not an exclusive employee of the crown. Some citizens feel King Ander isn't willing to make necessary sacrifices."

"You're talking about treason," I said.

"It's not treason to have your country's best interest at heart. I'd rather die than work against my king and queen. If anyone should understand what I mean, it's you."

I touched the brand. "I also understand the consequences of going against those in power. Rulers don't care about intent. What do you expect to receive for your service?"

"Power and influence. A stable life and, perhaps, a family."

I shook my head. "In my experience, at least half of those things are the goal of every schemer I've ever met. You make your living with lies and deception. Why should I believe you?"

"Maybe you shouldn't. Your friends don't. Perhaps this is all one big plot to ensnare you. But let me give you something else to think about. What would anyone gain entrapping a fallen, presumed dead, leader? Especially one focused on a suicidal mission more likely to fail than to succeed."

Before I could answer she stood and hurried away. True to her word, she left me something to think about. A short time later, my friends found me.

"Tindra left not long after you walked out," Crum said.

I nodded. "We talked."

"She told us she had to make travel arrangements. What did you talk about?" he asked.

"Her mission, my mission, and possible outcomes."

Crum raised his eyebrows.

"Maybe we should head back for breakfast," Grima said.

"Sounds good," I said, happy to focus on anything, but Tindra.

We walked quicker on the way back and soon the smell of food filled the air.

Einns greeted us at the door. "I set the outside table. Everything's ready to eat."

"We'll join you after putting our clothes away," Roi said.

He shook his head. "I ate before you got here."

Roi chuckled. "Why am I not surprised? Everyone hand me your clothes, I'll put them up and Grima can show you to the table."

"It's a wonderful morning to eat outside," Grima said.

We followed her to a stone table with benches down each side in a clearing surrounded by trees. Several trays of fresh bread, broiled meats, and stewed fruits sat in the middle of the table. Between the trays sat steaming pitchers of tea.

I took a spot on a bench and filled my plate. The first bite brought a smile to my face. Einns' cooking was amazing, with flavors and spices from both Croy and Varia.

"Are you sure he needs training, Grima?" I asked.

She smiled. "He learned enough at Geri's to figure out how to cook better once we got here. Still, he has much to gain from studying under master chefs. When it's his time, I want him to shine."

"If he was any better, I might never leave," I said, as Roi joined us.

"I'll make sure to tell him," he said, and sat.

Everyone ate their fill in relative silence. When we finished it seemed like we hadn't made a dent in the food.

"I can't eat another bite," Crum groaned.

"I think you speak for everyone," I said.

Mam burped and a blush spread across her face.

"Roi, are you riding with us?" I asked.

He looked at Grima. She blinked a couple of times before looking away. "I will if you insist, as I have sworn my life to you, but...my family needs a stable life."

"Say no more," I assured him. "I know the value of stability. Stay, love your wife, and raise her son. Still, I could call for you. If I do, it's because I have no other option."

"When the time comes, we'll be ready," Roi promised.

"All I can ask," I said. "Grima, thank you for your hospitality on such short notice."

"No thanks necessary. If not for you I would've never met Roi. I'd still be at The Trader's Cup."

"Want to take food for the trip?" Roi asked.

"If you don't mind," I said.

He groaned as he stood. "Crum, come with me. We'll get the saddlebags and find a way to pack some food."

Mam looked at me. "Are we waiting for Tindra?"

I shook my head. "She left without making plans to meet. It's on her to find me. After all, she said she didn't want me out of her sight."

She nodded.

"Grima, if Tindra comes by can you tell her we've left for the capital?" I asked.

"I head to work soon, but I'll tell Roi to give her the message. Do you think it's wise to let her sneak up on you?"

"From what she said earlier, I don't think I have anything to fear from her. Whoever she's working for could be another matter."

"Crum told me he doesn't believe anything she says," Mam said.

I nodded. "Mam, let's get the horses. Grima, do you know the best way to the capital?"

"Roi took us once. Keep this mountain range to your left, turn north through the first pass and keep the mountains on your right. You can't miss the capital."

"Anything we need to watch out for along the way?" I asked.

"Roi would know better, but the usual, big cats and bears."

"We've dealt with much worse. Simple predators would be a relief," I said, grinning.

We met at the front door and hurried to get everything secured. "Roi, anything to worry about on the trip? Other than predators, I mean," I said.

"No organized bandits in the area from what I know."

I hugged him. "It'd be nice to have you with us, but I understand why you're staying."

"No one's forcing you to do this," he said. "You could stay, make a home."

"If someone doesn't stop Eirickson, Varia may not be safe much longer. He'll use Satra to invade this country and maneuver to rule over everyone."

"Do what you must. Travel safe my friend," he said, before releasing me and turning to Crum. "I'd tell you to stay out of trouble, but I don't believe you can. Can I ask you to keep Fitzeirick safe and take good care of Mam?"

"With pleasure."

Roi wrapped his arms around Mam and picked her up in a hug. She squealed like a surprised child. "It's nice to meet you. May your journey be swift and safe," he said.

"Thank you for having us. I hope I see you again," she said.

Grima looked at me with tears in her eyes and walked into the house.

"She's never been able to say goodbye well," he said.

"Tell her I said I'm happy for her, and you," I said, after pulling myself onto Andale.

I told Crum the directions Grima gave me as we rode away.

Chapter 28

"Fitzeirick, did she say how far to the pass?" Crum asked.

"No."

"And you didn't think to ask her?"

"No," I said.

He turned to Mam. "You see, this is why I don't leave him alone too long. How are we going to figure out when to make camp if we don't know how long we ride to get to the pass?"

She giggled. "We'll stop when the time is right."

"Listen to her, Crum," I said. "There's much wisdom in the concept of 'live now and worry about later when it happens'."

"I think you two spent too much time together," he replied, before pushing his horse to pick up its pace.

Mam let out a whoop and took off at a gallop.

I shook my head and kept a comfortable pace. Soon enough, they quit playing. I caught them and noticed two things.

I saw a slit of light with my right eye. Maybe *the oil* is *helping*.

More concerning, we were slowly gaining on a wagon.

I decided to put on my hammer, in case.

Crum noticed what I was doing. "What has you so worried?"

I nodded toward the wagon. "Seems like a good idea to be careful."

"Want me to ride ahead and see if they're friendly?"

"No, we'll catch them in due time. Keep an eye out and make sure we know where Mam is," I said.

"Of course," Crum said. "Mam, keep close to me please. We don't know who's in the wagon."

She moved beside him. "But Grima said all we had to worry about were big cats and bears."

"Sometimes people are more dangerous than either of those. Remember the others in the tunnels?" I asked.

She shivered.

"Do you think it's impolite for me to put my bow together?" Crum asked.

"Maybe," I said. "A hammer hanging at my side is less threatening than a bow at the ready."

The wagon turned and stopped. Two dark horses pulled it, and dark fabric or leather covered the back. The driver got down and stood next to the front wheel. I didn't see anyone else moving about.

I pulled Andale's reins. "What do you think?"

"Maybe the wagon's having trouble," Mam said.

"If so, I'd expect a signal of some kind," I said.

"It's a strange trap," Crum said.

"I'm open to suggestions."

He looked from the wagon to me and back to the wagon. "I see two options and only one makes any sense. Let me get my bow ready. You ride toward the wagon. I'll be within range before you get close enough for a trap. If you turn away, I'll shoot whoever gives chase. If you get off your horse, everything's safe and we join you."

"If that one makes sense, what else did you have in mind?" I asked.

"We keep going like we didn't even notice them."

"I'll take the first option," I said.

"Ride ahead when ready."

"Keep Mam safe. If I go down, you two run. Full speed back to Swinter, to Roi."

"I won't leave you," Crum said.

"If I'm captured or killed, Roi needs to know."

"I see your point," he said, putting his bow together.

I pushed my heels into Andale, hoping some speed would make it harder for someone to target me. As I got closer, details became clearer.

The driver had short black hair. They wore the same outfit I saw Tindra in earlier, a light-colored shirt and dark pants with short boots. *Not a typical Varian outfit.* I made it almost to the point I'd have to decide to keep going or turn from an ambush when I recognized her.

Tindra waved.

I pushed Andale into a gallop and stopped when I got close.

"Wondered if you planned to catch up with me."

I dismounted. "Are you alone?"

"Yes"

"Is the wagon broken?"

"No. Why do you ask?"

"When the wagon turned sideways Mam thought maybe someone was having trouble."

"I decided it'd be easier to keep an eye on you while you caught up. Let me guess, Crum has you covered with his bow."

I nodded.

She laughed. "I'll give you credit, you don't go charging into a situation, do you?"

I touched my scar. "Not anymore."

"I see they're headed this way. You dismounting...the safe signal?"

I nodded. "Why a wagon?"

"I prefer to travel in comfort," she said, with a smile.

"Well stocked I suppose."

"Enough food and water to make the journey plus a day."

"We have plenty of food, too. If you'd have come by Roi's house you could've eaten with us," I said.

"I know when it's time to leave."

"You were welcome to eat with us," I said.

"Welcome...maybe, but I wasn't wanted," she said, with a smile.

"Where'd you steal this from?" Crum asked, when they reached us.

She laughed. "Working for those with power has benefits."

"It does? I was only friends with someone in power, never made my life much easier," he said.

"So, you say," I replied.

He chuckled.

"What's the plan?" I asked

"Depends. Can any of you drive a team?"

"It's been a while, but I could manage," Crum said.

"Never have," I said.

"I've ridden in a wagon," Mam added.

Tindra nodded to her. "So, two of us. Who wants to ride in the wagon?"

"We planned on riding until dusk, making camp before it got too dark," I said.

"Like I said, I like to travel in comfort. There's plenty of room. We can keep going well past moonrise with the lanterns."

"Hate to say it, but she has a good point," Crum said.

"I'd like to ride in a wagon again," Mam said.

Tindra smiled and tapped me on the shoulder. "Is she always —"

"Yes," I answered, cutting her off.

"You didn't let me finish."

"Doesn't matter. The answer to 'Is Mam always' is yes. I find it endearing," I said.

She shook her head. "Tie your horses to the back of the wagon. Crum and Mam, ride in back. Fitzeirick, I'd like you to ride on the bench with me."

"Did someone put you in charge without telling me?" I asked.

"My wagon, my rules."

"She's right," Mam said, dismounting and securing her horse. When she climbed into the back of the wagon, she squealed. "We get to ride on straw."

Tindra looked at me.

I shook my head while struggling to choke down a laugh.

Crum chuckled at Mam's glee. "I do have one thing to say before I climb aboard. You can't push your team much past nightfall, and our horses have never pulled a wagon. We *will* have to stop."

"I know what I'm doing."

He nodded to her, put away his bow, and climbed into the wagon after securing Sinar. I heard him say, "Yes, dear little Mam, I'd love to watch you weave."

Tindra looked at me again.

I smiled. "She is always."

She climbed into the seat. "We need to get going."

I tied Andale to the back of the wagon, hurried to the front, and climbed on.

"You don't smell of peppers. Have you applied oil to your face today?"

"Not yet. I'll to do it when we stop to eat. The swelling's gone down some. I can see some light."

"Good. I hope to have the swelling gone before you stand before the crown. It will be some time before the bruising goes away, but the visible damage supports your argument that killing Olver was self-defense."

"It *was* self-defense."

"I'm aware, but sometimes the crown decides to set an example," she said. "King Ander may not take pity on a tavern brawler plying his trade in Stone Roof."

"I'm not a —"

"Save your argument to convince the king and queen."

"Should be easy enough."

"You'd better hope so," she said.

I soon tired of the subject at hand and decided to look for more interesting information. "You never said how your employer knew I'd traveled to Swinter."

"Your friend isn't as discreet as he believes."

I squinted at her. "Someone in Crum's circle of support is providing information on him?"

She smiled. "I'm part of the same circle."

My eyebrows shot up. "Are you telling me —"

"Where do you think the funds came from for the free food, transportation, and rooms?" she asked.

"Not everything was free. Some of the aid came with a promise of repayment when I'm done."

She shrugged. "They receive compensation for their service. No one frowns on them asking for extra from those they help. Some ask, some don't."

"Crum wouldn't keep something like that from me."

"Can't tell you what he doesn't know."

"He's many things," I said, "but stupid isn't one of them. How'd he do all this work for the Varian crown without knowing it? I have no reason to believe you."

"You may not yet trust me, but why would I lie?"

"Like I said, he's not stupid."

"We can debate his merits later," she said, grinning. "Think. Beyond faith in your friend, what makes you think I'm misleading you?"

"It doesn't make sense. Why put together this conspiracy to gamble on the offhand chance some Croian decides to attempt a coup? Varia has soldiers and resources, why not attack? Direct action has a better chance of succeeding."

She shook her head. "War is messy. The Varian crown lost its appetite for messy some time ago. We have Eirick to thank for that, I suppose. Now, the power plays take place in shadows. Money and power flow from the court into the countryside. Small groups are organized to help each other. They don't know what they're helping with or why. If one is compromised, the others don't fall.

"Crum attracted the attention of our operation based in Nikulas' holdings. We once sought to use the skald to undermine Eirickson, but he didn't want to play. He's happy with the power he has now. Your sole focus is the downfall of our — now mutual — enemy. Your need for vengeance piqued interests."

"But everyone thought I was dead. You said so yourself," I said.

"Word you might be among the living came a few days after Nikulas secreted you out of his hall."

"If this group knows about me, Eirickson does too. Doesn't that diminish my value?"

"So far we have no reason to think he knows you escaped," she said. "We have a vested interest in keeping you secret."

"Why not get me to your king as soon as possible?"

"Some questioned your value after you killed our man at The Trader's Cup."

"Slode was part of this?" I asked.

"A bit too traditional for his own good, it would seem, but yes."

"Is Geri involved?"

"He isn't, as far as I know," she said.

"But he's the one who told me where I might find Crum."

She nodded. "Your friend used his services. We kept track of him through Slode."

"What about the guard who helped me reconnect with Crum?"

"Most of the skald's staff and guard are Varian agents."

That can't be right. She's just trying to confuse me...make me doubt my friends. "I won't listen to lies," I said, crossing my arms.

She chuckled. "Believe what you want. I told you he had our interest at one time. Surrounding him with our people was the best way to keep him safe."

"Nikulas told me he had contacts in Varia, knew people who could get me to safety," I said, recalling the conversation.

"If he only knew the truth," Tindra said, smiling.

"If you're telling the truth, then how many Varian agents were in my hall?"

"None, as far as I know. Sympathizers lived in your territory, and provided general information, but none of them joined your court. I suspect your mother kept them out. We contacted her shortly after you received your title. She wanted nothing to do with us. She chose Eirick and Croy."

Mother would've protected me. I tapped my finger on my chin a couple of times, then pointed at Tindra. "Can you tell me if Aesa's alive?"

She frowned. "Wish I could, but we lost our contacts when your territory fell. I can't help but think about what your fiancée would endure if taken alive. The Satran value themselves over all others, everyone else exists to cater to them. The prosperity of Satra is their only concern. To say they torture their captives changes the meaning of the word. I've never heard a word to describe what their victims suffer — especially women."

I shivered and took a moment to consider what she said. "But Crum saw Satran representatives meeting with Eirickson, discussing how to divide Varia."

"Eirickson is a fool," she scoffed. "In the end, no one benefits from a deal with Satra. They'll rip Croy apart for their own entertainment. Trust me or not, it doesn't matter. Marry me or not, it doesn't matter. Promise me you will kill your half-brother and lead your country against the Satran. So long as you work toward that goal, no money or power will set me against you."

The conviction in her voice almost convinced me she was telling the truth. "I've already promised myself."

We sat in silence for a long time. To be honest, what she said scared me. After listening to her rant about Satra, I almost hoped Aesa was dead. Nevertheless, I had to consider her intentions. Crum's warning came to mind again. *Had I let her get too close?*

Almost as if he knew I'd thought about him, Crum yelled, "When are we going to eat lunch?"

I looked at her. "Your wagon, your rules."

"Are we eating your food or mine?"

"I don't know what you brought, but ours isn't preserved. It'd be best if we eat it before it spoils."

She nodded and yelled, "Whoa!" As soon as the wagon stopped, she jumped down and unhooked her horses so they could graze.

Crum walked into view shaking his head.

"What's wrong?" I asked.

"Nothing. Mam spent the entire time making things from straw and taking them apart again. She isn't even tired; I can't believe it."

I smiled. "Probably best that she kept busy. Would you mind getting the food?"

He nodded and turned to get the food stored in our bags as Mam came around the wagon. She held a straw bracelet in her hand.

"For me?" I asked.

She shook her head. "I made it for Tindra. Do you think she'll like it?"

"Ask her yourself."

"Ask who what?" Tindra asked, walking past me.

Mam held out the bracelet. "I made this for you."

She looked from the bracelet to Mam and froze with her mouth open.

I nudged her.

"It's — I..." she stammered. "I don't know what to say."

"I believe something like, 'thank you,' is appropriate," I muttered.

"Thank you, Mam. I wasn't expecting this at all. Young Varian girls make these to pass time, but I see you put a lot of thought into this. I imagine this took some effort."

"I ask the straw how it wants to go together and help it," she said. "Some of the straw doesn't want to cooperate, those pieces get set aside."

"Her method is foreign to me, but I can't argue with the results," Crum said, as he got close.

"It sounds like early lessons taught to children. That's how I learned the beginning lessons for firesyths. Use the natural tendencies of fire and heat to make it easier to manipulate. Only later, do the stronger and more talented learn to bend it to their will," Tindra said.

"I've felt her energy. She's strong, but lacks practice," Crum said. "Why would she stick to only the early lessons?"

"Maybe, I never learned anything else," she said.

"Follows with her other youthful and outdated ways," Tindra replied.

"And there's nothing wrong with that," I said.

"Glad we've settled that," Crum said. "Let's eat."

I shook my head. "Never one to miss a meal."

"No sense in letting this wonderful food go to waste," he replied.

"We have no plates," Mam said.

"They're stored under the seat," Tindra said. "Fitzeirick, get them and a couple of waterskins."

"Be glad to, since you asked so nicely," I said.

I lifted the seat and found plates and eating utensils, several full waterskins, and bundles of cloth, Tindra's sword sat on top. Grabbing the items we needed, I returned to find everyone sitting in the wagon's shadow.

"I see you came prepared," I said.

"Told you, I like to travel in comfort."

We ate quickly and without conversation.

As Crum and I cleaned the plates, Tindra asked, "Mam, would you like to ride with me for a while?"

Mam looked at me and I shrugged. She turned to Tindra. "Why?"

"You made this wonderful bracelet for me. I thought you might like to take in the scenery as we go."

"Go ahead," Crum said. "Enjoy the trip."

"You won't miss me?" she asked him.

"The entire time, but Fitzeirick will keep me company," he said, grinning at me.

"Yes, I will."

"Settled," Tindra said. "We need to get moving. Load up while I harness the horses."

As I gathered the plates, Tindra grabbed my arm, "Wait."

Everyone stopped and looked at her.

"Fitzeirick, you aren't going to avoid this any longer. Put those away and get the pepper oil. We have to treat your face."

Having forgotten the need for that torture, I dragged my feet walking to Andale and grabbed the pot of oil.

"Why are you acting like a child?" she asked, taking the pot from me.

"I don't like this. It's not at all pleasant. As a matter of fact, it's painful."

"Only until the numbness sets in," she said, chuckling, before rubbing a generous amount of the pepper oil on the swollen part of my face, avoiding the area around my eye.

"Why not get it closer to my eye?" I asked. "I'd think it would help it open sooner."

"If the oil gets in your eye, it will burn long into the night," she said.

"Sounds like personal experience," Crum commented.

"Are you sure you're not a spion?" she asked. He laughed and shook his head as she handed me the pot. "Pack this away and we'll go as soon as you get into the wagon."

I noticed the lurching of the wagon was much worse seated on straw.

Crum laughed as we bounced around. I think he made himself a cushion in secret.

"Wonder what she's going to talk to Mam about?" I mused.

"Between humming those strange tunes and weaving, she hardly said a word to me. If I'd done so much work, I'd sleep for a week."

I nodded. "She gets nervous and doesn't know how to act when she's alone with you." The look on his face told me he didn't believe me. "What do you mean?"

"You're everything she isn't; confident, outgoing, and you crave attention. She has feelings for you, but doesn't understand them and has no idea how you feel. She's scared to get too close to you and scared to let you go."

"I only want what's best for her," he said.

"I know and I think it's her opinion you're what's best for her. She cares about me, but she cares for you."

"Are you saying she loves me?" he asked.

"I'm not so sure she'd call it love, but I'd say she's in love with you," I said. "I've asked you before, but how do you feel about her?"

"Assuming I remember what love is, I can say I love her. I don't know if I'm able to be the person she needs or the man she deserves, though" he said, frowning.

I patted his knee. "I have a feeling her life will be in turmoil not long after we get to the capital. If she is Jesca, we'll know shortly after the queen sees her. A mother *will* recognize her daughter. That's a fact."

Crum nodded, his expression thoughtful.

"You can be the man she needs if you make the effort to be her rock. Support her as much as you can. The things you'd do for me when I'm in trouble...do for her and you two will be fine."

"How do I stay near her if she *is* their daughter?"

"Talk to her now. Let her know you want to be by her side, to help any way you can. Make sure she knows she can depend on you. You know how to maneuver through the chaos of a royal court. Use your experience."

"And should it work...what then?"

"Who knows? Given some time there could be a wedding. Maybe you two can do right all the things your parents did wrong," I said, before clapping my hand on his shoulder.

"Don't mention my parents," he said, scowling.

"Sorry," I said, drawing my hand back.

"Apology accepted."

Desperate to change the subject I blurted out, "She's scared."

"Mam? Yes, I know. You told me already," he said, an odd look on his face.

"I meant Tindra. Tindra's scared."

"Scared of what, exactly?"

"Satra."

"A good thing to fear."

"And they may have Aesa," I muttered.

"Can't blame you for worrying about her, but don't let it distract you."

"Should the fate of my country be more important than my fiancée, my future?" I asked.

"You answered that question when you decided to plead your case to the Council of Thanes."

I stared at my friend for, what felt like, a long time. "You think I can kill Eirickson and lead Croy?"

"If I didn't believe in you, I wouldn't have looked for you when you disappeared. I wouldn't have traveled this far, especially with company like Tindra."

"If you believe in me, there's no way I can doubt myself," I said, smiling.

"You're the man your country needs, the man your *people* need. I'm not saying it'll be easy, but the outcome is certain...you will win."

I smiled. "Save the speeches for later. I'll need one to rally whatever troops I find. You've given me a lot to think about and my full stomach's telling me to nap."

"Sounds like a great way to pass the time. See, you're making important decisions already," he said, chuckling.

I tried to glare at him, but couldn't. "My next decision may be to push you out of the wagon, if you keep it up."

He yawned and shook his head. "You wouldn't hurt Mam's feelings like that." A smile spread across his face as he closed his eyes.

I waited until he started snoring before allowing myself to fall asleep.

Chapter 29

The wagon wasn't moving when I woke. Sunlight came from behind us. The slit of light I could see with my right eye grew larger.

I shook Crum. "We're stopped."

He snorted a few times, mumbled something, and opened his eyes. "We're stopped."

I nodded. "Nice of you to notice. Take a moment to wake up and I'll see what's happening."

"Sounds like a sensible plan."

Our horses didn't seem restless, but I crept out of the wagon, sending my talent out once my feet hit the ground.

The wagon wheels made a large area of pressure, impossible to miss. The horses were easy to find, and I felt two people standing next to the horse team, but couldn't detect anything else.

"Something wrong?" I called, when I saw Tindra.

"No," she said. "We decided to let the team rest and eat dinner now. The horses can keep pulling long enough to get through the pass before we stop for the night."

"Still planning to travel after nightfall?" I asked.

She nodded. "Only until we make it out of the pass. We'll stop when you find a place to secure the horses."

"Are you sure the lanterns will light our way well enough?"

"I have enough faith in them to risk my own life," she said.

"Good enough for me," Crum said.

I nodded. "What's the plan for eating?"

"Finish off all the cooked food and leave the containers here," she said.

"Makes sense," I agreed. "Did you turn the wagon to shade us?"

"Yes, we did," Mam said, sounding proud.

"Clever girl, this one," Crum said, pointing at Tindra. "I'm almost thinking about letting myself consider the possibility of starting to like her."

I noticed the quip confused Mam.

Leaning toward her, I whispered, "Don't try to figure it out...trust me."

She looked at me and smiled. "Can I get the plates?"

I nodded. "Bring water, too."

Tindra ate with urgency and everyone followed her lead.

"It seems such a waste to leave this behind," I said, as we finished.

"Sometimes one must make sacrifices," Crum said.

"Wise words," Tindra agreed, smiling. "You should listen to him, this time."

"I sense a real friendship developing between you two," I said.

"Never," they replied in unison.

Mam laughed and I shook my head.

Tindra stood. "I'll harness the team. Clean the dishes and secure your horses so we can get moving."

Mam ran to gather our horses while Crum and I cleaned. The three of us working together finished at the same time Tindra had her team ready.

"I think it best if Mam and I drive until dark, and you two get us through the pass."

I nodded and looked at Crum. "Get your bow ready; stow it and your arrows in the bench."

"I like the way you think," he said, before running back to his saddlebag.

I climbed into the back of the wagon and found a comfortable position as Crum jumped in.

The wagon lurched forward immediately.

"Tindra said she'd get the wagon moving before I got in. She was almost right," he said, before laughing.

"What is it between you two?"

"Professional discourtesy," he said, smiling.

"What do you mean?"

"She's a deceiver and a manipulator. I don't like people who do that."

I shook my head and chuckled. "But aren't you a manipulator?"

"Do I embellish stories to make them, and myself, more interesting? Of course. But I'm not deceptive simply to twist a person to my purpose. I'm a storyteller, but I'd never lie to get someone to do what I wanted."

He pointed toward the front of the wagon and continued. "Tindra will tell you what she thinks you want to hear and use you to her advantage. I entertain. I appreciate whatever I gain from my stories, but I don't demand anything."

"Still doesn't explain 'professional discourtesy'."

"She sees me as a competitor and treats me as such. I'd never lower myself to her level. The thought of using seduction, lies, torture, or whatever makes me ill. Still, she acts like I'm working against her, so I respond in kind." He smiled. "One might consider it a sign of respect...if I could respect someone like her."

I pursed my lips. "Are you saying she never tells the truth?"

He shrugged. "I'm sure she does when it suits her purpose. I also have no doubt she'll threaten, beat, and torture someone to get what she wants."

"I understand what you're saying. Still, considering what I have to do, violence is sometimes a necessity."

"Of course, but I never want to live where it's the preferred option."

"I see your point."

"Also, you're her assignment," he said.

"I won't forget. She's made it clear the Varian court wants someone other than Eirickson ruling Croy."

"What do you want?" he asked.

"I want him dead. As far as being ruler, it seems Nikulas has no interest in anything beyond his skati, so I'm their next choice."

He raised an eyebrow. "Have you asked him?"

"The last time we spoke it wasn't part of the conversation. I was looking for you."

"What makes you think he wouldn't want to lead Croy?" he asked.

"Tindra said he's content with what he has."

"And you took her at her word?"

I shrugged. "No, but I've never known him to be aggressive. Also, she claimed to have inside knowledge of his situation."

Crum nodded. "It's not secret he has strong ties with Varia. Odds are they'd back him against Eirickson."

I put my hand on his shoulder. "If you believe her," I tightened my grip, "he's surrounded by Varian agents and doesn't know it."

"What do you think she meant?" he asked, eyes opening wide.

"Most of his guards and confidants are either Varian or sympathizers."

His face lost some color. "Even the ones —"

I nodded and took my hand away. "Even the ones you worked with looking for me."

He sucked in a deep breath. "Too many people know you're alive."

I shrugged. "If Varia wants me as an ally, they'll keep me safe."

"So, you aren't at risk as far as we know," he muttered.

"I have a feeling we'll be fine."

I could tell by his expression that he was in deep thought and decided to let him work things out on his own. Nothing else Tindra and I spoke about was his concern anyway. Everything was quiet for a while until he blurted out, "This is my fault!"

"Only if you believe Tindra," I said, smiling.

"Maybe she fed you information to make you doubt me."

I nodded. "Except, she was elaborating on things Nikulas told me."

"So, it *is* my fault. Because of me, Varia sent a spion after you." He put his face in his hands.

I patted his back. "It's not so bad. I'd end up in Varia anyway. Where else would I go? I couldn't stay in Croy and Satra isn't an option."

The wagon stopped. Crum and I looked at each other before looking out the back of the wagon.

It would be dark soon.

He made it out ahead of me. Mam wasn't there when I reached the front.

"She went around the other side. I expect she's about to climb in now," Tindra explained, before I could ask.

"Are you going to leave us something to light the lanterns?" I asked.

"Get them for me and I'll light them now."

"Crum, get the other one," I said, grabbing the lantern hanging near me.

"I need a piece of straw."

He handed her the lantern and jogged to the back of the wagon, returning with a handful of straw.

"Can you put some together into a thick piece?" she asked.

He nodded, forced three pieces together, and handed it to her.

"Still warm," she said, with a grin. "Thanks for the help." Closing her eyes, she rubbed her fingers over the end of the thick straw. Tiny wisps of smoke drifted upward; she opened her eyes, and the tip burst into flame. She lit the lanterns and stared at the burning straw for a moment. It flared before going out, not even giving off any smoke.

"Pay attention, and go slow when it gets dark. If the first stand of trees after we exit looks safe, stop there. If not, keep going until you find someplace to secure the horses," she said, and hurried to the back of the wagon.

After the lanterns were in place, Crum snapped the reins to get the team moving.

"Best if we keep quiet and stay focused on what we can hear," I said.

"Sounds like an excellent strategy," he said, nodding.

As twilight took over, the sounds coming from the movement of the wagon grew louder. Once the light surrendered to full darkness, I wanted to shout at the wagon to be quiet. I think Crum would have questioned my sanity — and I wouldn't have blamed him.

If it had been a cloudy evening, we would have passed the break in the mountains where we needed to turn. Who knows how long we would have wandered around in the dark looking for the pass. I noticed it as the sudden appearance of more stars to the left and pointed them out to Crum.

He turned the team and slowed as we entered the pass.

The horses seemed reluctant to walk into the passage. Shortly after we entered, the noises from the wagon echoed from all directions. It created a perfect cover for anything or anyone stalking us as we continued into the darkness. I considered extinguishing the lanterns because they made us an easy target, but the small pool of light was necessary.

"It's too loud in here," I whispered.

He nodded.

"Good, glad to know I'm not the only one worried. Can you get the horses to walk faster?" I asked.

"I think they're afraid of walking past the edge of the light."

I peered into the darkness ahead of us. "I'll be happy when we're out of here."

"Makes two of us."

We settled back into silence and time slowed to a crawl. Snapping the reins resulted in unneeded noise as the horses kept to their plodding pace.

Just when I was starting to think we might still be in the pass at daybreak, we entered an open prairie, and I choked back a cheer. "Grima said to turn north after the pass."

He turned the wagon and snapped the reins.

"I'll watch for trees," I whispered.

He nodded.

We both spotted treetops in the distance and he steered the wagon toward them. He stopped when we got close and handed me the reins. "Hold them here. I'll look for a way in."

After placing his hands on several trees, he returned. "The trees are too dense."

I frowned. "Not what I wanted to hear."

"Think you can make a pen for the horses?"

"Let me see what I have to work with," I said, handing the reins back.

I checked the area as soon as my feet touched the ground. "The dirt's shallow. I should be able to raise a rock wall to keep the horses safe. We can sleep in the wagon. What do you think?"

"If that's what it takes for us to stop for the night, I'm all for it," he said. "What do you need me to do?"

"Have some food and water ready. I'll need it."

I walked several paces before finding a suitable spot. Dragging my foot in the dirt to mark the edge of the pen gave me something to focus on. I knelt, placed my hands on the line, closed my eyes, and breathed deep.

Clearing my mind of distractions, I focused on the idea of a wall. After taking a moment to prepare, I pushed energy into the rock below. At first, the old stone resisted my effort. I drew another breath and pushed more of my will into the ground. Beads of sweat formed on my forehead before the rock moved.

A smile spread across my face as the stone breached the surface and continued upward. I made sure to keep my hands touching the rock until the circular wall stood slightly over my head. We had someplace to keep the horses safe.

I breathed heavily and wobbled, light headed from exerting myself.

Crum brought me a waterskin. "Looks good, but I have a question."

I took a long drink. "What?"

"How are we going to put the horses in there?"

I forgot the opening for the horses. I dropped the skin. "Give me a bite to eat and a little time to recover."

He tossed me a small bag. "I'll get the horses."

Taking a few strips of dried meat from the bag, I chewed until it was moist enough to swallow. Feeling better, I placed my hand on the still warm wall and forced an opening large enough for Andale.

Crum arrived with Tindra's team. "It's amazing to see you work so much stone."

"And I'm not as powerful as Roi," I said, before taking another mouthful of food.

He led the two horses into the pen and stepped back out. "Keep them in there while I get ours."

I picked up the waterskin and quenched my thirst. Once our horses walked in, I moved the rubble back in place to seal the animals inside.

Yawning, I handed the waterskin and bag of dried meat back to Crum. "I need sleep."

"Get in the wagon. I'll put this away and then join you."

I pulled strength from the ground to carry myself the short distance and climb into the wagon. Falling into the straw, I bumped into someone.

"Wha —" Mam mumbled.

"Shh. It's me, Fitz. Go back to sleep."

I noticed Crum climbing in soon after.

"Did you put out the lanterns?" I asked, half awake.

He groaned. "No. I'll be right back."

I fell asleep before he returned.

Chapter 30

CRACK!

"Fitzeirick! We need you out here!" Crum shouted.

My left eye opened wide, but my right struggled to open halfway. Aches and pains flowed through my body. *Where am I?*

Someone was snuggled next to me in the back of the wagon. I looked closer, having trouble seeing in the dim light. Tindra pressed herself against me.

CRACK!

"What's that?" she mumbled.

"Don't know, but I have a feeling Crum does." I groaned, making my way out of the wagon.

CRACK!

The sound came from the horse pen. "One of the horses wants out," Crum explained.

Mam stood near him, cringing. "Why is it making —"

CRACK!

"that sound?"

"One of them is kicking the wall," I said, hurrying to the pen, Crum and Mam not far behind.

CRACK!

Placing my hands on the wall, I willed an opening as hooves struck again. With my talent intertwined in the stone, the impact felt like a kick to my chest, knocking the breath out of me. "Get them..." I wheezed, "...out."

Crum rushed into the pen as I stumbled out of the way and lay on the ground.

Andale charged out alone.

Tindra got out of the wagon as he ran past.

"Whoa!" she yelled. The big horse slowed. She secured him to the wagon and then jogged to me.

"Andale was in a hurry," Mam said, leading Sinar and Aspeit. "Crum said he was trying to kick your wall down."

Crum followed her with Tindra's horses. "Shoe marks were too high to be any of the others."

"Are you going to live?" Tindra asked.

"Give me a moment to catch my breath. I'll make it."

"Need help getting to the fire?" she asked.

"Now that I feel like I can breathe again, I'll walk to the capital if need be."

She stayed close as I shuffled toward the fire.

"What's the plan for breakfast?" I asked, sitting.

"I think we need a pot," Mam said. "I didn't find one in the bench."

"If only we traveled in comfort," I said, loud enough for Tindra to hear.

"I hadn't planned to take time to cook," she replied.

"What do you have in mind, Mam?" I asked.

"Crum and I decided it would be tasty if we boiled some of the dried meat with a few of the peppers you had," she said.

"Tindra, get the peppers from my saddle bag. I'll make a pot."

"You can syth metal?" she asked.

I shook my head, made my way to the messy hole in the stone wall, gathered a few rocks, and carried them to the fire.

Tindra was already back, the bag of peppers in one hand and the pot of oil in the other. "A stone pot?"

"You've never seen one?" Crum asked.

"I also brought extra rocks to make bowls for each of us," I said. "Mam, will you get spoons?"

She ran to the wagon.

I steadied my breathing and focused on the stone in my hand. It was big enough to make a pot twice the size we needed. I worked the bottom until it was flat and smooth before turning it over and directing my attention to hollowing it. My finger traced a circle before pulling out handfuls of softened rock and dropping it next to me. They hardened on their way to the ground. Fatigue from making the pen the night before slowed my progress, but I managed to make a workable pot.

"Here." I held it toward Crum. "Once you fill it, I need some water and something to eat."

"As I expected." He placed the pot in the middle of the fire. "Mam, give him the other waterskin and a couple of hard rolls."

I broke a piece off a roll, put it in my mouth, and took a long drink from the skin. Once the bread softened, I chewed and swallowed everything. After eating the first roll, I made four bowls.

Once those were ready, I ate the second roll. "Make sure there's enough for at least two bowls for me. I'm going to lay back and rest."

"Do you want your face to burn before breakfast or after?" Tindra asked.

"Go ahead and get it over with," I said, with a sigh. "I don't like it, but it *is* helping."

She dribbled a little oil on my forehead and then rubbed it into my face. It felt nice, relaxing even, to have someone taking care of me. Still, I had to remember the person involved had questionable motives. I hissed as the burn started.

"Tindra, do you like doing that?" Mam asked.

"Treating his injury?"

"No, touching him. It seems...I'm not sure I know the word."

"Intimate," Tindra supplied. "Most likely the word you're looking for is intimate."

"I don't know what that means," Mam said.

"A deep personal or private connection," Crum said.

"That's one meaning," Tindra added.

"Yes," Mam said. "It seems intimate."

"Mam, what she's doing is necessary. For an intimate connection, I would have to be glad she was touching me," I stated flatly.

"It's not that simple," Tindra scoffed, pouring more oil on my cheek. "I don't mind intimate contact. Especially with someone I find attractive. I've had worse assignments."

"It's not worth arguing...just hurry up," I said.

"But doesn't the oil burn? How can you like hurting him?" Mam asked.

"It doesn't burn like fire, more like spices in your mouth. What I'm doing is helping him heal faster," Tindra said. "Generally, I take no pleasure in hurting people, unless it's necessary. When I do have to cause pain, I try to enjoy myself."

"Oh," Mam said.

Crum crossed his arms and stared at Tindra. "Can we not talk about what you enjoy?" he asked, through clenched teeth.

"She has to learn about the world she's missed, sooner or later," Tindra said. "Why so apprehensive, smooth talker? Afraid she'll find out you enjoy the darker side of life from time to time?"

"Drop the subject," he growled.

"It seems I've touched —" Tindra started.

That's about enough. I grabbed her wrist. "He asked nicely. How about you respect his request?"

"Seems we're all a little touchy this morning," she said, as I released her arm.

I figured she was smiling by the sound of her voice.

"I think we — meaning Mam, Crum, and I — are all concerned about what awaits us in the capital," I said, sitting up.

"No one forced you to leave Swinter. I didn't *make* you travel with me," Tindra countered.

"You came to see if I was in Swinter and, if so, bring me to the Varian royal court, correct?"

She nodded. "From a certain perspective."

"What do you mean?" Crum asked.

"Fitzeirick was my target. Delivering him immediately wasn't necessary for a successful mission."

"You're not making any sense," I said.

"Observe, gather information, get to know you, and start a relationship...that's my mission. At some point, I would arrange a meeting."

"Getting to know me, marrying me into becoming a Varian ally? That's a long game to play considering the slim chance of success," I noted. "Your people had to know plans for my wedding were underway when this all started."

"Marrying you?" Crum exclaimed. "You aren't very good at your job if you don't know how dedicated Fitzeirick is to Aesa."

Crossing my arms, I stared at her. "By now, you know he's right."

She frowned. "The marriage part wasn't necessary, or...even...in the original plan."

I scowled at her. "Explain yourself. And I expect specifics."

She looked at the ground. "Can you and I discuss this on the way to the capital? You know...alone?"

"Why the sudden fear of an uncomfortable conversation?" Crum asked. "You seemed all too happy to make Mam squirm."

"I'm looking —" she started.

"I don't care what you're looking for," I said. "As of now, you're no longer in control. I'm halfway tempted to find a way to force the truth out of you. Two things are stopping me. First, I have no doubt you know how to avoid simple interrogation and endure torture. More important, anything I might do to you would upset Mam. I won't do that to her."

She looked at me, defiance in her eyes. "Torture is a hollow threat from you anyway. You don't have it in you to —"

SMACK!

I think the sound of my hand hitting her face echoed.

Mam's gasp stopped me from slapping her again.

Tindra acted like she didn't feel a thing, but the fire flared.

My stomach burned and the ground quivered. "You don't know what I have in me. Whatever information you have on me, assume it's wrong. Here's what's going to happen. We're going to eat, then you *will* drive us to the capital. You and I will talk about whatever it is you need to discuss with me. If, at any point, I feel you're lying or manipulating me, we stop and I bury you to your waist. We, the three of us, will continue the journey while you dig yourself out. If you have a problem with any part of the plan, start walking now. Am I clear?"

She nodded once and turned away from me.

"Food's ready," Crum said. "I crumbled a few hard rolls into it to thicken it."

"How are we going to get it into the bowls?" Mam asked.

"I'll make a scoop," I said.

"Nonsense," Crum said. "You're tired, I'll make one."

"I'll make one from straw," Mam offered.

"Are you sure?" Crum asked.

"Yes. I need to practice."

She ran to the wagon and returned with a smile on her face and a large straw spoon in her hand.

"Can I see it?" Crum asked.

She nodded.

He looked it over before plunging it deep into the pot. "Who wants the first serving?"

I held my bowl out.

He smiled. "Of course, sir."

I cradled the bowl in my hands, inhaling the aroma rising from the crude meal, before taking a bite. The odd mix of bland meat, mushy crumbs, and spicy water was warm and filling, but not much else.

Crum made sure Tindra was served last.

As hungry as I was, Mam finished her bowl first. "Tasty."

"There's plenty more," Crum said.

"No, thank you," Mam said. "I'm full. Do you think I'll meet the queen?"

Before I could answer, Tindra cleared her throat. "I'd expect to, if I were you."

I looked at Crum.

He scowled at Tindra.

"Should I make her a gift?" Mam asked.

Before Tindra could say anything, Crum put his hand on Mam's knee. "I don't think it's necessary."

Tindra smiled. "Seems you like making gifts."

Crum's face turned red.

"I do," Mam replied.

"Go ahead. There's no harm in it," Tindra said.

He looked at me.

I read his expression and shook my head.

"Maybe a bracelet," Mam said, to no one in particular.

"I think that'd be fine," I said, before Tindra caused any more trouble. "Tindra, would you mind putting out the fire?"

"If you need me to."

"Thank you." Before the second word was out of my mouth, the fire was gone.

"Anyone want more stew?" I asked.

Crum patted his stomach. "Far as I'm concerned, it's all yours."

Mam giggled and copied him.

Tindra said, "I'd like a little more...if you don't mind."

"Glad to share. How much do you want?"

"I can serve myself," she said.

"Go ahead."

She added a couple of modest scoops to her bowl. "The rest is yours."

"Mam, we should make sure everything's ready to go." She nodded to Crum and they walked away as I emptied the pot into my bowl.

"Consider not being a thorn in Crum's side. You might regret it otherwise," I warned, before taking a bite.

"I can take care of myself," Tindra said. "Much better have tried to kill me, yet I'm still here."

"You're as much at fault as he is."

"It will always be that way between he and I. It goes beyond firesyth and woodsyth. We're too much alike in what we do. Professional discourtesy will always cause animosity between us."

I laughed. "He said the same thing."

"My point's made," she said, smiling.

"Maybe."

She finished her stew.

I wanted to get moving again, so I put the bowl to my lips and tilted it to gulp the rest down. "I meant what I said earlier. I will leave you in the ground."

"I have no doubt," she said.

We walked together to the wagon.

Crum had the team harnessed.

"Are we leaving everything here?" Mam asked.

"Do we need the bowls and pot?" I asked.

"If we don't get delayed, we'll make the capital by midday," Tindra said.

"Leave everything, but the skins and spoons."

Mam nodded, took the spoons and waterskins, and placed them in the bench.

I started to thank her, but she ran to the back of the wagon and jumped in before I could get the words out. I assumed Crum was already inside.

"Seems to be in a hurry," Tindra said.

"She's lived on the move a long time."

She nodded and snapped the reins.

The wagon jerked into motion.

I felt content to sit quietly and enjoy the sun, but wondered what Tindra had on her mind. She sighed several times before asking, "Are you ready to talk with me?"

"Of course."

"Where should I start?"

"Start where you feel most appropriate, keeping my expectations in mind."

She sat silent for a while, looking back and forth or nodding her head. "The plan. The plan was to bring you to a...council...of sorts. A group of individuals working toward a common goal."

"Which is?"

"I'm getting there. It centers on the territory you used to control. In the beginning, the council focused on advancing our ability to do battle, inventing ways to ensure victory over Croy. When you, a half-Varian, were given control of the region, their focus changed. They sought to gain control of the territory through subversion instead of an overt war."

"But my mother wouldn't cooperate," I said.

She nodded. "From what I know, she was loyal to Eirick, despite the venom his wife directed at her. No one foresaw the Satran invasion. After you disappeared, the group's focus shifted back to war. Then you showed back up. Now, they want to align you against Eirickson and the Thanes. The assumption is you want power again. Their plan: convince you an alliance with Varia is the only way to get your authority back."

"And the marriage?"

"All my idea." She hung her head.

"Are you ashamed?"

"Only of my motivation."

"You mean your motivation isn't to do your job?"

"I saw you fighting in Stone Roof and a single thought flashed across my mind: a way out. Marrying you would get me out. If I could bring you to power in Varia, as my husband, I'd no longer be a spion."

"I'm a career change?" I barked, through clenched teeth. "Not much of a professional if you're so easily distracted from your job."

She flinched. "Was I in love when I laid eyes on you? No, that would be absurd. Was there an attraction? Yes. The way you fought, the passion and the rage, but always thinking. I saw it in every move. I was told you were kind, gentle... that you had good leadership qualities but no heart for battle. I saw a man who wouldn't back down. You fought like you already knew you'd be the victor. I had to test you; hence the dance. Sure, I took you down, but you were already tired and hurt."

"Out of curiosity, are you in love now?" I asked. "Not that it matters, Aesa will always have my heart."

"If it doesn't matter, I won't bother answering," she said, shrugging. "What if I told you she's dead?"

"You already said you didn't know so, one way or another, you're lying."

"But if I told you she's alive..."

"Still a lie," I said, crossing my arms.

"She can't be both."

"I know, but sooner or later I'll find someone I can trust who can tell me where she is."

"Can't fault a man for loyalty," Tindra replied, frowning.

"Quit trying to distract me and get back to their plan. What about the war preparations?"

"I assume they're still underway, but I'm not privy to all the council's activities."

"Does this council operate under the blessing and approval of the Varian crown?"

She frowned. "It's possible my king knows the council exists, but doubtful he knows their plans."

"By going along with them, do I chance being branded a traitor in two nations?"

She shook her head. "The council doesn't work against King Ander, but he won't approve of every plan they have."

"Because?"

"Some on the council consider King Ander a pacifist," she said. "They believe he disapproves of improving our ability to wage war."

"What's this mean when we get to the capital? Where are we going first?"

She shrugged. "I haven't worked all those details out yet."

"What details do you have?"

She looked away from me. "None, really."

"How much longer until we reach the capital?"

"If we keep our current pace? Less than four hours."
I folded my arms across my chest. "Stop the wagon."

Chapter 31

Tindra looked at me, eyes wide and upper lip trembling. "You can't...are you going to...I can help you."

I think she knows she can't best me in a fair fight, but I'd better be ready. "Get down, walk five paces away, and wait for me."

"Are you going to leave me food and water?" she asked, sparks showing in her eyes.

Don't show weakness or give her an opening. I gave her my best evil smile. "Do as you're told, and I'll make sure you live."

She growled while climbing from the wagon, walked a little further than I expected, and flopped to the ground.

I hopped from the bench and hurried to the back of the wagon. "Crum, you aren't going to like it, but I need your help."

He stuck his head out of the opening. "What do you need?"

"Come with me."

He hopped out. "Where are we going?"

I pointed to where Tindra sat, hunched over. "There."

"What'd you do to her?"

I chuckled. "Nothing. She thinks I'm going to bury her and leave her here."

"And what are you going to do?"

"Maybe something worse," I said.

"What?"

"We need a plan. She knows details and I trust you. Put your skills together, figure out how we get into the capital while avoiding attention, and where we go from there."

"No reason to work with her; I'll get us in myself," he said.

"How?"

"Find a place to hole up until we figure out our next move."

"All the while we risk discovery and waste time? Not our best option." I pointed toward Tindra. "I want...no, I need you two to put aside your differences. Throw professional discourtesy to the fire."

Crum tensed. "And if I refuse?"

"I'll leave both of you here," I growled.

"In all seriousness...are you kidding?"

"Don't tempt me. I'm more serious about this than anything else ever in my life."

"Fine, I'll do it, but you'll owe me a huge favor," he said.

I put my hand on his shoulder. "Crum, work this out, see me through to Eirickson's death, and I'll pay any price."

He nodded and walked to Tindra.

I heard a noise and turned to see Mam clambering out of the wagon. "What's all the yelling about?" she asked.

"I need Crum and Tindra to work together. He didn't want to cooperate."

She nodded. "He doesn't like her. He told me she lies and to not trust her. Do you trust her?"

"Maybe. I hope I'll be able to answer better after we get to the capital."

"Would you like to see what I made for the queen?" she asked.

"Of course," I said, smiling.

"They're inside the wagon," she said, and climbed in.

"They?" I asked, following her.

"I made two, in case she lost the other one."

"The one you are going to give her?" I asked, confused.

"No, the one I made her."

"I don't understand. Are you talking about the bracelet you made on the way here?"

"No," she said, "that would be silly. How can she lose one I haven't given her yet? I mean the one I made when everyone called me Jesca."

"Do you remember, for certain, she's your mother? You remember making her a bracelet before you were in the tunnels?"

"I'm not sure I'd call it remembering, exactly. It's more like a strong feeling this is the right thing to do because I've done it before," she said. A tear welled in the corner of her eye.

My heart ached. *I wish I could take the pain from her.* "Sounds like remembering to me. No matter what you call it, follow your feelings and hope for the best." I smiled at her, trying to cheer her up.

"Do you think she'll like these?" she asked, holding identical, simple, delicate bracelets.

"Well, I've never met Queen Ines, but anyone should appreciate the work you've done."

"Thank you," she said. "How long are we going stay here?"

"Depends on how cooperative they are," I said. "I'd go check on them, but I'm afraid an interruption might compromise their progress."

She looked at me like she wanted to say something. Instead, she nodded, closed her eyes, and hummed.

I listened to her for a little while. The unfamiliar tune was relaxing. Much like the bracelets, it was simple, but it was important enough to her to make it beautiful. I hated to interrupt her, but curiosity took over. "What did you and Tindra talk about?"

"She tried to get me to tell her things about me and you and Crum and the tunnels, but I acted like I didn't know anything."

"Did she tell you anything?" I asked.

"I asked about the capital and the king and queen. I didn't tell her they're my parents. She thinks the king doesn't always know what's best for his people, but he tries to do what's right. She said the queen's a nice woman, loyal to her husband and popular among her people."

"Did she say anything about their children?"

"They have one living daughter, Stina, and they hold a big memorial for Jesca every year," Mam said, tears welling in her eyes again.

I sighed. "Please don't tell me we'll get to the capital in time for the memorial."

"No, it was a few months ago."

"Thank —"

"Fitzeirick, we have a plan!" Crum yelled.

"Want to join me?" I asked Mam.

"Do you think I'll be part of the plan?"

"Traveling with us, I'm sure you'll be involved."

"Then we should go together," she said, smiling.

I motioned for her to go ahead of me and we walked to the seated conspirators.

"Sit," Crum said. "This could take a little while to explain."

I sat facing Crum and Tindra. Mam planted herself beside Crum.

"What do I need to know?" I asked.

Tindra tilted her head toward Crum.

Interesting show of deference.

He cleared his throat. "I'll drive the wagon into the capital with Mam sitting with me. Fitzeirick, you'll ride in the back while Tindra hides under the straw. If the guards let us in, she knows someplace we can stay until we are granted an audience with the king. If they deny our entry, we turn around and ride away. Tindra comes back under cover of darkness and starts working contacts to get word to the king. The goal is to avoid the council until after we have spoken with, and gained favor from, King Ander."

I raised my hand and looked at Tindra. "Why are we avoiding the council? And why not go straight to the king?"

"The council doesn't know about Eirickson conspiring with Satra. King Ander needs to hear about the threat before they do. I can't go barging into the castle because there's a...blockade, I suppose, is the right word, between King Ander and me," she said.

"What sort of blockade?" I asked.

"Queen Ines suspects I garnered inappropriate attention from her husband. A baseless accusation, believe me, but no one questions the queen. I was fortunate to escape in one piece. Never figured out who got me out of that mess."

I shook my head. "Continue please, Crum."

"I'm a Croian citizen fleeing the Satran invasion, protecting a poor Varian girl who lost everything. I swore to her dying father to keep her safe and get her to her extended family. Fitzeirick, you're a fugitive, captured in an early Satran raid. You escaped and made it back to Croy. Everybody knows no one escapes Satran capture, so you were accused of defecting to Satra, coming back to spy for them. The court couldn't prove your treachery, so you got branded a traitor instead of executed."

"Why am I traveling with you?"

"In exchange for transport out of Croy, you keep us safe."

I nodded and motioned for him to continue.

"Tindra must stay hidden. Most, if not all, of the guard know her by sight. If they see her, the plan's sunk."

"I can do my part. Mam, how do you feel about this?" I asked.

"Do I need to say anything?"

Tindra shook her head.

Crum added, "We thought of that. I'll tell the guard you're so distraught you've quit speaking."

Tindra nodded. "Keep your head down, look at your feet. Don't look at the guards and *do not* say a word."

Mam nodded. "I can do that."

I looked from Crum to Tindra and back a couple of times. "It seems like a well-thought-out plan. Simple and direct, easy to follow. When do we leave?"

"Climb in, get her hidden. We'll get moving shortly," Crum said.

I followed Tindra into the wagon.

"Have you ever done anything like this before?" I asked.

"I know how to hide. Clear the straw away from the front of the wagon. I'll lie there, you pile it on top of me. Sit with your back leaning against the front wall."

"You plan to make the rest of the trip buried in straw?"

"I'll do what I must," she said.

The wagon lurched into motion while we cleared a spot for her.

She lay down, facing away from me. "Cover me."

"Remember, you agreed to do this," I said, before shoving straw over her. I did the best I could to keep the lump uniform. Once I felt it would pass a casual glance, I took my place leaning against the wall. I felt a slight movement as she breathed. The steady rhythm made me think she was asleep. It wasn't long before I was, too.

• • • • ● • ● • • •

I woke as the wagon jerked.

A face I didn't recognize appeared at the back of the wagon. "You there, get out here."

I grunted.

"You heard me. Get out here."

"A little stiff, moving a little slow. Give me a moment."

"As long as I see some movement," he said. "If I have to drag you out of there, we're going to have trouble."

I moved as slowly as I thought I could get away with, grunting and groaning on my way out.

"What happened to your face?"

"Disagreement over a spilled beer," I said.

"That where you met your two traveling companions?"

"No. They picked me up long before that fight."

"And the brand on your face? Did it come from a fight?" he asked.

I rubbed it and frowned. "No, sir, it came from the fact my homeland doesn't believe the truth."

"What truth would that be?"

"I escaped Satran captivity."

He squinted at me. "There's a hard truth to swallow. Try convincing me."

"I got captured. Most of my fellow warriors died, but one of those savages thought I'd make a fun play toy in a fighting pit. I won him, and his friends, some money and gained his trust...big mistake on his part. Killed him in his sleep and disappeared into the woods. Killed a few more before I made it back to Croy...back to what, I thought, would be safety."

"Figured they'd give you a hero's welcome."

I nodded. "They even sewed my head up...to stand trial. Accused of being a spy and branded a traitor because I did something almost no one else ever has."

"You have to admit, they had a pretty good reason to be suspicious. The Satran don't let people go."

I glared at him. "This scar across my head came from a Satran sword. I killed the guy who tried to cut my head off. Does it sound like they let me go?"

"You have a good point there," he said. "What can you tell me about these horses?"

We forgot about our horses.

"These three horses here?" I asked, stalling for time to think.

"Yes, these three horses."

"Well...the big one...he's mine. Found him in the forest, making an awful racket, surrounded by wolves. Ran them off and kept him. The other two, they were with the wagon when I started traveling with Crum and Mam."

"What did you say their names were?"

"The horses?" I asked. "I call mine Andale, the other two...I don't know their names."

He shook his head. "No, the couple you're traveling with. What are their names?"

"Oh, the man's Crum...or at least it's what he told me to call him. I suppose he could go by another name, but it's not my business. The woman, she doesn't speak, far as I know. I call her Mam...out of respect."

Another guard walked back and looked over the horses and their gear.

"Excuse me," the second guard said. "Where'd you get these saddles?"

Why do they keep asking about the horses? "A Varian. He runs a stable. We stayed with him for a little while, a day or two, but I don't remember his name. I think it started with a V. Most Varians I've run into have funny sounding names."

"Did the other two seem to know him?"

I nodded. "Crum. He seemed kind of friendly toward him...umm...V something."

After rubbing my chin for a moment, I continued. "Veckman maybe or Vecar. Wait, his name was Veck. No, that's not right either. But it's close to Veck. Vecka...Vekela...Vekel...maybe it was Vekel? Yeah, I'm sure. The guy running the stable was Vekel." I smiled. "That a common Varian name? I can't think of anyone in Croy who'd name someone Vekel."

The second guard nodded. "I've heard of Vekel. He runs a stable, but why'd he give you saddles?"

"He didn't want us to ride them bareback. Said it wasn't good for the horses. We did some work for him. I promised to pay him some more once I come across some honest work," I said.

He nodded and walked away.

"What did you say your name was?" the first guard asked.

"I tell most people to call me Fitz. A nickname I picked up because some people think I can be a mean bast —"

"Good enough," he said, interrupting me. "Anyone else traveling with you?"

"I haven't seen anyone else in the wagon, but you can have a look for yourself," I said, stepping away from the opening.

He scratched his chin and looked inside. "Why's the straw piled at the front?"

Another unexpected question. "Helps my back. I got hurt a couple of times, fighting, and the support keeps me from locking up."

"Fighting in the pits?"

"Yes, exactly," I said, nodding.

"What do you expect to do here?"

I shrugged. "Find work, settle somewhere...maybe start a family."

He nodded. "Once you get through the gate, go two streets in and turn right. Stop by the second building on the left and ask for the watch captain. He can put you to work."

I smiled and held out my hand. "Thanks, I'll make my way there as soon as I've seen them safe to wherever they're going. I'm a man of my word."

"Loyalty and integrity are admirable traits. It's Croy's loss for not believing you. Need help getting back in the wagon?"

"Appreciate the kind words. I've made it in and out of this wagon, plenty of times, should be able to manage it now."

"May your travel be smooth," he said, turning away.

Groaning while climbing back into the wagon, I kept up my act to cover my nerves. My heartbeat raced and beads of sweat ran down my forehead. I closed my eyes and took long, calming breaths. Shortly after I settled, the wagon lurched. Worry crept back into my thoughts until I heard hoof steps echoing off stone.

We're in.

Chapter 32

"Does Crum know where we're going?" I asked.

Tindra shifted beneath the straw. "I made sure he knows where to go. There's nothing to be concerned about."

"We're sneaking into your capital city to avoid turning me over to the people who hired you. All things considered, I have some concerns."

"We're going to a community where the deaf, blind, and mute live together, take care of each other. The residents of the House of Daufi are the outcasts of Varian society. No one thinks about them," she said.

I chuckled. "Hiding among outcasts seems appropriate. How long will we be there?"

"At least until I contact the castle, arrange the meeting."

"And if you can't?"

"In a few days, go the castle. Tell anyone who will listen about the meeting between Eirickson and Satra. That should keep the council from getting to you while someone investigates your claim," she said. "You'll have to figure out what to do from there because I'll most likely be dead."

"I suspect you're more useful to me alive. I don't want to work my way through the Varian royal court without a competent guide."

"I'll do my best," she said. "Help me get uncovered before —"

The wagon stopped.

"We shouldn't be at Daufi yet," she said.

"Wait here," I whispered.

I heard a scream and hurried out of the wagon. Pushing my talent into the ground as soon as my feet touched the road, I felt two people blocking the street. Another moved near the front left of the wagon and a fourth stood near the front right.

Mam screamed again and Crum's feet hit the ground.

I grabbed my hammer and ran toward her. A dirty, heavyset man grabbed her as I arrived.

Bones snapped when my hammer smashed into his arm.

He bellowed in pain and backed away, holding his now useless left arm.

The two people stopping the horses ran toward him. "What happened?"

His face pale, he pointed toward me and spoke through clenched teeth. "Came outta nowhere. Broke my arm. Kill him. Grab the girl. Filip, quit playing over there and come help us."

"This one's too quick," Filip yelled from the other side of the wagon. "I can't get a good hit on him."

I smiled. "Only warning I'm going to give. Leave, and you get to live."

"No one threatens us on our territory and gets away with it," one of them snarled.

I softened the ground under them, and they sank to the middle of their chests. While they struggled to get out, I hardened the ground to hold them in place.

Grabbing Mam, I took a few steps toward the back of the wagon and felt someone stonesything.

The injured thug was trying to free his friends. Pulling some strength, I threw the hammer at him. With his focus on his two friends, he never saw it coming. The impact to the middle of his chest knocked him to the ground.

I scooped up Mam and ran to put her inside the wagon. "Stay in here. Tindra will keep you safe," I said, and hurried to help Crum. Rounding the back of the wagon I yelled to distract Filip.

He turned to look at me, leaving Crum an opening.

As the thug drew his hand back to throw a knife, Crum kicked his knee.

Filip screamed in pain, dropped the knives, and grabbed his injured leg. Crum punched him in the face, grabbed his head, and rammed his knee into Filip's nose.

He slumped to the ground.

"You hurt?"

He raised his arms to show me several cuts trickling blood. "Nothing I can't live with for now."

"Good. Come with me. I want answers."

"Be right there," he said, lifting the top of the bench.

I jogged to the captives, still stuck in the ground. Stooping to retrieve my hammer, I confirmed the big man was dead.

Crum joined me, Tindra's sword in hand. "We need to hurry before we draw a crowd."

I nodded and tapped the nearest bandit on the shoulder with my foot. "Who sent you?"

"Sent us?" he said, before spitting at me. "No one sent us, we own this street."

"So why jump us?" I asked.

"You come through here in a wagon with extra horses. You must have money or cargo, so you pay to use the street," he said.

"Ohhh, I think there's been some misunderstanding. Totally our fault. You see, we're not from around here. *We* didn't know toll collectors are so zealous in the enforcement of their duties." I turned to Crum. "Did you *not* notice their uniforms?"

He shrugged and looked at the cuts on his arms. "*I* was too busy keeping myself from getting carved like a slab of meat."

The second bandit laughed. "These two idiots think we work for tha king."

"Wouldja shut up?" the first one yelled.

"Wait," I said, rubbing my chin. "You *don't* work for King Ander?"

"*I can't believe it,*" Crum added, throwing his hands up. "I often run into toll collectors who take innocent women as payment."

I rested my boot on one of their heads. "Now, we have a problem. We've never met, so I can't blame you for not knowing I'm a man of my word. I don't make threats, I make promises, and I keep them. It's a point of pride, you see. I told you to leave us, and you could live. So how do you want to die?"

Crum looked at me and shook his head.

"Go, make sure Mam's unharmed," I said.

"What are you going to —"

"Exactly what I said."

"You can't kill them," he argued.

"Why not? What were they going to do to Mam? What was Filip trying to do to you? They had their chance to walk away," I said.

"But they're no longer a threat. You can't kill someone who can't fight back."

"What he said. Listen ta him," the bandit, supporting my boot, said.

I tightened the ground around him. "Keep your mouth shut."

He nodded.

"What should I do?" I demanded. "Let them go so they can rob, rape, or kill the next group coming this way?"

Before Crum could answer a loud groan came from the other side of the wagon. We turned and saw Filip wobbling, unsteady on his feet.

"This isn't over!" he yelled, hobbling away from us.

I looked at Crum.

He glared at me and said, "I don't like this," before turning to walk to the back of the wagon.

I'm doing what must be done. You don't have to like it. "How many others have they hurt?" I snarled. "It stops now."

"Whatcha gonna do?" one of the trapped men asked.

I didn't say a word while tracking Filip. With little more than a thought the ground opened under him and the others. The live ones didn't have a chance to react before I closed the dirt and stone around them.

I gathered Filip's knives, and carried them to Crum. "These might come in handy."

"What did you do?" His face was pale.

"Buried them."

"Alive?"

"Better than they deserved," Tindra said.

"Kill or be killed," Mam said. "Thank you, Fitz."

Crum looked at her and his jaw dropped. "Is that how you feel?"

"Mam," I interrupted. "Do you want to ride back here the rest of the way?"

She nodded.

"I'll keep her company," Tindra said.

"Thank you," I replied. "How much farther?"

"Not far, just keep following this street until it ends," Tindra said.

"Let's get moving," I said.

Crum scratched his head as he put Tindra's sword away. "Where'd you bury them?"

"Right where they were."

After climbing onto the bench, he said, "I can't even see a ripple in the road."

"Unless someone looks for them under the surface, nothing will change until they rot."

"I still can't believe you've become so cold," he muttered, snapping the reins.

"I did what I had to."

He shuddered.

Chapter 33

For the first time since we passed through the gate, I got to see the buildings and houses in the Varian capital city. There was a comforting uniformity of sizes and shapes. Some displayed an ornate door or stonework facade, but otherwise they all looked similar.

I also noticed the ever-worsening conditions as we continued to the outskirts. It started as something simple, homes with a damaged shutter or broken stones around the door. As we went further, the areas became dirtier and less maintained.

The road ended at a large wall, overgrown with vines. The only obvious entry was a wooden, double door, large enough for the wagon to fit through with room to spare.

"We're here...I guess," Crum said.

"I'll try knocking," I said.

Walking to the doors, I looked around, but didn't notice anyone about, nor did I see anywhere someone could watch us. Rapping my knuckles against the door, I waited for a response.

"Knock harder," Crum said.

I pulled a little strength from the ground and landed three, hard blows, stepping back when I heard stone slide against stone.

"Who's there?" a voice called out, from the greenery.

I paused, unsure of what to say.

Crum said, "We've come seeking shelter."

"Shelter from whom?"

"Those who wish us harm."

"If your words be true, enter in peace," the voice said.

I hopped on the wagon as it passed.

Two large men stood next to the opened doors. At a glance, they looked like twins, and both had milky, white eyes. They pushed the thick, wooden doors closed behind us without so much as a grunt.

We entered a large, well-kept courtyard. People of various ages and builds moved about, tending bushes and vines along the wall or minding a garden. A few walked a winding, stone path snaking its way around the interior of the walled compound. A man and a woman, holding hands, walked out of an archway in the middle of what looked like a large, stone barracks.

"Hold there and identify yourselves," the man called out, his right hand raised.

They both looked like they had lived hard lives. In contrast with their well-groomed silver and gray hair, their skin looked like old leather, worn and wrinkled. They wore rugged-looking, simple clothes and thick-soled leather boots. The woman's eyes were dark in color, I couldn't see his.

She looked from Crum to me.

Tindra ran past and embraced the couple "Mother, Father...I have some people I'd like you to meet."

Crum and I looked at each other.

That's why she considers this place safe.

He smirked and whispered, "Time for you to meet the parents. You two haven't even been out...unless you count the Stone Roof."

I glared at him and hopped from the wagon.

"Crum, tell Mam it's safe," Tindra called out.

She turned to me, grabbed my hand, and placed it in her father's. "Father, this is Fitzeirick. Fitzeirick, I'd like to introduce you to Mikael, my father."

I looked closer at his face as we shook hands and noticed both his eyelids were sewn shut. Out of habit, I spoke with a formal tone. "Mikael, it is my pleasure to meet you. Tindra has been a helpful assistant in our recent travels."

"She's a good girl, but spends so much of her time in service to the crown. I'm surprised she's made any friends. Sounds like you're Croian and of their court."

I was so shocked I almost forgot to answer. "Yes...yes, sir. I am Croian and spent much time in the court. How did you know?"

"Your voice, manner of speaking...your accent," he said, smiling.

She pulled my arm and placed my hand in her mother's. "Mother, this is Fitzeirick. Fitzeirick, this is Margit, my mother."

"I see where Tindra gets her beauty," I said, falling back on manners I'd practiced my whole life. *Even if I don't like her, or trust her, she is attractive.*

Margit raised her left hand and moved her fingers in various patterns.

"Mother says you are too kind," Tindra said.

"She's mute?"

Margit nodded.

My eyes opened wide. "Oh. Please accept my apology. I didn't mean to be rude."

Her fingers moved in a blur and she nodded.

Tindra coughed. "She doesn't take offense so long as you learn from your mistake."

I bowed to her. "Yes, of course. I will be more mindful of my actions. Also, I thank you for your hospitality. My friends and I will do our best to not be a burden on your people."

"Nonsense," Mikael said. "Anyone traveling with our daughter is welcome. We don't often get visitors here anyway. It's a pleasure."

"Thank you for the kind words," I said, releasing Margit's hand and stepping to the side.

"Crum," Tindra said. "This is my father, Mikael."

Crum shook his hand. "Nice to meet you, sir."

"Another Croian," Mikael said.

"Yes, sir. A lifelong friend of Fitzeirick."

"You're with him in the courts?"

"Not as much as he'd like," Crum said.

"Still, it's good to have someone to rely on," Mikael said.

"And this is my mother, Margit," Tindra said.

Crum took her hand, bowed deeply, and brushed her knuckles with his lips. "Always a joy to meet a beautiful woman."

Margit blushed.

"It was love at first sight. Back when I could see," Mikael replied, with a laugh.

Margit took her hand from Crum's and made some gestures.

"She would thank you for the compliment, but she's seen your kind before," Tindra said, snickering. "She says she'll be keeping an eye on you."

He bowed again and moved next to me.

"Father, this special, young girl goes by the name Mam," Tindra said, placing Mam's hand in her father's. "Mam, this is Mikael."

He bent down and kissed her hand. "Welcome to our home."

It was Mam's turn to blush. It took her a moment to regain her composure. "Thank you. I find all the plants refreshing."

He smiled.

Tindra pulled Mam toward her mother. "Mother, I'd like you to meet Mam. Mam, this is my mother, Margit."

"You have a beautiful name," Mam said, and curtsied.

Margit smiled and made some signals to Tindra. "She said thank you and welcome. She also said each of you should feel at home here."

Mikael cleared his throat. "Tindra, take your friends to the guest rooms. Dinner will be at the usual time. You're all welcome to eat in the hall. Someone will see to the horses and wagon shortly."

"Thank you, father. The food under the seat goes to the kitchen. Everything else goes to my room. Have the saddlebags in the back taken to a guest room. We'll sort them later."

"Excuse me, sir. I have a question," Mam said.

"Yes, young lady...Mam, I believe it was," he said.

"How'd you know about the wagon and the horses?"

"Since I have no eyes?" he asked.

"Yes."

He smiled. "The creaking of the leather harness. Hooves scraping the cobblestones. I can smell the horses too, but the other sounds tell me there is a wagon here. Also, I'm a stonesyth. I feel where they stand."

"Oh!" she exclaimed. "Fitz can, too."

"Fitz?" he asked.

"She means me, Fitzeirick."

"Are you blind?" he asked.

"No, sir. I learned to do it to survive."

"Clever. A valuable skill for those who master it," he said.

"Yes, it has come in handy."

"Again, I hope you all enjoy your stay here. I have responsibilities demanding my attention," he said, before they walked, hand in hand, back into the stone building.

I stepped close to Tindra. "I have questions."

"I expected you would. Follow me."

We walked behind her into the House of Daufi.

Candles set into alcoves lit the stone hallway. I almost asked Tindra why, but remembered not everyone living here was blind. Reaching out through the floor, I found her parents near the end of a hall to the left. No one else was near, as far as I could tell, and there was a hallway below us.

She led us into a hallway and stopped in front of an open door. The next three doors stood open also. "Wait here. It looks like these rooms are empty. Let me check."

She looked into the room, nodded, then checked the next two. On her way back, she closed the doors. "I was right, no visitors. Still, we must follow proper protocol. It doesn't matter who takes which room, they're all the same. The uniformity is comforting to the blind."

"Where are you staying?" I asked.

"In my room, of course."

"Near here?" I asked.

"Not far. I'll explain everything when we get there."

She led us further down the hall, turned left when it ended, and right through an archway leading to another hall. Turning right, she stepped onto a staircase, heading down.

I stopped. "Where are you taking us?"

Her sigh echoed off the smooth, stone walls. "I told you, to my room."

"You live underground?" I asked.

"Most of the permanent residents here do," she said. "Relax. You're free to come and go as you please."

I nodded and she was on the move again.

The stairs emptied into a hallway, like the one above.

"Is every floor the same?" I asked.

She nodded. "Uniformity."

"How many floors are there?" Crum asked.

"Last time I was here they had recently finished the third floor. You'd have to ask my father to see if there are more now."

"Impressive," I commented.

"He'd be glad to hear you say that."

We turned left, followed the hall, and stopped at a single door in the right wall.

"Wait a moment," she said, opening the door.

Chapter 34

A chill spread through the air and Tindra called out, "Candles are lit. Come in and get comfortable."

I walked in and looked around. The room was a contrast between practicality and comfort. No artwork or tapestry hung on the plain, stone walls, but a beautiful, wooden table stood in the middle of the room, holding an aged, silver tea set. Two overstuffed, fabric couches sat against the wall. Her bed was a stone slab projecting from the wall holding a large cushion and blankets. The fourth wall contained a small fireplace and a simple, wooden desk with an ornate, well-padded chair.

"Sit and we'll talk," she said. "Should I put on some tea?"

"Sounds good," I said.

She nodded. The air chilled again as she lit small logs.

"Your parents," I said. "I assume they haven't always been outcasts?"

She took the kettle from the table, looked inside, and frowned. "If you'll excuse me a moment, I need water."

"Is it a long walk?" Mam asked.

"Where?" Tindra replied.

"To get water. I could walk with you...if you don't mind."

"Oh. While I've come to appreciate your company Mam, I don't have to go far. My room has its own bathing area with water available all the time."

"I don't believe you," Crum said. "Do they keep your bath filled even when you aren't here?"

"What? No. That would be an incredible waste of time and effort. Each bathing room has a tap to control the flow. There's a large cistern behind the main house. Pipes bring water to the lower levels."

I stared at her.

Crum spoke before I did. "I still don't believe you. Show me."

She laughed. "Follow me."

We walked through an arched opening and found the floor sloped down, into a large bathing tub. In the far wall, over the tub, was a wooden tap, much like you would see in an ale cask. Tindra placed the kettle under the tap and twisted it. Water flowed free.

"How do you warm the water to bathe?" I asked.

"A small fire pit, under my bed. Hot air flows through a passage under the tub before rising through a chimney in the wall."

Crum and I said, "Amazing," at the same time.

"I take it your home didn't have such features, Fitzeirick?" Tindra asked.

"I don't think anyone in Croy has such things in their homes," I said, shaking my head in disbelief.

"Well, they aren't common in Varian homes, but not unheard of either. Get comfortable and I'll put the kettle on," Tindra said.

We returned to the common area. Mam and Crum sat next to each other on one couch and I took a spot on the other. Tindra placed the kettle over the small fire before joining me, sitting so close she was almost in my lap.

I pressed my lips together and shook my head before moving away from her.

She gave me a crooked grin. "Now, you asked about my parents. I'll tell you, but please don't interrupt me. I'm not sure I can tell the whole story if I have to stop and start."

We agreed to stay quiet.

"The simple answer is no; they haven't always been outcasts. They grew up in Southern Varia, the land now under Satran control. Father's the youngest of three brothers. His family had a farm while Mother, an only child, lived behind her parent's tailor shop. Their families lived near each other and often traded food for clothes.

"Father was almost of age when some men found him minding the farm on his own. They beat him and cut out both eyes. By the time his family returned from the market, he'd almost bled to death. His brothers rode off in different directions to retrieve any herbalist they could find.

"Several people worked on him over the next few days. The bleeding stopped, but the damage done was horrible. One of the herbalists said it would be best to sew his eyes shut to ward off infection. Mother volunteered her services. They were already close when she moved in and helped him learn how to live as a blind man. With her parent's blessing, they married."

She cleared her throat. "One morning, while helping my grandmother gather eggs, Mother walked past a skittish horse. The horse kicked, hitting her throat hard enough to damage something. It's a wonder her neck didn't break. Several herbalists tried to fix her voice, but she never spoke again."

Mam started to say something, but Tindra held up her hand.

"When the Croian invasion started, both families loaded everything into wagons and fled. My parents made it to the capital alone, don't know what happened to their families. They lived in a wagon outside the city because the guard wouldn't let them in. After selling enough of their belongings to bribe their way inside, Mother worked as a seamstress and servant until they saved enough to buy this lot and build a haven for outcasts."

Tears streamed down Mam's cheeks. Crum and I looked at each other, shocked.

I had no idea what to say.

The whistling kettle broke the silence.

"I'll take care of it," Crum said.

Soon we each held steaming cups of tea with plenty left in the kettle.

Tindra looked composed after her first cup, so I asked, "How do they communicate?"

She smiled. "He speaks to her, of course, and she touches his hand in special patterns. They worked out the system of touches together. Everyone living here learns at least a little of it. The same with her hand signs, created with the help of other deaf residents."

"And you understand it?" Crum asked.

"I'm out of practice, but well enough to get along," she said. "How are the cuts on your arms?"

He shrugged. "Not bad, but I should probably get them looked at."

She poured another cup of tea, walked to the desk, and took a small bag from the drawer. "Let me see if I can help. Tell me about the attack."

"Four guys, one a stonesyth and another named Filip. I killed the stonesyth and buried the other three alive," I said.

Crum hissed as she applied some kind of ointment to several small cuts. "Seems I'm out of practice when it comes to fighting unarmed against a knife."

"Sorry. I should've warned you this would sting. Several of these larger cuts need stitching. It won't be pretty, but I can do it."

"Go ahead," he said.

She turned to me. "Sounds like a typical group of street rats."

"Is this a common problem?" I asked.

"Not if you ask the capital guard," she drawled, stitching a cut. "So long as the bandits leave the wealthy alone, the problem's ignored."

I shook my head. "Can't believe anyone allows such a thing. I'd never allow criminals to prey on anyone in my skati."

"Sometimes the leaders have to make do with the resources they have," she said, shrugging. "In a city this size, there's no way to secure everyone inside from everything, except the outside. I'm not saying I agree with it, but I accept it.

"One of my early assignments was to infiltrate one of the more violent groups, kill the leader. The idea was 'cut off the head and the snake dies' but killing the leader splintered the group, made them harder to control. The royal court decided to let the situation handle itself as long as the groups fight among themselves. So far, it's worked well enough; greed and infighting keep the gangs in check. Of course, all it would take is one strong leader to bring them all together again, and we have no plan to deal with them."

"When are we going to meet the king and queen?" Mam asked.

"I have to make some preparations first," Tindra said.

"Don't you work for him?" Mam asked.

"Even when I was in good standing, I couldn't just walk in and demand an audience."

"You mean the king and queen don't welcome visitors?" she asked.

"King Ander has an open court, but he doesn't like surprises. I fear we'll present a bit of a problem, if we show up without warning."

"What sort of problem will we be?" Mam asked. "I don't want to be a problem for anyone."

Tindra finished stitching Crum's wounds and turned to Mam. "There are a few things about us which could cause concerns...each in their own way. First, the suspicion I'm under from the queen.

"Fitzeirick ruled territory taken from Varia. Now, he's branded, disgraced, and looking for aid. He'll present accusations against his half-brother which will be the source of many discussions. I expect questions regarding his intentions.

"There's you, Mam. You look enough like Ander and Ines' daughter to fool many people. You can't be Stina, but you could claim to be Jesca. Reminding them of their eldest will be painful for them. Questions will come. Accusations will fly. The court will resist accepting her sudden appearance.

"Crum's the least of the potential problems. It's obvious, at least to me, he's in love with you. Should the king and queen determine you aren't their daughter, there's no problem for them. You two are commoners working out your feelings for each other. But if you *are* their daughter, he is a concern for the crown. How will they handle Princess Jesca returning with a Croian suitor?"

Crum glared at Tindra.

"I think I need to rest now," Mam said, looking away.

"Crum, can you take Mam to a guest room and help her get settled?" I asked. "I still need to talk to Tindra."

He took Mam's hand. "My pleasure."

"Try to relax. Tight muscles could tear the stitches out," Tindra said, smiling as she put the bag away.

"I appreciate your concern," he said, scowling, and led Mam out of the room.

"Are you ever going to not take unnecessary jabs at him?" I asked.

"He and I cooperated when we had to. I'm certain we will again if it becomes necessary. For now, let us have our fun."

"I'm positive that wasn't fun for him...or Mam."

"No, but he's already plotting his retaliation. Sometimes the entertainment is in the anticipation. The royal court will eat her alive if she can't handle uncomfortable truths. Crum's presence won't make any difference."

"He and I both know that. But I didn't stay behind to discuss them."

"I figured," she said. "I propose we continue our conversation while soaking in a hot, relaxing bath."

"I'm not going to bathe with you. It's improper."

"That's something else we need to talk about," she said, shaking her head. "If you're going to stay in Varia long enough to get the help you need, you're going to have to adapt to some of our customs."

"Why?"

"Because it's how things are done," she said. "It's not uncommon for business deals to be negotiated while soaking in hot springs. Men and women bathing together is not a problem, unless you don't trust yourself."

"It's not a matter of trust. It's a matter of respect."

She nodded. "In that case, you need to learn to respect this custom. No one is going to take you seriously, if you're not willing to join them when invited to soak."

"I'll have to think about it. Can we talk over tea?"

Her shoulders slumped. "Sure, we'll talk over tea. I'll bathe later. What do you want to talk about?"

"How do I get an audience with the king?"

"I'll send a sealed letter to someone close to King Ander. I hope to receive a reply after dinner or first thing tomorrow. So long as the reply is favorable, we'll see Ander as soon as possible."

"And if the reply isn't favorable?" I asked.

She shrugged. "I go to the council and deal with whatever consequences come my way. You'll have to make a decision. Do you work with them or go it alone?"

"Dare I ask about your courier or who will receive your letter?"

She laughed. "Not everything I do is so secret nor are all my confidants undercover. Society, in general, shuns this house, but my parents maintain a relationship with Ander. Two house members serve as advisors to the king and the court. It isn't unheard of for messages and requests to go from here to the castle. No one will even think twice."

"We wait and hope for the best," I sighed.

"Yet I'm sure you're already preparing for the worst."

"Spend enough time in someplace like those tunnels and it becomes second nature," I said. "Is it too early to ask about dinner?"

"I'm going to clean up before I eat. Head back to your guest room. I'll come get the three of you."

"Thank you," I said.

"While you wait, I want you to put some serious thought into what I said about our customs."

I nodded and hurried to my room. On the way, I passed several people in the corridors, but no one stopped me or seemed to notice my presence. I felt people tracking me through the floor.

Other stonesyths know when I reach out with my talent.

Maybe my discovery wasn't so unique. As I considered the implications, I found Crum standing outside a room with the door closed.

"Mam's inside, resting," he said. "Your room's the last one, saddlebags are on the table."

"Thanks," I said. "Tindra's coming soon to lead us to dinner."

"I'll wait out here and wake Mam when she gets here."

I opened the door and stepped into the room. It was simple, with a bed like Tindra's. I noticed a storage trunk against one wall and a small table with a couple of plain, wooden chairs. Like he said, my saddlebags sat on the table along with my hammer.

After changing into fresh clothes, I sat and waited for Tindra's arrival.

Chapter 35

My eyes flew open when Crum stuck his head in the room and said, "She's here. Ready to eat?"

The fight must have taken more out of me than I realized. "Dinner sounds good," I said.

"Did you have a good rest, Mam?" I asked, when I saw her.

"Yes, but the bed is almost too soft."

"Are you lying down to sleep now?" I asked.

"I'm trying," she said. "It still seems strange."

"All you can do is try," Crum said, putting his hand on her shoulder.

She smiled and patted his hand.

Tindra led us to a large room with people sitting at rows of long tables. We stood in line, moving with everyone else through a passage in the far-right corner of the room. People picked up trays, and someone handed out large bowls of thick stew before placing a stone plate and a wooden cup next to it. As we moved, servers put various vegetables and some bread on the plate. Tindra took a rolled-up cloth from a basket at the end of the line and we followed her example.

"Do you mind if I sit with my parents?" she asked. "I haven't seen them in some time."

"I don't mind at all," Crum quipped.

I chuckled. "Go be with your family. We'll find seats ourselves."

"Thank you," she said. "We can meet back at the guest rooms later."

"Don't feel obligated to spend any more time with us," Crum said.

"If you insist," she said.

"I do," he said, before I could answer.

She flashed him a big smile and walked away.

"Fitz, you look better," Mam said, as we sat.

"The swelling around my eye is almost gone. I can open it all the way." I unrolled the cloth. It held a knife, fork, and spoon inside.

Crum looked into a couple of pitchers sitting nearby. "One looks like water, the other's milk."

"Hmm...milk for me please," Mam said.

He poured their cups full of milk while I filled mine with water.

"I'd like to take a bath," she said.

"Ask someone. I'm sure there's someplace to clean up here." I said.

"Perhaps we can go exploring and find out ourselves," Crum said.

"Sounds fun," she said, and took a bite of bread.

"That's what we'll do. It's been too long since I've had some fun," Crum said.

I swallowed and looked at him. "Remember, we're guests here. Don't cause trouble."

He nodded. "Of course, no trouble. You know I wouldn't risk getting Mam in trouble...at least not on purpose."

I looked at her. "I'd tell you to keep him out of trouble, but I'm sure you can't."

She smiled and giggled.

I turned my attention back to him. "If you find you can't keep yourself out of trouble, I trust you to keep her safe."

He nodded. "I'll be on my best behavior."

"All I ask."

He swallowed another mouthful and washed it down with some milk. "What's the grand plan to get an audience with the king?"

Between bites, I explained Tindra's idea to get us into the castle.

"You're placing a lot of trust in her," he said.

"You have a better way?" I asked. "I can't walk up to the front door and expect a warm greeting. Ignoring what I represent, my credibility is tarnished by the brand on my face. Her contacts clearing a path to the king is our best move."

He shook his head and swallowed. "You're right. It would take too long for me to establish my own contacts here. Unless they're already in place by some Varian spion."

"Can I help?" Mam asked.

"Get us in the castle? Doubtful," I said. "If someone believes you are who you think you are, you may be able to sway some opinions later. I'm concerned about people deciding you're lying and trying to gain favor through deception. It could cost us our lives."

"I want to help," she said, frowning.

"I'm sure you'll help as much as you can," Crum said. "For now, let's finish our meal then go exploring."

"Might want to stop by your rooms and get a change of clothes," I said.

He nodded. "Thanks for the suggestion."

They finished their dinner and left for their adventure.

I took my time eating, taking in the sights and sounds. It seemed everyone here looked after each other as best they could. Several families lived here; young children sat with parents while older kids had a table to themselves. Other groups looked drawn together through their various situations.

The more I looked around, the more happy faces I saw. I couldn't understand why these people were outcasts. Was Varia willing to ignore them simply because of their physical challenges? Storing the thought for future reference, I finished my meal, and headed back to my room.

Reaching out through the floor, I found someone pacing in front of our rooms. I slowed, moved against the wall and glanced around the corner. It was Tindra. She'd knock on one door, wait for a moment, move to the next, and knock.

"Are you lost?" I asked

She jumped. "No, I was looking for you, and didn't know which room you picked. No one answered when I knocked."

"I'm in this room," I said, opening the door. "Why not go in one and look for my stuff?"

"House rules. No one enters a closed room uninvited."

I chuckled. "Hope Crum doesn't barge in someplace by accident."

"Why would he?"

I explained their plans to explore the grounds.

"Please tell me he has some amount of decency or at least common courtesy," she said.

"Believe it or not, he does."

"Maybe we can get through your stay without an incident," she said, with a sigh.

"Now that we have that matter settled," I said. "What did you need me for?"

"Wanted to let you know the courier left for the castle. I handed him the letter after I ate."

"And you expect an answer..."

She smiled. "When it arrives."

"I suppose one can't expect a king to ignore everything to address someone like me," I said.

"No, but I put enough bait on the hook to expect a big bite sooner rather than later."

"Do I dare ask?"

"Relax. I didn't write a single falsehood. Do you doubt my ability to tantalize someone? I do a good job at creating interest when necessary," she said, with a predatory smile.

"You can try," I replied, with a smile of my own.

"You wound me," she said, clasping her hands over her heart. "I know Ander well. I know how to get his attention."

"Do I need to know anything?"

She shook her head. "I told you, everything in the letter's true. Relax, go to sleep. I'll see if I can find Mam and Crum before they cause an incident by mistake."

"Good idea. I'm sure he wouldn't go looking to cause trouble. Sometimes, often, trouble happens to find him."

"Rest well my...friend," she said, closing the door.

Blowing out the lantern, I flopped onto the bed. Though I felt tired, there was too much on my mind for sleep to come quickly. I tossed and turned for some time before slumber finally took over.

• • • ● • ● • ● • • •

I jumped when someone pounded on my door.

"Fitzeirick, get up," a woman's voice yelled.

I sat up and rubbed my forehead.

"Fitzeirick, let me in."

Tindra. I misjudged where the edge of the bed was and fell to the floor. "Give me a moment!" I yelled back, struggling to untangle myself from myself.

I dressed and opened the door. "What's so important?"

"The official response. It's in Ander's hand, bears his seal. We need to move now. I have people getting the wagon ready. Put on one of the hooded robes out here while I wake Crum and Mam."

"Wait. Where are we going?"

"The castle, but no one can see us go in," she said. "Move."

Rushing out of the room, I tripped over a pile of dark clothes on the floor.

"Pick yourself up and get a robe on," she said, turning toward Crum's room.

After the fourth time she knocked, I heard his voice. "What?"

"Wake Mam, we need to move," she said.

We were ready to leave when Mam said, "I need to get the bracelets," and went back in her room.

"Are they necessary?" Tindra asked.

"It's important to Mam," I said.

"They're necessary," Crum added.

She returned shortly, bracelets in hand.

Tindra gave us instructions as we hurried out of the building. "Get in the back of the wagon. When it stops, we all get out as fast as we can. Someone's waiting for us. As soon as we arrive, we need to hurry inside, get out of these robes, and get ready for our meeting."

Sweat stung my eyes by the time we reached the wagon.

After we climbed into the wagon, Mam asked, "What's the king like?"

"I haven't dealt with him in a while," Tindra said. "The last time I worked for him it was...intense. Some have concerns about his ability to focus outside our borders, but no one can question his passion for his people and this country. In my opinion, the defeat he suffered from Eirick caused him to be more defensive in his thinking. He seems to always be planning for an attack that, at least until recently, wasn't coming."

"And the queen?" Mam prodded.

"Depends on which Ines you are asking about," Tindra said.

"What do you mean?" Mam asked.

Tindra sighed. "The queen has many faces. I've seen two. The public face, the one most people see, is one of a happy woman. To her subjects, she's a loving, nurturing wife to her wise and benevolent husband. Behind closed doors, she's like a protective mother bear. Even when presented with evidence to the contrary, Ines acts like Stina can do no wrong. The queen shows no mercy to those who say otherwise. She'd as soon slit their throat and watch them bleed to death as she would wave to them."

"Oh," Mam said, voice quivering. "Which one do you think we'll face?"

"I suspect you'll see both before it's all said and done. Who knows? Maybe you'll see a side of her I never have."

"Mam, you won't face this alone," Crum said.

"Thank you," she replied.

Soon the rhythm of the hoof beats slowed, and the wagon stopped.

"Everyone out," Tindra said.

We clambered out of the wagon as fast as the billowy robes let us. Tindra was the last one out. She pounded twice on the wagon as soon as her feet hit the ground and it sped away. I pushed my talent out and found no one else around.

Tindra hurried to the nearby wall, shoved open a hidden door, and motioned to us. "Move...inside, before anyone sees you."

We ran through the door into a dark hallway. For a moment, it reminded me of the tunnels, except there was a light at the end.

"Leave the robes here," Tindra said.

"What's going to happen to them?" Mam asked.

"No idea, not my concern," she replied.

"I can't see a thing," Crum muttered.

"This hallway's straight, head toward the light," Tindra said.

"Where do we go from there?" he asked.

"We'll follow Lars to King Ander's meeting room."

We got close enough to see someone standing in the room. "Is that him?" I asked.

"I'm almost blind, but not at all deaf," Lars called out.

Tindra laughed, as I apologized.

He told us to wait once we stepped into the entry room and left through an arched passage to our right.

I looked at Tindra. "I thought we were following him. What are we waiting for?"

She shrugged. "Don't know, but it might be a good idea for you to check for anyone coming."

I nodded and Mam started humming one of her odd songs. Crum put his arm around her shoulders after I glanced at her. *One less thing for me to worry about.* I gave him a quick nod and closed my eyes to concentrate.

There were no hidden passages into the room. The only ways in and out were the hallway we came in from along with arched openings to our left and right. Every hallway was clear for as far as I could reach. I felt movement near me. It was Tindra, shifting her weight from one foot to the other.

I opened my eyes when I felt movement in the hall behind us. "Tindra, were you expecting anyone else?"

"No," she said. "Why?"

"Two people coming behind us. One's stumbling."

We turned as a guard walked in with a woman leaning against him.

"You know to stay away from those places," he said to her.

"What difference does it make?" she yelled. "You don't care...no one does. I know Mother doesn't care. If my —" She lifted her head off the guard's shoulder and opened her eyes. They locked onto Mam. "Who are you?"

My legs trembled when I saw the resemblance. "You must be Stina."

The guard let go of her.

She stumbled backward a few steps before falling to the floor and giggling.

"Identify yourselves," he demanded, as his sword cleared its scabbard.

"You know who I am. We're waiting to meet with King Ander," Tindra said, stepping between the guard and me.

"Liar!" he yelled. "The king doesn't meet with anyone at this hour."

"I have a letter with his seal. He sent for us. Lars let us in, told us to wait here," Tindra said, stepping toward him. "Is Princess Stina ill?"

"She's not your concern," he said, pointing his blade toward Mam. "Who is that girl?"

Tindra took another step. "I'm a citizen of Varia, and work for our king, which makes Stina my concern. This woman is a friend of ours and needs to meet with King Ander and Queen Ines. May I look at Stina? I'm afraid she might be sick or hurt."

Stina sat up, looked at Mam again, and pointed. "She looks like me."

"I told you the princess isn't your concern. Stay back," the guard ordered.

I felt Tindra shift her weight. *Don't do it. Don't attack the guard.* My head turned toward the hall Lars left down, two more people were headed our way. "Tindra," I said. "More people are coming."

She stepped back, looked at me, and nodded.

"Why does she look like me?" Stina asked, wide eyed.

Mam whispered, "Is she my sister?"

"Stay behind me, Princess. I'll protect you," the guard said.

I looked at Crum. He whispered something in Mam's ear.

Lars and another man walked in.

Hopefully, one of them is the voice of reason.

The man looked around the room. "What is going on here?"

The guard spoke first. "Captain Torsten, glad you're here, sir. These four claim they're meeting with King Ander."

"Ingvar. Put your sword away before Tindra takes it from you, or worse you cut yourself," Torsten said. "They *are* here to meet with King Ander. Why is Princess Stina sitting on the floor?"

"She...went...out..." Ingvar said, putting his blade away. "But I found her and brought her back."

"Not soon enough, it would seem," Torsten barked. "Get her to her room. Be quiet about it. I hope, for your sake, the queen is in a good mood when she finds out. Lars, go with them."

"Of course," he said, and bowed.

Ingvar scooped Stina off the floor.

She howled. "Why does *she* look like *me*?"

I looked at Mam and saw a tear on her cheek. *Not the welcome home any of us expected, but I'm not sure if it's better or worse for us now.*

Torsten shook his head as they left the room with Lars trailing behind. "I'll apologize for the princess," he said. "And for what I have to ask next. Are any of you armed?"

"Are you questioning my loyalty?" Tindra snapped, putting her hands on her hips.

"I'm not sure you know where your loyalty lays, Tindra. Even if I ignore you, I have standing before me a branded traitor, a second man who looks untrustworthy at best, and a woman bearing a troubling resemblance to Princess Stina. The four of you will be in the presence of my king. I'd be negligent in the extreme, if I didn't make sure you pose no threat."

"I've never made a move against the crown," Tindra countered.

He stepped toward her. "Doesn't matter. Are you armed?"

Good to know I'm not the only one unsure of her.

"How often am I not armed?" she replied, smiling.

He frowned and held out his hand. "Are you going to hand it over or do I need to search you?"

"Understand this is one of my favorites. I expect it back," she said, before reaching down the front of her shirt and removing a knife and sheath.

"I should have known," he commented, as he took it from her. "Now, you three...armed?"

"No, sir," I said, trying to look non-threatening.

Crum said, "I have a couple of knives," and pulled the blades Filip had used on him from his boots.

Torsten took them and looked at Mam.

She shook her head and looked at the floor.

"Tindra, can you assure me or do I need to search them?"

"I can assure you they aren't armed."

"It's your head if they are," he said, smiling.

"I know. Take us to King Ander."

He grunted. "Follow me."

The captain led us through a short hallway to a set of stairs. They spiraled upwards high enough that we were breathing heavily when we reached the top. We kept walking until we reached a door with two guards. "Is he in?" Torsten asked.

"Ready and waiting, captain."

This is it. The rest of my life and the future of Croy depends on this meeting.

My heart beat hard and fast when he pulled the door opened and motioned for us to enter.

Chapter 36

Tindra led us into a room with a long table and chairs facing a raised dais with two ornate thrones. The room reminded me of the Council of Thanes' chamber. I looked around and shivered as fear and suspicion shot through my body.

Hope I'm not making a mistake coming here.

Reaching into the floor with my talent, I found comfort at having natural stone under my feet. The fear drained away, but nervous apprehension remained, keeping my heart beating hard in my chest.

The man sitting on the larger of the two thrones looked older than my father had when he died. He wore a bright-red shirt, black pants, and polished, black boots. A simple, gold circlet sat on his head, binding his long, white hair. His skin was darker than I expected, as if he spent a lot of time outdoors. He looked frail, but something gave me the impression it was an intentional façade. It was his eyes. The dim light hid their color, but they had a youthful energy to them.

He waved us toward the table. "Sit."

Tindra bowed. We followed her example, before sitting at the table.

"Tindra, it has been some time since I've seen you," he said.

She stood and bowed again. "If only I could visit more often."

He nodded and she returned to her seat.

"I am Ander, King of Varia. Please stand and introduce yourselves."

Small tremors shook my legs as I stood. After bowing, I said, "I am Fitzeirick, former Skald of the far eastern skati of Croy. Son of Eirick of Croy and Sar'sa of Varia. Thank you for seeing us on such short notice. I recognize your time is valuable and hope you do not feel it wasted."

He stared at me, lips pressed together. "I'm curious why you requested an audience. Surely, you don't expect the current status of your territory to afford you my pity."

"I do not come looking for pity. Instead, I bring information about a common enemy," I said, returning to my seat.

Ander squinted and tilted his head for a moment. "Next."

Crum stood and bowed low. "I am Crum, son of Elgin and Hanna, both of Croy."

"May I ask why you are here?"

"To support Fitzeirick, my lifelong friend and leader. Additionally, I have firsthand information on a subject of interest to you and your country."

As he sat, Ander nodded. "Tindra, you did not tell me this was going to be such an interesting game. The last guest has already caught my eye."

Mam stood and curtseyed. "Fitz named me Mam, though I am almost certain it's not my real name. Will the queen be joining us?"

He leaned forward, placing his elbows on his knees, and stared at her for a moment. "I would not expect my wife to attend this meeting."

"I have gifts for her. May I give them to you?"

"My eyes are not what they used to be," he said. "I think I need a closer look at you."

She curtseyed again and hurried to the raised dais. Slipping the straw bracelets off her arms, she held them out.

He gestured for her to come closer. After taking the bracelets, the king studied them in detail before taking a long look at her. "You said Fitzeirick named you. Is Mam your birth name?"

She shook her head. "No, sir. I don't believe it is."

"How can you not know your name?"

"I had forgotten it," she said.

He bellowed, "Torsten!"

Mam jumped and took a step back.

The captain burst into the room, sword in his right hand, dagger in his left. "Here, Sire."

"No need for weapons. Put them away," Ander ordered. "Bring my wife...and tell her to bring the bracelet."

"The bracelet?" he asked.

"She'll know. Do as I ordered...and be quick about it."

He shifted his focus back to Mam. "Do you mind waiting here?"

She bowed her head. "Not at all, sir."

"I'm not sure I believe what I'm seeing," he said, after a moment. "Please, come closer."

She took a hesitant step toward him.

She's taking this better than I thought she would. Maybe part of her recognizes him?

He passed the time by looking back and forth from the bracelets to Mam. A couple of times he shook his head. His lips moved, but I couldn't hear what he said.

While we waited, I checked for hidden threats and tried to take in the details of the room since the few lanterns didn't cast much light. A large, unlit chandelier hung from the ceiling. *I'd feel better if it was lit.* When my talent reached the king's feet, he focused on me.

"Fitzeirick, what are you doing?" he asked.

Tindra and Crum both turned to look at me.

My cheeks warmed. "Please excuse me, Sire, it's a habit. I was trying to get a feel for my surroundings."

"By reaching out like a blind man?"

"If it is not too rude of me, the reason will be clear in due time," I said, and bowed my head.

"I look forward to it. I trust you can also explain the brand on your face?" he asked.

"Yes, your majesty, I can. No doubt you will understand both after I tell my story."

Ander nodded and turned his gaze to Tindra. "Before my wife arrives, how are you involved with these three?"

"Fitzeirick was a job. They came with him."

"I didn't send anyone after him," he said.

"No sir, I am...was...working for another party," she said, and looked away from the king.

"The war council? They sent you without word reaching me...interesting."

She gasped. "Yes, but I was under the impression —"

He interrupted her with a laugh. "Young woman, do you believe such a group operates without my knowledge, to say nothing of my blessing? Simply because I choose to not take part doesn't mean I'm ignorant of their existence."

"Of course. It's foolish to think they could operate anywhere in Varia without your approval, Sire," she said.

"I trust they pay you well," he said, smiling.

"Not as well as the crown," she said, "but good enough to keep me interested."

"Good to hear. I know you're worth more than you make."

Without warning, the door creaked. Captain Torsten stepped in. "All rise and bow to Queen Ines!"

We stood in unison.

Ander moved to conceal Mam.

A few more candles lit by themselves as she stepped into the room.

The door closed, and we took our seats, but the king remained standing. The queen looked a few years younger than her husband and carried herself with the grace of a firesyth.

She wore a simple, pale-green gown complementing her long, sandy blonde hair, almost the exact color of Stina's and Mam's. I noted the aged, straw bracelet on her right arm. From where I sat, it looked identical to the ones Mam made.

While the shape of her face and the skin tone told the story, the color of their eyes sealed it. All three had the same green eyes, the color of grass, wet with morning dew.

Mam had to be Jesca.

Ines looked at Ander and raised her eyebrows.

"Introductions are in order," the king said. "Tindra, you and my wife know each other already."

She looked at Tindra. Ines' expression looked like she'd bitten into a rotten piece of fruit.

"My lady," Tindra said, and bowed.

"Yes," the queen replied.

Tindra sat, as he continued. "To her right is Fitzeirick, son of Eirick and a Varian woman named Sar'sa. Eirick placed him in control of the conquered lands, now under Satran control."

Her expression did not improve much. She stared at me for a moment. "At least you are half Varian. Well met."

I bowed to her and sat.

"Next, we have Crum, son of two common-born Croians, lifelong friend to Fitzeirick."

She tilted her head. Her mouth twisted into an odd, crooked grin as she studied Crum. "Do you serve a useful purpose or simply ride the bastard's cape?"

My friend stiffened his backbone. "Some believe I'm only a smooth-talking scoundrel. Yet, I serve my liege in many useful ways both in his court and in his personal life. As point of fact, I was the one who introduced him to his fiancée."

Ines looked at her husband. "Is this what you had me awoken for? To meet with three people of no consequence?" The flickering flames around the room reflected her worsening mood.

"I saved the best for last," he said. "A gift." He presented the bracelets to her.

She glanced at them. "They expect to win me over with such paltry, childish things?"

He cleared his throat. "Look closer. I think you might find them interesting."

She sighed and the flames grew brighter. After looking longer at them, she lifted her arm to study the one she wore before looking back at Ander.

He cocked his head. "Do you think there is a resemblance, an interesting similarity?"

She whipped her head around to look at us. The flames flared brightly. "Where did you get these?" she screamed. "Guards! Torsten! In here now! Arrest these three. I want them tortured until they tell me where my daughter is. They know where Jesca is. Make them tell me."

The flames stayed bright as the door burst open and three men ran in, drawing weapons as they moved. I felt at least one of them drawing strength from the floor.

I did the same. Jumping to my feet, I shoved Crum behind me and lifted my chair.

I'd rather have my hammer, but the chair will work until I take a sword from one of them. Don't know how this will end, but I won't be taken captive.

King Ander shouted, "Stop!"

His voice seemed to come from everywhere at once and echoed several times before it faded. Everyone in the room stood still as a statue.

"I doubted my eyes at first and wanted you to confirm my thoughts. I believe Jesca is right here," he said, then sat so his wife could see her eldest.

Queen Ines studied her before asking, "Who are you?"

Tears ran down her cheeks. "Fitz called me Mam, when we met. Now, I believe I'm Jesca, your daughter, but I don't remember much of before."

Ines breathed heavy. "Before what?"

She hesitated. "Before I was living in the tunnels."

"What do you mean?" Ines asked. "What tunnels?"

She looked down and shuffled her feet for a moment. "There were tunnels...in Croy...under...Sir kept me safe."

I cleared my throat, put the chair back on the floor, and looked back to Crum, still sprawled on the floor. Mouthing 'sorry,' I offered to help him to his feet before facing the queen. "I may be able to explain better than she can."

She looked at me, rage burning in her eyes. "How can *you* know what she is going to say?"

"Because I am the only other person in this room who knows where she was."

She looked back to Mam. "What did he do to you Jesca? Where has he kept you all this time?" She glared at me again, a chill moved through the room, and the candles in the chandelier flared to life. "I don't know what you did to her, where you kept my Jesca, but you will suffer. Until you draw your last breath your life will be agony."

Grabbing a nearby candle and forcing the flame to burn uncomfortably bright, she held it before her eyes. "I'll light the fire and laugh while you scream in agony. I will watch you burn alive."

"He rescued me!" Jesca yelled. "He saved my life." She ran from the dais, crouched between me and Crum, and started humming.

Ander cleared his throat. "Everyone, calm down. Torsten, your men are not needed. Please, return to your posts."

They bowed and left the room.

Ander looked at his wife. "Ines, did you not hear her? Fitzeirick saved her from something. Try keeping your wits about you long enough to find out what happened to our daughter."

The candle went out as she put it back, but her expression did not change.

I stood, bowed to the king and queen, and told the story again. Describing, in horrific detail, how Eirickson bound and branded me before tossing me into the pitch-black nightmare. I explained how Mam and Sir found me, how we settled on their names, and helped each other survive. It was difficult to find words powerful enough to express my elation once I discovered a possible way out. At the end, I emphasized how hard I worked and how Sir sacrificed himself so we could escape.

They seemed to understand the reason for cutting her hair. The queen's expression softened when I described Jesca's horse riding exploits. Ander chuckled at his daughter knocking me out by accident. I pointed out all the time I spent in Varia including reuniting with Roi and his new family. The fight and killing at Stone Roof made the king grimace, but he didn't stop me. I praised the good people at the House of Daufi.

My speech ended with an oath to see Eirickson dead.

King Ander shook his head when I finished. "I...I don't know if I can put into words what I feel. It was horrific and yet you triumphed. How many times you should've died. And my daughter...how did she survive all those years?"

"We can't figure out how long she was in there," I said.

"We lost her almost twenty-two years ago. I don't understand how she lived all this time," Ines said.

"What?" I blurted. "How old is she?"

Ines dabbed at her eyes and looked at her daughter. "She was nearly nine when she disappeared."

"Then she's —"

Ines interrupted me. "Almost thirty years old."

"What?" Crum yelled. "She looks so young."

Mam looked at Crum. "Is that why —"

He nodded before she could finish.

"Why what?" Ines asked.

"Queen Ines, before I answer your question, I should tell you and King Ander what I discovered while searching for Fitzeirick," Crum said.

"Go ahead," Ander said.

He described Eirickson's meeting with Satran leaders emphasizing how they would divide Varia.

Ander's face was pale when Crum finished.

The king looked at me. "Do you have anything to add?"

I nodded. "Eirickson claimed Varia was planning an attack from the north. It was his excuse to leave me defenseless. Considering his refusal to return warriors to my border, a conspiracy with Satra only makes sense."

King Ander put his head in his hands and rubbed his forehead. After a little while, he looked to his wife, smiled, and turned his attention to Tindra. "Setup a meeting with the war council for me."

"I must warn you, many on the council do not agree with you on certain subjects," she said.

"I know what they think, and their opinions can go to the fire for all I care," he barked.

"I will see it happens at your earliest convenience, Sire."

Ines cleared her throat. "Jesca, come to me...please."

Her daughter looked at her. "Are you going to be angry again? Are you going to threaten my friends?"

The queen gave a weak smile. "No. I could never be angry with those responsible for returning you to me."

Jesca nodded and looked at me as she stood.

I smiled at her and she hurried to her mother.

The queen stood and pulled her into a tight embrace before sobbing so hard it shook both of them.

"Does anyone know why they took her? How did it happen?" I asked.

Ander looked away from his wife and daughter, covering his face with his hands. When he looked back at us, he wore an expression of sadness and relief. "We were vacationing in the south when the invasion started without warning. We considered

Croy friendly and had no army in the area, so the invaders captured land and kept moving. By the time we received word, the battle raged near our doorstep.

"We fled at moonrise, using the cover of darkness to hide as much as possible. Sometime during the third day, while we slept, Jesca disappeared. Of course, we wanted to find her, but we were defenseless. With the Croian army snapping at our heels, we had to keep moving or risk capture. I sacrificed my daughter to save my country. For weeks and months, we expected a ransom demand, an offer to trade me for her...something, but none came.

"After a year we sent messengers, pleading for proof our daughter was at least alive. Not a single messenger returned. We lost many spies trying to discover what happened to her. Now we find out she spent some, if not all, of that time struggling to survive in a lightless, barren dungeon."

He took a deep breath, looked back at his wife and daughter and shook his head. "Someone will pay for this."

"If I may be so bold," I said. "Our goals are the same. The question is, can we work together to remove the corrupt leadership in Croy?"

"Before we move on to that discussion, I want Crum to clarify something," Ander said.

He stood. "I will do my best."

"When my daughter asked you if that was why, you said yes. What did you mean?"

Before he could speak, Ines looked at him. "Yes, explain yourself."

Chapter 37

Crum's face lost all color. For a long, uncomfortable moment, he was speechless. "Umm...well...I...have a reputation," he stammered. "A reputation for being a bit —"

Tindra coughed.

He turned and stared daggers at her. Turning back to the king and queen, he put his fists on his hips and squared his shoulders. "Fine...I am a ladies' man. I don't pursue women; I simply don't refuse their attention when it comes my way."

Ines pursed her lips and raised her hand.

He stopped talking.

"I want to make sure I understand," she said. "You're telling us you simply walk into someplace —"

"Like a tavern," he interrupted.

She scowled. "Like. A. Tavern. And women come running in your direction?"

He wilted under her attention. "Rarely does that happen. When I'm out, I enjoy being the center of attention; I'm a storyteller. I never outright lie, but if a slight embellishment to my tale amazes my audience...who does it hurt?"

Ander added his voice to the pressure. "I still haven't heard how this involves Jesca." *Say it, brother...tell them how you feel. You can do this.*

He cringed, took a deep breath, and held it for a moment. "She...and...I...no, I am *not* going to speak for her. I have feelings —" He paused and shook his head before squaring his shoulders again. "There's no way to skirt the words without lessening the meaning. I love your daughter. I love Jesca."

I wanted to jump out of the chair and hug him. Good sense prevailed, limiting my approval to a smile and a nod.

"No," Ines muttered. Sparks flashed in her eyes. "No! My daughter will *not* associate with commoners!"

I stood and put my hand on his shoulder. "Crum may be common born, but he isn't a commoner. He's loyal to a fault and proven his worth to me, and my court, many times over. I trust him with my life. This man earned your daughter's trust through kindness, caring, and patience. He helped her rediscover her woodsything talent and did everything he could to nurture and encourage her. I know it's not my place, but I think you should ask *her* before making a rash decision."

Ander nodded to me. "My family will discuss this in private. Do you trust we will make no decision in haste?"

"Yes, Sire, I take you at your word. Thank you," Crum said.

Ander nodded. "I believe it's time for breakfast. Would you three join us?"

"It would be my honor," I said.

"Also, mine," Crum added.

Tindra looked at Queen Ines. "I don't want to cause problems."

"Eat with us," she said.

"Only if you are certain, my lady," Tindra replied.

Ines stepped away from Jesca and stared at her face before returning her focus to Tindra. "You helped return my daughter. You filled the hole in my heart. I have never been more certain."

"Torsten!" Ander yelled.

The captain stepped in the room with his hand on his sword. "Here, Sire."

"Send someone for Stina. She will join us for breakfast to hear the good news."

Torsten looked toward the floor. "I am afraid Stina is...feeling poorly, this morning my liege."

Ines whipped her head around and glared at him. "Who guarded her?"

"A man new to my command, my queen. Ingvar. I ask your mercy on his behalf. Despite all warnings, he underestimated how cunning she can be."

She pursed her lips and tapped her chin for a moment. "Since I am in an exceptional mood, I will leave Ingvar to my husband. My love, before meeting with this council, please impress upon him how much I care for my daughter. Make sure he understands the importance of her safety."

Ander nodded. "Of course. Do not allow such business to sour your happiness. Consider it done and think of this incident no more."

"Thank you."

Ander pointed to Torsten. "The order stands. I want her with us at the table this morning. Your only limit for getting her out of bed is physical harm. If she shows up looking like a drowned cat, so much the better, as far as I am concerned. Sooner or later she will learn."

"Yes...of course, Sire," he said. "I thank you on behalf of Ingvar for the queen's mercy."

The captain bowed and hurried out of the room.

"What if she *is* ill?" Jesca asked. "She didn't look good coming in earlier."

Ines raised her eyebrows. "You saw her?"

"We did," I answered. "She was rather drunk."

"And upset because I looked like her," Jesca added.

"I'm sorry you saw that," Ines said, "and apologize now for the spectacle which may occur while we eat."

"Perhaps we should eat elsewhere and let this be a family matter," Tindra offered.

"Nonsense," Ander said. "If my youngest wants to sneak out and mingle with the lowly in some dark, dank, ale house, she can deal with my ire."

"Tindra does make a point to consider," Ines said.

"No," he barked. "You will *not* continue to defend her actions. We have ignored her disgraceful behavior for too long."

She put her arm around Jesca. "I'm sorry. This isn't the homecoming I envisioned for you, dear."

"Is there anything I can do to help?" Jesca asked.

"We will see," she said. "For now, we'll make our way to the table."

Ander led us out of the room, and Ines held Jesca's hand as they walked behind him. Tindra, Crum, and I fell into step behind them. The guards moved next to Ander as he walked out the door.

Ander's pace convinced me he wasn't as frail as he appeared. He moved so fast I couldn't keep track of the turns before descending stairs into a large dining hall. Several people stood when they saw who entered the room.

He turned to the men flanking him. "Get something to eat. I doubt we'll need your services anytime soon."

A faint energy flowed past my feet and his voice came from the stone in the room. "Good morning, loyal subjects and servants. I apologize for interrupting your meal. Carry on as you were."

As people returned their seats, he led us to a door in the far-left corner of the room.

We entered a small dining room. Baskets of apples and pears sat in a line down the middle of the table and a serving buffet stood along the right wall. The wall opposite where we entered also had a door. The large fireplace in the left wall looked like it doubled as a cooking area.

King Ander moved to the head of the table. "Please sit. My staff will bring hot oatmeal, bread, and roasted meats out shortly, along with water and milk. Help yourself to fruit while we wait."

Queen Ines sat to his left and Jesca sat across from her.

Crum moved to sit next to Jesca, but a quick glance from Ines made him move one chair away. I sat across from him, and Tindra sat to my left.

"If you don't mind, I'll wait," Jesca said.

"Of course, we don't mind, dear," Ines replied, reaching for a pear.

King Ander smiled and nodded before taking an apple for himself.

Silence hung in the air like an oppressive blanket, its weight loading my shoulders. I didn't have to use my talent to feel Crum bouncing his leg.

"Your highness, how soon would you like to meet with the war council?" Tindra asked.

Ander swallowed and his eyes moved back and forth, as if reading something. He squinted and looked at his wife. "Do we have anything planned for this afternoon?"

"No, but with the return of our daughter, I assumed we would spend time together as a family."

We all jumped when the door behind him groaned open.

A soaking-wet Stina, dressed in the same clothes as earlier, stumbled into the room. The door closed behind her.

Ines stood. "Stina, dear, we have exciting news."

The princess grumbled something I couldn't make out and meandered toward the table. She fell into the chair next to her mother and looked at Jesca. "She here to replace me?"

Ander cleared his throat. "No, Stina, this is your sister. This is Jesca."

She never looked away from Jesca. "My sister's dead."

Ines took her hand. "I know this may be difficult for you to understand, especially considering your current...state. We know this is Jesca. Our three guests rescued her. They kept her safe and returned her to her rightful place."

Stina pulled her hand away. "I'm wet because an idiot guard dumped water on me while I slept. I don't feel well, and now I'll catch my death. This girl is a liar. Look at her hair, she's almost bald. A Varian princess would never do that, it's not proper."

Jesca slammed her fist on the table. "I had to cut my hair because it was matted and filthy. Proper or not, I was uncomfortable. I assure you I'm not dead."

"You are *not* Jesca. You are a liar and a fraud. How much you plan to take from them?" Stina asked.

"She's not a liar," Crum barked. "She's your sister, and a wonderful person."

Jesca bristled. "I want nothing from the king and queen. I've been without a family for so long, I'm content to stay with Fitz and Crum."

"You will not," snarled Ines.

I stood. "No disrespect, but I know Mam...Jesca...better than anyone here. King Ander, Queen Ines, you both need to understand she looks at life differently than most. She keeps a firm grasp on the here and now without thought for the future. Stina, I don't know you, and you have no idea who I am, but the woman sitting across from you is your sister. She is Jesca."

"Ha," Stina spat out. "You're a liar and a fraud, too. You called her Mam."

Jesca hit the table again. "It's the name he gave me when we met because I forgot who I was."

Before Stina could respond, King Ander motioned for me to sit. "Stina, I think it best if you kept your thoughts to yourself for now. Breakfast will be here soon and we all should enjoy a good, hot meal. Your mother and I appreciate your enthusiasm in defending us against deception, but this is your sister. Consider the matter settled."

The door opened and servants paraded in. No one said a word as the table was set. They served our food with the precision of a troupe of well-practiced dancers. Their tasks complete, the servants bowed in unison and left the room.

Ander tapped his cup with a spoon. "Enjoy."

Stina set upon her food like a starving predator. She ate so fast there was no way she could've tasted the food, much less enjoyed it. After devouring everything in front of her, she swallowed the cup full of water in one gulp and finished with a belch loud enough to scare most people.

Standing, she looked at each of us, then said, "I'm done with breakfast. You can sit here and talk about how my fake sister is going to make us a big, happy family again, but I am leaving."

Ander grabbed her arm as she passed. "You will sit and keep a civil tone, or I will confine you to your room until —"

"Until you feel bad for locking me away?" she interrupted. "We both know it won't last long."

"No," he replied. "You'll be confined until Jesca convinces me to allow your freedom."

She glared at him and yanked her arm out of his grip. "We both know Mother won't let that happen."

The queen flew out of her chair and slapped Stina so hard the sound echoed around the room. "How dare you defy your —"

Ander interrupted her with a roar. "Enough! Both of you sit...now. Stina, you may sit of your own free will or I will make you sit."

"Fine," she snarled, and returned to her chair.

Jesca sobbed. "I...I am sor...sorry. I should...not...have come. We'll leave after we eat...unless you...would prefer we leave...now."

Ines gasped. "We don't want you to leave —"

"I do," Stina said.

Her mother slapped her again, this time hard enough to knock her and the chair over. I thought I felt the impact from where I sat.

Jesca covered her face with her hands.

Crum moved to put his arm around her. "Shhh...dear little Mam. Calm yourself, you're fine. If you want to leave, I'll make sure you get out."

"Her name is Jesca and you will do no such thing," Ines said.

He faced the queen square on. "Lady, I told this lovely woman I would do her bidding. I gave her my word. I will see my vow through to the end or die trying."

I stood. "Can I ask everyone to calm down before something we all regret happens?"

"That is the wisest thing I've heard since I asked everyone to enjoy their food," Ander said. "Everyone sit and keep quiet until we are all done eating. The next person who disturbs the peace will finish their breakfast behind bars. Furthermore, they will remain there until the rest of us have eaten our fill."

Crum and I sat, and we all ate in silence.

Stina rested her head on the table.

Crum finished his oatmeal and made a sandwich to eat while he went to the buffet and refilled his bowl.

I decided to forgo a second helping, hoping to escape this awkward situation sooner.

Ander ate as slowly as he could.

My shoulders drooped once I understood this was part of Stina's punishment.

If not for the changing morning light shining through the windows behind me, I'd swear time had stopped. I remembered Jesca's saying, "No sun, no moon, no stars, no time," and bit my lip to keep from laughing. There was no doubt King Ander would make good on his threat, and I didn't want to deal with the consequences.

Crum finished his second bowl of oatmeal while the king took his time.

He took a piece of meat and studied it in extreme detail before taking a small bite, chewing slowly before swallowing.

Tindra tapped my leg with her foot.

I looked at her, shook my head, and shrugged.

Ander finished his meat and turned his attention to the bowl. He scooped a spoonful and blew on it even though there was no possibility it was hot.

Stina groaned. "You can't be serious."

He dropped the spoon into his oatmeal. "Guards!"

The door behind him swung open and two men drew their weapons as they entered the room.

He pointed to Stina. "Arrest her. Take her to the dark box."

Ines' and Stina's heads snapped toward him in unison.

"No," Ines gasped. "I won't let you."

"Silence, or you will join her."

"Father, no," Stina cried.

"With all due respect, my lord, there is a prisoner in the box," one of the guards said.

"Move the prisoner to nicer confinement."

"As you wish, Sire," he replied, and moved toward Stina. They stood a respectable distance from the princess and asked her to come with them.

"I said *take* her!" Ander barked.

The guards stepped forward and grabbed Stina's arms.

As they pulled her from the chair, Jesca grabbed her father's hand. "Don't lock her away in the dark."

"Why not?"

"Because, I know what it's like. I'd never wish it on anyone."

"Listen to her!" Stina screamed, as the guards dragged her out of the room.

"What would you have me do?" he asked.

Screams echoed in the hall.

"I don't know. Almost anything is better than being locked away in the dark."

He turned his attention to me. "Fitzeirick, in your time as a leader you handed out punishments...correct?"

"Yes."

The screams slowly faded.

"What would you consider appropriate punishment in this situation?"

I sat up straight and tapped my fingers on the table for a moment. "I believe the best way to advise you is by knowing what you want her to learn," I answered. "Punishment without a purpose in mind is not very effective, in my experience.

He looked at me for a moment and nodded. "Very wise answer. I agree. Tindra, you know where they're going. Tell them to bring her back."

Looks like I am gaining his trust. I tried to hide my smile as Tindra jumped from her chair and ran from the room.

"Why?" Ines asked.

"I need time to consider what she should learn and how best to teach her."

"Father?" Jesca asked.

"Yes?"

"Does everyone have to be here while you talk with Stina?"

"Why? What did you have in mind?"

"I'm feeling...I'd like to be outside. Mother could escort Crum and me. It would give us a chance to talk, to get to know each other."

"I should be here when your father deals with your sister," Ines said.

She frowned. "I guess I understand. Crum and I can make our own way around."

"No one here knows about you yet," Ander said.

"And you don't know your way around. You could be lost or get into trouble," Ines added.

"Crum will keep me safe."

"You may trust him. We do not," Ines said.

Hope I'm not pressing my luck. "If I may? When the guards return with Stina, have one of them escort Jesca and Crum," I suggested.

"For Jesca's benefit, I'll allow it. Crum must swear to be on his best behavior," Ines said, after Ander nodded.

"I promise to act with honor," he said.

"So agreed," Ander said.

"Thank you," Jesca exclaimed. I'm not sure whose smile was bigger, her's or Crum's.

I couldn't understand the yells coming from the hallway, but it was obvious Stina was berating the guards. I think she threw some choice words at Tindra for good measure.

Tindra entered the room ahead of the other three and every flame flared. I felt heat coming from her when she sat next to me.

Stina entered next, a step ahead of the guards, wearing a smug look.

"Stina, sit," Ander commanded.

"I prefer to stand. I don't plan to be in here much longer."

"Sit and be quiet!" he roared, loud enough to shake the room.

The poor girl paused for a moment before hurrying to her chair.

"I need a guard to show my daughter, Jesca, and her friend around the castle and the grounds. Which one of you wants to do this for me?" Ander asked.

The two men looked at each other before one stepped forward. "I would be glad to do this for you, Sire."

"Excellent. Thank you. Please make sure Torsten knows I gave you this assignment. Keep them safe and entertained."

"I will do my best, but...permission to speak freely, Sire?"

"You may."

"How can she be Jesca?" he asked. "I've always heard Jesca was dead. The resemblance to Queen Ines and Princess Stina is obvious, but it does not mean —"

He raised his hand. "The queen and I have determined she is our daughter. She wants some fresh air and you will see she is safe."

He bowed low. "Of course, Sire."

"Thank you," Jesca said, as she got up and walked toward the guard. Crum stayed silent and moved to her side.

"Make sure they get lunch and have them back for dinner," Ines said.

"Of course, my queen," the guard replied. He bowed again and left the room with my friends close behind.

"You," King Ander said, addressing the remaining guard, "close the door on your way out and wait in the hall. We may need your services again, soon."

"Yes, your majesty."

"Now, Stina. Fitzeirick raised an important question. What's the point of punishing you? What lesson should you learn? I've been pondering this since sending Tindra to retrieve you. I believe I know what I want you to learn, but I'm unclear on how to teach it."

"Do what you will," she replied. "It doesn't matter. I've proven over and over you can't control when I come and go."

"That's what troubles me about anything less than locking you away," he said.

"What do you want to teach her?" Ines asked.

"I think it's time she learns to be thankful for what she has and learn what it means to be humble."

"Send her to the House of Daufi. Let them put her to work," Tindra suggested.

"But those people are —" the queen started to say.

"My parents founded that house. They are good for our community even though everyone is blind to their involvement. Most do not appreciate the irony."

The queen again looked like she was eating something rotten before forcing a smile. "My apologies."

"An interesting suggestion," Ander said. "Can they keep Stina on the grounds?"

"Keeping her shouldn't be a concern considering what they face every day," Tindra said.

"And she would be safe there?" Ines asked.

"Yes."

"How would we arrange such a thing?" Ander asked.

"I'll contact my parents, explain what's needed. I'm sure they'll have questions and concerns, but they should be willing to help."

"You said concerns," Ines said. "What kind of concerns?"

"Everyone who lives there works as they are capable," Tindra said. "If Stina refuses to work, what are they allowed to do to her?"

"I don't —" Ines started to say.

Ander interrupted her. "What do they do to their own when they refuse to work?"

"The first step is public humiliation. They stand in the most populated area while it's announced they refuse to work. They must stay while the others berate them. Often, that's all it takes. If it's not effective, they go hungry. No solid food, only liquids. If they still refuse to work, they are turned over to the beggar's house and considered dead. To the best of my knowledge, it's only happened once."

"My youngest daughter will not go to the beggar's house," Ines asserted.

"She'd better work," Ander replied. "How would we make arrangements for her to live at House of Daufi?"

"Meet with my parents. I'd expect they'll want specific terms. Things like how long she'll stay or the condition for release."

He turned to his wife. "Do you have an objection to Stina moving to House of Daufi?"

"I won't keep you from sending her there."

"I have an objection," Stina said.

"I did not ask you," Ander said.

"How long are you going to leave me with the outcasts?"

"Your mother and I will discuss it with them." He paused, then called for the guard. The guard stepped into the room. "Yes, Sire?"

"Secure Stina in the northern tower, the highest room. I want at least two men stationed outside her door day and night, and two men watching each outside door and window, day and night. She will remain there until I send for her. No one else has the authority to take her from there. Do I make myself clear?"

He bowed. "Yes, Sire. I understand and will see to it personally."

"I thank you for your service. Be on alert; she can be a slippery one."

"I am aware of her reputation, your majesty."

"Off with you two," Ander replied.

"I will not stand for this!" Stina yelled, when the guard got close.

He stopped and looked at his king.

"Take her," Ander growled.

The guard nodded once and grabbed Stina by the arm. She struggled. He held her tight.

"You are hurting me," she screamed.

"Stop fighting," Ander said.

"Ander!" Ines exclaimed.

"She put herself in this position," he said. "Take her to the tower."

"I will not let her be manhandled," Ines said.

"She should conduct herself as a proper lady. Our family is whole again, you will stop overlooking her behavior," he said, before turning back to the guard. "Why is she still here? I ordered her taken away."

He nodded once and forced Stina from the room.

The screams started as she passed the door.

"I think it might be best if I take a walk until you calm down," Ines said.

"I am calm," Ander said.

"All the same," Ines said, as she stood and walked out.

Tindra cleared her throat. "In light of the trouble with Stina, when should I contact you to arrange the meeting with the war council?"

"My family doesn't take priority over my country. I give you leave to arrange the meeting. Take Fitzeirick with you; his involvement will be crucial. I will have Lars contact your parents. Once you have things in place, ask a guard or servant to get word to me."

"Yes, your highness," Tindra said, as she stood.

I stood and bowed. "Until we meet next."

"I'm already looking forward to it," Ander replied, as we left.

We walked in silence until we were well away from the room.

"That was —"

I cut Tindra off sharply with a hand on her wrist. "Did you notice Ander projected his voice through the stones around him? I don't know if he can listen through them also."

"Can stonesyths hear through walls?" she asked, glancing around.

"I can't, but I didn't know one could send their voice out through stone either. I think it best to wait until we're outside to carry on any meaningful conversation."

Chapter 38

Tindra nodded and led me to the nearest door out of the castle. She made sure the door closed behind us and waited until we were away from the castle before speaking again.

"Do you think Mam...I mean Jesca, will be safe?" she asked.

"Your concern surprises me," I said. "Crum's looking after her, she'll be fine."

"She's a good person who deserves better than what life's given her so far."

"True. How long until we reach the war council?"

"It's not so simple. I have to contact someone and ask them to get the word out. I agree with Ander; the meeting needs to happen soon. However, some of the council may not share his opinion."

"How many council members are there?"

"I don't know if I've ever seen them all in one place, but I have a feeling it's more than the few I've dealt with in the past," she said.

"Where are we going?"

"Blacksmith shop, not much farther."

"One of the members is a blacksmith?" I asked.

"I wouldn't be surprised if some are, but not this one. He owns the shop, uses it to hide his...activities."

"But if King Ander knows about the council and this man is doing something illegal —"

She cut me off. "Ander's lack of acknowledgment protects him from detractors if something goes wrong. He can claim they're a rogue group of conspirators involved in all sort of illegal and immoral things, hiding among the good people of Varia."

"Perhaps you shouldn't be so free with the king's secrets," I said.

She winked. "I only talk secrets with those I trust."

Before I could respond, she pointed toward a wooden sign. A bucket on its side with horseshoes spilling out. "There's the place, Kurt's smithy. I wonder who he has pounding metal now."

"What do you mean?"

"The front of his shop seems like a never-ending line of workers. The good ones either gain responsibility in his crew or go to work for a more reputable shop. The bad ones stick around until Kurt gets tired of them."

"Doesn't sound like a good way to do business," I said.

"I figure he'd be out of business if he relied on income from smithy work."

When we reached the shop, we found the door bolted and the windows shuttered.

"Strange," Tindra said, rattling the door one more time. "Guess we'll check the back."

We turned the corner, into an alley, and saw a slender man leaning near the back door. At first glance, he reminded me of Crum. "Recognize him?" I asked.

"Can't say I do. Let me do the talking," she said. When we got closer, she called out, "Well met. Do you happen to know if Kurt is in today?"

He stood, putting himself between us and the door. "Shop's closed. Whatever you need will have to wait until tomorrow."

She looked him up and down. "I need to talk to Kurt, important business to discuss. Today."

"I told you the shop's closed. No business today."

"Can you get a message to him?" she asked.

"Depends on what the message is and what's in it for me."

"I've been paid handsomely to get this information, not just anyone should hear it. Come here, I'll whisper it to you."

"I still haven't heard how I benefit," he said.

"I'll tell you after I've given you the message."

He stepped closer and leaned over.

Tindra put her lips close to his ear.

He nodded a couple of times before she raised her voice. "Do what I've asked, and I'll put in a good word with Kurt."

"How about I kill you and take the package to him myself?" he asked, drawing a knife. Before I could react, she swept his feet out from under him. He yelped, dropping the knife as he fell to the ground, and she grabbed it. "I want him on his knees while I decide what to do."

Best to follow her lead, I guess. I hurried to grab him and, lifting by his neck, pulled him into a kneeling position.

Tindra stood in front of him, tested the blade's edge with her thumb, and nodded. "You should have cooperated. Good thing you keep this sharp; it won't hurt as bad."

"What are you talking about?" he asked, struggling to get free of my grip.

"A sharp knife removes an ear with less pain than having it ripped off," she said.

"You're not going to take my ear!" he yelled, struggling to stand.

I pulled some strength to hold him in place.

She smiled. "I asked you, nicely, to do something for me. Not only did you disrespect me, you threatened to kill me. If word spread that I didn't do something about that, my reputation would suffer. Other people might think they can get away with disrespecting me. That would make my job more difficult," she said, looking at me. "Hold him still. If he squirms too much I might slip and cut his throat."

Guess she wasn't lying when she said she'd dealt with these kinds of people before. I clamped my hand tighter on his neck. Part of me worried she might slit his throat anyway.

When she touched his ear, he screamed so loud it hurt my ears.

Before she could do anything else, the back door creaked open about halfway.

I looked over to see a man's head poke out. It looked like solid muscle.

"Kurt wants ta know what all tha noise...Oh, hullo Tindra."

She waved and the head retreated into the building.

He yelled, "Kurt! Tindra's here!" I heard a muffled reply and he yelled back, "I dunno! Lemme find out! You there. Holding Botel. You with Tindra?"

I tilted my head. "Yes. I came here with her."

He nodded, went back in, and yelled, "No! She's not alone!" I still couldn't make out what was said, but he replied, "I dunno. Lemme find out." Out popped the head again. "Tindra. Kurt wants ta know if this is him."

"Holven. Tell Kurt it is and I said he needs to hire a better class of thug."

He pulled his head back inside and yelled, "She said it is and ya need better thugs!"

"Holven," she said. He stuck his head back outside. "Why not let me in and I can tell Kurt myself?"

"I dunno. Lemme find out." He pulled his head back inside. "She wants in!"

"Is this normal?" I asked.

"Holven?" she replied. "I'd say he's acting normal for him. Lots of muscle, not much thinking power though."

"No," I said. "Well...yes, him, but also this whole situation."

She shook her head. "This isn't normal for Kurt. Something's going on."

The door opened and Holven stepped out. He stood at least a whole head taller than Roi, maybe more. I guessed he weighed at least twice what I did, solid muscle. His face was unremarkable. He had long, black hair that looked thick as yarn and wore threadbare clothes.

"Kurt said ta check for weapons," Holven said.

"I'm unarmed," I said.

"I have Botel's knife," Tindra said.

Holven smiled. "Gimme tha knife. Follow me."

Tindra looked at me. "Bring Botel. I'm not finished with him."

I pulled him to his feet and followed them into a small room.

Holven pointed to a door on the left. "In there."

Tindra led us to an office. A blond-haired man with a groomed beard sat behind a desk. Two men sat across from him, one bald, the other with curly, black hair. They turned to look at us when we walked in.

"Why'd you bring Botel?" the man seated to our left asked.

"Introductions before explanations," Tindra said. She pointed toward the man on the far side of the desk. "Kurt. To our right is Tyres." She pointed to the curly-haired man. "I don't know him."

He stood, or at least got out of the chair. He was shorter than Tindra by about half a head. "I'm known as Folke. Now, I want an explanation. Why does he have my man by the neck?"

Tindra sighed. "You're almost as disrespectful as he is. Introductions are not yet complete. Kurt, Tyres...this is Fitzeirick, son of Eirick." She inclined her head to the short man. "Folke, I'm Tindra. I assume you paid attention when I introduced Fitzeirick."

His face turned red before he nodded.

"Good, that's an improvement. Now for explanations, first me, then Kurt. Your man's here because he can't follow directions. Also, he does *not* respect his betters."

"That's a lie," Botel blurted out.

"Keep him quiet," she barked.

I nodded and squeezed his neck.

"I'm not sure I understand," Folke said.

"I asked him to let Kurt know I was here, nothing more. He tried to take advantage of my trust and threatened to kill me, so I decided to take his ear. It's still attached because Holven interrupted."

"I suppose I see your point," Folke said. "But I have to know, what makes you think you're his better?"

The candles flared. "We came here unarmed, but I handed Holven a knife before he let us in. Whose knife was it?"

Silence hung in the air.

She turned to Botel. "Answer the question. Whose knife did I have?"

"Mine."

"And how did I get your knife?"

"I dropped it, when you knocked me down," he said.

She nodded and turned back to Folke. "An unarmed woman easily took his blade. Any further doubt as to why I say I'm better?"

Kurt cleared his throat. "Folke, take your man and leave. I'll contact you when I have time to spare."

"What about Botel's ear?" Tindra asked.

"What about it?" Folke responded.

"I do my best to keep my word. Bad for my reputation if I don't."

"Kurt," Folke said, face turning a deeper red. "This is no way to start a new business arrangement. Do something about this."

Kurt shrugged. "She's an independent. I pay for results. I *don't* make demands outside of the job."

The short man sighed. "What's it going to cost me to let Botel keep his ear?"

Tindra stepped closer to Folke, forcing him to crane his neck to look her in the eye. "I like Kurt, he treats me fair. You and he are working a deal of some kind?"

"Yes, but it's no concern of yours," Folke said.

"You never know what the future holds," she said. "New business arrangement? So...negotiation, compromise, that sort of thing...correct?"

"I think you know it does," Folke said.

"How about *I* offer a compromise?"

"I'm listening," he said.

"Your man leaves the capital and doesn't come back."

"And if he doesn't?"

She shrugged. "If I see him, I'll take what's mine. It's a big place, our paths may never cross, but is he willing to take that chance? Are you going to let him risk it?"

"You don't want coin?" Folke asked, patting a pouch, hanging from his belt. "No way I can pay to cover his mistake?"

Tindra looked at Kurt. "You understood me, right?"

He nodded.

She slapped Folke. "I think I'm starting to see where Botel learned his behavior. Should I add something of yours to the agreement?"

Folke drew strength from the stone floor.

I raised my eyebrows. *Little man might be tougher than he looks.* "I could crush his neck," I warned. *If that doesn't discourage him, this could get ugly.*

Folke looked at Kurt. "Control your hired hands."

Kurt shook his head. "Learn your place. You came to me looking to make a reputation for yourself. Tindra...she's as solid as it gets. She can put names in King Ander's ear. Those names can find their way to the guard. It's hard to get much work done with them riding your back."

"I see your point," Folke muttered, and turned back to her. After clenching and relaxing his jaw a couple of times, he said. "My lady, I apologize for any slight directed toward you. You won't see him again."

"All I needed to hear," she said. "You may take him and leave. Now."

Folke stepped around her and punched Botel in the knee. "Try to keep up."

I let go of his neck and stepped aside while Tindra took the empty seat.

"You sure know how to make an impression," Tyres said.

"All he had to do was follow directions," she said, and looked at Kurt. "What's Folke offering?"

Kurt rolled his eyes. "He wants to move merchandise for me. He's a street rat with enough money to hire some muscle. I figure he'll get himself killed on his first job."

"How did a rat that short get money? I figure someone would've stepped on him," Tindra said, her hand at Folke's height. "Speaking of street rats, do either of you know anything about a gang robbing people on the way to the House of Daufi?"

Tyres shook his head and Kurt said, "No, why?"

She nodded. "Four of them jumped my wagon yesterday. They didn't live to regret it."

"Their mistake," Tyres said.

Kurt chuckled. "I hadn't heard you were back. Dare I ask how you managed to sneak in with him?"

"You can ask, but I won't tell," she said, smiling. "However, I will give you some good news, no extra charge."

"What do you mean," Tyres asked.

"You don't know who he traveled with."

"Of course, we do. He had some crazy girl with him when he met up with this Crum," Tyres said.

"She's not crazy," I interjected.

"As a matter of fact, she's Princess Jesca," Tindra said, with a wide smile.

"Can't be. Someone's playing a game. Everyone knows Jesca's dead," Tyres said, shaking his head.

Tindra looked him in the eye. "I don't lie to my employers. She's alive and...well."

"I don't want to believe it, but you don't play games with me," Kurt said, stroking his beard. "The Jesca? You're sure?"

She nodded.

"Does Ander and Ines know yet?" Kurt asked.

"Not only do they know, he wants to meet with the council."

"You told him about the council?" Kurt said, looking concerned.

"He already knew," she said.

"Wait. Because of Jesca, he wants to meet with us?" Tyres said.

"No. Because of Fitzeirick, he wants to meet with the *whole* council," Tindra said.

"When?" Kurt asked.

"Soon. Today, if possible."

"It will take some time," Tyres said.

"What's in it for us? How do we know he won't throw us all in the dungeon?" Kurt asked.

"Because of Fitzeirick," Tindra said. "Also because of what Crum knows."

"Crum's a tavern snake. There's nothing —" Tyres started to say.

I stood as tall as I could, crossed my arms, and glared at him. "Consider what you say about one of my closest friends."

Tyres held his hand up. "Apologies, I didn't know he was important to you."

I shifted my gaze from him to Kurt. "More important than anyone in this room."

"Understood," Tyres said.

"As I was saying, he stumbled onto a meeting between Eirickson and Satran advisors while looking into Fitzeirick's disappearance. They were discussing how to divide Varia after a successful invasion."

"When?" Kurt blurted out.

"We don't know," I said.

"This changes everything," he said. "We have to move up the schedule."

Tindra shook her head. "Don't do anything rash. Get the word out. Meet with Ander. Gain his support and you get supplies, maybe men."

He pursed his lips for a moment. "Tyres, start rounding up people...now."

Tyres nodded and left the room.

"Most of us are seeing to business away from the capital. How should I contact you?" Kurt asked.

"Leave word at House of Daufi. I'm staying there."

"I guess the last thing I need to know is where will we meet?" Kurt asked.

"I don't know yet. How many do you think will show?" Tindra asked.

"Given what we know now, all fifteen should," he said.

"Pick a location and let me know," she said. "I'll get word to Ander."

He shook his head. "After all this time, the war council is going to work with the crown. You know we had plans to —"

"You won't need them," she interrupted.

He nodded. "Right. But now, we have so much more to do...and soon."

"Get to it," I said.

He glared at me. "You're *not* in charge, Croian. I don't take orders from you."

"Not yet," she said. "We'll be in touch."

"Yes, we will," Kurt said, as she stood.

"By the way," she said. "No one else knows about Jesca. It's best you keep it secret."

"I see no reason to say anything to anyone," he said, nodding.

"Make sure Tyres feels the same way," Tindra said, before turning to leave.

Chapter 39

I followed Tindra out of the office and waited until we were well away from the smithy before I spoke. "Wasn't sure what to expect, but I don't think that was it."

She shook her head. "It wasn't. I've never seen Kurt close his shop for an unknown. Interested in a tour while I gather my thoughts?"

"Don't have anything better to do. Wouldn't hurt to get to know the area."

We walked for several hours while she showed me different places she found interesting. In general, the buildings were in better condition than the places near House of Daufi.

At the edge of a busy market square, Tindra said, "We're near one of my favorite eateries."

"I could eat."

"Follow me."

She moved through the crowd like a dancer. I charged through like an impatient bull. We managed to reach the eatery without getting into a fight.

"Ever had Satran food?" she asked.

"No. There's Satran food in the Varian capital?"

"Tudal's family left Satra generations ago. He's Varian by birth, but continues their cooking traditions," she replied. "It's a nice change from the bold spices we favor. Sound interesting?"

"Sure," I said, "but I'm not eating anything raw."

She laughed and shook her head.

We stepped into the front of the eatery. I smelled fresh bread with an earthy, herbal aroma and heard meat sizzling. Every seat was taken.

"Looks like we'll have to wait," I said.

"Don't worry, Tudal takes care of me and my guests."

A young girl ran toward us and wrapped herself around Tindra's leg. At first glance, the girl looked Varian. After a moment, I noticed her honey-colored hair had faint, silvery streaks and her skin carried a rosy gray tone.

"Papa, Tindra's here," the little girl squealed, before looking me up and down. "And she brought a man."

Tindra chuckled. "Nolwen, his name is Fitzeirick, a good friend of mine. Fitzeirick, this is Nolwen, Tudal's daughter."

I bowed to her. "Nice to meet you, Nolwen."

"You have a long name. Can I call you Fitz?"

Tindra laughed.

"Yes, you may call me Fitz, if you like," I said, grinning.

A slender man, about my height, walked out of the back. He had mottled-gray skin with matching long hair. "Tindra, it's good to see you. Lena will be happy you're here. Who's your friend?"

"Tudal, this is Fitzeirick. He's never had Satran cooking before. Care to treat him to a surprise?"

He looked me up and down, much like his daughter had, and stared at my scar. "Anything I should be concerned about?"

I held out my hand and smiled. "Nothing at all. Tindra speaks well of your cooking."

He shook my hand. "I can't take all the credit. The recipes were in my family long before I was born. And my wife, even if she is Varian, does unbelievable work in the kitchen. Your usual spot, Tindra?"

"Only if it isn't an inconvenience," she replied, looking at me. "You don't mind sitting in the kitchen, do you?"

"Closer to the food, right?"

Tudal smiled. "Nolwen, go set our table. Tindra, good to see you've found a man who thinks like I do. If you want my advice, marry him."

She shrugged. "I'm trying."

I narrowed my eyes and growled her name.

"He's not cooperating," she said, smiling.

"For good reason," I countered.

She raised her hands. "I know, I know."

He shook his head and waved us toward a small table in the back of the kitchen. "Lena, look who's here."

A squat Varian woman looked up from the large stove where she held court over various pots and pans. Her honey-blonde hair was twisted into a roll on the back of her head. The heat from the stove colored her rosy cheeks a deeper, red. She smiled at us. "Tindra, so good to see you. Come, give us a hug."

I took a seat while Tindra walked over to hug Lena. "You look well. Nolwen's growing so quick. She's seven now, right?"

"I'm almost nine," Nolwen said, placing two cups on the table.

"How'd you get so old?" Tindra teased, as she sat down.

"We often ask ourselves the same thing," Tudal commented.

"She looks like your wife," I said.

"I hope it makes life easier for her. There's some amount of dislike for my ancestry," he said, shaking his head.

"You seem to have a good business."

"Food this good sells itself and a Varian cooks most of it. But Tindra didn't bring you here to talk about problems. The treat for today is three-meat-stew pie. Be right back."

"What's in it?" I whispered to Tindra.

"I don't want to spoil the surprise. It's delicious."

He returned and placed a plate holding a large pie between us. Tindra plunged a fork into the top crust, twirled it a couple of times, and pulled out some meat. She blew on it, pushing the scent toward my face, and put it in her mouth.

"Mmmm," she hummed, as she chewed. After swallowing, she said, "I have to know how you get the meat so tender."

Tudal laughed, but Lena yelled, "Don't give away secrets,"

"Amazing, as usual," Tindra said. "I'm never disappointed when I come here. My compliments to the cook."

He bowed. "You are too kind. Enjoy."

Tindra pointed her fork at me. "Satran dishes are meant to be shared. This is for both of us. I can't eat it all."

The crust broke like thin, hard bread, and exposed a thick stew. I had no problem finding some meat with my fork and cooled it before taking my first bite.

The broth from the stew had a strong flavor, reminding me of being in a forest for some reason, along with fleeting tastes of lemon. The tender meat seemed to melt in my mouth. The first flavor was lamb, seasoned to perfection. Pork, carrying a citrusy taste, followed close after. The third meat took me a moment to pick out. I finally decided it was rabbit with a slightly nutty flavor.

Tindra broke off a piece of crust and scooped some thick broth.

I followed her example and experienced a new variety of flavors. The woodsy, tangy flavor of the stew faded behind sweet and sour from the dough with a light, peppery flavor. "This is amazing," I said, around a mouthful.

Tindra smiled. "And they won't tell anyone how they make it."

"Lena, if you ever find yourself in Swinter ask someone to introduce you to Einns. The two of you would be unstoppable in the kitchen," I said.

"Who's that?" Lena asked.

Tudal turned from his work. "Are you trying to set my wife up with another man?" Tindra laughed.

"No, no," I said, smiling. "Einns is my best friend's stepson. He learned to cook in a busy inn, but his talent with flavors blossomed after they settled in Swinter. Please don't let him know I said so, but...this is my new favorite food."

"Another convert!" Tudal shouted.

Tindra looked at me. "Don't give him any more praise or he'll start singing and dancing."

"What's wrong with my singing and dancing?"

"Nothing, my love," Lena said, before shaking a fork at him. "But it keeps you from working. If you don't get the meat ready, we won't be serving dinner before moonrise."

"Fine, fine," he said. "Work before fun."

Tindra chuckled during their entire exchange.

I couldn't help but smile. The light mood in the kitchen helped me relax, a welcome change from the stressful breakfast earlier.

Their playful banter continued until Nolwen interrupted to let Tudal know she needed him out front.

Finally, I decided I couldn't eat another bite and let out a long sigh. "As good as this is, I'm stuffed." Tindra looked from the remains of the pie to me. "I can't leave without paying Lena for our meal. Tudal would refuse. He insists I'm the reason his little eatery remains busy."

"How many people have you brought here?"

"Ohhh," she said, drawing the word out while she thought. "I recommend this place to everybody, but I only bring those I want to share a meal with."

She left the table, hugged Lena, and slipped coins into her pocket.

I stood near the door and waited for her. "That's not an answer."

"But it's the truth," she said, as we left.

"It also doesn't tell me what you've planned for the rest of the day."

"I think I need to introduce you to my favorite weapon maker. It's time you got a proper Varian fighting hammer."

"I like my hammer. I've had it most my life and Crum kept it safe for me."

"It's so primitive, it's almost a tool. You can do so much better," she said, and walked faster.

I sighed and sped up to stay with her. She took unnecessary turns and seemed to seek out narrow passages. As we walked, I wondered if she ever took a direct route anywhere. Out of frustration I finally asked, "Are you doing this on purpose?"

"What?"

"Taking the long way to wherever we are going."

"Habit," she said. "Makes it easier to notice someone following me. It's saved my life before."

"Makes sense, but it's still frustrating."

She laughed.

After a while, she stopped in front of a pair of large metal doors set into the wall of a long stone building. She pulled a rope hanging out of an opening near the top of the wall and a bell rang inside.

One of the doors swung out without making a sound and Holven stepped out. Instead of threadbare clothes, he wore heavy leathers meant for working around hot metal.

"Tindra. So nice to see you. How long have you been in the capital?" he asked.

"You saw her earlier at Kurt's," I said. "You let us in."

Tindra smiled.

"No. I've been here working since before sunrise." He scratched his head. "Is Holven back at Kurt's?"

She nodded and chuckled

"You aren't Holven?" I asked.

"No. I'm Per. Holven's my brother. I assume you're here with her."

"Yes, he's a friend of mine," Tindra said.

I held out my hand. "Fitzeirick. I apologize for the confusion."

"Happens all the time," he said. "Nice to meet you, but the mark on your face makes me question her judgment."

"He came out on the wrong side of a family squabble," she said.

The big man cringed. "Must have been a serious disagreement. When my family has squabbles, someone usually ends up knocked out on the floor."

"Something like that happened too, right after the branding," I said.

"I'd like you to show him some battle hammers," Tindra said.

"Stonesyth?" he asked.

"I am."

He nodded. "Come with me."

We stepped into a large, open space with a searing firepit taking up most of the far wall. Several men were working with glowing metal. He led us through another large room where men and women finished various items. I glanced around and saw everything from small knives to large cooking pots. We stopped in a third room, about half the size of the other two. A wide assortment of weapons hung on the wall and stood in stands around the room.

"What did you have in mind?" Per asked.

I shrugged. "This was her idea. I'm happy with my hammer."

"You have a rock on a stick. Per, show him something special."

He smiled and reached for a large hammer with a long handle. It looked like someone formed it from a single piece of dull, gray metal. The handle had a line of holes near the end.

I noticed he lifted it off the wall with little effort, and taking into consideration how much bigger he was, I pulled a little strength from the floor as he turned to me.

"This is the best we have. A special piece indeed," he said, presenting the weapon.

Bracing for the heft, I took it from him, and nearly threw it at the ceiling. It weighed almost nothing, like an empty shell. I guess I didn't hide my surprise well because he chuckled.

It rang like a bell when I tapped my knuckle on the head. It *was* hollow. It even had a hole in the middle of the striking faces. "This is all wrong," I said, handing it back.

He nodded. "What would you change?"

"First, I can't imagine anyone fighting with a hollow hammer. Even if it didn't collapse at the first impact, it wouldn't carry enough weight to do any damage. Second, the balance is wrong. Varian's must fight differently than how I learned. I'm sorry we wasted your valuable time."

"Tell me *exactly* what you'd change," he said, grinning.

I looked at him and wondered if his thinking ability was closer to his brother's. "The head should be solid, heavy, dense stone. But you need some weight in the handle as a counterbalance."

"Can you syth metal?"

"No, only stone."

He handed the hammer back to me before walking to a pair of wooden doors set into the wall. Reaching in, he pulled out a block of something shiny and black. "How's this feel?" he asked, offering me the block.

I let the weight settle in my hand. It weighed a little more than my current hammer's head. *I'm holding the mold for a hammer.* "I think it would do," I said.

"Give me the stone and hold the head toward me," he said.

Turning it so a striking face pointed toward the ceiling, he gripped the bottom tightly, closed his eyes, and brought the stone toward the upturned face. As soon as the shiny black stone touched the metal, it melted and flowed into the hole. The head grew heavier as the dark liquid disappeared into the metal form. "I need a moment to catch my breath."

If I thought the balance was wrong before, it was terrible now. But I understood what he was doing. "What stone is this?" I asked.

"We don't know exactly. It comes out of the ground with raw iron, but it doesn't act like iron. See if you can syth it."

Touching it through the holes, it didn't feel like metal, but was denser than any stone I'd felt. I pushed a little energy and felt it respond. "I can."

He smiled. "Good. Now the handle. Are you familiar with Olivine?" He reached back into the closet and pulled out a large lump of bright-green stone.

"Can't say I am. Mostly work with Granite and Hornblende."

"Hornblende isn't quite dense enough to make up for what's in the head. See what you think with this in the handle."

I turned the handle toward him.

Again, he closed his eyes and let the stone flow into the metal handle. "Try it now."

The hammer was much heavier now, but the weapon didn't feel awkward; the balance was close to perfect. "The head's a touch too heavy. Adding a little weight to the end of the handle would help, but I can live with it."

"No need to live with it when we can get it exact," he said. "Give me your hammer."

He took it and reached back into the closet. I couldn't see what he did, but when he handed the weapon back to me, handle first, it felt warm.

"How about now?" he asked.

It was perfect. Heavy, but relatively easy to swing. "What did you do?"

"Took out some of the Olivine and added Lead in its place. Want to try it out?"

"I'd love to, but I don't want to hurt anyone."

Tindra and Per both chuckled.

"We have practice targets," he said. "Come with me."

He led us out to a courtyard well stocked with various styles of targets made of different materials. "Have a swing at those."

I walked to one of the sacks and took a tentative swing. The hammer felt good and hit the sack with a slight 'whuff.'

"You're not trying to make friends with the sack. Swing the hammer like a man," Per jeered.

I looked at him, snarled, and swung with all my natural might. The smooth metal slipped a little, but the impact was solid, making a loud "whack." It stung my hands when the force traveled through the handle. I dropped the hammer and shook my hands.

"Some get stung, some don't," he said. "Give me your hammer and wait here."

Tindra walked over. "What do you think?"

"I like the weight, but the handle hurts my hands. A wooden handle absorbs the blow."

"Per's the best, he'll fix it."

"I hope you're right," I said. "It's different, but I like it. Although I'm not sure how I'm going to carry it."

"He'll have something for that too," she replied, approaching a rack of wooden swords. She worked through several attacks and parries before Per walked back out.

The hammer had a leather strap wrapped around the handle. It started with tight wraps near the head spreading further apart as it made its way to the end of the handle. The leather didn't cover the holes in the handle.

He handed it to me. "Give it a try."

As I prepared to swing at the sack, I noticed the leather gave a better grip. After another solid impact into the middle of the sack, without any sting, I smiled. "Tindra said you're the best."

"Now, for the fun part," he said, without acknowledging my compliment. "Make one face have a spike."

"I told you my sything isn't strong enough for metal."

He shook his head. "A stone spike."

I reached toward the head.

"Not that way. Can't you push your talent through the handle, into the head?"

I looked at him for a moment before wrapping my hand around the handle again. My fingers fell onto the smooth, green stone through the holes. Closing my eyes and pushing energy through the Olivine. I found where it bonded with the shiny, black stone and visualized a short, sharp spike forming through the hole in one of the faces.

The balance of the hammer changed slightly. I looked at the head of the hammer and there it was, a spike about as long as my finger.

"Good. Hit the sack."

I took a swing and penetrated the woven fiber with ease. Sand flowed from the hole after pulling the hammer back.

"Might come in handy some time," I said, pulling the stone spike back into the head.

He nodded. "Tindra...are you fast enough?"

"Of course," she said, through a crooked grin.

"Fast enough for what?" I asked.

"To avoid you hitting her while you learn how to fight," he said.

"I know how to fight."

"Not with that," he countered.

"I've practiced fighting with a hammer most of my life," I said.

"Not this one," he said, shaking his head. "But feel free to show me."

Tindra raised the wooden sword, screaming, as she charged.

Caught by surprise, I took an awkward swing at her to slow her down. She ducked my less than graceful defense, slapped my wrist with the flat of her wooden blade, and rolled away as I stood stunned.

"Again!" Per shouted.

She stayed quiet this time, but charged from the same direction. I knew what to expect and swung the hammer to block a sword stroke toward my chest. She adjusted and struck me below my shoulder.

"Would you like a demonstration?" Per asked, as Tindra smirked.

"Sure," I said, tossing the hammer to him.

She backed off several paces and charged.

He squared his stance and stood still, keeping one hand near the hammer's head and the other held the end of the grip.

She hesitated.

He took the opportunity to swing the handle at her head, forcing her to break off her attack. "Again," he said.

She backed away and changed tactics, stalking toward him.

He still held the hammer with his hands at the extreme ends of the handle.

She was close to striking range when she made her first fighting move, a low thrust toward his leg.

He pushed the hammer down to deflect the strike and she changed her target.

The low thrust was a fake.

She stepped back and lunged, thrusting the sword high.

I saw Per smile as he brought the hammer upward, using the handle to deflect the sword. At the same time, he made a quick move to the left and the sword passed over his shoulder. He roared and swung the hammer toward her. The weapon hit the ground so hard I felt the force from the blow where I stood.

"Enough," he said, and turned to me. "You learned to use a weapon with a wooden handle." Standing the hammer on the ground, he patted the handle. "Metal handles make hammers more versatile. You can parry and strike with the handle. It won't be a powerful blow, but it can distract or frustrate your enemy. If nothing else, it can create opportunities for you to smash them. Create a spike, and you can penetrate most armor with a good, solid hit."

I pursed my lips and nodded.

"So much fun," Tindra chimed in, with a big smile.

"You need to train him," he said, then pointed at me. "Make sure you don't hurt her."

"I'll do my best," I said.

"He has yet to best me anyway," she said, and laughed.

"I'll let you two settle that. I need to get back to work."

"Before you go, how am I supposed to carry this?" I asked.

"Wait here, I'll get you a proper back sling."

"Have you ever trained with a sword?" Tindra asked.

"Only enough to know I'm not good with one. Why?"

"I think you'd have an easier time learning blocks and parries if you had some sword experience."

"Only one way to find out," I said and held the hammer out like Per had. "Come at me."

Tindra moved slowly while I concentrated on blocking her various strikes and thrusts. It didn't take long to learn not to use the areas near my hands where she could hit my hand instead of the hammer handle.

I started picking up speed when Per returned carrying an odd, leather pouch with straps attached.

"Take a break while I get the sling to fit you." He fastened a belt around my waist and buckled a strap across my chest. "Put the hammer over your right shoulder and guide the head toward your left hip. Magnets in the sling hold it in place once it's cradled."

I did as he said and felt the hammer click into place after I adjusted it a couple of times. The end of the handle stuck up above my right shoulder. The weight was noticeable, but not uncomfortable.

"You can ride most horses without having to go unarmed," he said.

"This will take some getting used to, but I see how it can work," I said, offering him my hand. "Thank you. What do I owe you?"

He shook it and looked at Tindra. "Are we even now?"

"More than. You have to accept something for this."

"Not money. Get King Ander to do business with me and we're good."

"I can't promise anything," she warned.

"But you can try. You have more influence with him than anyone else I know."

She nodded. "I'll do what I can, but if he won't listen to me, I'm bringing you coin."

"Don't bother," he said, smiling.

"Thank you again," I said. "You're sure I can't pay for this?"

"Maybe next time," he said, and walked away.

Before I could say anything else, Tindra turned, raised her sword, and charged.

We concentrated on basic skills as if I had no experience at all. Our shadows grew long before I held her off enough to make counter attacks.

"We should think about where we're eating this evening," she said.

"Tudal's?"

She laughed. "One taste of Satran food and you forget about everything else?"

"It's different. I enjoyed it."

"What about your friends?" she asked.

I shrugged. "Don't know if they'd like it or not."

"I mean, maybe we should try to find Crum and Jesca and see where they're eating. I thought you'd like to see how she's doing."

I nodded. "You're right. We should find them. Can we make it back to the castle before nightfall?"

"We can, but only if we hurry and don't worry about anyone following us," she said.

I rested my hand on the handle of my new weapon. "I'm not worried."

She put the wooden sword back on its stand. "But I'm unarmed."

"I have a feeling you're no less capable of defending yourself."

"Only against several, armed attackers," she said, and headed for the door.

I followed her and we both said our goodbyes to Per.

Chapter 40

"What did Per mean when he asked if you two are even now?"

"None of your business."

"Fair enough," I said, "but it seems you do business with a lot of people and I haven't seen much coin change hands."

Tindra nodded. "I've worked hard to establish myself as someone worth paying for. People know I'm worth paying up front because I get results. Most of my jobs pay, some very well. Some I do for favors repaid later or a simple exchange of information or services. Rarely — almost never — do I work simply out of kindness. Getting Jesca back to the king and queen was a kindness."

"Was it?" I asked, pointing at her. "You didn't know who she was when you met her."

"Despite my doubts when I first saw her," she said, smiling, "the longer I was around her, the more I believed it was possible. Seeing how important those straw bracelets were to her convinced me. I thought returning her might regain some good will with Queen Ines. But still, it was a kindness. Don't expect it to happen again."

"At this point, I don't know what to expect from you," I admitted, shaking my head.

She laughed. "Good. It will make your life a little more interesting."

"Lately, my life's been more interesting than I'd like."

Darkness replaced twilight by the time we reached the castle walls. Tindra showed the guards a small stone with the royal crest embedded in it and they let us inside.

We walked into a hive of activity. Servants hurried about the grounds. Nobles flitted from one group to another, making their presence known.

"I wonder what's going on," I said.

Tindra shrugged and approached a group of servants. "What's all this about?"

A young man turned toward us. "Haven't you heard? Princess Jesca has come home."

"Thank you for letting me know," she replied, turning to me. "This not good."

"Why?"

"Do you think she's ready for all this attention?"

"No, but word had to get out sooner or later."

"True, but what's the royal family do about Stina now? Someone will question where she is when the celebration happens."

"As harsh as it sounds, Stina isn't my concern."

"Neither is Jesca — now."

"I think she'll always be my concern," I argued, rubbing my chin. "I saved her...brought her home."

Tindra shook her head. "Exactly. She's back with her mother and father. No doubt they're grateful, but they won't pay much attention to your opinions regarding their daughter. You're neither family nor advisor — or even Varian. Best you prepare yourself to accept this fact now and consider how you might use Crum."

"I don't use my friends," I said, crossing my arms.

"You misunderstand. If Jesca insists he stay by her side, Ines may allow it, but you'll lose your best friend. I'm sure you know better than I how hectic life in the royal court can be. If he can gain the trust of the right people, he can help you, but is he ready? If not, he'll be chewed up and spit out."

She's right. Crum's always helped me before, no reason he can't now. "I need to talk to him," I said, slumping my shoulders.

"Yes, you do," she said. "Servants know everything happening inside these walls. There are more servants in the kitchen than anyplace else. Someone there will know where he is."

The kitchen workers moved around each other in a well-rehearsed dance to an unheard band.

Tindra approached an older woman stirring a large pot. "Beg your pardon. Do you happen to know where Princess Jesca might be dining this evening?"

"No need to beg pardon, I don't mind. You're breaking the boredom. It's wonderful she's back home," the woman said. "I don't know where she'll eat. I'm working on the guard's meal." She turned and pointed to a tall man near the center of the room. "He'll know."

Tindra looked at me and sighed. "Wait outside. Both of us trying to move through here would be a disaster."

I nodded, made my way back outside, and stood well away from the door. She found me a short time later. "Where do we go?" I asked.

She frowned. "Bad news. They're eating with Stina in the tower. We may not be able to get in."

"If Crum's with them, I can get in," I said.

"Or he can get thrown out."

"Against Jesca's wishes?" I asked.

"Until today, I've been unwelcome here for quite some time. I don't want to push my luck."

"But we can try," I said.

"We'll ask, but if the guards turn us away, we go."

I nodded. "Lead the way."

We dodged people moving around the grounds and arrived at the tower. Guards stood at their posts as ordered by King Ander this morning. "Are King Ander and his family inside?" I asked.

"I am assigned to guard this door, not talk to...you," one said, eyeing me.

"I'm a guest of King Ander," I said. "May we enter and see if he is here?"

"I have no instruction to allow guests inside."

Tindra produced her royal crest. "I was at the table when King Ander gave his order this morning. I know who you're guarding and assure you we aren't here for her in any capacity."

The two men looked from the stone to Tindra. "You are free to enter."

"Thank you," we said together and entered the tower.

We walked into an empty sitting room with a large fireplace on the right wall.

"Take the stairs to the top floor," Tindra said.

"Have you been in here before?" I asked, as we made our way up.

"Not as a guest, but I've escorted a few people to these cells."

"Seems rather nice for a prison," I said.

She nodded. "Much nicer than the dungeon. Of course, our dungeon is luxurious compared to what you and Jesca lived through."

We made our way to the top floor and two guards posted at the door.

"How long have you two been here?" I asked.

"We escorted King Ander and his family in a short time ago," one of them said.

"Was Crum with them?" I asked.

"The Croian man?" the other asked.

"Yes."

"He's with them."

"May we go in?" I asked.

"We have no instruction to let anyone enter," the first guard said.

"Can one of you get a message to King Ander?" Tindra asked.

The two men looked at each other, one shrugged. "I don't see any reason why not."

"Tell him Fitzeirick and Tindra are here and would like to speak with him," she said.

He nodded and walked into Stina's room. It didn't take long for him to return. "Crum will be right out."

"Not exactly what I asked for," Tindra said.

"But what King Ander allowed."

I nodded, said, "Thank you," and glared at Tindra.

She crossed her arms and made an exaggerated turn of her head to look away from me.

The door opened and Crum stepped out. "I wondered if you two got lost or something."

"We've been making the rounds and I have a new battle hammer," I said, reaching for the handle.

Both guards gripped their swords.

"Maybe I can show you later," I said, lowering my hand.

"Good idea," Crum said, grinning. "What did you need?"

"We wondered what you and Jesca were doing for dinner. I think it might be a good idea for us to talk, especially you and me."

He glanced back at the door. "We're eating right now. The king and queen wanted to have a quiet meal as a family this evening. At first, I wasn't invited, but Jesca insisted I stay at her side."

"One of my concerns," I told him.

"Why?"

I shook my head. "Not here."

He nodded.

"Where are you sleeping tonight?" I asked.

"The unasked, uncomfortable question of the evening." He chuckled. "I'm almost certain the answer will not be Jesca's room. Wouldn't do it anyway."

Raising my eyebrows, I cocked my head.

He shrugged and nodded. "I know, sounds strange coming from me."

I smiled, pride filling my heart. "I think Sar'sa would've liked hearing you say it."

He responded with a weak smile.

"Tindra and I will see to our own meal. Maybe we can get together tomorrow morning?"

"I'll do my best," he said.

I looked at Tindra. "Any advice?"

"Stay in your guest room at House of Daufi."

"It would be easier to meet with you there," Crum said.

"If you're allowed to leave the grounds," Tindra said. "If you're with Jesca, they're not going to let her leave without an armed escort."

"I can take care of her," he protested.

"An armed escort they trust," she countered.

He frowned. "Understood. I'll either come to you or send word as early as I can."

"Enjoy the rest of your evening. Please express our regret for interrupting the family's meal," I said.

"I will. Don't do anything I wouldn't do," he said, before hurrying back into the room.

"Can we make it to House of Daufi in time to eat?" I asked, as we left the tower.

"I won't go hungry in my parent's home. If there's nothing ready, I'll cook for us," she said, smiling.

"Do you think the residents of Daufi can keep Stina inside the walls?"

She chuckled. "They can't do any worse than the castle guards."

"What happens if she gets out?"

She shrugged. "That's between my father and King Ander. I know Father won't agree to anything that puts his people at risk. House of Daufi members will take care of her, but she *is* her parents' responsibility."

"Do you think Ander will agree?"

"What other option does he have?" she asked. "Do you believe Ines will let him keep her locked away in the tower?"

"When you put it that way, no," I said.

"On to a more pleasant subject...can I interest you in a bath after we eat?"

"I'm still not comfortable with the idea of bathing in mixed company," I admitted.

"What are you afraid of?"

"Betraying Aesa's trust."

"Even if you don't know —"

I interrupted her. "Because I don't know."

"Your loyalty is showing again."

"I see no reason to hide it. If I don't have my principles, what good am I?"

She smiled. "I guess I'm used to men without principles. They make my job easier."

"Am I still your job?"

I expected an immediate answer, but she stayed quiet as we walked. We weren't far from House of Daufi when she spoke. "No, the job's over. I'd say now you're my project, perhaps an ally, and — maybe — a friend."

"Your project?" I repeated, cocking my head to the side. "What do you mean?"

She sighed. "Of the things I said, you question that? I'm teaching you things, introducing you to people who can help you, and training you to fight. Doesn't that sound like a project?"

"More like student and teacher."

"Except, I see you more as an equal, someone I may learn from as we work together."

"You're the street-smart, talented, well-traveled spion for hire," I noted. "What could you learn from me?"

"Principles. Let's talk about them while we soak."

I chuckled. "You're not going to give up, are you?"

She shook her head. "You want me to help you get things done, this is the first step. Would you feel better if I called it a lesson in Varian society?"

"Fine," I conceded, crossing my arms. "I'll soak with you, but only because my muscles could use it after training with my new hammer."

She shivered and sighed loudly when the walls around House of Daufi came into view. "I couldn't wait to get away from here when I was younger. Now, I appreciate the feeling I get when I see these overgrown walls."

"Maybe one day I'll know how it feels, to have someplace special."

"You don't feel that way about your home?" she asked.

I shook my head. "I haven't seen my home in about a year and, from what Roi said, it's gone. It was never a home anyway, more of a symbol of my authority."

"I hope you're able to find your place someday," she said, paused for a moment, then added, "with Aesa."

We entered the courtyard and I marveled at the number of people working in the near dark.

She noticed me looking around. "The blind don't need light to work."

"Never thought about it, makes sense though."

"We should hurry to see if there's any food left," she said, and sped up her pace.

I walked faster to keep up with her and soon we were in the almost empty dining room. "People are still eating. Maybe you won't have to cook, after all," I said.

"You almost sound relieved."

"While I trust you don't cook badly enough to make yourself sick, how do I know you'd make something I enjoy?" I teased, grinning.

"You ate raw snakes and rats," she said. "I couldn't cook anything worse — even on purpose."

"Did it to survive, not because I enjoyed it."

"I stand by what I said."

"Either way, you don't have to cook."

She responded with a grunt and made her way to the serving line.

I followed her and came away with two sandwiches and a bowl of vegetable soup. There were plenty of empty seats in the dining room, but Tindra chose to sit at the edge of the room.

She took a couple of bites of her sandwich. "I want to ask you something, but I'm not sure you'll like the subject. I don't want to upset you."

"If it's about a marriage, keep your questions to yourself."

"It's not about marriage, exactly. At least not to me. You never talk about Aesa, except to insist on honoring your engagement. Would you tell me about her?"

"Why?" I asked, furrowing my brow in suspicion.

She cocked her head. "Maybe it's my curious nature. I admire the fact you feel so strongly for another person. Make me wonder about the woman who has your complete commitment."

I considered the question while chewing a big bite. "She's the most beautiful woman I've ever met. You could say I fell for her the moment we met, but Crum tells the story much better than I do."

"Would he tell me if I asked?"

I nodded. "I suspect he would if you told him I said he could. In many ways, she's everything I'm not. She's lean and graceful, like most firesyths. To be honest, you're built like her, but her personality isn't as outgoing as yours. She's much more reserved, a reflection of growing up in different environments I think."

Tindra smiled. "You like her cooking?"

I shrugged. "Don't know, she never cooked for me. No need since I was already a skald when we met."

"And as a lover?"

I frowned. "The proper answer to your improper question is none of your business. The honest answer is I don't know."

"You mean you never —"

"Not with her."

"Oh."

"Principles," I reminded her. "I love Crum as a brother, but we don't agree on how to best handle relationships with women."

"It would seem," she said, through a smile.

"While we're on the subject...how about you? Any significant man in your life — ever?"

She looked around the room before answering. "I chose my career early on, to get away from here. This life doesn't lend itself to long-term relationships."

"Sounds like something Crum would say."

"Do you think he'll stay with Jesca?"

I shrugged. "One thing I know for certain about Crum is to never try predicting what he'll do. He's always looking for an adventure. I think his feelings toward Jesca are unmapped territory for him. The real question is will he find a place in this new land where he can settle? From what we've talked about, I think he can, if he's honest with himself."

"If he does too much exploring with her, he'll have to choose between settling down or living in the dungeon," she said, grinning. "And if he breaks her heart, he'll have to answer to Queen Ines. It won't end well for him."

"I agree with you there. Something else he and I need to discuss. Now, I have a question for you."

"What do you want to know?"

"You said I'm a project and an ally. Why are you so interested in helping me?"

She nodded. "This lifestyle's losing its luster. I've never been much at planning for the future. I plan my jobs, as necessary, and once the job's done I relax and go where my whims take me. After hearing about Eirickson's plans, I'm thinking about the future...both mine and my country's. Helping you means I may save my country. After that, I'll start fresh...away from my old life."

"So. Walk away now. You can survive, maybe even thrive, doing something else. What can you do?"

"You mean other than deceive, seduce, gather information, and fight?"

"Yes."

She shrugged. "Pretty much sums up my skills."

"You said you can cook. Go work for Tudal until you can open your own place."

"No, I can't stay here," she said. "Too many contacts, people expecting me to keep doing what I do best. If I'm going to get out, I have to leave my old life behind. Let me help you. If, in the future, you choose something more between us, I'll accept with pleasure. If we part ways, I'll miss you, but I'll understand."

I nodded. "I'd be a fool to refuse help from someone like you. You know how I feel about anything else."

She frowned and sighed. "Time for a hot bath to relax and unwind."

"As friends," I said, pointing at her.

"If you consider me a friend."

"Despite the fact you can be aggravating on occasion," I allowed. "Let me get a change of clothes and I'll meet you in your suite."

She nodded and left the table.

After taking my time enjoying the last of my soup, I headed to my room. To my surprise, the clothes I'd left on the floor were clean, folded, and sitting on the bed. I took off my new hammer and its harness, grabbed fresh clothes, and headed to her suite.

Chapter 41

Warm air and the echoes of splashing water greeted me when I walked into the room.

Tindra sat at the table with two steaming cups of tea.

A knot formed in my back as I sat. I tapped my finger on the table and locked eyes with her. "To be clear, this isn't a date or anything."

She grinned and handed me a cup. "Friends can have a relaxing cup of tea together."

"Of course," I said, not really relaxing. "Friends often drink together. The bathing together afterward tends to break tradition. In Croy, it's considered improper for unmarried couples to go naked together. Especially when they aren't engaged to each other."

She raised her eyebrows. "Are we a couple now?"

She has to know she isn't helping. I shook my head. "We're friends...at best."

"Then there's nothing improper if we keep our distance. Wait here, I'll check the water." I finished my tea as she called out, "The water's perfect, come in."

Her naked back was toward me when I walked into the bathing room. Despite my reservations toward bathing with Tindra, I'd be lying to myself if I didn't admit to a physical attraction. She had a certain beauty despite, or maybe because of, several obvious scars.

She was different than Aesa. My fiancée was tall and thin. Tindra was slightly shorter and showed more muscle. Both of them moved with the grace typical of their talent, but each carried it differently. Aesa had the silky-smooth movements of a trained dancer. Tindra moved like a predator stalking her target, smooth but ever alert to her surroundings.

"If you're going to stare, at least keep your mouth closed," she said.

"I —"

"What? Weren't staring?"

"I didn't have my mouth open."

"Do you like what you see?" she asked, glancing over her shoulder.

"Be lying if I said I didn't."

"Why are you holding back?"

"Because I don't like who I see."

She turned to face me as I undressed. "Fair enough." Stepping into the tub, she sighed as she sat, before taking some soap from a small alcove in the wall.

I walked into the water and sat well away from her. The warm water soothed some aches I'd been ignoring.

"What do friends talk about in a situation like this?" she asked, while cleaning her hair.

"On the rare occasion I used a public bath, the conversation tended toward recent events or tavern gossip. Did you have a topic in mind?"

"I think it might be a good idea to discuss how we're going to pass the time until the council meeting," she said.

"Any idea when it will be?"

She shrugged. "I expect less than a week, but it could take longer for everyone to get here. Plus, there still isn't a location."

"From what Kurt said I doubt they'll meet in the castle," I said.

Tindra nodded, but frowned. "Meeting outside the walls will cause a delay."

"Why?" I asked.

"Arranging security, putting guards in place — important details," she said.

"Is the council hostile toward their king?"

"No, but the royal family never leaves the grounds without a guard detail. Except for Stina, but she sneaks out."

"Do you have any suggestions, within reason, of how we pass the time until the meeting?"

"Why'd you have to bring reason into the discussion?" She faked pouting.

"Principles."

"Of course." She smiled. "Would your principles let you wash my back for me?"

"Wash your —"

"I can't reach my back," she said, interrupting my question.

"Who washes it when you're alone?" I asked.

"It takes longer to get clean when I'm alone. If you help, the bath will go quicker."

I sighed. "Turn around."

She shivered when I first touched her. While sliding the soap across her skin, I brushed against a scar below her left shoulder.

"Sword."

"What?"

"The scar is from a sword strike," she explained.

I touched another, lower on her back.

She giggled. "Knife. Sneaky woman stabbed me in the back."

"Why'd you giggle?"

"It did something to me inside," she said. "Tickles, when someone touches it just right."

I placed my hand over a large, burn mark on her right shoulder blade.

"Mistake during firesyth training. Learned we aren't fireproof, the hard way."

"You remember all your scars?"

"Each one is a lesson. How could I not remember them?"

I shook my head and splashed water onto her back, rinsing the soap away. "All clean."

She looked over her shoulder "You sure you're done?"

"Yes," I answered, moving away from her.

"I'm curious about something you said earlier," she said. "When I asked why you were holding back, you said you didn't like who you saw. How do I change that?"

I crossed my arms. "You don't change how I feel. I do. By asking what you could do to change my feelings, you're asking how you can manipulate me, which I won't allow. Have I not made myself clear?"

She nodded. "Your opinion is crystal clear, but your judgment is clouded. We could make a good team. We may not desire the same things, but we can fill needs for one another."

I glared at her and frowned. "I *need* to finish my mission and save my country. I need to find Aesa, for love or closure...whichever it may be. Where your needs complement mine, we stand together. Where those needs aren't in line with mine, we stand far apart."

"Do what you must," she said, the water steaming around her. "I'll be there with you, for you, ready to give whatever you need along with whatever you decide to take. For now, I think it'd be a good idea for you to get to know some of the guards. You also should spend time training with your new hammer."

"I thought I'd train with you."

"Training with a single teacher is a bad idea. You'd get too comfortable with my style and wouldn't learn to deal with other tactics. Besides, I wouldn't want you to get too attached to me."

"I suppose you have a point. What will you do while I'm not training with you?"

"Tying some loose ends. Let me wash your back."

"Just my back," I said, and turned around.

It felt pleasant having someone work their hands across my slippery skin. As she worked, she did more caressing and massaging than actual washing. It felt nice but didn't take long before my body started to betray my principles.

"Enough. Thank you," I said, before dunking under the water to rinse. The warm water made my scar sting. *Will the pain ever go away?* "Do any of your scars still hurt?" I asked, after my head came out of the water.

"What do you mean?"

"Hot water makes the brand sting. Do you have anything like that with any of your scars?"

"Other than the ticklish one, no. Give it time. I'm sure it'll get better. If not, it proves every scar's a lesson," she said.

"I suppose you're right. I think it's time I dry off and get some sleep," I said and walked out of the tub.

"Can I convince you to sleep down here? I'm not in the mood to be alone tonight," she said.

I sighed. "Sounds like a bad idea."

"Sometimes those are the best kind."

I looked her in the eyes. "No. I'll see you in the morning."

Dressing quickly, I left before I changed my mind.

• • • ● • ● • ● • • •

Once I reached my room, I lay in bed trying to force myself to sleep. My slumber was fitful, often waking between dreams intertwining Aesa and Tindra.

I woke to loud pounding on my door, followed by Tindra shouting, "Fitzeirick, are you in there?"

"One moment." I rolled out of bed and opened the door.

She held a tray of flatbread and meat, a couple of small pitchers, and two cups. "My parents wanted us to eat with them this morning, but I thought it'd be best if we talk about last night."

I stepped aside so she could come in. "Nothing happened I didn't consent to."

She placed the tray on the table. "Milk or juice?"

I haven't had fresh juice in a while. "What kind of juice?"

"A spiced blend of apple and pear."

"I'll give it a try," I said, sitting.

She poured some juice into the cups and sat across from me. "I know I didn't take advantage of you, as such, but —"

"Would you apologize to anyone else for what happened last night?" I interjected.

"No."

"So why me?"

She looked away. "Because I care what you think about me."

"But you can't look me in the eye and say it?"

"It wouldn't mean much, coming from me," she said.

"It is a sign of trust, a show of honesty."

She shook her head. "Not from me. I have no problem lying to someone while looking them in the eye. It's a necessary skill in my line of work. I could look you in the eye and convince you even the most outlandish lie is the truth. I don't want to look you in the eye because I'm afraid you'll see —"

I scoffed. "You don't think I know how you work? You're a deceiver. You even said as much last night. I agreed to let you wash my back and let it turn into something else. I also decided to stop before it became something I'd regret," I said. "I know to keep you at arm's length —"

"Crum?" she interrupted, smiling.

I nodded. "You may get the impression I've opened my trust to you, but that's not the case. I won't lie to you, I hold myself to a higher standard, but I don't expect honesty from you."

"I *am* being honest when I tell you I'm sorry for my behavior," she said.

"And I believe you," I assured her. "You earn trust, over time, through actions. Being honest with me helps. Treating me and my friends with respect helps. You know how to use trust. What you need to learn is how to build it."

"Regardless, I feel bad," she said, looking down again.

"I accept your apology. Thank you."

We both focused on eating although she still seemed upset. I thought she was about to say something, but a knock on the door stopped her.

"Who's there?" she called out.

"It's Crum."

"Come in, come in," I said.

He opened the door. "Wasn't sure I'd find you here, but it seemed like a good place to start. Why's she in your room?"

"We're talking over breakfast. Clearing the air, I suppose," I said.

"About?" he asked.

"Nothing of your concern."

Tindra raised her eyebrows, then nodded. "Just as well he's here, I'm full and have some things I need to see to."

"Should I look for you later?" I asked.

She shook her head. "I'll find you if I need you. If nothing else, meet me in the dining hall for dinner."

"Sounds like a good plan," I said.

She closed the door behind her.

"Here by yourself?" I asked, as Crum sat.

"Not exactly. We all came with Stina. Her family's meeting with some of the caretakers. Mind if I eat?"

"Help yourself," I said. "There's more than enough."

"What was on your mind yesterday?" he asked, before taking a bite of bread.

I explained my concerns about Jesca, pointing out what a relationship with her would mean both to him and to our friendship. I also wanted him to know I approved of their relationship, so long as he conducted himself with honor.

He nodded at the appropriate times while eating, exactly as I expected.

After a long drink of milk, he looked at me and smiled. "My behavior will be beyond reproach."

I eyed him with suspicion. "What do you mean?"

"I think I've found what I've been looking for. I introduced you to your lifelong partner by accident, and I think you did the same for me."

My expression didn't change. "Do you mean what I think you mean?"

"An engagement? No, not yet," he answered. "But when the time is right, things have settled, and the country's used to the idea Jesca's alive...it could happen."

I smiled, feeling happy for him. "And the king and queen agree?"

He laughed, loud and long. "No. Ander tolerates me because I played a part in getting her home, but Ines hates me. If it wasn't for Jesca insisting I stay nearby, I think Ines would have me escorted back to Croy at spear point."

"Doesn't sound like a good way to start a relationship."

He shrugged. "I've had worse."

"But not with someone you were serious about making a life with."

He nodded. "True. There's one downside to this whole situation, though. I'll have to stay with Jesca. I won't be able to go back with you."

"Figured as much," I replied, frowning. "Can't say I look forward to fighting without you or Roi at my side, but I understand."

"And I won't get a chance to spend much time with you before you leave, I'm afraid."

"Regrettable, but necessary. I'd value your insight as plans are made. Can you find a way to attend the council meeting when it takes place?"

He nodded. "I'll see if I can get away."

"Offer to escort Ander."

"Good idea," he said, smiling. "If you aren't going to be with Tindra today, what are your plans?"

"She woke me with breakfast. Haven't had a chance to make any plans," I said. "She suggested I meet some of the guard and learn how to fight using my new hammer."

"I know who can help."

"Captain Torsten?"

He shook his head. "I'll introduce you to Lieutenant Aerison. He showed us around the castle and the grounds yesterday. He's personable and quick witted, I think you'll like him."

"Coming from you that's a big compliment. Sounds like I should meet him."

"Grab your hammer and we'll head back to the castle. It might take some asking around, but I'm sure we can find him," he said, smiling.

I strapped on the pouch and placed the hammer in it.

"Impressive."

I reached over my shoulder and handed him the weapon.

"Heavy, but pretty well balanced. How'd you come by this?"

"Tindra introduced me to a weaponsmith yesterday. Big man. Does amazing work. Seems this balanced some debt between them," I said.

"I can't wait to see how you fair against some trained fighters," he said, smiling.

"Have a sword with you?"

He shook his head. "I borrowed Tindra's when those guys tried to rob us on the way here. Haven't needed one since. Why?"

"I've always respected your ability to handle a blade. Thought it'd be interesting to see how we do against each other."

"You'd need to be a little worn out first," he laughed.

We walked to the castle. The entire way he smiled, waving to everyone who looked our way. "What are you doing?" I asked.

"Setting everyone at ease. People like a friendly face. If I'm to wed Jesca someday, they need to know I'm welcoming and approachable."

"Spoken like someone learning to work their way through a royal court," I said, chuckling.

"I can charm any court member you put in front of me," he said. "Lest you forget, I've done it most of my life. Getting the commoners on my side will take more time and effort. I can't hang out in the taverns and talk my way into their good graces. Well, I could, but then I couldn't stay near Jesca."

"So, you're a changed man?"

"Changing," he corrected, grinning.

I stopped walking. "You're serious!"

He took a few steps and turned to face me. "I'm trying to be. I think I need to ask if you're going to let me be."

"Be what?"

"Serious. Are you ready for your happy-go-lucky brother to settle? Is this something you can accept?"

I pulled him into a hug. "I think I can learn to accept it. I'm proud of you...Sar'sa would be, too."

He embraced me for a moment before pushing away. "You miss her."

I sighed and ran my fingers through my hair. "Of course, I do. How could I not miss my mother?"

"I wasn't asking a question," he said.

"What do you mean?"

"You talk about Aesa more than your mother," he said. "I'd wondered if you missed her."

"Have no doubt. Aesa is always on my mind, but I relied on my mother more than most people realize."

"And Eirick...do you ever miss him?" he asked.

"Hard to miss a man who wasn't around enough to get to know."

"Then your feelings for your father won't get in the way when you go to kill Eirickson?"

Heat flashed across my cheeks before I growled, "No."

He nodded. "Good to know. Now, we should pick up our pace so you can get a good training session in before lunch."

"Why are you so interested in my training?" I asked.

"I want to know I'll see you again. I want to know you've done everything you can do to win when you face Eirickson again."

"I won't be alone this time, and he won't catch me by surprise."

"You may not be alone, but you won't be with me or Roi," he said. "Answer this: do you trust anyone else with your life?"

"Not yet."

"For the best," he said.

We reached a gate to the castle grounds. A guard greeted Crum by name and allowed us to enter without question.

"Friendly and approachable," he said, after we were well inside the castle wall.

"Why didn't mister friendly and approachable ask where Aerison might be?" I asked.

"Because I know a better place to ask." He took a direct route to a long, unremarkable stone building and knocked on the door.

It took a little while, but someone finally opened the door and looked out. He looked like an older member of the guard. His close-cut hair matched the salt-and-pepper colored stubble on his face. "Can I help you?" he asked.

"I hope so. I'm looking for Lieutenant Aerison," Crum answered.

"The captains have him running new recruits around the grounds. Seems it's his reward for an easy assignment he took yesterday."

"I'll have to talk to someone about his reward," Crum muttered. "Any suggestion where I might find them running?"

The man rubbed his chin and stared off into the distance for a moment. "Not much of one. Not sure how many prospects they had, but they run until half collapse. For all I know they could pass by here sooner or later."

"Good to know, but not much help. I guess we'll look around until we see a group of men running."

"Who are you anyway?" he asked.

He held his hand out. "Crum, a close friend of Jesca. The good lieutenant escorted us yesterday."

The guard's eyes grew big as he shook Crum's hand. "Jesca really is back...like he said?"

"She is," I answered.

He turned his gaze to me, eyes locking on the brand. "And you are?"

I held my hand out. "Fitzeirick. Crum's best friend and the man who rescued Jesca." Instead of taking my hand, he bowed. "Everyone here's in your debt."

"I did what any decent man would do."

"Maybe there aren't enough decent men left outside these walls. Let me help you find the lieutenant."

Crum shook his head. "No, see about your duties here. I'd hate to cause someone else to get a special reward on my behalf."

"If you insist," he said. "I'd say your best chance to catch the runners would be to head toward the northwest."

He gave the guard a quick bow. "Thank you for your help."

The door closed as we stepped back.

"Gives me a chance to show you some of the sights while we look for Aerison," he said.

When we passed crowds, I let Crum greet them and ask if they'd seen the men running. We turned a corner and almost tripped over a young man on his hands and knees, gasping for breath.

"Is everything all right?" I asked.

At first, he nodded, then shook his head and collapsed.

Crum knelt next to him. "He's still breathing."

"Either he's sick or we found a trail," I said. "Maybe the runners were here recently." The young man rolled onto his back and pointed.

"I'd say it's a good route to follow," Crum said, as he stood.

"Should we help this one?" I asked.

The young man shook his head.

"I'd take that as no," Crum said.

"Doesn't seem right," I said.

"It's their way. Leave the man with his pride," Crum said, and started off.

"If they're running, how are we going to catch them?"

"We're going to take shortcuts," he answered, through a sly grin.

Along the way, we passed two more young men lying on the ground.

"Must be getting closer," Crum commented.

As we cut through the market, I mentioned the Satran eatery.

He looked at me and wrinkled up his nose. "Satran food?"

"Have you ever tried it?"

"I figured those savages ate their food raw," he said.

I laughed. "No. Tudal and his wife cook old family recipes with amazing flavors."

"Well, I'm not hungry right now, anyway."

"Last one down! Halt!" someone yelled ahead of us.

"Sounds like Aerison," Crum said.

We slipped between two buildings and almost stepped on another downed recruit. A few paces away stood four young men, breathing heavily. They all looked some combination of worn out, relieved, and proud. Nearby, a man about my size, but in much better shape, looked over the prospects. He didn't look any worse for the run.

"Lieutenant," Crum called out.

He turned, saw Crum, and smiled. "You planning on joining after all?"

Crum laughed. "No, but I have someone I want you to meet. You remember how Jesca went on and on about Fitz?"

"How could I forget?"

Crum patted my shoulder. "Allow me to introduce you to Fitzeirick. My best friend and Jesca's liberator."

I stepped toward the lieutenant and held out my hand. "You made an impression on Crum. Few people do that. Nice to meet you."

He shook my hand. "Jesca credits you with saving her life. We're all in your debt."

"Second time today I've heard that," I said, smiling. "If I hear it too often, I might start to believe it."

He laughed. "Is this a social call or is there something I can do for you?"

"I think there's something we can do for each other," I said.

"Do tell."

"I have a new battle hammer, much different than what I'm used to fighting with. I'd like to train with the guard. Crum and Tindra both think it's a good idea."

He looked me up and down and shook his head. "Can't have you beating my men into pulp."

"Not exactly what I had in mind," I said, shaking my head. "I need to learn how to use it for defense. I know how to smash things."

Aerison stared at me long enough to make me uncomfortable before nodding. "I'll make you a deal. Run with us to the training ground and, if you make it, I'll let these four have a go at you with some wooden swords."

I heard four distinct groans.

"Hadn't planned on going for a run today, but I think I can hold my end of the bargain," I said.

"What about me?" Crum asked.

I looked at him. "If I'm running, you're running."

His groan sounded a lot like the prospects'.

Aerison yelled, "Move out, on me," and started running.

Crum and I fell in behind the four prospects. We took a meandering path back to the building where we started our search.

I enjoyed hearing people cheer or yell words of encouragement as we passed.

We stopped in a large field like Per's courtyard except with archery and lancing targets.

As we slowed to a walk, I noticed Aerison was finally breathing hard. "Men, take a moment to catch your breath before getting a wooden sword. When you're ready, circle the man with the big hammer."

I drew my hammer, smiled, and nodded, before noticing Crum picking out a wooden sword. My smile turned into a frown.

He checked its balance, took a few practice swings and thrusts, and a mischievous grin spread across his face.

I stood surrounded by five men.

Chapter 42

"One at a time for now," Aerison warned. "He's learning, like most of you. Remember, this is practice, not a time to hurt someone. If a blow lands on Fitzeirick, it's his fault, but don't try to injure him. Don't aim for his head. Any blows below the beltline better hit his knees or lower. Understood?"

"Yes, sir!" everyone, except Crum, responded with enthusiasm.

"Show this Croian what you're made of! First strike, whoever's ready!"

I pushed my talent into the ground to track everyone.

Someone on my right flank decided to make a move. Pivoting, I brought my hammer up like Per showed me the day before. The recruit shifted his weight wrong and took an awkward swing. His wooden blade sliced through the air an arm's length from me. I stepped forward and pushed him while he overextended.

He stumbled and fell.

The recruit behind me charged while I was off guard. I tried to dodge. He landed a solid strike across my back as I turned.

"Nice," Aerison called.

I nodded and bowed to the young man before offering my hand to the one I knocked to the ground.

"Fitzeirick, why did you pursue the initial attacker?" Aerison asked.

"One less attacker to worry about with him on the ground."

"You left yourself wide open. You're surrounded. Unnecessary movement puts you at a bigger disadvantage. Your goal should be to move for defense or to get your back covered. If you can get your back covered, you are at an advantage. Does anyone know why?" Aerison said.

Crum cleared his throat. "We have to avoid our fellow soldiers. Fitzeirick only has to worry about not getting hurt."

"Exactly," Aerison said. "Five on one is only an advantage if the five know how to fight together. Many untrained attackers on one, well-trained defender are apt to thin their own numbers. Now, positions and attack again."

The recruits took the same positions except Crum and the recruit who first attacked switched places as the man right in front of me faked a thrust.

I dodged right into Crum's strike.

"One at a time!" Aerison shouted.

"He didn't attack," Crum said.

"We're teaching him defense, not proving superior numbers can overwhelm him. No more than one attacker moving toward Fitzeirick. You can shift sideways to create confusion. Understood?"

Everyone shouted, "Yes, sir."

"I want to try something different," I said.

"What'd you have in mind?" Aerison asked.

"Other than Crum, who's the most experienced sword fighter?" I asked.

Two of the recruits pushed the one who landed the strike on my back into the circle.

"What's your name?" I asked.

"Ravel."

"I want you right in front of me."

He nodded.

I pointed to the pushers. "Names?"

"I'm Bor," one of them said. He pointed toward the recruit I knocked down earlier. "He's Stig."

"Either of you have much experience with swords?" I asked.

"A little," Bor said.

"Not much," Stig said.

"And you?" I asked the last recruit.

"Ollie. I grew up hunting with slings and bows. Never even held a sword before."

I nodded. "Ollie, Crum's a bowman like you, but can handle a sword well enough. You spend time with him. Bor, I want you on Ravel's left side. Stig, work with Crum to learn a little, too."

Aerison scratched his head. "I thought I was running the training here."

I nodded. "Hear me out. If you disagree, we'll go back to what we were doing. If I have several people attacking me who haven't handled a sword, we aren't learning anything. Ravel can work with me while Bor watches and steps in. I'll learn, and so will they. Crum's no expert, but he can teach them the basics and you get better recruits for it."

He cocked his head. "I guess we can give it a try."

"Thank you," I replied, before turning my attention back to the men in front of me. "Ravel, attack me as you will, keeping my safety in mind. I'll give you the same courtesy. I'll be defending, parrying and deflecting your attacks. After several strikes, step aside, and let Bor have at me. A landed blow is a signal to take a break. Sound good to you two?"

"Sure," Ravel said.

Bor nodded.

"When you two are ready."

Ravel went from casual and relaxed to attacker in the blink of an eye and let loose a battle cry, surprising me. He got close with his first attack, but I managed to block it, more out of luck than a planned parry.

I stepped back to create a little room and make him move, hoping he'd give away his next strike. He stepped toward me and unleashed a flurry of blows, each one getting closer to an actual hit. Finally, I anticipated one of his attacks and managed to catch his sword in mid-swing. I pushed it back into his chest and shoved him away from me.

Bor picked that moment to step in. His strategy was a stark contrast to the maniac attacks from Ravel. He moved slower, more tentatively, but didn't look afraid. The first few weak attacks, I knocked away with ease, but Bor gained confidence as we worked together. The clack of wood striking metal came more often.

"Switch!" Ravel yelled, moving toward me as Bor backed away.

He pressed the attack and kept me moving. Shifting from swipes and thrusts at my midsection to slicing at my sides and legs, he threw me off balance. I had a moment to plant my feet after knocking away an attack, but didn't get my hammer back into position.

Ravel followed with a quick thrust to my stomach.

"Break!" Aerison yelled.

Ravel smiled wide and I bowed to him. "Well played," I said.

"Yes, it was," Aerison agreed. "You figured out how to play the strength of your weapon against a weakness in his."

"It took a little while for me to notice," Ravel said. "I caught on watching Bor. His slower attacks let me study how the hammer moved. Fitzeirick has less control than I have with my sword."

"I did good?" Bor asked.

"Did fine if you ask me," I said.

"Saw you gaining confidence as you went. I take it as a good sign," Aerison said.

Bor smiled at the praise.

I looked toward Crum and his two trainees in time to see him disarm Stig with a quick flourish. The poor recruit stood there looking at his empty hand.

"Looks like Stig will take some work," I said.

Aerison shook his head. "Good runner, but...we'll see."

"Ready for another round?" I asked.

"Bor, you start this time," Ravel said.

I took a deep breath as Bor moved toward me, making tentative attacks again. It didn't take as long this time for him to speed up the timing of his blows. He'd learned from watching Ravel and started forcing me to block more to the side. Switching my blocks forced his weapon high before I stepped back. His follow-up thrust toward my chest found air.

The first few times he grunted in frustration. He adjusted by hesitating before trying a follow-up attack. The change of pace made my job easier.

"Switch," Ravel called out.

I barely had enough time to prepare before he charged. Sidestepping his wild attack, I let him run past me. He took another wide swipe as he circled to my left.

I pivoted to keep him in front of me and blocked a couple of feigned thrusts as he moved toward his intended spot. He shifted his weight and came at me again. I used the block up and wide strategy, but Ravel wasn't having it; he reversed his swing, keeping me from returning to a more neutral position.

As I looked for a way to slow him or throw him off, he changed his focus to my legs and caught me unprepared to protect low. I had to jump over the first couple of swipes and soon learned what happened when I blocked a low attack upward. My second block placed Ravel's sword in the exact spot he wanted, and I took a solid blow on my arm.

"Break!"

"You got me again," I said, and nodded to Ravel, impressed with his raw ability.

"But you made me work for it."

"I noticed when you changed what you were doing, but I'm not sure why you did it," Bor said.

"To see what you would do," I said. "You slowed your attacks and gave me the advantage."

"I need to keep pressing the attack — always?" Bor asked, scratching his head.

"It doesn't hurt to study an enemy's change for a moment," Aerison said. "But you need to press hard again soon. You gave Fitzeirick time to catch his breath while you worked out how to adjust — not a winning strategy."

"Anyone else thirsty?" I asked.

"I think we could all use some water," Aerison said. "Stig, run back to the barracks, bring back water for everyone."

"Yes, sir," the young man responded and ran off like an arrow loosed from a bow.

Crum walked over to me. "Learning anything?"

I nodded. "Teaching anything?"

"Ollie might make some progress with more training. He doesn't have any bad habits to break. Stig is — he's trying too hard."

"I'm sure they can work that out of him. He seems eager to follow orders anyway." Crum nodded.

I heard wood clack against wood. Ravel and Bor squared off against each other. Watching the two of them, it was obvious Ravel was better, but Bor wasn't too far behind. He had a lot of untrained potential.

"With a good mentor, they'll both make excellent swordsmen," I said.

"I think I agree with you," Aerison said, before shouting directions to the two recruits.

I moved a few steps away and sat to watch. Crum plopped next to me. "You looked pretty good."

"I'm starting to get comfortable with it. It's different than fighting with a short-handled hammer, though."

"Mind if I ask you a touchy question?"

"You know you can ask me anything," I said.

He nodded. "How's Tindra figure into your future?"

I shrugged. "She's working to get the pieces in place. I expect she'll be in planning and strategy meetings. Wouldn't surprise me if she takes an active role in the fighting. Beyond that, she's not part of my future."

"Sounds like you trust her."

I chuckled and cocked my head. "To a certain extent, yes."

"Why?"

"I understand what she is and how she works," I replied. "She'll do what she thinks benefits her most. Where my interests are the same as hers, she'll do what I need. When those interests move apart, so will we. I don't want to face off against her again, but there's a chance it could happen. If she stands in my way, she'll get pushed aside or worse. Why are you so worried about this?"

He frowned. "You were — are — a good person and she's...not. I know it seems like a good idea to have her on your side, but she's never on anyone's side except her own. It sounds like you understand. I only want to make sure you come out of this whole situation better off. Whatever she has planned, it won't be in your best interest. She'll make sure to come out on top. Trust her to do nothing else."

"I may have my focus on a specific goal, but, believe me; I haven't lost sight of what's going on around me."

"And yet you missed seeing Stig's back," Crum said, as he stood.

I looked over my shoulder and, like he said, Stig stood near Aerison with several waterskins. I walked over to get a drink.

"Lunch in about two hours," Aerison said. "You two can join us, if you earn it."

"Any idea when the royal family will be back?" Crum asked.

"I don't know their schedule," Aerison said.

"In that case, I'll be happy to eat with the guard," Crum said.

"You'd be happy to eat anyplace that provides food and drink for free," I teased. "I appreciate an opportunity to eat with the guard."

Aerison smiled. "Back to training!"

Everyone took their previous positions and started mock combat again. Finally, Aerison said, "I figure it's about half an hour before we eat. Time to run back to the barracks."

We all groaned in unison, then made the mistake of letting Stig set the pace. He proved himself quite the runner.

This dining hall reminded me of the one at Daufi, except the layout emphasized efficiency instead of socializing. There was a constant stream of men moving in and out of the room. They served stew and some bread. Mugs of water waited for us at the table. Crum and I found two empty seats and ate in silence. The bland, but filling meal was soon gone, I asked Ravel to let Aerison know we appreciated the practice, and we left the dining hall.

"What should we do now?" I asked.

"Anything but run," Crum said, grinning.

"I'd like to bathe."

He looked at me for a moment and nodded. "And I need to find out when Ander, Ines, and Jesca will be back at the castle. I can show you where a bathing pool is in Daufi. After we get clean, we can see if the royal family is still there," Crum said.

"Sounds like a perfect plan," I said.

· · · · ● · ● · ● · · ·

We arrived without incident and headed straight for the guest rooms.

"Can I move our stuff into your room for now? Neither Jesca nor I will be staying here. Might as well leave the rooms for someone else."

"Why not take it to the castle when you leave? Oh, I bet you find your clothes cleaned and folded on the bed. I'm not sure who did it, but the service surprised me."

"Better than any inn or tavern I've ever stayed in," he said, before walking into his room.

He returned with saddlebags over his shoulders and a change of clothes in hand.

"Drop those anywhere and lead me to the bath," I said.

"Yes, sir."

We walked deeper into the compound than I'd ever been, but he knew exactly where to go. It was about twice the size of the private chamber in Swinter. Several people were already in the water. They greeted us, but otherwise seemed indifferent to our presence.

We undressed and stepped into the lukewarm water.

I shivered. "I prefer my baths warmer."

"Hard to complain when it's free."

"True enough."

After a quick wash, we dried off, got dressed, and made our way back to my guest room.

Tindra was there when we walked in. "Wondered where you'd gotten off to," she said.

"Would you happen to know if Ander, Ines, and Jesca are still here?" Crum asked.

She nodded. "Going over the last details of Stina's stay. The queen and Jesca are with Stina, trying to have a civil conversation. From what I've heard, it's not going well. Stina's furious. Jesca's sudden arrival is the spark that lit the fire, I guess."

"Maybe spending time here will change her mind," I offered.

"Not your concern," Tindra said. "I have some information about the meeting. We need to talk."

"Anything you'd say to me you can say in front of Crum," I said, glancing at him.

"Is he going to attend?"

"If I have a say, he will," I said.

"And I wouldn't object, for whatever my word's worth," she said. "The meeting's scheduled day after tomorrow. Everyone's going to meet before dawn in Per's courtyard."

"Why there?" I asked.

"It's easy to secure, neutral, and Per wants to impress the king. I hear both sides will finish planning security details no later than midday tomorrow."

"Is there any chance someone would consider an attack on the meeting?" Crum asked.

"This group exists because some people don't agree with Ander's opinion on various topics. An actual attack would surprise me, but someone could get stupid."

"This is one aspect of the royal court I don't miss," I muttered.

"And one I don't ever want to get comfortable with," Crum added.

"What do you need us to do before the meeting?" I asked.

"Crum should stay near the king as much as possible," she said. "Do you have his trust?"

"He hasn't been hostile toward me, not compared to Ines, but I wouldn't say I have his confidence," Crum said.

"Be available to him. If you see a chance to offer sensible advice, take it. Do what you can to build trust, but don't aggravate him," she said.

"In my best interest anyway," Crum agreed.

"And what should I do?" I asked.

"I'd prefer you stay with me. I want both sides to look to us as the bridge between them. We have more control if they consider us crucial members while planning. It's best if people see you and me together, being friendly."

"How friendly?" Crum asked.

She scowled at him. "It's none of your business, but friendly — nothing intimate or improper."

"Simply watching out for my liege," he said, smiling. "And so, I'm off. I'll stop by and grab the saddlebags before I leave for the castle."

"May your trip be smooth," I said.

He gave me a quick bow and left.

"What have you been up to?" Tindra asked.

"Crum introduced me to Lieutenant Aerison. I trained with my hammer and ate lunch in the guard dining hall."

"Sounds like a fun morning."

"It was, but I'm sure I'll be sore," I said.

"Take it easy for the rest of the day, nap if you want. We'll eat dinner out and, after moonrise, hit a couple of taverns."

"Why?" I asked.

"The council has eyes and ears in most of the larger towns. Remember, they knew someone new showed up in Swinter shortly after you arrived. We need to make some appearances and let them see we get along. Afterwards, we can soak together. Nothing like hot water to soothe sore muscles."

It's better for me if she stays focused, not emotional. "So long as you're not setting yourself up for regret later."

She crossed her arms. "I rarely make the same mistake twice."

I nodded. "Back to Swinter. Jahon? Is he on the council?"

"No, but he has connections."

"Crum was working with the council most of the time?" I asked.

"No direct link, but most of the people helping and guiding him have ties."

"I can't believe he didn't figure it out. He's usually better than that."

She shrugged. "He was desperate, running for his life and looking for you. Plus, no matter how good you are, there's always someone better. Rest and I'll come get you when I'm ready to go."

I nodded. "It would be nice to have an easy, relaxing evening."

As she left, she turned back and said, "I'm glad you think we can have a relaxing evening together," before closing the door.

As soon as my head hit the bed I was asleep and didn't wake until someone shook me.

Chapter 43

I grabbed the hand on my shoulder and rolled over to see who risked touching me in my sleep.

It was Tindra.

"You slept through Crum coming in and getting everything?" she asked.

I squinted at the question then looked past her. Their saddlebags were gone.

"He headed back to the castle a while ago," she explained.

"Oh. Guess I needed the rest."

"And now you're refreshed for an evening of fun," she said, with a smile, and dropped something on the bed. "Change into these."

"What's this?"

"Clothes. More appropriate for my plans for the evening."

"Am I going to regret this?" I asked, releasing her hand as I sat up.

"I doubt it. Silk shirts and leather pants are the current fashion among dance troupes."

"I don't dance," I said, gruffly.

She shrugged. "Never hurts to be prepared. I'll come get you when I'm ready." She closed the door as she left.

My arms and back felt stiff, sore from the earlier sparing, and my legs were tight from running. *If I'm going to be any good in a fight, I have to get in better shape.*

The dark-blue silk shirt was soft and cool. It's smooth texture against my skin felt almost slippery. All the leather I'd worn before was heavy and stiff, but the black pants were thinner and moved with ease. I couldn't imagine why a dancer would favor them, but Varians had different ways of looking at things.

I walked slow circles around the room to get used to moving in these new clothes. After completing my sixth circle, someone knocked on my door.

"Come in."

Tindra opened the door and took my breath away. She wore a tight-fitting, black, silk top. The long sleeves were bright red at the cuffs with the red dye growing darker as it went up her arms, fading to black near her shoulders. Her black, leather pants looked like mine, but fit much tighter. She wore matching, black, lace-up boots that flared right below her knees.

"Can you breathe?" I asked.

She responded by taking a deep breath, which showed off her body even more. "Good enough?"

"I'm convinced, but isn't this an evening out as friends."

"This is an evening out to get noticed," she said. "Are we not friends?"

"I've never had a friend who dressed like that."

"Then you've never had a friend like me," she said, with a laugh. "We need to get going. We'll dine at The Stag Pub, one of the more high-class places to get noticed.

Afterwards, we'll make our way to a couple of the seedier taverns for drinks and, maybe, dancing."

"I don't dance."

"But the evening's not yet begun. Many strange things may happen before the night is through," she said, turning to leave.

"What do you mean?"

She held her arm out for me. "I mean we're doing this to make an appearance and make the right impressions. Play the game right and you'll have all the support you need to overthrow Eirickson."

I took her arm. "But I don't dance."

"Try to be flexible. It could be important," she said, and laughed again.

"Stonesyths aren't known for their flexibility."

She shook her head.

We left the compound and she drew attention as we approached the first crowd.

"Are you armed?" I whispered.

"Why would you ask me such a thing?" she replied, sounding shocked.

"We — you — are attracting quite a bit of attention. I'm feeling exposed without my hammer," I confessed.

"We need to get you a boot knife. I'd offer you one of mine, but they're too long to hide in your short boots."

"So, you *are* armed."

"I rarely go out without a way to take care of myself," she said, with a sly smile.

"How much farther?" I asked, watching for anyone paying us too much attention.

"It depends."

"On what?"

"How much longer I want to keep you on edge," she answered, grinning.

"Why aren't you paying attention to what's going on around us?"

"What makes you think I'm not?" she asked.

"Because you're at ease."

"Of course, I am. I have you at my side. Also, this area of the capital is safe, for the most part. Nobles, even the lesser ones, complain too much if the guard lets them get jostled."

"In other words, the moneyed get protected and the poor get preyed upon?"

She nodded. "So long as they choose to stay inside their safe area, otherwise they play at their own risk. A few of our noble families seem to have a taste for...adventure. It's not unheard of to bump into them in even the most dangerous taverns when the mood hits. We're safe here. Do you remember how to be a noble?"

"Been one most of my life," I said.

"Get ready to show it. You can start by opening the door for me."

I'd been so focused on the people around us and our conversation I missed the tall building in front of us. Large, wooden stag heads projected out from the corners. Two of them held a cloth stretched between them, shading the entryway. It looked like a log cabin with at least three floors. The entrance was two, wide doors, decorated with hunting scenes. I hurried to the door on the right and opened it for her.

She gave me a respectful nod, walked in, and waited for me to enter.

A tall, well-muscled, young man strode toward us. He wore a tailored, green-and-brown hunting outfit. "Who do we have this evening?" he asked.

I cleared my throat. "I am Fitzeirick, escorting Tindra."

The man narrowed his gaze and looked me over. "Rooftop dining this evening. Follow me."

We climbed three flights of stairs to the roof. Torches along the short wall cast a soft light on the roof and candles lit each table.

Tindra stepped out and each of the candle flames shrank to an ember. The torches near us flared for a moment before everything went back to normal. Everyone turned to see what had happened.

Our guide whispered, "Nice entrance."

She gave him a quick nod and he led us to a small table near the center of the roof.

We took our seats and he asked, "Drinks?"

I looked to Tindra and she smiled. "Do you have any sharp, apple-and-pear cider?"

"Of course."

"Excellent, we will each have a mug, warmed and mulled, as well as cups of cold water."

"The lady knows her drinks. I will have them on the table as soon as they are ready," he said, and hurried away.

"I'm guessing you planned all this," I said, looking around. "What are we eating?"

"A salad will come with our drinks. Soon after we'll each get a plate with broiled, seasoned red deer and roasted potatoes. Dessert will most likely consist of a stewed-fruit sweet pie."

"Eat here often?"

"Not as often as I'd like. The view from the roof is amazing as the sun surrenders the sky to the moon."

She was right. I could see beyond the city wall in every direction and took the opportunity to admire the land around the castle before the sun set.

"Ah, moonrise. A most beautiful sight," she said.

"Especially over land like this, with a good meal and the company of a...remarkable woman." *Hope I don't regret saying this.*

Her jaw dropped. "Wait...did you compliment me?"

I smiled. "While I have issues with you, I can't deny the fact you are remarkable, in several ways."

"The evening's already getting better," she replied, and smiled back.

Two young women, dressed like our host, carried trays to our table. "Your drinks," one said, as they placed cups and mugs on the table.

"Your salads," the other said, "prepared with minced horseradish. It complements the sharp, mulled ciders, contrasting with their sweetness."

I nodded like I understood and plunged my fork into the leafy greens. After about two chews into the salad a heat tickled inside my nose. I swallowed and took a drink of the warmed cider. The spices in the drink did improve the taste of the salad. "Well done."

The server nodded and walked away.

"I'm surprised you like the horseradish," Tindra said.

"I've never tasted it before, but I can taste why Varian cooks find it useful."

"Your mother never used it while cooking?" she asked.

I shook my head. "I'm not sure it's found in Croy. I don't recall ever hearing anyone peddling any in my skati."

"And the spicy cider?" she asked. "You like it?"

"It tastes excellent, to be honest, and goes well with the salad. Thank you for ordering it."

"I wasn't sure they would have it. Try the water."

The wooden cup felt cool. "How'd they find water so cold?" I asked, after taking a sip.

She smiled. "They didn't find it, they made it."

I gave her a questioning look.

"Have you ever noticed when a firesyth draws heat from the surrounding area the air grows chill?" she asked.

I nodded.

"The kitchen workers use it to their advantage. They keep pitchers of water near ice cold by moving heat around to cook."

Before I could say anything, a light breeze carried the faint scent of cooked meat to my nose.

"I suspect our meal will be here soon," Tindra said.

I heard sizzling meat and turned to find the source. The same servers from before stepped onto the roof, carrying wooden platters.

They put the platters on the table, refilled our drinks, and picked up our salad plates. A metal plate, dominated by a large cut of meat with some potatoes on the side, sat on the platter. "Mind you, don't touch the metal. It's hot," one said.

They bowed and walked away.

I pushed a fork into the steak and found it so tender it almost fell apart before I touched the knife to it. Placing a small piece in my mouth, I found the various flavors were almost overwhelming. The meat tasted smoky, but was tender and moist. I couldn't even start trying to identify all the spices used to season the meat. "This is amazing," I said, after swallowing.

Tindra's smile seemed to generate a light of its own. "I'm happy you like this."

I was already chewing another piece so all I could do was nod. Inside, I wondered why I felt comfortable talking with Tindra this way. Perhaps I was caught up in the moment, glad for time away from all the stress. Maybe it was her, something she'd done...or maybe it was just me being lonely.

"Make sure you try the potatoes. I don't know of anyplace else that prepares them this way."

I swallowed and cut into one of the potatoes. The skin was crisp to the point of being fragile, but the flesh inside was soft. Steam escaped through the cut and carrying a whiff of herbs. I scooped out a bite of the white insides. The flavor wasn't complex like the steak, but still pleasant; much better than the typical bland root prepared over a campfire.

"I like the steak better," I said, after swallowing.

"Try them together," she said, spreading some potato on a slice of steak.

I followed her example. "I can't say the potato makes the meat taste any better. If nothing else, it seems to cover some of the steak's flavor."

She shrugged. "To each their own. I think it makes for a good change of pace during the meal."

"To each their own," I echoed, and smiled.

I noticed her watching me savor the last of my meal. "Something on your mind?"

"Wondering what it will be like to watch you lead."

"Lead what?" I asked.

"People — an army, a battle, a nation."

I chuckled. "What makes you think King Ander or the council will allow me to lead anything? As you've said before, I'm not Varian."

"No, but you *are* a leader. You have to lead the battle against Eirickson, otherwise it won't be you who takes control of Croy. One uprising against a tyrant will be shocking enough to your country. Do you think it would survive two?"

"I'll see Eirickson fall — die. I'll control my country, but I won't be a tyrant."

"I believe you," she said. "But if you don't lead the fight against him, the council's chosen will rule, and before long Croy will become part of Varia. Of course, the support you need won't be free."

"No doubt the King and the council expect repayment after I've settled my debt with my half-brother."

"But are you prepared to pay the cost?"

"Do you know something you're not telling me? If so, what's it going to cost me to get you to share?"

"I have my suspicions, but nothing I know to be fact," she said, looking at something behind me. "We'll discuss it over dessert."

I turned and saw the servers again.

"Warm, cinnamon milk to go with sweet-and-sour cherry pies," one said, as dessert plates replaced the empty platters.

"Perfect," Tindra said.

I looked at the golden-brown pastry with coarse sugar sprinkled on top and pushed a fork through the crust. It gave way with an audible crunch. The stewed fruits inside were pliant, but not mushy. The taste was an ideal end to the wonderful meal.

"Your suspicions?" I asked, as we ate.

"The council will want a trade agreement, something favorable to their interests."

"Not a surprise. Given a fair chance, I'll negotiate something they find satisfactory."

"I think Ander's demand will trouble you more."

"What do you think he'll want?" I asked.

"I expect his cost will be twofold. It seems foregone he'll demand you ally with Varia against Satra. I think it likely he'll use you to fight the battle as Varia's proxy. He'd much rather have others dirty their hands while he benefits."

I nodded. "So long as he can supply Croy's needs."

"The second part of his expectation is where I expect trouble."

"Why?"

"He'll demand you return conquered lands to Varian rule," she said.

"My skati?" I asked, eyebrows raised. A knot formed in my stomach.

"Exactly."

"I will have trouble with that," I admitted, frowning.

"As I expected. Remember everything's open to some amount of negotiation. Regardless, King Ander won't come out short."

"I appreciate your insight," I said, and decided to focus on my pie, hoping the sweet taste would distract me from sour thoughts. "You don't have a purse with you. Am I to pay for this?" I asked, after swallowing the last bite.

"You just now thought to ask?"

I shrugged. "Maybe I've been relying on the kindness of others for too long."

"I paid for the meal when I made the arrangement earlier today," she said.

"And what will it cost me to repay your kindness?"

"We'll negotiate on the way to our next destination," she answered, through a crooked grin.

"Should I dare ask where we are going?"

"The Witty Fool. Crum's kind of place."

"So, not as nice as this?"

She chuckled and shook her head. "I doubt they would allow many of the Fool's regulars through the door here."

"I suppose I should go check it out, in case Crum decides to return to his old ways," I said, grinning.

She chuckled and drank the last of her milk. "Then we're off."

I followed her down the stairs. Several people watched as we moved from one floor to the next. I made certain the host knew how much we enjoyed the meal.

"We look forward to your return," he said.

The streets were even more crowded now that night had fallen. Torches along the sides of the street lit the way with bright circles.

We walked arm in arm, but I had no doubt who led the way.

Chapter 44

"I'm almost afraid to ask, but what am I going to have to do to repay you?"

"Dancing," she answered, smiling.

"No."

"Dancing."

"I don't dance."

"I think you do, but you don't realize it," she said.

"I'm certain I don't."

She tilted her head. "Ah, but you've forgotten. We've danced once before."

"It wasn't a dance, it was a fight," I corrected her.

"I recall it was a dance." She tapped a finger on her chin, then nodded. "It must have been. Had it been a fight, there would've been blood and injuries."

"Remember the bruise on my face? Eye swollen shut?" I asked.

"You fought with...what was his name?"

"Olver."

"Yes, Olver," she agreed, nodding. "You fought with him, but you *danced* with me. I remember it well. I even got your feet moving."

"You hit me in the knees and ankles."

She laughed. "Compromise?"

"What's your offer?"

"One dance...after a few drinks."

"It would take several drinks," I said.

"One dance after several drinks. I'll make sure the barkeep makes them strong."

"You're not going to take no for an answer, are you?"

"No," she said, before sticking her tongue out.

I chuckled and clapped my hands together. "Fine, one dance — after drinks." *Nothing wrong with letting her think she's in control.*

"How many drinks?"

"Let me think about it before I answer," I said.

She nodded. "You have little time, use it well."

I took her advice, weighed my options, and soon settled on three. Three seemed like a good number. *I can stretch them out without looking like I'm stalling. With any luck, she'll get bored and I'll talk her into leaving before humiliating myself in public.*

"Three," I told her. "Three drinks."

She nodded. "Only three?"

I smiled in return to disguise my plan.

As soon as we stepped into the large room, I realized The Witty Fool was a place for entertainers. An older man stood in the center of a raised stage. He told some sort of story with musical accompaniment. People sitting at tables around the stage laughed. I wanted to listen, but Tindra tugged me toward the bar.

"Barkeep!" she shouted. "Six shots of your best brandy."

I frowned, having agreed to three drinks — she just ordered three for both of us. *I suppose there's no shame in an expert outfoxing me.*

The young man behind the bar looked no older than fifteen. He glanced at me. "Don't serve his kind here, got standards. You can stay, but he's gotta go."

I don't have to take that from him. Standing up straight, I leaned toward him. Tindra put her hand on my chest and locked eyes with the boy. "What, exactly, is the problem?"

"He's not Varian and he's branded. Don't want his kinda scum in here."

"We should leave," I said.

"Wait," she said, pulling a small, leather pouch out of her shirt. "He's in Varia at the invitation of King Ander. How would it look if he told the king you refused him service? If you can't decide on your own, ask Tyres what he thinks. Assuming he's here. I suspect he's busy planning for the upcoming meeting."

"What meeting?" the boy asked.

"I understand now," she said, with a nod. "You aren't trusted. Fine, get me someone with some authority."

"I'm in charge'a da bar."

"Prove it," she demanded. "Serve us or face whatever comes. Do you think Tyres will look kindly on you when the guard starts frequenting his tavern?"

The boy shivered, placed six, large cups on the bar, and filled them to the rim with a dark-amber colored liquid. "All good?"

The boy's arrogance may play to my favor.

Tindra reached back into her pouch and placed something in the boy's hand. With practiced ease, she slipped the pouch back between her breasts. "Keep the extra," she said.

He nodded and smiled before moving to the other end of the bar.

"Not as dull witted as I first thought," she commented. "He didn't check the amount I tipped in front of me. I appreciate the respect. Now, have you ever had brandy before?"

"Not that I recall. What is it?"

"Think of it as extremely strong, spiced wine," she said. "I asked for shots so we could down the three drinks quickly. These will take a little time. It seems his mistake may be in your favor after all," she said, and winked at me before taking a drink. "This is pretty good. You might want to take a few sips to get used to the taste."

I lifted the full cup with care. The smell of alcohol hit my nose and made me feel like I might sneeze. Doing my best to ignore the sensation, I took a sip. A combination of strong grapes and hot peppers spread across my tongue. I must have made some kind of strange grimace because Tindra snickered.

"Well?" she pressed.

The peppery burn continued down my throat when I swallowed. "Considering Varian cooking, I can see why this is popular."

"It's an acquired taste, but I think you'll grow to like it if you give it a chance. It gets easier after the first one."

"If you insist," I said, and sipped again. Somewhere about halfway through, I stopped noticing the smell and the burn. "This is starting to taste pretty good," I admitted, after finishing the cup. "But I think I should take my time drinking the rest."

She was halfway through her second drink. "It's pretty bad when a strong guy like you can't keep up with a little thing like me."

"I have to get used to something new. How long have you been drinking this stuff?"

"Years...I guess," she answered, with a shrug. "I have an offer."

I eyed her with suspicion. "What?"

"We dance now and call it a night. We can go back to my suite, clean up, and get some sleep."

"Dance, bathe, and go to sleep — alone? Nothing more?"

"I won't ask you to do anything you aren't comfortable doing," she promised.

"And these drinks?"

She shrugged. "Someone will finish them."

"Why make this offer now? It seems you have something planned."

"Because I think if you drink all three of those you won't be able to walk, much less dance," she said, grinning.

"And if I find that insulting?"

She shrugged again. "Suit yourself. Drink up, but if you can't walk, I won't carry you."

I laughed. "You *can't* carry me."

"That's beside the point. What do you say to my offer?"

I put the cup back on the bar. "You have a deal."

"Barkeep!" Tindra shouted.

The boy appeared almost immediately. "Yes, ma'am?"

"How do I get the band's attention? It's time to dance."

"Make your way to the stage and tell them what to play."

She nodded and led me through the crowd. We had to wait for another storyteller to finish. He told a tale I'd never heard before, something about a fight between two Varian families. As the tale unfolded, two men joined him on stage and acted out the fight in mock combat. A few coins flew past us, landing at the feet of the performers.

I considered leaving as they gathered their pay, but I was a man of my word.

"Follow my lead, and try to keep up," she said, before dragging me to the center of the stage.

No doubt all eyes were on us when she looked toward the band. "Play something spirited."

The band struck up a song with a quick beat. I did my best to sway in time with the music as Tindra slithered her back against me. She finally turned to face me and put her hands on my waist, putting pressure in the direction she wanted me to move. I followed her lead, like I'd done for most of my time in Varia. She moved us around the dance floor to the whoops and cheers of the people seated around the stage. I did my best to ignore them and focus on her to keep from making a bigger fool of myself.

As we moved back to the center, she leaned against me and said, "Catch me when I jump," before sauntering to the edge.

I only had a moment to understand what she meant before she ran full speed and leapt. I caught her with my hands on her waist.

She moved us around the stage again as the band built to a climax.

"Kneel on one knee and drape me over your leg."

My knee hit the stage as the song ended.

Tindra lay against my leg, placed her hands on my cheeks, and pulled my face to hers.

At first, I resisted, but she smiled and whispered, "Trust me." Our noses touched and we looked each other in the eye.

I have no idea what she saw, but there was no mistaking the sparks in her eyes. For the first time since I met her, I had to admit, I could fall in love with her if I wasn't careful. A cold shiver shook me. *I'd best be careful.*

"Ready to make an exit?" she whispered.

My mouth felt like sunbaked dirt. "S...sure."

"Stand, throw me off the side of the stage, and stalk me where I land."

"What about the crowd?" I asked.

"Do it. They'll move."

I did as she said, and the room burst into cheers and yells.

When I reached her, she said, "Carry me out."

I nodded and scooped her up. As I walked out men gave me knowing nods and patted me on the back. Someone even opened the door for me.

"Put me down," Tindra said, after we were a few paces away from the tavern. As soon as her feet touched the ground, she let out an unladylike whoop. "That was way too much fun."

"I'm glad *you* liked it," I said. "I could've done without all the attention."

"Nonsense. That's why we came. We'll be the talk of the town for a few days. Believe me, this will help you in the long run."

"I'm afraid I don't understand —"

"Well, what do we have here? Unless I am mistaken it is Kurt's pet and her tag-a-long," a voice I'd heard before, said from nearby.

I immediately reached out with my talent and found three people standing in a dark alley.

"Folke, right?" Tindra said, turning to face the voice.

"Got it in one guess, lovely lady. I'm impressed," he said.

"What brings you here?" I asked.

"I don't believe it's any of your business," he said.

"*Little* man," Tindra spat, "I've had a wonderful evening. Spoiling it with rudeness wouldn't do."

"Rudeness?" he squealed. "You want to talk about rudeness? You two barged in on my business meeting — made Kurt dismiss me. You should apologize for the trouble you caused."

Tindra shrugged and reached to scratch her leg, putting her at eye level with Folke. "Kurt makes his own decisions. As far as our interruption of the meeting...wasn't my fault. Your man caused the confrontation. I won't apologize for doing exactly what I said I would. I doubt Kurt would appreciate your attitude here. I think it best if we act like we never saw each other and part ways."

"I agree. It's best if Kurt doesn't hear about this. Botel, Elis — kill them," he ordered.

I felt them sything as they rushed us. I softened the ground in a few places to slow them.

"Want a blade?" Tindra asked.

"I think I'll be fine," I replied.

"Good," she snarled, and all the torches around us went out.

The thugs shouted in surprise. I circled toward Folke, while Tindra used the confusion and moved to attack the two men from the side.

Folke hurried around a corner and pressed himself against a building. There was no way to get past him.

Good thing I'm not planning to get by him.

I heard something strike the torch post we'd been standing near followed by a yelp. It wasn't Tindra. The injured man stood, but wasn't steady on his feet.

"Elis?" Folke yelled.

"Crazy bitch cut my leg," Elis said.

Another yelp. He fell to the ground and rolled around. I heard Tindra yell and the rolling stopped.

"Elis?" Folke yelled again, panic evident in his voice. "Botel?"

"I think he's down," Botel answered, before letting out a yelp of his own.

I knew exactly where he went to one knee.

Before Folke could call out again, I rushed toward him and planted my foot in the middle of his chest. I heard his lungs empty and ribs crack as his chest collapsed.

He grabbed my leg, pushing against my weight until he went limp and slid down the wall. I slapped him a couple of times to make sure he wasn't faking.

"No, no——NO," Botel screamed. "My ear! You cut off my —"

He didn't finish his sentence.

I hurried back to Tindra. "You alright?"

"Perfect," she said, and sighed. "Some people insist on learning the hard way. Where's Folke?"

"Dead in the alley over there."

"How poetic," she drawled. "I'm more than ready to go home."

We hurried through streets and alleys to reach House of Daufi without another incident. Once inside, we made our way to Tindra's suite. She started the fire while I opened the tap to fill the tub.

"Will Folke's death cause any problems with the council?" I asked.

She shook her head. "Kurt will understand."

It didn't take long for the tub to fill, but heating the water took a while. I made tea while Tindra did her best to get the water hot.

"Thank you," she said, when I handed her a cup.

I nodded and emptied my cup in one drink.

She finished hers slower. "I think the water's ready. Go ahead and get in the tub. I'll add a little more wood and join you."

I undressed and stepped into the hot water. It was hotter than I preferred, but I knew my muscles would benefit.

Tindra walked in naked and sat at the edge of the tub dangling her legs in the water. "Would it be too forward of me to ask if I could sit with you...and...maybe...cuddle?"

"I don't think —"

She stepped into the water. "I know, I know...but maybe it's time to not think and simply act, at least a little."

"I'm afraid I might violate Aesa's trust."

"I think you're more afraid of forgetting her," she said, approaching me.

"Never. I'll never forget her."

"So, it won't be a problem to hold me, let me feel the way I felt while we danced," she said, sparks in her eyes again.

"About that..."

She nodded. "I saw the fear and conflict in your eyes. I respect you and your feelings. Please, believe me. I'm prepared to fight by your side, to die for you. The least you can do is hold me for a little while. I'll honor your principles — and make sure you do, too."

"I won't let you manipulate me," I warned her.

"I have nothing to hide from you, no secrets, and no hidden agenda. Do I want you? More than I've ever wanted anything in my life. Am I going to steal you from your promised? No. You're too good to treat that way. I'd surrender my life to Aesa instead of taking you from her if those were my only options. I only want you to hold me."

All I have to do is keep her on my side until I get the support I need to end Eirickson.

"Fine. I'll hold you, but nothing more."

She smiled and sat with her back against my chest and wrapped my arms around her.

My body soon betrayed feelings I wanted to hide.

Tindra sighed while I focused on how many of her scars I felt against my chest. I tried picking them out to distract myself. Instead, I noticed how her breasts felt moving against my arm as she breathed.

"You moved well after the torches went out," I said, attempting to focus on something else. Anything else.

"Growing up here you learn how blind people make it through life. Those amateurs had no idea how to be quiet, which helped."

"An advantage in your line of work."

"Use every edge to come out on top." I could hear the smile in her voice.

"Did you cut off his ear before you killed him?"

She laughed. "Yes."

"Why?"

"I told him I would. Keeps my reputation intact."

"And you want to get away from this life?" I asked, with a laugh.

She nodded. "I know you think it's funny, but I'm good at what I do."

"Sounds like something Crum would say."

"It amuses you to think he and I are alike. I mean, we are, to a certain extent. The biggest difference is why we do what we do. But why are we talking about your friend when we should be talking about us?"

"There *is* no us," I countered.

"A matter of perspective. Romantically, there is no us. Sad, but true. Professionally, we need to act as a team for the meeting. Both sides consider me a biased member working for the other side. You're a resource for them to exploit. The king and the council both want to see what they can get from you. You and I need to work their plots to our...*your*...advantage."

"Crum will be there."

"He'll present his information to back-up your story and motivate the council. At least, it's how I expect Ander to use him," she said.

"Because it's how Ander works?"

"Exactly. He looks for leverage to move resources into place without overt involvement. His attitude allowed the council to be born. I'm starting to think Ander intended for it to happen."

"If he's as good as you say, he's already planning ahead of us. It might be best if you focus on how we use the council instead," I said.

"He's good, but not perfect. I'll have to be at my best and ready to react when he starts working the council. I hope I see it coming before anyone else. Do you trust me?"

"No."

She sighed again. "For the meeting?"

"I trust you to work for your best interest," I allowed.

She pressed into me harder. "I told you I'd fight and die for you. No different than Roi and Crum have said. You never question them."

"Never compare yourself to them. They're the best friends anyone could ever ask for. Neither of them have their principles for hire. Roi isn't a schemer or a manipulator. Crum, well, he does it...did it...trying to fill a hole in his life. I think the hole may be gone. Both of them have sworn more than their life to me. They have, each in their own way, already given them."

She laced her fingers through mine. "Will you ever let me?"

I'm not going to lie to her...I'm better than that. "If you're ever able to prove to me you can, I'll start to consider it."

She nodded and shivered, but didn't say anything.

I held her a little longer before I said, "What are we doing tomorrow? I'm about ready for bed."

"I'm open to suggestions."

"I'm considering going back to the guard to see if I could train with them again after I breakfast. Train until midday and find some lunch. After lunch, I'll figure out how to keep busy until dinner, and then bed."

"Sounds like a full day," Tindra quipped. "Can I convince you to sleep on a lounge in here? I'll keep to myself on my bed, I promise."

"Is this another lesson on Varian social customs?"

"No. I don't want to be alone and it saves time."

"Your wants are not my concern," I said, frowning, "and how would it save time?"

"I don't have to get you from your room in the morning. We can get up together, eat, and train either with the guard or alone. We'll have lunch at Tudal's and spend some time planning for the meeting before dinner, a bath, and back to bed. Everyone will be at Per's before sunrise and I'd like to arrive first, or at least ahead of King Ander and his men."

"My principles overrule your desire to save such a small amount of time," I told her. "Why do you want to get to the meeting so early?"

She squeezed my hand. "To explain about Folke and his men. No doubt, Kurt will know what happened by then. Also, to prove I'm not working for Ander."

"Sounds like it's time to get out and get ready for bed," I said, pulling my hand from hers.

"Water's getting too cool for my taste anyway," she said.

After drying off, I put on a cloak, and went to my room to sleep. For the first time in recent memory, I slept soundly through the night.

Tindra woke me. "I'd like to eat with my parents this morning."

I yawned and stretched. "Is there something I should know?"

"Other than I care about them and want to spend time with them?"

"This isn't a setup or a trap or something?" I asked, dressing.

"No. It's a meal with my parents. Do Croians not eat with their family?"

I smiled. "They do, often. I wanted to know if I should prepare myself for uncomfortable questions."

"My parents know what I do and how I work. They quit asking uncomfortable questions years ago."

"I look forward to a nice meal then. Lead the way," I said, motioning toward the door.

Chapter 45

The dining hall was about half full when we arrived.

"We're eating in the private room," Tindra said, leading me through a door in the far corner of the hall.

It shocked me to find Stina sitting at the table with Mikael and Margit.

"Stina," Tindra said. "A pleasant surprise to see you this morning."

"Someone has to keep an eye on me it seems," she snapped.

"Good morning to you too," I quipped.

"Our food will be here shortly," Mikael said. "While we wait, I thought you two could talk to our guest. Maybe help her understand why she is here."

"I'm here because my parents are going to replace me with the memory of my older sister," she snarled.

"I don't believe that's why you're here," I said.

"Of course not. You're the one who brought the imposter. She isn't Jesca. Jesca's dead."

I shook my head. "I never knew Jesca before. I've done everything I could to keep her safe and help her remember her life. You don't believe me, but I have no doubt she's exactly who she says she is."

"And I know King Ander well enough to know he'd never replace you. He wants you to learn some humility and self-control — a lesson we all need at some point. He won't leave you here for the rest of your life," Tindra said.

"Fine. When can I leave?"

"As we've told you, when you've learned and changed," Mikael said.

The door opened and servers entered, carrying large serving bowls of boiled grains and fruit as well as pitchers. They placed everything in the middle of the table and left.

Tindra kicked me in the ankle when I reached for the serving ladle in the grains.

I squinted at her.

She shifted her eyes from me to her mother.

Margit smiled and filled Mikael's bowl before serving herself.

Looking back to Tindra, I received a short nod and decided to follow Margit's example, serving Tindra before myself.

Stina grabbed an apple and bit into it like an angry animal.

Margit gestured to her. "Stina. Eat a full meal. You'll have a busy day today and it's hard to work on an empty stomach," Tindra translated.

"The only thing I plan to do is figure out how to leave this place," Stina said, scowling at Tindra.

"The people who live here are the kindest, most welcoming, you'll ever find. This house will do you some good, if you let it," I offered.

"What would you know? You're a royal bastard who lost his territory. I suppose you like it here considering you're an outcast too, and a branded traitor no less."

"You shouldn't talk about something you know nothing about," I said, wagging my finger at her. "This brand comes from a tyrant, a coward. My half-brother betrayed Croy and sacrificed me to cover his own treason."

"My parents have shown you more grace than I would," Tindra said. "If it were up to me, you'd be eating in the dining hall."

"If it were up to you, you'd still be having improper meetings with my father."

The candles flared as Tindra shot a burning look at the princess. "Never have I conducted myself as less than professional with King Ander."

"Prostitutes get paid. It's what makes them professional."

Without warning, Margit slapped Stina so hard she fell out of her chair.

"Choose your words with care when talking about my daughter," Mikael said. "I think it best if you finish your meal elsewhere, spoiled child."

Tears ran down Stina's cheeks and she fled the room.

"Thank you," Tindra said. "I was ready to do worse."

Margit moved her fingers across Mikael's hand.

He squeezed her hand when she finished. "I'll get word to Queen Ines as soon as possible."

"I don't understand," I admitted. "Stina should be happy her sister's alive and back with her family. Instead, she seems angry at everyone."

"I think she believes Jesca's return threatens her standing in her family. Stina's done as she pleased without consequence. Her exploits went ignored because the king and queen still mourned. With her sister home, she fears Jesca will get all the attention and they'll force Stina to behave. At least it's how I took all the conversations we had with the king and family," Mikael explained.

"I guess we saw some of it over breakfast the other day," I said.

Tindra nodded. "We need to finish eating and go to the barracks to arrange for some training this morning."

"You two be careful," Mikael said.

Margit nodded.

"We will," I said, before eating fast enough to keep up with Tindra.

I thanked her parents for the meal, and we left. I didn't see Stina when we walked through the dining hall. We stopped by my room to get my hammer, jogged to the barracks, and knocked on the door.

"Who's there?" someone shouted from behind the door.

"Fitzeirick, looking for Lieutenant Aerison."

"He took some new recruits to the training field."

"Perfect. Thank you," I said.

We hurried to the training field where a few recruits sparred under the watchful eye of Aerison.

"Can we join in?" I asked.

"Both of you?" he asked, looking at Tindra.

"She can best me," I said.

He nodded. "You two can use the field, but try to not distract these rookies too much."

"Thank you," I said.

Tindra went to get a practice sword. She took two.

"Why two?" I asked, when she returned.

"It'll be more fun," she said, grinning.

We moved away from everyone else and she launched into a furious attack with both swords.

I struggled to keep up. Just before I decided to let her land a strike so I could take a break, she slowed her pace and threw me off balance. As I recovered, she slapped the flat of a sword across my thigh.

"Not bad," she said, "but adjust to changes quicker."

"I'm still learning."

"Time for another lesson," she said, before coming at me again.

This time she started off slow and increased her tempo before changing the timing. I managed to hold her off until my arms burned before she placed the blade against my neck.

I smiled at her and stepped away to catch my breath.

She let me relax almost long enough to recover and then started at me again.

Soon, we fell into a pattern. She attacked and pressed until she got past my defense. Then she'd let me almost catch my breath.

After a while I collapsed, gasping for breath. Stinging sweat blurred my vision. My fingers cramped, clutching the handle of the heavy, battle hammer. I couldn't let it go.

"Stay down," Tindra said, wheezing herself. "Stay down and you'll die."

She's lost her mind. "What?"

"As soon as I catch my breath, I'll be on you and you *will* die," she said.

"I think..." I breathed heavy. "You...need to...calm down...a...little."

"Eirickson and his men won't calm down. They'll come at you until you're dead."

I struggled to push myself up to a knee. "I know. That's why I'm training now."

"Are you ready to run?" she asked.

"No. I'm not sure I'm ready to walk yet."

Aerison laughed.

"What's so funny?" I asked.

"She's worn you out and wants you to run? I thought *I* was rough on the new men. Hope she never wants to join the guard."

Tindra turned to him. "What I'm preparing him for is far worse than anything most of them will ever face."

"I'm starting to think *you* might be worse than anything any guardsmen would face," he quipped.

"It's best you keep that impression," she said. "On your feet, Fitzeirick. It's time for lunch."

I groaned, forced myself to stand, and put my hammer in its pouch after peeling my fingers from the handle. Exhaustion kept me from pulling stamina from the ground.

"The sooner we get to Tudal's, the sooner we eat," she said, putting the swords back on the weapon stand.

She jogged toward the market district. I'd almost lost sight of her by the time we reached Tudal's eatery.

"Tindra!" he called out. "So good to see you again! Fitzeirick, you don't look well at all."

"He needs water. Could use some myself," Tindra said.

He eyed her. "Of course, follow me to your usual table."

She shook her head. "Not today. I want people to see us together today."

"Sure," he said, clapping his hands together. "Pick a table."

She selected a table where everyone could see us. "This is perfect."

"Water coming right out. Am I to assume you want the usual meal or will that be different, too?"

"One of your stew pies would be perfect," I said.

"Unfortunately, it's only two-meat stew today. We haven't had any rabbit delivered lately."

"Fine with me...unless the slave driver sitting across from me has an objection."

She ignored me.

"Nolwen, water for our guests — lots of it!" he yelled, walking toward the kitchen.

"Tindra!" Nolwen squealed, when she saw us.

She smiled. "It's good to see you again."

"Papa said you two are thirsty. I'll leave the pitcher."

"She's so cute," Tindra commented, as Nolwen left.

"Yes, she is."

Between the two of us, we managed to drink about half the pitcher before Tudal brought our meal.

We thanked him and proceeded to devour the savory pie.

Nolwen brought out more water and looked surprised at how much we ate.

"We worked hard this morning," Tindra explained.

"It usually takes three people to eat that much," the girl said.

I laughed.

"Would you see if your mother could come out for a moment?" Tindra asked.

"Right away!" she shouted, with childish enthusiasm and ran toward the kitchen.

We picked at the remains while waiting for Lena.

"Tindra," Lena said. "So good to see you back so soon."

"Thank you."

"The meal was wonderful," I said. "Didn't miss the rabbit."

"I appreciate your honesty," Lena said. "Some of our customers miss the extra flavor. No one will say why they can't go hunting, but I've heard rumors about Satran soldiers wandering into the southern forests."

"Don't worry yourself over rumors," Tindra said, dropping coins in Lena's apron pocket. "We'll try to come by again soon."

"Thank you again and tell your parents to come by. We haven't seen them in months."

"I'll pass on your invitation," Tindra said. "Now, get back in the kitchen before Tudal messes something up."

She laughed and hurried back to her domain.

Nolwen stepped out and said goodbye as we left.

Tindra waved. "Hope to see you again soon."

"Where to now?" I asked.

"I think we should get cleaned up and relax. We can discuss strategy before dinner and get to sleep early."

"A workable plan, but I'd prefer we stay apart while we bathe. Last night was —"

She interrupted me. "My fault."

"I was going to say a bit too intimate, but I agreed to everything. Why do you feel it's your fault?"

"I pushed you, asked for something I shouldn't have," she said. "It'd be a lie to say I didn't enjoy it — and I think you did, too."

"I haven't held anyone that way in a long time. If I were a lesser man, I'd be happy do it again."

"I know and I don't want you to be a lesser man," she said, and pursed her lips for a moment. "I want you to make me a promise."

"I have to know what you want first."

She nodded. "Understandable. I want you to promise you'll keep me at arm's length from now on."

"I've been trying to do just that all along," I admitted. "Why?"

"Principles, both yours and the ones I need to learn."

Maybe, she's finally starting to listen to me. Either way, I don't have to be on guard around her if she keeps herself in check. "You have my word," I said. "I'll do the best I can to keep you at arm's length. Next time I see him I need to tell Crum you agree with him."

"If you do, he'll find a way to use it against me."

"He still feels like he owes you some payback, so I guess I won't give him any advantage."

"Thank you," she said, grinning.

"It's the honorable thing to do."

She snorted and sped up.

I kept up with her and it didn't take long to get back to her suite.

"Same as yesterday? I start the fire while you fill the tub?"

I laughed. "Considering you're the firesyth, I think it's the best arrangement."

After undressing, I took a seat in the tub while waiting for it to fill. Tindra waited until the water heated before coming in.

"Any idea what we're getting into tomorrow?" I asked.

She shook her head. "I don't want to think about it, or anything else, right now. I want to relax for a while."

"No argument from me," I said, and closed my eyes.

Exhaustion and full stomachs conspired with the hot water to lull us to sleep.

· · · · ● · ● · · · ·

Cold water hit my face. I woke shivering.

"Too cold in here for me," Tindra said, through chattering teeth. "Get out. I'll s-start a f-f-fire and m-make s-some t-t-tea to warm us up."

It took me a moment to realize where I was and why I was so cold. "S-s-s-sounds good."

She hurried out of the tub, leaving without to drying herself. I took the time to dry before heading into the main room. She had a small fire burning in the fireplace, but couldn't stop shivering long enough to help it grow. "G-g-grab a cloak for me. Under the s-sofa cushions."

I hurried to the padded seat. "Hope this helps," I said, handing her a cloak.

"Thank you."

The fire flashed bright and she tossed a couple more logs on before closing her eyes and letting out a sigh of relief.

"So," I began. "Tomorrow?"

"I assume it will come at its scheduled time."

I sighed. "The meeting."

"I suspect it will also come at its scheduled time," she said, and laughed.

I sighed again, louder.

"What are you so worried about?"

"Last meeting I went into unprepared ended with me branded and thrown down a hole. I'd like to avoid repeating the experience," I said, rubbing my cheek.

"Oh," she said. "When you put it that way, I suppose it makes a little sense. Would it put you at ease if I told you Per doesn't have any dungeons under his property? At least none I know of."

"I doubt Per's going to take issue with anything tomorrow."

"No one on the council runs any sort of prison. They usually make their problems disappear. I'm not sure where they dispose of the bodies though. Could use a hole," she said, scratching her head.

"I think I'm safe from them. They sent you to get me. Have a hard time believing they'd kill me now. It'd be a waste of money."

She nodded. "And you brought Ander his daughter back and provided him valuable information."

"But I foisted Crum onto his family," I noted, pointing my finger at her.

"I see your point and the king does have a dungeon. I suppose he'll be your biggest concern," she said, grinning.

I shook my finger. "Are you going to take this seriously?"

"I intend to take this with the sincerity it deserves, but you need to calm down"

"Don't like going into this not knowing what to expect."

"Here's what *I* expect. Ander will call the meeting to order and speak first. Chances are his speech will be meaningless bluster to disguise his demands. Once he's done, someone, Kurt I'd guess, will reply and make counter offers. They may suggest a compromise before presenting their demands. Ander will posture some more, trying to maneuver the council to his benefit.

"Afterward, one side will present its idea of an opportunity to you. They'll tell you what they can do for you and let you know what they expect in return. This is, most likely, a test both to see how you react and what you offer in return. At some point, the other party will feel left out and start their maneuvering. Sooner or later, we'll all grow tired of the game and come to some agreeable solution."

"All things considered, what makes you think you have this figured out at all?" I asked.

"Nothing," she replied, smiling. "I'm likely wrong about every assumption I've made."

I groaned in frustration. "So why give me the explanation?"

"An apparently misguided attempt to get you to calm down. The only thing you can control is how you handle yourself tomorrow. Focus on that."

"And your role?" I asked.

"From the council's perspective, I work for the crown. From Ander's perspective, I'm a mercenary working for them. Of course, they don't know they're both wrong. I'm on your side. I believe you'll win when you fight Eirickson, and I can get out of this life much easier backing the winner."

I smiled. "I appreciate your support and your confidence, but I can't make you any promises."

"I know," she chuckled. "I've never met anyone like you. You don't see how you inspire others to be better than they are. Your leadership quality is interesting, and it doesn't seem like you even try. People respect you and follow you, not because you wield so much power or even demand their respect. They do it because it seems like the natural thing to do."

"I think the cold water affected your mind."

She laughed again. "Just wait."

"I'll wait for you to come to your senses when your mind thaws"

She shook her head and smiled. "Better to wait and see how the meeting turns out tomorrow."

"So long as I don't end up down a hole."

"How about we dress and go for a walk? A nice change of pace, I think," she said.

"A change of pace sounds good. Where?"

"We'll walk the grounds here. There are several places to relax and enjoy some peace."

"Peace would be nice," I said.

We dressed and she led me out the back of the main house. The path wound through a well-tended garden. People smiled and waved or called out greetings when they noticed us.

The garden gave way to clusters of trees. Each was its own private area. Beyond the tree shelters was the fruit orchard. It rivaled any I'd seen.

"Why doesn't the house doesn't sell fruit and vegetables in the market?" I asked.

"Who's going to man the store? The people live here because they're outcasts. Varian society is content having them out of sight."

"Such a shame," I said.

"Yes, but it all works out."

"What happened to our horses?" I asked, as we walked.

"Want to walk by the stables?"

"Yes."

Several people worked cleaning and maintaining tack. A couple more trained horses to pull carts and wagons. Tindra stopped at one of the trainers and waited for him to look her direction.

He saw her and smiled. She made some signs with her fingers. He signed back and pointed toward the back of the stables.

"They're in the pasture out back," she explained.

We walked through the stables. Everything was clean and well maintained. When we reached the gate, I spotted Andale, Aspiet, and Sinar grazing. All three looked to be in excellent condition.

Seeing Aspiet reminded me of something. "Do you know anything about Vairan Parade horses?"

She tapped her finger on her chin for a moment. "Haven't seen one in a long time. Why?"

"Jesca remembered them, but no one seems to have seen one since Croy took my skati from Varia," I said.

"Ask Ander."

"I'd hate to open a wound best left closed," I said.

"Suit yourself," she said, shrugging.

"I assume they have Jesca's special saddle stored somewhere."

"Of course, and I expect it's cleaned and any damage repaired. Would you like to see it, too?"

"No, but I should remind Jesca or Crum it's here. It upset her to ride on a normal saddle."

"He'll be at the meeting tomorrow, correct?"

I nodded. "I'll tell him then."

"We have some time before dinner starts. Care to take the long way back?"

"Excellent suggestion," I said. "A long walk should help build my appetite."

We made our way to the dining hall and took our place in line. I noticed Stina working in the serving line.

"Looks like someone finally calmed down enough to do some work," I said.

"Best we stay quiet. Upsetting her now could be a disaster."

"I agree."

Stina scowled as she ladled stew into my bowl. I gave her a little smile and a nod, but she snorted in reply.

We took the first available seats and ate while the hall filled.

I still hadn't become accustomed to the odd cadence of conversations going on around us. Some spoke while others signed, it broke the typical to and fro pattern most groups spoke in and felt like I was eavesdropping, only catching half of a conversation.

"Takes a while before it seems normal," Tindra said.

"What?"

"It's easy to see your unease," she said.

"Is it obvious?" I asked, looking around to see if anyone else was staring at me.

"If you know what to look for," she said, and smiled. "Eat. We have an early start tomorrow."

"I hope I can sleep," I said. "I'm starting to worry about tomorrow."

"I can help," she said, sparks flashing in her eyes.

"No."

"A back rub," she said, eyebrows raised.

"Arm's length," I said, shaking my head.

"As I asked for," she said, frowning.

We finished our meal and went our separate ways.

Despite my worries, I was able to settle my mind and get to sleep.

Chapter 46

I woke and questions flooded into my mind. *What am I getting into? How will the council treat me? How will Ander treat me? What made that noise?*

The door opened. "Fitzeirick, wake up," Tindra said.

"I'm awake."

The air chilled as she lit a couple of candles.

"Get dressed. Wear something to project strength and confidence. You need to look ready to lead. If you look submissive, both sides will tear you apart," she said.

I shivered and the hair on my neck stood up. "I had the same conversation with my mother before I left to confront the Thanes." I sorted through my clothes until I had a suitable outfit. A heavy, unbleached, cotton shirt with a black, leather vest and the pants I wore for our evening on the town. "Are we going in armed?" I asked.

She cleared her throat and pointed to her scabbard. "Of course." She wore an outfit identical to what she had on when I met her the first time, without the head cover.

I put on the pouch for my hammer and fixed it in place. The familiar weight brought me comfort. "I thought Per's place is neutral ground."

"It is," she said, "but the king will still have guards on the grounds. The council will have some number of enforcers nearby. If this meeting breaks out into a fight, we need to take care of each other. At this point you're the only person there I trust to have my back."

"Crum —"

"He'll have *your* back. I don't expect he'll spare a single thought about my fate."

"He's a good man to have on your side."

"But he'll never *be* on my side."

The argument isn't worth the time. "Ready to go when you are."

"Let's go."

The sliver of moon did little to light our way as we walked through town, avoiding the castle. "No sense in causing the guards any unnecessary alarm," she said.

Not far from Per's, I felt people hiding in shadows and dark corners. *She guessed right; the council's posted people all around.* I wasn't expecting four castle guards at the smithy entrance.

"Tindra and Fitzeirick, here for the meeting," she said.

"No one goes in before King Ander's personal guard," one of them replied.

She produced the royal seal she carried. "I work for the king. Fitzeirick's here at his personal invitation."

The four men took positions around us, resting their hands on their swords. "Your seal doesn't carry any weight in this situation. You can wait, away from here, or you can miss the meeting because we tied you up and had you carried off. Your choice."

"Look," I interjected. "We aren't here to cause trouble. Do any of you answer to Lieutenant Aerison or Captain Torsten?"

"Of course, we do."

"Good," I said, with a nod. "How about we do each other a favor? I can tell them you four did your job well in exchange for letting us in."

"Your praise won't carry any weight, Croian traitor."

I pursed my lips. "I never like to say this, but do you know who I am?"

The other three men mumbled something. Their chosen spokesman said, "I can tell you're Croian and a branded traitor. Don't need to know anything else."

I cocked my head toward him. "True, but do any of you have any idea why I might know a lieutenant and a captain by name?"

"Because you've been in trouble often enough to remember their names?"

"If so, you'd recognize me," I countered.

"He's right," one of them agreed.

"Another question," I said. "Do you know Lieutenant Aerison escorted Jesca and another Croian around the castle grounds?"

"The lieutenant's duties are none of our business."

"I brought her home. The other Croian, Crum, is my best friend. He's currently staying at the castle, as a guest of the royal family. Do you want word getting to the royal family, you four barred my entrance into this meeting?"

"But the king's safety —"

"I rescued Jesca from a dungeon no one knew existed," I said, pointing at myself. "I risked my life to bring her back to her family. Why would I threaten your king's safety?"

"Has a point there," one of the guards muttered.

The spokesman shook his head. "We have our orders."

I groaned and pointed to the man who'd kept silent. "What's the worst duty you can think of?"

"Scrubbing cells in the dungeon."

The others nodded.

"Sounds pretty bad," I agreed, and glanced at Tindra.

She nodded.

"If we can't reach an agreement," I continued, "I'll make sure King Ander considers assigning it to all four of you. While you're down there, I'll see if Torsten can find something worse once you finish."

"Your word doesn't carry enough weight with the king to back such a threat," the first guard said.

Before I could reply, Tindra spoke. "That may, or may not, be true, but consider *my* word. You all know what I do. One could argue I'm among the king's most trusted agents. If Fitzeirick makes a claim and I support it..."

"She's not wrong," the second guard said.

"Let them in. I'm sure they'll put in a good word for us," the quiet one said.

I nodded.

Tindra added, "Of course we will. You can get rewarded or you can get punished, doesn't matter to us. We only want to get on with our business."

Three of the guards stepped away but the first one stood fast.

"I don't like threats."

I nodded. "No one does."

He grimaced and stepped aside. "Do *not* get in trouble while you are in the capital."

"I appreciate the advice," I said, giving him a shallow bow.

Tindra knocked on the door and kept an eye on the guards while we waited for someone to let us in. It felt like hours passed before Per looked out and invited us in. We stepped inside and he closed the door.

"You're here early," he said.

"First ones?" Tindra asked.

"Other than the royal guard," he said.

"Any arrangements for food?" she asked.

"According to the king's delegation, they'll bring breakfast. He'll send for any other meals if necessary."

"Just paranoid enough," she commented. "We'll wait in the courtyard if it's alright with you."

"Makes me no difference."

"Please, tell Kurt I'd like to speak with him if he arrives before Ander and his people," she said.

"I'll let him know."

"How does Kurt plan to get past the guards out front?" I asked.

"What do you mean?" Per asked, forehead wrinkling. "Their orders are to let anyone here for the meeting in."

"They insisted we wait for the king's personal guard," I said.

"We bullied our way in," Tindra added.

"That wasn't the agreement," Per said. "I'll go talk to them."

"Doubt they'll listen to you," I said.

"If you insist," Per said, looking toward the door.

"Leave it," Tindra suggested. "It won't hurt to let the council figure out how to deal with those four. For all I know, Kurt won't get here until after King Ander has arrived."

"I'm still going to say something," Per said. "Oh, and don't scare the archers in the courtyard."

"Thanks for the warning," Tindra said.

We stepped out into the pool of light left by the open door to the courtyard. A chorus of bow strings, drawing tight, broke the silence. Pushing out my talent showed me six men posted along the wall.

"Hold!" I called out. "We are here for the meeting at the invitation of both King Ander and the council."

"How do we know you're telling the truth?" replied a voice from my right.

"We wouldn't have made it past the guards outside," I said.

"Do we take him at his word?" another voice asked.

"Will you stand down long enough for me to get something from my pocket?" Tindra asked.

"What good will it do?" the first voice asked.

"I can show you the seal proving I operate with the blessing and authority of King Ander."

"Any tricks and we let fly."

She reached with care and pulled out the seal.

"Evert, check it out. We have you covered."

I tracked someone moving toward us from the left. It didn't take long for him to step into the light.

Tindra held out the seal.

"It looks legitimate, Henrick!" he shouted.

"Back to your post!" Henrick yelled. "You two take a seat — middle of the table."

"Thank you!" I yelled back. We walked straight to the long, stone table in the middle of the courtyard.

While we waited, the archers paced. I kept myself occupied by tracking their movements and Tindra slumped forward and went to sleep with her head on the table.

The door creaked and Captain Torsten yelled, "Attention!"

The archers quit moving. I fought the urge to stand, but Tindra didn't even flinch.

"Henrick!" Torsten yelled.

"Yes, sir!"

"Servants are here with the food. I secured a small table for the guard. Foot traffic will be constant. Stay alert, but do not act unless necessary."

"Understood, sir!"

Torsten held the door open as porters paraded into the courtyard. The first two carried small torches and lit candles on the table and large torches around the wall.

Once the yard was lit, a small, wooden table was placed away from the main one. The next group placed large platters of baked goods along the main table. A smaller tray went on the guards' table. Another group carried pitchers. They set them between the platters and left a couple on the guards' table. Finally, a group set plates, cups, and utensils at each seat. The guards only got cups.

"Torsten, can we eat now?" Tindra asked.

"Bad form, I'm afraid. Wait for King Ander."

I frowned and looked over the spread, piles of rolls, cakes, and flatbreads. The pitchers had lids, so I had no idea what they held. With a table full of temptation, I questioned the wisdom of arriving first.

It seemed like hours passed after the food arrived, so I asked Torsten when he expected Ander.

He glanced toward the top of the wall. "Don't see the first signs of sunrise. He'll be here no later than first light."

I was about to say something when someone stepped out of the building. "Are you the captain?" he asked Torsten.

I'd heard the voice before.

"I am. Who are you?"

"Kurt, with the council. Here to meet with our king."

"Any with you?" Torsten asked.

He nodded. "The other council members are outside."

"They may enter after King Ander," Torsten said.

"If it must be."

"Kurt," Tindra called out. "Come. Sit. We need to talk."

He looked our direction and squinted for a moment before nodding.

"I suppose we do," he said, sitting. "It seems someone left a mess outside of Tyres' Fool. Know anything about it?"

"I suspect you know I do," she said.

He nodded. "You can't deny you two were there and the cut off ear...hope you have a good explanation."

"Ah yes, the dance," she said, and sighed. "Everyone remembered it?"

"Oh, you made an impression," he said, smiling. It turned into a frown. "And then, it seems, you made a disturbing exit."

Tindra chuckled and shook her head. "We were heading back to Daufi when Folke and his thugs ran across us. I tried to get him to leave in peace, I swear. He decided it'd be better to kill us. Once the fight started, the runt proved to be a coward. Fitzeirick ended him while I made short work of his two friends."

"Three bodies, and messy," he said, shaking his head. "Bad for business. Tyres isn't happy."

"He needs to hire better help anyway," she said. "The young barkeep almost got on my bad side."

"Not how he told the story," Kurt said. "He claimed you two came in looking for a fight. Said he was about to throw you out himself, but you paid him not to. According to the boy, you two all but said you'd kill someone before the night was over."

"He's a liar," I insisted.

"Strong words from a branded traitor."

I puffed out my chest as my hands balled into fists.

"Relax," Tindra said, grabbing my arm. "Fitzeirick's right, the boy lies. We'd finished a fine meal and intended to spend time drinking and dancing. Tyres' young barkeep had a chip on his shoulder. I nudged it a little, and he changed his mind. He served us the drinks I ordered, I paid him and left a tip, a generous tip. We danced the one dance and decided to leave. Neither of us threatened anyone or even suggested anything violent would happen. We even left drinks on the bar."

Kurt's eyes shifted from Tindra to me and back. "I'll talk to Tyres after the meeting."

With that settled, we waited for King Ander's arrival. It didn't take long. More guardsmen hurried into the courtyard, taking positions near the door.

"All rise," Torsten shouted.

Kurt, Tindra, and I stood.

King Ander strode into the courtyard with Crum behind him. A few moments later, Tyres led a small parade through the door.

Ander took his place at the head of the table. "Fitzeirick, please sit at my left."

I nodded and moved to sit across from Crum.

Glancing toward Tindra, I noticed Tyres standing next to her.

Ander looked everyone in the face, pausing at each person, before nodding. "I propose we eat before conducting official business. Any opposed?"

No one said a word.

"Please sit and enjoy this...modest...breakfast."

We stood, motionless, until Ander sat down. Once seated, we waited until he placed a piece of flatbread on his plate before reaching for food.

With the formalities over, it became organized chaos. I managed to grab a couple of everything near me and poured a cup full of milk. Crum grabbed more than me, as I expected.

While eating, I grew tense again. Nervous energy conspired with anticipation and I worried about the meeting turning against me. Crum looked at me and smiled. His show of optimism made me feel a little better, until I remembered he rarely saw the worst in any situation.

Ever brighter sunlight made the candles unnecessary as the eating continued. As the sun peeked over the courtyard wall, King Ander stood. "I believe it is time to call this meeting to order. Any opposed?"

Everyone responded by dropping whatever they had in their hands.

"Excellent," he said. "Of course, it may be the last thing we agree on for a while, but at least we have an agreement to start. I ask Fitzeirick to introduce himself, describe what he went through, and tell you why he's here."

I nodded to him and stood as he sat. "For those I haven't met, I am Fitzeirick; son of a Varian woman named Sar'sa and the deceased Croian Jarl, Eirick. Younger half-brother of the current Jarl, Eirickson, and former Skald of the far-eastern, Croian skati, now lost to Satra."

Continuing, I described the ill-fated meeting with my half-brother and told them how he branded and imprisoned me. Murmurs arose as I spoke of the wretched conditions along with the escape. While telling the story of my travels, the aid I received, and lives I had taken, a few on the council looked angry because I killed a Varian. I mentioned reuniting with Crum, but said he had his own information to contribute. Toward the end of my speech, I channeled my fear and apprehension into power and declared Eirickson the true traitor to Croy.

My body shook as I swore to see his corrupt tyranny ended by my hand, leaving no doubt I wouldn't rest until Jarl Eirickson drew his last breath.

Several council members nodded; a couple wore slack-jawed expressions of surprise. The rest I couldn't read.

Ander put his hand on my shoulder. "Take your seat and calm yourself. It's time for Crum to speak."

I looked at him and nodded.

Crum stood and started his story with the bravado I expected. He wove a tale of mystery around my disappearance, emphasizing the fear and desperation he felt while searching for me. He went into fine detail about the various places he haunted and contacts he made in the Croian capital.

My heart pounded as he spoke about the discussion between Eirickson and Satra, stressing their plot to divide Varia.

I fought back tears while he expressed the gloom and terror of fleeing for his life and breathed easier as he finished the story on a high note. With a bright smile, he described our reconnection and journey to the safety of Varia.

His performance was met with mumbles and whispers.

King Ander stood and Crum moved to sit.

"Wait," Ander said. "It seems some here don't think you're telling the truth. I believe there are questions."

Crum stood still and stared at me.

I raised my eyebrows and mouthed, "Good job."

Kurt cleared his throat and stood. "How is it you are the only person who's heard of this supposed alliance between Croy and Satra? We have...people placed in Croy and none of them have reported any sort of meetings."

Ander nodded. "A fair question. Do you have an explanation?"

Crum smiled and turned to Kurt. "Can I explain why I'm better at gathering information in my home country than your people? No. I can't tell you why your money and effort isn't well spent. I know what I saw and every word I've spoken is true." Raising his eyebrows, he asked, "Any further questions?"

No one responded to his challenge.

Ander nodded and motioned for Crum to sit. "Now is the time for the council to speak. Kurt, am I to assume you're the mouthpiece for these men?"

He stood. "For the purposes of this meeting, I am granted authority by majority consent."

"The table is yours," Ander said, sitting.

"Thank you, my king," he said, and bowed. "The loss of the conquered land to Satran invasion wasn't understood at the time. Now, we have a much clearer description of what happened. Crum gained the attention of our agents operating around the Croian leader, Nikulas. Through him, we learned of the disappearance of Eirickson's half-brother. Fitzeirick's unexpected arrival in Varia presented an interesting opportunity and we sought to bring him to our side. We seek to pledge our support to any action Fitzeirick may take. Assuming we can reach an agreement securing all necessary concessions, of course."

"What concessions would those be?" I asked.

King Ander cleared his throat. "Negotiations will happen in due time."

"I beg pardon for speaking out of turn," I said. *Now seems like the ideal time to settle this, if you ask me.*

"We should expect some misunderstandings on your part. Continue, Kurt."

"The council exists to improve our ability to do battle. It has spent many resources developing tools and machines for the battlefield. Due to the secretive nature of our work they remain untested. This was all done for us to lead an overt attack, but a growing alliance between Croy and Satra limits our time to act. We believe a small, covert team can make a precise strike on the Croian leadership," Kurt said.

"We can discuss plans and tactics later," Ander said. "Do you have anything else to add?"

"No, Sire," Kurt said.

"You may be seated. It is time I spoke on this matter. The members of this council believe they operate in secret, without my knowledge. The existence of this group came to my attention some time ago. I've monitored your activities for several years now, making sure you didn't endanger my country. Your continued existence has been at my consent. Some of your associates have enjoyed the benefits of being on my payroll at various times."

He coughed and took a drink. "I know how this council feels about my pacifist views. Your opinion was valid, but things have changed. In light of the threat described by Crum, I feel it is time to make moves to protect Varia and take back what is ours.

"It is no secret I, like many Varian, lost more than land and belongings when Croy invaded. Many of us lost family. I lost my eldest daughter, changing the way I looked at life. I feared risking further losses. The Varians here have attended the annual memorial service held in Jesca's honor. Some have attended a few. I have attended every one. We will no longer hold the memorials. Instead, we will soon have a celebration because Jesca is home."

Several men gasped as he paused for another drink. "Here is my proposal. While I will not recognize this council in public, I will provide *some* support. I ask you to improve our security and our ability to fight the coming war. In exchange, I will continue to turn a blind eye to your other...activities."

Do his bidding and keep collecting spoils. Interesting manipulation.

King Ander paused until the murmurs between councilmen stopped.

"Assisting Fitzeirick and stopping this alliance is the goal, but find a way to do so without drawing undue attention to Varia. Any attempted coup needs to look like it originated inside Croy's borders. I also propose we look to Tindra as liaison and will present my expectation of spoils after the council accepts this offer. Does the council need time to discuss my proposal?"

A chaotic uproar began after King Ander sat.

Is this about to go bad? I slowly reached for my hammer and glanced at Tindra. She shook her head, motioning for me to stop.

Kurt attempted to settle his group, but no one paid attention to him. He resorted to climbing onto the table and yelling for silence. Finally, he walked down the table and kicked one man out of his chair before everyone got quiet.

I fought back a laugh.

He jumped to the ground and stomped back to his seat, his face bright red. "King Ander, please accept my apology for such an uncivilized display. Some of my associates forget their manners when presented with surprising offers. There should be no problem working with Tindra. She has earned the respect of several councilmen. We do need time to debate the merits of your generosity. Some may feel we should stay independent as we have our own interests to consider. We prefer to negotiate benefits for ourselves if we decide to enter into an agreement."

"Understood," Ander said. "How much time do you need?"

Kurt looked over his group. "Would it be possible to table your proposal, let us weigh our options, and meet again over lunch?"

Ander stared at Kurt long enough that the council spokesman started wilting. "I hoped to have the preliminaries worked out before we left here. If we reach an agreement now, future discussions can happen under less formal circumstances."

"Can we ask you and the other non-council members to go inside while we discuss this?" Kurt asked.

"You may speak freely," Ander offered.

"Only a fool prepares negotiations in front of those he negotiates with. I didn't get where I am by being a fool," Kurt said, crossing his arms.

"Point taken," King Ander agreed, with a nod. "It is easier for a few to leave than many. In the spirit of compromise, Crum and Fitzeirick would you please join me inside? Kurt, what would you have Tindra do?"

"She should go with you. I'll send someone to tell you when we have an answer."

"And the guards?" the king asked.

"They may stay."

"Please debate quickly. I don't like to wait," King Ander warned, as he left the table. Crum, Tindra, and I followed him.

My future rests on the decision of a table full of outlaws.

Captain Torsten closed the door behind us.

Chapter 47

"Kurt doesn't trust you?" Crum asked Tindra.

"This is council business, I'm not on the council."

I looked at Crum. "Remind Jesca her special saddle is still at House of Daufi."

"Special saddle?" Ander asked.

"She insisted on riding sidesaddle," Crum explained.

The king scratched his chin for a moment, then chuckled. "Of course. When she was taken, sidesaddle was in fashion for women."

"Speaking of riding," I began, "what happened to the Varian Parade horses?"

Ander glared at me, pursed his lips, and flared his nostrils before closing his eyes. "Jesca loved those animals. It wouldn't do for even one to fall into foreign hands. We killed them before fleeing the Croian invaders. After we made it back to our castle, the Parades stabled here served as a painful reminder of our lost ,little girl. Ines became almost inconsolable when she saw one. We decided to put them down to save our sanity. They're gone forever."

A tear rolled down his cheek when his eyes opened.

A knot formed in my gut. "Please, accept my apology," I said, bowing. "I didn't mean to cause sorrow."

"You didn't know, couldn't know," he murmured, before walking away.

"I thought you said you'd avoid the subject of those horses," Tindra whispered.

And now I wish I had. "After he asked about the saddle, I thought he might relate it to the special horses."

"Instead, you reminded him of what he lost," Crum said.

I wanted to change the subject and take focus off my mistake. "Crum, any idea of how involved you'll be in this business?"

"If you are asking me to fight at your side, I won't refuse, but my heart won't be in it. I'd like to stay with Jesca."

"Good to know, but not exactly what I was asking. Do you have any indication of how much King Ander might involve you in this situation?"

"We haven't discussed it."

"Then he doesn't intend to use you," Tindra said.

"But he's all too ready to use you," Crum said.

"He knows me, knows what to expect. You're a Croian who has his daughter's heart which, I'm sure, causes him some trouble."

He pointed at her. "What are you trying to say?"

I stepped between the two of them. "No fighting, not here."

He looked at me, nodded, and walked away.

She waited a moment, then whispered, "He thinks you chose me over him."

I shook my head. "He knows better."

She smiled. "The Crum you remember knows better. The man who just walked away may not."

"What do you mean?"

"He's confused and changing, a bad combination. You didn't stand next to him, support him, just now. Instead, you stood between him and me. He may think you're moving away from him, starting to take my side. He doesn't know I'm already on your side."

"Trust me, Crum has no doubt where he and I stand," I argued.

A knock on the door interrupted our conversation.

Captain Torsten opened it. "They're ready. Go back out, and I'll get King Ander."

After taking my seat, I studied Kurt, but his blank expression gave nothing away.

Everyone clambered out of their seats when the door opened again.

I noticed Crum wasn't with the king.

"Sit," King Ander ordered, from the head of the table.

Everyone except Kurt sat. "We would like to clarify some points before giving our answer."

"Understandable," Ander said.

"First, where's the other Croian?"

"I sent him back to the castle. His part in this meeting is completed."

Kurt nodded. "What did you mean when you said some of the council members have been on your payroll?"

"Exactly what I said. Individuals received payment for services or information. I will not betray anyone's trust nor will I tolerate sudden deaths of anyone here or their relatives. Any such incident will receive extraordinary attention from the guard."

Kurt nodded again and opened his mouth, but the table rumbled with Ander's voice.

"I demand everyone state their understanding."

Everyone sat in stunned silence for several moments before a chorus of voices expressed acknowledgment.

I still don't understand how he projects his voice through stone.

He smiled and nodded. "Any more questions?"

"What type of support are you offering?" Kurt asked.

"Anything I provide cannot draw undue attention to the Varian crown. Coin is easy enough as are other materials. People would be a bit problematic, though I can make arrangements if there is no other option. What do you foresee needing?"

"If I could see the future I wouldn't have to ask," Kurt said.

The king smiled. "I will address the requests as they come. What else?"

"I believe you have addressed our concerns. Your proposal is acceptable," Kurt said, with a nod and a smile. "What do you expect from us in return?"

"Nothing more than you've said you are ready to give. Support Fitzeirick in his fight and stand ready to defend his claim to Croian rule once Eirickson is dead."

"But what about action against Satra?" Kurt asked.

"I expect those plans will require many more meetings. Considering the evidence, taking Eirickson out of power should delay their movement," King Ander said.

"What am I going to pay for this support?" I asked.

"Once you overthrow Eirickson and secure your country, I expect you to lead the attack on Satra," Ander answered. "After you secure that victory, you and I will work out a beneficial agreement."

I crossed my arms. "I stand ready to do what's necessary, but I won't give you the land of my birth."

He shook his head. "Carts don't pull horses. We will negotiate at the proper time."

Ander best understand my skati is not part of the negotiation. I gave him a small bow and turned to Kurt. "And the council's demands?"

He shrugged. "We believe they are of little concern to you. We are all businessmen at heart. We want to do business in Croy same as in Varia."

"Not without limits," I warned.

"We aren't evil. We're necessary, in our own way," he said, sweeping his arm toward his peers. "If not us, someone worse could come in and keep their activities hidden from you until they are too big to get rid of. We control ourselves and do our best to avoid unnecessary attention."

"I will not condone any type of slave trade and children are off limits," I said, crossing my arms.

Kurt looked at King Ander. "Sire, how many slavers operate inside Varia?"

"None," Ander replied, smiling. "You did away with the slave trade almost ten years ago."

"Without involving the crown. Children are safe from our activities unless they choose to involve themselves. We frown upon putting anyone's child in harm's way, but we don't discourage them from working for us."

"*You* say they choose to involve themselves, but who's the judge? And who enforces the rule?" I asked.

"We all understand what is and is not acceptable and control each other's actions. Anyone who decides they are beyond the authority of the council is soon found out. We have ways to teach them how wrong they are."

I turned to Ander. "And you condone this?"

He nodded. "Considering I take no action to discourage them, one could argue I do. The council's self-rule allows me to devote more resources to our society. It is rare for me to address major crimes."

Why should I welcome these men, outlaws and thugs, into Croy? Just because I need their support? "I'll have to consider this before I can agree." I glanced sideways at Kurt, "Can we agree to move forward while I weigh my options?"

"For now," he said, "but it's best you decide soon...for everyone's benefit".

I nodded. "Where do we go from here?"

"If King Ander has no objections, I would like to lay out our current plan," Kurt said.

"I didn't expect negotiations to end this quickly, but I'm pleased with the progress. Yes, enlighten us."

"I believe everyone knows we've surrounded Nikulas with Varians and earned his trust. We used our connection to present the idea of establishing a trade agreement with him. The original intent was expanding operations, generating more income, and moving weapons in secret. Now, we should send our emissary with a large enough trade caravan to convince him we are serious. A large caravan needs protection. We want to hide Fitzeirick and five of our men among the caravan guard. Before we reach Nikulas, those six leave, ride to the Croian capital, and find a way to assassinate Eirickson. Fitzeirick, are six men enough to kill Eirickson and overthrow the Croian government?"

I thought for a moment before answering. "Do you have any information on the current number of his personal guard or surrounding forces? Hard to say without knowing that information. After his death, executing the Council of Thanes would be necessary, but easy. Then I'll need men to secure my claim to rule. Six won't stand against much resistance."

"Our agents around Nikulas are the closest we can get to Eirickson," Kurt said. "We know nothing about his personal security or the possibility of rebellion."

King Ander cleared his throat. "Can you get into the capital the same way you escaped?"

"No," I replied. "The escape tunnel leads underground with no exit. We *could* approach the capital that way, but some of the mountain paths are treacherous and I'm not sure how to best gain entry."

"Get the lay of the land, when you get closer, and decide then," Kurt said. "Any other details to address?"

"Me," Tindra said. "I'm not in the attack party."

Several of the council members laughed. Tyres shook his head.

"No, you're not," Kurt said, "as there's no reason for your involvement."

"No reason other than I'm *perfect* for this mission," Tindra argued, slapping her hand on the table. "I'm one of the best at infiltration, gathering information, and finishing my target. Also, to represent King Ander's interests, or do I speak out of turn, Sire?"

The king laughed for a moment. "I regret risking such a valuable resource, but it might be impossible to keep you from going. You have my support."

Tyres groaned, but Kurt shook his head. "Then it will be Fitzeirick, Tindra, and four of our men."

"Who?" Tindra asked.

"We haven't decided yet," one of the council members at the far end of the table said.

"When do we leave?" I asked.

"This will take time to put together," Kurt said. "Sizable trade caravans don't simply appear overnight. Our best estimate is two months to get this together and moving toward Croy."

"What can I do to help?" King Ander asked.

"Horses, wagons, and guards," Kurt said.

"Horses and wagons, I can provide, but no men — no guards."

Kurt shook his head. "This needs to be a sanctioned, trade caravan carrying the crown's full support. No one would suspect an escort of guardsmen. As a matter of fact, it would look strange if it weren't guarded."

"He's right, Sire," Tindra added.

"Fine, but I won't *assign* men, volunteers only. How many would you need?"

"Ten wagons, four guards per wagon. At least forty men," Kurt said.

"Torsten!" the king yelled.

The captain came running with his hand on his sword. "What do you need, Sire?"

"Send a runner to the barracks. I need at least forty men to volunteer for guard duty on a trade caravan to central Croy. It will leave in approximately two months."

"I will send word immediately, my king," he said, and hurried back into the building.

"A suggestion, if I may," I said.

"Of course," King Ander said. "We value your input."

"If we're going to blend in with the Varian guard, shouldn't we look and act like them? I think the six of us should train with the guard," I said.

"Well, I don't see how —" Kurt said.

The king cut him off. "Outstanding idea. Makes sense and creates the perfect disguise. What do you see wrong, Kurt?"

Kurt raised his eyebrows. "I think it may be difficult for our men to spend time among people they avoid out of habit."

"It would be even better if everyone involved commits to living with the guard. Let them learn to act like a true Varian guard unit," King Ander said.

Tindra raised her hand. "A point. The guards are men."

King Ander rubbed his chin for a moment and looked off in the distance before returning his eyes to her. "You insisted on taking part. You're a clever one. I'm sure you'll figure it out."

She snorted. "Another point. If the six invaders are living with the guard, this won't stay secret. We'll have to tell someone we're going to split off at some point. It exposes our mission."

"She's right, my king. The more people who know the secret, the more likely it's discovered," Kurt said, smiling.

"The six need to spend as much time as possible together, so I'll have rooms in the southern tower for them. They report to the barracks for breakfast and leave after dinner. I'll arrange the special treatment with the officers," King Ander said. "Will that work for you?"

She nodded. "Yes, my king, a wise solution."

"No need for flattery."

"A request," I interjected.

"So long as it is reasonable," the king said.

"May we have Lieutenant Aerison assigned as our trainer? I've worked with him recently and agree with his methods," I said.

"I hope he appreciates the assignment."

"Thank you."

"There is one other thing we should consider," Tindra said.

"Enlighten us, please," the king responded.

"Two months from now is near the beginning of the raining season. We could travel through bad storms for at least part of the journey."

"Which proves how serious we are about establishing trade," Kurt said.

"Kurt, I agree. Anything else we need to address?" King Ander asked.

"No, other than when to start putting things into motion," Kurt said.

"I expect your men to report to the barracks tomorrow morning. Turning people into trained and disciplined guardsmen takes time. They train every day until the caravan is ready. The faster you prepare, the sooner we strike. Remember, time is of the essence here. For all we know the first surge of a Satran invasion could happen any day."

"Tomorrow?" Kurt barked.

"Is this a problem?" the king asked. "You claim you've been planning something for a while now. I would think you have suitable men already selected."

"Oh...umm...yes," Kurt stammered. "We *have* been planning, but not for this exact situation. We have men, but not the...resources...the trade goods."

"Gather your goods quickly. I'll see to transportation and food," the king said. "May I suggest we adjourn the meeting now, so you can start making preparations? It's not as if I have nothing to arrange myself."

"Of course, my king," Kurt said, and looked down the table. "Does anyone have any objection to ending the meeting now?"

From what I saw everyone shook their head or said, "No."

No one moved until King Ander stood. "Make your way with haste and safety," he said, before walking toward Per's shop.

Tindra made her way to me as everyone else walked away.

"Train with the guard for two months?" she said, throwing her hands into the air.

"I think it's a good idea," I said.

"Kurt talked Ander out of housing us with them, at least. Still, the tower isn't as nice as my suite."

"The mission's more important. Do you know who the council will send?"

"No idea."

"What should we do now?"

"Get our stuff and head for the southern tower," she said. "We'll have our pick of the rooms."

"Sounds like a good idea," I said, as we left the courtyard.

Per stopped us as we stepped inside. "Tindra, King Ander put in an order. It's big enough we have to stop working on everything else to meet his schedule. I didn't have to discount any of my prices."

"Good," she said. "I hope it turns into a long, profitable relationship."

"As do I," he said.

She nodded and we left the smithy.

"I'll have more things to bring than you. Do you mind carrying some for me?" she asked, when we got close to Daufi.

"Not at all, assuming you don't plan to treat me like a mule."

"A strong stonesyth like you should handle the load without a problem," she said, with a wink and a smile.

It took no time at all for me to put my belongings back in the saddlebags. I entered Tindra's suite and found her filling a second bag. She looked at me. "As much as I enjoy this suite, I think I'm going to miss hot baths the most."

"What do you mean?"

"The tower doesn't have water running, much less heated tubs. The guards bathe under a waterfall. Only officers have access to a heated bath."

"No hot baths for two months?"

"The mission's more important," Tindra mocked. "It'll be more than two months, if you think about it. We're on the road as soon as the council's ready to start the caravan. What happens after you kill Eirickson? How soon will you gain control of your country? It could be quite some time before you see another tub of hot water."

"Oh," I said, frowning. "I hadn't thought of that."

Her eyes lit up. "I'll start a fire. If you want to fill the tub."

I shook my head. "Tempting, but I think it best if we show our commitment by preparing for the mission."

"I hate being the example," she said, buckling her bag closed.

"You insisted on going," I reminded her, through a grin.

"Only to help you win. Without Crum, who's going to watch your back?"

"I'm supposed to trust you like I trust him?" I asked.

"You will," she said, smiling.

I sighed and shifted my saddlebags on my shoulder. "Are you packed yet?"

"Yes," she said. "Take this bag, I'll carry my other one."

It was heavier than my own. "What's in here?"

"Only the essentials," she said, and laughed.

We stopped at the stairs. "Are you going to say anything to your parents?"

"Not now. They're used to me disappearing without notice. I'll try to see them, say goodbye, before we leave for Croy."

Chapter 48

We arrived at the tower and found a guard posted at the door. "We need two rooms," Tindra said.

"I expect six men tomorrow morning," he said.

"We're two of them," I said. "The others report tomorrow."

He opened the door and moved aside. "The tower's empty. Rooms are first come, first served."

"Thank you," Tindra said.

The guard nodded as we walked by.

"Which room do you want?" I asked.

"Doesn't matter, they're the same," she said. "I prefer the one farthest from the entrance."

"Why?"

"If someone attacks, they go to the closest room first — usually. Assuming they don't surprise you, the fight will get my attention and I can help."

"I'll take the first room," I said, smiling.

I followed her to the second door, dropped her bag, and went to what would be my home for the next couple of months.

It was a slightly larger version of the guest room at the House of Daufi. It had a bed against the far wall, a table with four chairs in the middle of the room, and a fireplace in the left wall. From the quick glance I'd had of Tindra's room, they were mirror images.

I dropped my saddlebags near the foot of the bed along with my hammer and its pouch, lit a few candles, and lay down to think about how my life was about to change.

A knock on the door interrupted my contemplation. "Fitzeirick, are you in there?" Tindra asked.

"Where else would I be?"

"Care to join me at Tudal's for lunch? May be the last time we get to eat there for a while," she called.

I jumped from the bed. "You don't have to ask me twice."

We weaved through the crowds in the market and walked into Tudal's eatery. His daughter saw us first. "Dad, Tindra and the man with the long name are here again."

"I told you to call me Fitz."

She blushed. "I only remembered you have a long name."

Tindra laughed as Tudal walked out from the kitchen. "You want to sit out here or be social with us?"

Tindra replied, "I think we're feeling social today."

"Nolwen, go set the table and pour them..." Tudal stopped and looked at me.

"Water."

"Water," he repeated.

The young girl hurried into the kitchen and had everything ready by the time we arrived.

"Back so soon?" Lena asked, as we sat.

"You may not see us for a while, so I thought we'd pay you a visit," Tindra told them.

"Why not? Where are you going?" Tudal asked.

"Royal business," I said. "We can't talk about it."

He waved his finger at me. "You better be careful. Tindra's one of my favorite customers *and* my best spokesman."

"The usual?" Lena asked, trying not to laugh.

I was about to say yes when Tindra stopped me. "If we're going to be away for a while, would it be too much to ask for something special?"

"I could've started something this morning, but we're getting ready for lunch," Lena said, with a slight frown.

"One of your meat pies will be fine," I assured her.

"Perhaps I can add a little something to make it memorable," Tudal suggested, thoughtfully.

"What are you thinking?" Lena asked. "We don't have anything else ready."

"Dear wife, you don't know all my tricks," he said, laughing.

The lanky man went to work. I couldn't remember the last time I'd watched a talented cook working at a frantic pace. *For all I know, this is his typical pace.* It looked like he was in several places at once, dodging around his wife as he worked on our meal.

She eventually threw up her hands. "I'm going to sit until you're finished."

If he heard her, he didn't react and kept working on his creation.

"Do you know what he's making," Tindra asked, as Lena sat.

"It started like a meat pie, but took a strange turn somewhere." She shrugged. "I've never seen him do this before."

"I didn't mean for him to go to so much trouble," I said.

"Oh, this will do him some good. He loves to create. Let him have his fun."

Finally, Tudal slid the deep pan in the oven and wiped his brow. "I had to clean some thick dust off that memory, but I think I got the recipe right. Should be worth the wait."

"Care to let me in on the secret?" Lena asked.

He laughed and shook his head. "Only after they taste it. Don't want to spoil the surprise."

"Back to work for me," she said.

Tudal stayed near the oven, watching over it like someone guarding a treasure, until he pulled the pan out and the smell of earthy spices erupted into the room. "It has to cool a little."

My nose became used to the spices and I was able to pick out the smell of pork, potatoes, and something sweet. "You're not going to give us a hint?" I asked.

He shook his head. "I want to see the look on your face."

I looked at Tindra. She shrugged.

"Warm some sage bread and this will be ready to serve," Tudal said.

"I have a couple of loaves fresh from the oven," Lena said.

He nodded and said, "Put one on the tray," before placing his creation on the table and stepping back.

I pushed my fork through the crust on top. It wasn't as crisp usual and the filling wasn't as heavy with sauce. I speared something firm — a piece of cubed pork, a chunk of potato, and a small piece of something else. It was white and resembled the potato, but wasn't the same.

I put the food in my mouth and let it sit for a moment to figure out what I was eating. It was a mix of spicy, salty, and sweet, but I couldn't figure out what the third thing on my fork was. "This tastes amazing," I said.

Tudal smiled.

"You've outdone yourself," Tindra said.

He smiled even wider.

"Lena, you have to try this," Tindra said.

She came to the table with a fork and took a bite. "Pork, potato, and pear?"

"Yes," he said, "but stir it around a little to get a good coating of sauce."

We all stirred and tried the new flavor, much sweeter than before.

"Honey," Lena practically cooed.

"Now, try it with sage bread," he said, with a big grin.

I tore us each a piece of bread and we demolished the crust, dipping it at the same time. The sage enhanced the various flavors.

Lena smiled, nodding as she chewed. "Next time add more sage to the crust."

"I'll try to remember," Tudal said.

"You two should join us," Tindra suggested.

Lena shook her head. "One more bite for me and then back to cooking."

"Nolwen can't mind the front by herself yet," Tudal said, turning to go check on his other customers.

"This may be the best tasting thing I've ever eaten," I said, after gulping another forkful.

"I'm going to miss this place," Tindra said.

"Why do you sound like you'll never eat here again?"

"Because, I don't believe I'll be back."

"I don't intend this to be a suicide mission," I told her. "I plan to survive, to win."

"We shouldn't talk about this here," Tindra said, glancing at Lena.

"You don't trust her?"

"Of course, I do, but this isn't her business. Shared secrets have a way of traveling on their own. We'll talk later, at the tower."

I nodded and ate my fill.

Tindra paid Lena and we returned to the tower. I knew the amount of free time I had was fast growing smaller and suspected Tindra felt the same way.

She followed me into my room, closed the door, and sat at the table, while I replaced the candles. I sat across from her. "Why don't you think you'll ever be back at Tudal's"

She laced her fingers together and rested her elbows on the table. "If you win, I plan to stay in Croy. If you lose, I'll likely die there. Either way, I won't see them again."

"Maybe I'll hire them to be my cooks," I mused and smiled.

"Doubt it. You'll summon Roi as your right hand, he'll bring Grima and Einns. The boy will be your cook."

"I suppose."

She laughed. "You know I'm right."

I nodded.

Her expression changed and she fixed me with a serious look. "There's something I want to make sure you understand. I'm on your side, no hidden agenda. No one has hired me. During training, it's us against the four from the council. Once the caravan gets underway, you're in charge as far as I'm concerned."

"We have to work together, the six of us, to keep our cover as guards. It can't be us against them."

"I'll do what I must, and so will you, but when it comes to the end, I'm on your side. Win or lose, live or die, I'll be there. I know you don't trust me, but you'll see."

"You know I don't love you," I said, shaking my head, "I barely like you. Why do you care if I trust you?"

"Because you can't do this alone. Eirickson's death ends a threat to Varia...spares the lives of my countrymen and helps secure our future. In order for you to win, someone has to watch your back. I'm sure the council wasn't pleased with your lack of commitment to their demands. It wouldn't surprise me if they decide to slip a knife in you before Eirickson dies, so they can claim Croy. How are you going to stay safe if you stand alone?"

"I hadn't considered it," I admitted, shrugging.

"Because you're focused on the end. You need to watch for traps waiting for you to get there."

"I used to depend on Roi for that. I need some time to think this over, alone."

She nodded and said, "You better think fast. Your time alone grows short," before leaving.

I moved to the bed to lie down and think. Was I so focused on the destination I overlooked the journey? Being honest with myself, it's been a fault of mine for some time. This all started because I wasn't able to conceive of Eirickson's treachery.

Can I trust Tindra? She thinks Kurt plans to stab me in the back. Would Kurt and his group do such a thing? She took me to Ander instead of the council for some reason. Her argument made sense, from one perspective, but would King Ander let such a thing happen? Of course, he wouldn't be present when we attacked. It would be the council's men explaining how I died. With no one to tell my story, their word would be the truth.

I had to pay close attention to Tindra. *If she proves herself by the time we leave for Nikulas' skati, I have to trust her.*

Satisfied I could push my concerns aside for now, I let my thoughts wander to Aesa. I knew nothing about her situation. *Alive or not? If alive...is she free and safe?* If she *was* alive and free, she would have fled to Varia. I'd have heard something by now. If she was a captive, was she a war trophy or worse — a slave? Considering what I'd heard about the Satran, I wasn't sure there was a difference between the two.

Aesa, my promised...my love, where are you? Did you die with mother? If so, should I feel relieved...happy you didn't suffer? I curled into a ball as my stomach churned and cried myself to sleep with a sour taste in my mouth.

• • • ● ●● ● • • •

Someone banging on the door woke me to a dark room and a foul mood.

"What?" I shouted.

"I decided to have dinner at Daufi and tell my parents goodbye," Tindra said, through the door. "Would you like to go with me?"

I wasn't in the mood for family, but where else would I eat? I opened the door to reply. "Sure. Now?"

She looked at me and frowned. "What's wrong?"

"I did a lot of thinking and fell asleep."

"Mmhmm," she hummed. "Looks like you cried yourself to sleep."

I nodded.

"Aesa?"

"Yes." Admitting my sorrow brought an odd, unexpected sense of relief.

"I'd tell you to cheer up, but I think you're allowed *and* it's none of my business," she said.

I rubbed the crust from my eyes. "Glad you understand."

Once we got inside Daufi, Tindra asked someone to find her parents and tell them to meet us in the private dining room.

We got our food and waited in the small room. Several times, Tindra looked like she wanted to say something, but never did. Each time I felt a little more aggravated.

Finally, the door opened.

"To what do we owe this pleasure?" Mikael asked, walking in with Margit.

Tindra stood. "I'm leaving town in a couple of months. I'll be busy and may not get a chance to see you two again. I wanted to have a last meal with you."

Margit's hands were a blur.

"No, I'm not dying," Tindra said.

"You have to admit it sounded final," Mikael said.

She nodded. "We...*I* have to...help Fitzeirick with something important. Something vital to the future of Varia — and Croy." She sniffled. "This isn't easy."

Margit's hands moved again.

"Nothing is wrong, Mother."

"You're scared of something," Mikael pressed.

Tindra took her mother's hand. "I *am* scared. I doubt I'll be back in the capital or back in Varia, for that matter, again."

"Fitzeirick, what do you have to say about this?" he asked.

I shook my head. "I told her not to go. She wants to do this, volunteered."

"And if I ask you to keep her safe, for us?" he asked.

"I'll do my best, but I'm risking my own life. I can't give you my word."

"We can't ask for more than your best," he said.

Margit pulled her daughter into a tight hug, before pushing her away and signing some more.

"No, Mother. I must go. I promise, I'll send word back when I can," Tindra said.

Margit left the room, crying.

Poor woman. I wonder if my mother was upset after I left. At least Tindra can give her a proper goodbye.

"Can you tell me what you're involved in?" Mikael asked.

"It's better you don't know," Tindra said.

"Is this the reason for Fitzeirick's bad mood?" he asked.

"How'd you know about my mood?"

"Heard it in your voice," he said.

I nodded, before remembering he couldn't see me. "They're related. I was thinking a lot this afternoon. Uncomfortable memories."

He smiled. "I know something about uncomfortable memories. They're pretty much all I have. Memories of when I could see. Would you like some advice?"

I shrugged. "What could it hurt?"

"Don't focus on what was, or you'll miss what is and what may be," he said.

The part of me nurturing my foul mood wanted to say something harsh back, but my more reasonable side didn't want to sound ungrateful. I managed to utter an almost sincere, "Thank you."

"Enough sorrow. Let's enjoy this meal if it's to be our last together," Mikael said, sitting.

"What about Mother?" Tindra asked.

"I'll have someone help me find her later. Your leaving always upsets her. This is just the first time you've seen it."

"Oh," Tinda murmured, before sitting and focusing on her meal.

I thought about what Mikael said, what it meant to me. In a sense he was right; if I keep looking back, I can't lead anyone forward. *My future isn't certain enough to distract me from my past. Victory saves two nations, but I've lost so much already. Defeat is death. At least then my loss will stop. Which would I rather have?* Those thoughts distracted me enough to let father and daughter have their moment together.

Margit returned before we finished eating. She hugged her daughter again and sat at the table.

"Sorry I upset you," Tindra said. "I'll do my best to stay safe while I help Fitzeirick. Helping him is the important part. Rest assured, I'll do everything possible to make sure you know if I'm well or not."

"We can't ask any more of you," Mikael said, expression grim.

"Fitzeirick and I should go. We have an early start tomorrow."

Mikael stood, and Tindra walked to him and hugged him tightly. "Wherever your travels take you, keep us in mind. We love you," he said.

His words reminded me I never had a chance to say goodbye my fiancée. I had missed my chance to tell her and my mother how much I loved them. I took a deep breath and did my best to hide my feelings as my heart shattered.

Margit moved toward me and held out her arms. I embraced her and looked at Tindra. She smiled at me.

Margit let me go, took my hand, and placed it in Mikael's.

As he shook my hand, he said, "Whatever it is you must do, do it with everything you have. Commit to your task and you cannot fail."

I couldn't stop the tears, but I managed to say, "Thank you," and followed Tindra out of the room, back to the tower.

I fell asleep thinking about Sar'sa and Aesa again and promised them both I wouldn't fail.

Chapter 49

Knocks on my door woke me.

"Are you awake?" Tindra yelled.

"I am now."

She stepped in. "Get moving. I want to get to Aerison before the other four."

"Why?" I asked, changing clothes.

"It makes an impression."

"He knows what to expect from me."

She folded her arms across her chest. "I'm not concerned with impressing *him*. I want to make an impression on the council's men."

"What difference would it make?" I asked, closing my door as we left.

She sighed. "Professional discourtesy. You and I have to put them in their place."

"Not this again," I moaned.

"Trust me," she said, walking faster.

The area around the barracks was busy. I looked around, didn't see our mentor, and asked someone near me, "Have you seen Lieutenant Aerison?"

He pointed to a building about fifty paces away. "Mess hall."

"Thank you," I said.

We arrived at the mess hall and found Aerison talking to four men I didn't recognize. Tindra growled.

"Calm down," I whispered.

"They got here first."

"Doesn't matter, we're all on the same team."

"Exactly what they want you to think."

Does she ever give up?

Aerison waved us over. "Fitzeirick, Tindra — nice of you to join us. First lesson: you're a team so you do everything together. Since everyone's here, you can eat," he said. "Wait here for me after you finish."

We stood in line for two bowls, one with a watery stew and the other held a lump of bread soaking in milk. I looked around and everyone seemed to consider their meal with the same unhappy expression. I took the first bite of stew after sitting and immediately understood why. The barely warm stew tasted bland. At least the bread and milk added some kind of flavor.

The six of us took our time eating the mediocre meal. The lieutenant hadn't returned by the time we finished so we sat looking at each other until I couldn't stay quiet any longer.

"I'll start," I said. "My name's —"

"We know who you two are and why we're all here," the one seated closest to me said, interrupting. "I'm Sabast." He pointed to the two seated across from him. "Brothers, Albin and Anifas. Albin's the one with a hairy chin. Big man is Halmar."

Sabast looked boyish at first glance, but his age showed in the defiant look to his brown eyes. He looked like he would argue any point I might make, just to disagree with me. His curly, black hair seemed to reflect his attitude; it couldn't agree on which direction to lie.

The brothers were average sized with deep-blue eyes and wavy, brown hair. I couldn't tell which was older. They both wore friendly expressions. Halmar reminded me of Roi. Large and solid with soulful, dark-brown eyes and rust-colored hair cut short in contrast to his bushy beard. Like Roi, he was hard to read.

I offered my hand to Sabast. "Nice to meet you. Did everyone agree you'd be the spokesman?"

He gripped my hand tight. "I've worked for Kurt the longest and he gave me the responsibility to make sure everything goes to plan. Tyres sent the brothers and Halmar's one of Arne's enforcers."

"Good to know."

"Halmar," Tindra said, smiling. "Long time, how ya' been?"

"Well enough," he grumbled.

She nodded and turned to the brothers. "I've heard of you two. Archers...right?"

"Good to hear our reputation precedes us," Albin said.

"Heard of you too," Anifas said, with a sly smile. "Looking forward to getting to know you."

Now, he reminded me of Crum.

Tindra chuckled before turning to stare at Sabast. "If you've worked for Kurt for so long, why don't I know you?"

He returned her glare. "Lots of things you don't know."

"Including the name of one of his trusted men, it seems."

"I get things done. All you need to know."

She opened her mouth to respond, but I spoke first. "We can all work together. This is an important mission."

Before anyone could say anything else, Aerison appeared. "Good to see everyone had a healthy appetite. Now, we get you fitted. Follow me."

"Fitted for what?" Sabast asked.

"Armor."

"We shouldn't need any armor," Sabast replied.

"Shows what you know," Tindra said. "We have to look and act like Varian guardsmen. We wear armor."

"Who put you in charge?" Sabast asked.

Before Tindra could say anything, Aerison backhanded Sabast. "King Ander put *me* in charge. I don't care how much weight you think you carry with your thugs, you answer to me now. I give an order and it gets carried out — immediately and without question. Understand?"

"Yes, sir," Sabast muttered.

"What? I didn't hear you!" Aerison shouted.

"Yes, sir!"

"I think there are five other people here who have not spoken up. Do you understand?"

"Yes, sir!" we all shouted, not exactly together.

"Not bad, but you all have a lot to learn," Aerison said. "Now, on me, to the armory."

We rushed to the armory and stood side by side at his instruction.

"I have two archers...correct?" Aerison asked.

"Yes, sir," the brothers said together.

"Ellit, fit these two with our standard leather for archers."

"And the other four?" the old man asked.

"Three swordsmen and a hammer swinger...correct?" Aerison asked.

"Yes, sir," we answered.

"Hand to hand gear, lamellar over leather."

"Even the woman?" Ellit asked.

Aerison looked at Tindra. "Even the woman."

"Plain leather suits me better," she said.

"Unless you want to be an archer, you get metal over leather" Aerison said. "Wait for Ellit to fit you. Training starts when I get back."

I'd never heard of lamellar armor and soon learned it was a coat of metal plates about the size of my hand sewn together with sinew to be flexible. It gave an extra layer of protection over my chest and back. The extra weight made me wish for plain leather.

The bulky armor made Tindra look much less feminine compared to her usual attire. Ellit offered to have some made to fit her better, but she refused, explaining it was important she looked like the rest of the guard.

Aerison came back near the end of the conversation and smirked when he saw us. "You all look like you've never worn armor before. Time to see how you handle it. On my command, we run until three of you fall. Understood?"

We all groaned. "Yes, sir."

"Not good enough!" he yelled. "Now, we run until four of you fall. Understood?"

"Yes, sir!"

"Better!" he shouted. "Now run!"

The six of us stood stunned for a moment before chasing Aerison. He glanced over his shoulder at the first turn and slowed a little to let us catch up.

I knew I wouldn't be one of the last two standing, but I decided to not be the first one down.

We started as a loose pack of six chasing one man, but soon turned into a line of six trailing behind him. The line stretched longer as we ran. Tindra led with Sabast and Anifas on her tail. Albin was a few paces from his brother. Halmar and I fell behind. It didn't help he and I were the heaviest in the group.

I thought about using my talent to boost my stamina, but decided it would be cheating until I felt little quivers in the ground with every footfall. *No doubt Halmar's a stonesyth.* Two wrongs don't make a right, but I wasn't going to be the first man on the ground so I followed suit.

Albin fell farther back from the front three, started limping, and grabbed his right thigh before falling.

I sped up a little. Soon, my legs let me know running faster was a bad idea. The combination of stinging sweat in my eyes and pain shooting up my legs convinced me to go to the ground. Halmar followed my example and the other half of the team ran out of our sight.

Albin approached, still limping, as Halmar and I tried to catch our breath. "What do we do now?"

"I don't know." I wiped sweat from my forehead. "Guess we walk back to the training grounds and wait."

"Sounds good," Halmar mumbled.

"After we rest," Albin said.

I nodded and focused on breathing for a little while. Once my heart quit pounding and my legs forgave me for the punishment, I pulled a little strength and stood. "Time to head back."

Albin and Halmar moaned and groaned, but they walked back with me.

We made it back to the empty training grounds.

"What do we do now?" Albin asked.

"Wait," I said.

"For what?" he asked.

"For everyone else to get back."

"And what do we do while we wait?"

He's just full of questions. I looked at him, trying to figure out if he was being aggravating on purpose. Before I said anything, Halmar put his hand on Albin's shoulder. "Sit. Rest."

The big man's suggestion sounded like a good idea and I hit the ground at about the same time Albin sat. Halmar joined us soon after.

"Is it true?" Albin asked, after sitting for a while.

"Is what true?" I asked.

"What they say about you, how you got the scar on your face."

"Shut up," Halmar growled.

I frowned at the big man. "If we're going to work together, we have to trust each other. What have you heard about this scar?"

Before he could answer Aerison, Tindra, and Sabast came jogging toward us.

"We seem to be missing a man," Aerison said. "Where is Anifas?"

Albin shrugged. "Last I saw him, he wasn't far behind you three."

The lieutenant turned to the last two standing. "Neither of you saw him go down?"

"No, sir," Tindra snapped. "I kept my eyes on you, focused on running."

"I lost track of him myself," Sabast said.

Aerison shook his head. "Not even midday and we've already lost a man. Albin, go find your brother. You four work with practice swords until they get back."

I stood. "No disrespect meant, sir, but I prefer my hammer."

Aerison smiled. "But you didn't bring it, so you'll use what's at hand."

I hung my head. "Understood, sir."

"Show me what you can do," Aerison said.

Sabast smiled and came at me hard.

At first, my attempts to defend myself were awkward. The wooden sword was nothing like my hammer. I took several hard hits before parrying a few of his slower attacks.

"You aren't any good," he said, at one point.

"Not with this," I replied.

"I don't think you can best me regardless," he said, pressing his advantage.

I held my tongue and concentrated on doing my best. Sweat stung my eyes again by the time Aerison yelled, "Halt! Stand down!"

I lowered my sword.

Sabast got in one more blow as the brothers walked past us.

"Beginning to wonder if I'd lost you both," Aerison said. "Where were you?"

"I couldn't run anymore, so I sat and waited for someone to tell me what to do next," Anifas said.

"Next time, you come back here," Aerison said, first pointing to Anifas then thrusting his finger toward the ground. "Everyone put up the weapons and hurry to the mess hall for lunch, if there's any left."

We tromped into the nearly empty room and got bowls of overcooked stew and large mugs of warm water.

"Eat fast," Aerison said. "When I get back we're on the field again."

After our leader walked out, Anifas said, "This isn't training. It's torture."

"It's not training yet. Aerison's testing us," I told them.

"Eat," Halmar grumbled.

"What do you know?" Anifas snapped. "You're just muscle anyway, Halmar."

Tindra slapped her hand on the table. "He knows you volunteered for this mission. We all did. Did we expect this? I know I didn't, but it doesn't matter. We're here to see the mission through to the end or die trying."

"Fine," Anifas muttered, dipping his spoon into the stew.

I felt less than excited about eating, but my hunger didn't care. Looking around the table, I think the rest felt the same way.

"Albin," I said. "You asked me about my scar earlier. What have you heard?"

"Drop it," Halmar said.

I chuckled. "Halmar, you seem like a nice enough fellow, even remind me of a friend of mine. I mean no insult when I ask this: can you say more than two words at a time?"

"When necessary," he mumbled.

I sighed and looked to Tindra for help. She shook her head.

Before I could say anything else, Aerison walked back in. "To the field."

We jogged to the field and got the practice weapons again.

"You two," Aerison said, to the brothers. "Any hand-to-hand training or do you just fling sharp sticks?"

"Daggers," Albin answered. "We work well with daggers."

"I'll have to see if I can find some for you to practice with," he said, and rubbed his chin. "For now, you use swords."

They moaned in unison before grabbing wooden swords.

"I don't care who attacks who, but no more than two on one," he said. "Try to avoid injuring each other. Go!"

Sabast was on me again, landing several, hard blows, before I could react. He kept at it until Tindra used her wooden blade like a paddle and smacked him across the butt. He cried out, more from surprise than pain I think, and turned toward her.

"Figures," he muttered.

I took the opportunity to exact a little revenge on my attacker and the tide turned against him. Soon it became a game of four against two or three on three, depending on which side Halmar took.

"Water break!" Aerison yelled.

Our sword tips dropped, and we dragged ourselves to a keg of water with cups on top.

"Tindra and Sabast, you two know what you're doing. Halmar, your size is *not* an asset. You need to move more. Albin and Anifas, I haven't found any wooden daggers. I'll have some made this evening. Fitzeirick, I recommend you remember your hammer tomorrow."

"Why does he get a real weapon and we have wood?" Sabast whined.

"Because I've watched him train with it. He knows how to not hurt people," Aerison said. "Back at it!"

This time we started roughly equal, with Tindra sandwiched between Halmar and me. I heard her laugh, using our bodies as shields, while landing blows when she saw openings. The strategy worked well for her until Halmar switched sides.

We worked with and against each other until Aerison yelled, "Put them away and follow me! Time to clean up!"

We put the weapons on the rack and followed him on a long walk to a waterfall. "Strip and rinse off," he said. "I recommend rinsing your clothes as well."

"What do we wear after?" Anifas asked.

"Wet, clean clothes are better than sweat-soaked clothes," Aerison said.

We groaned as we peeled off our armor.

Tindra and Sabast seemed to be in a race to get undressed first.

I noticed Anifas leering at her, and I leaned toward him and whispered, "Don't let her catch you."

"What's it to you? You telling me you have some claim?" he asked, under his breath.

I raised my hands. "Nope, no claim, but I know her pretty well. If she doesn't like you, you'll pay for looking."

"I can handle myself...and her."

I smiled and shook my head as I walked under the falling water. I didn't feel the cold until I stood about waist deep in the pool under the falls. I let out a yelp and everyone laughed. Still, it felt refreshing to cool off, to wash away the sweat and grime from the day's work. Even with the relief, I found the sting of falling water unpleasant.

We all washed our clothes in the pool and got dressed on the shore.

"Take your armor with you. After you eat, go to the armory where Ellit will teach you how to clean and care for it. After the lesson, I recommend you find a bed," Aerison said.

"I know how to care for leather," Tindra said.

"And now you'll learn our way," Aerison replied, calmly.

Every muscle in my body disagreed with me by the time reached the mess hall. We stood in line for our food, keeping our armor with us. Several guardsmen gave us knowing looks. I was too tired to care what they served us and ate without paying attention to anything before making my way to the armory.

Ellit handed me a small, leather sack. "Take these supplies and have a seat. We'll start when everyone is here."

I sat on the floor and considered investigating the contents of the sack. Before I gave in to temptation, my teammates arrived with several other recruits.

"Everyone sit," Ellit ordered. "Wait for your supplies."

Once everyone was ready, he started the lesson.

I never knew keeping leather and metal clean and maintained was so much work. By the time he told us to finish on our own, my fingers cramped, and my forearms burned.

"Do this every evening before bed. Take care of your armor now and it will take care of you when you need it," Ellit said, before dismissing us.

"I'd offer to race everyone to the tower, but I'm too tired," Sabast said.

"A race would be a waste of effort," Tindra said. "Fitzeirick and I already have the first floor."

The four other men groaned and slowed.

Chapter 50

I fell asleep quickly and all too soon, like the day before, a knock on my door woke me.

"Best get up and get going or you'll be late and face punishment," someone I didn't recognize said, though the door.

I forced myself out of bed, changed into fresh clothes, fought to get my armor on, and almost left without my hammer. At least I wasn't the last of us to report to the mess hall.

The training and torture started with a run after we ate. At the training grounds, Aerison gave the brothers wooden daggers. Their hand to hand combat skills showed themselves right away. I learned skill, quickness, and agility often beats brute force.

We settled into the same daily routine. Rise, dress, eat, run, train, eat, train, bathe in the waterfall, eat, go to your room, clean your armor, and sleep.

Shocking news swept through the guard during our fifth week. Word Stina was missing spread at breakfast. Somehow, she'd gotten out of House of Daufi.

I looked at Tindra when I heard someone talking about it. "Is it possible?"

With her eyes wide, and face a little pale, she shrugged. "Of course. It's not like my parents run a prison. Stina seemed pretty convinced she wasn't going to stay."

"Your parents live in Daufi?" Anifas asked.

"They own it," she said.

"But there's nothing wrong with you," he said.

Tindra sneered.

"Watch what you say, Anifas," I warned.

"Listen to Fitzeirick," she agreed, looking away.

We weren't allowed to volunteer for search duty. Instead, we kept to our normal routine.

A few things were certain by then. We were all in better physical condition, blended with the other guards, and worked together better. The initial, underlying tensions seemed to be gone as well. I let myself start believing things were going to work out for the best.

Training continued, rain or shine. The next break in our routine came during lunch, almost two months after the training started.

King Ander walked into the mess hall, unescorted and unannounced. It took a few moments before anyone noticed him and everyone stood at attention.

"Sit, finish your meal," he said. "I'm here to speak with Aerison and his charges."

"Aerison is in the officer's mess," someone said.

"Let him know I need him here," the king said, approaching us.

"Of course, Sire."

I moved from my seat to give King Ander the head of the table. "Unnecessary," he said, "but thank you."

I bowed and found a nearby seat.

Tindra looked away from him.

"According to what I'm told, your training goes well. Good to hear because the caravan leaves tomorrow," he said.

We all gasped and looked at each other. I saw expressions of disbelief and relief.

"I'll say no more until your lieutenant arrives."

"A question, if I may, Sire," Sabast said.

"So long as it does *not* pertain to the caravan."

"Although we weren't allowed to help search for your daughter, I'm still concerned. Any word?"

I saw Tindra shiver before the king spoke.

"The search continues, widens every day. There are rumors of sightings. By the time we act on the information, there's no sign of her."

"No word of who took her?" Albin asked.

"I don't believe anyone took her," King Ander said. "I, as well as others, believe she found a way out herself. I'd like to address one matter now, though. Tindra, would you please show me enough respect to look at me?"

Tindra turned to look at him. There was no color in her face.

"I don't blame your parents or anyone in their house. Your father and I discussed this possibility before he agreed to accept Stina. All is well between us."

Tears formed as she said, "Thank you for your mercy and understanding."

"I am nothing if not fair," the king said, with a nod.

"You sent for me, my lord?" Aerison said, bowing after he entered the hall.

Out of habit, we all stood when we heard his voice.

The king chuckled. "Sit. Lieutenant, it appears your training has forged these six into a tight group. Would you agree?"

"I believe so," Aerison said.

"These six are to report at first light tomorrow, ready for the caravan, to Sergeant Elias in the marketplace," the king said.

"I take it the sergeant knows of their mission?" Aerison asked.

"He's aware they will leave before the caravan reaches its final destination. He doesn't know why, doesn't need to."

The lieutenant nodded. "Understood. Is there anything else?"

"I want to emphasize upon each of you the importance of success. We must stop Eirickson at all costs. I prefer Fitzeirick overthrow him, but the success of the mission is of greater importance. You must protect Varia."

"What are you saying?" I asked.

"I'm saying, should you fall, everyone left must press on. Do not give up the fight until Eirickson is dead. Retreat is *not* an option."

"Understood," I replied, frowning. *We both want Eirickson dead, but Ander doesn't care if I live or not. We're training as a team, but I can't depend on anyone but me. Nothing like a little doubt to change your focus.*

Aerison said, "I believe we all understand what's needed, my king."

King Ander nodded. "I'll leave you to your preparations."

We stood and bowed as he left the hall. "Report to the stables for horses and saddlebags," Aerison ordered.

"Lieutenant," I said, "I have saddlebags of my own and a horse currently at House of Daufi. Can I use them?"

He scratched his chin for a moment. "Can't imagine why not. Anyone else with gear of their own?"

No one answered.

"The five of you with me," Aerison said. "Fitzeirick, make haste. We still have to get packed."

"Yes, sir!" I shouted and ran to the stables at Daufi after stopping by the tower to grab my saddlebags. The stable hands helped me tack and saddle Andale. I rode straight to the guard stables and found my teammates mounted and waiting.

"I understand you each have your own weapons, so I'm not going to send you to the armory," Aerison said. "Go to the warehouse. Tell them you need the load-out for the caravan to Croy. After you're loaded, take the day to rest. Best get to bed early so you can do me proud. Most likely, I won't see you again for a while. Travel safe and do your job."

We rode together to the warehouse and found several people loading up wagons. I dismounted Andale and waited for one of the porters to walk by. "Excuse me," I said. "Lieutenant Aerison sent us here to get the load-out for the caravan to Croy. Can you help or tell me where to go?"

"Oh, I can tell ya where to go," he said, and laughed. "But I don't want trouble 'cos ya got offended."

I smiled. "I suppose I deserve that. Can you help us?"

He nodded. "Go round to the other side of the building. Tell 'em what ya told me. They'll load ya up."

"Thanks. Keep your sense of humor."

He laughed and went about his task.

"Looks like we go to the other side of the building," I said.

There was no one there. We stood outside a closed pair of wooden doors, big enough to allow wagons through. I tried to open them, but they seemed barred from the inside. I shrugged, looked at my companions, and knocked.

We waited, but no one answered. "Halmar, let's see if we can get someone's attention," I suggested.

He slid down from his horse and stood next to me. Together, we pounded on the doors hard enough to crack the wood.

"Not so hard!" someone yelled. "Whatcha need?"

"Supplies!" I yelled back. "For the caravan to Croy!"

"Go round tha other side! Porters'll take care a ya!"

I looked at Halmar.

He shrugged and shook his head.

"No!" I yelled back. "Open this door and give us supplies, or I'll knock the door down and take what we need!"

"Fine...but I can't open tha doors by ma'self!"

"Unbar it and we'll open it."

The sound of wood scraping against wood filled the air. Several of the horses whinnied at the noise. "Open!"

I pushed against the large door.

It creaked in protest.

"Little help?" I asked, looking at Halmar.

He pushed me away from the door and shoved against it, moving it much easier than I had. I heard him laugh inside the warehouse, and he was still smiling when I walked in.

No one was waiting for us. Whoever moved the bar was gone.

Is someone playing a joke? If so, it's not funny. I pulled my hammer from my back, sythed some strength, and focused on my frustration, slamming the weapon into the stone floor. The impact knocked dust from the beams overhead.

Everyone froze and looked at me.

"I need supplies for six guardsmen going out with the trade caravan tomorrow morning. Lieutenant Aerison sent us here at the direct order of King Ander. Either we get taken care of now or I send word to the king."

Three young men ran to me and bowed. "Be glad ta set ya up, sir. Please bring yer men and horses in."

I stepped outside, waved the others in, and led Andale and Halmar's horse behind them.

Two of the young porters had already taken the saddlebags from the first four while the third waited for me. Halmar and I mounted after they removed our bags.

The young workers strained under the load of bulging bags. "Sir. Made sure ta pack extra, fer yer trouble."

"I appreciate your efforts and attention," I said. "Tindra, drop them a small tip."

She shot me a look before dropping some coins into the closest boy's hands. "Share."

"Course, sir," he said, smiling. "Swift 'n safe travel."

"Do we dare to eat dinner outside the mess hall?" I asked, as we left the warehouse.

"What did you have in mind?" Sabast asked.

"Have you ever had Satran food?"

"You aren't serious!" Tindra shouted.

"You think it's a bad idea?" I asked.

"Why would anyone want to eat Satran food?" Sabast asked.

"If Tindra thinks it's a bad idea, we shouldn't go," Anifas added.

"Quit trying to get on her good side, brother," Albin drawled.

"She's smart and fights well. Why is agreeing with her trying to get on her good side?"

"Because you're trying too hard," Tindra said. "And you've *been* trying too hard for the past two months."

"Oh," he said, and looked toward the ground.

"Tindra, are you saying Tudal wouldn't like the business?" I asked.

"I'm sure he would, but won't it look strange having six guards at the only Satran eatery in the capital? And, think about the mission...it's a bad idea for us to go out when we need to be up and ready early."

"She's right," Halmar grumbled.

"Fine," I said, and sighed. "To the mess hall."

We found Lieutenant Aerison waiting for us outside the mess hall. "You won't be eating here. Tie your horses and come with me. Someone wants you in the officer's mess."

I looked at Tindra. She seemed as surprised and confused as I felt. The faces of my other four teammates looked much the same. Still, we had an order, so our training kicked in.

He led us past the barracks, to a building none of us dared enter before. Opening the door, he stepped aside. "I'm not invited."

I walked in first and immediately caught a whiff of pork. My mouth watered. The room was palatial compared to the minimal comforts of the guard's mess hall. There were round tables and padded chairs. The table in the middle of the room held a large roast pig.

A man stepped into the room and said, "Please take a seat. Your hosts will arrive soon."

His instructions didn't clear up my confusion, but we sat. After almost two months of bland food, all eyes locked on the luxurious meal in front of us.

"Yes, wine for everyone," Jesca's voice said, behind us.

Whipping my head around, I saw her and Crum standing hand in hand. Bounding toward my best friend, I almost knocked over the servants bringing drinks.

Crum grunted when I hugged him tightly.

"Good to see you," I said.

He chuckled. "If it was much better to see me I think you might crush me to death."

I let him go and bowed before Jesca.

She giggled and said, "Look at me."

She was radiant, looking better than I'd ever seen her. Her hair was growing out, almost to her shoulders. She looked happy.

"You look wonderful," I said.

With a tear in her eye and a smile on her face, she asked, "Are you ready?"

I laughed and glanced at the pig. "Ready to eat."

"This feast was her idea," Crum said.

"And it's time it began," Jesca added.

They sat at the table with me and Tindra, but I tried to talk Crum into spending time with Anifas. "You two have similar personalities."

"I'm a changed man — well, still changing. But I'm not the man I was."

"Your doing?" I asked Jesca.

She shook her head. "All his decision."

After pouring the wine, the servants carved the pig and placed platters of meat on the tables.

I lifted my mug. "To friends, old and new, and to my fellow guardsmen."

"To friends," everyone replied.

"How have you been Crum?" Tindra asked.

He didn't look at her.

"You're not the only one who's changed," she continued.

"Be civil," Jesca whispered to him.

"Busy, I've been busy. Life with Fitzeirick was so much easier before all this. But meeting Jesca and growing closer to her is worth the sacrifice."

"Enough talk for now," Jesca said. "It's time to eat."

She didn't have to say it twice. The six of us ate like a pack of ravenous wolves.

Crum sat stunned for a moment when he saw how desperate I looked grabbing for the meat. I smiled between bites.

There was no conversation over the meal. Everyone ate and drank their fill.

After everyone had finished eating Jesca stood. "I take it everyone enjoyed the meal?"

A loud chorus of "Yes!" filled the room.

She smiled. "At the risk of being rude, I'd like to ask everyone to leave. I want to talk to Fitzeirick." She paused and looked at Crum. "Alone."

As everyone stood and made their way out of the room, Crum looked at me. "I'll see you outside."

As soon as she heard the door close, Jesca sat next to me, put her hands on my cheeks, and looked me in the eye. "Say you are ready. I need to hear it from you. Tell me you're going to kill Eirickson. I must know, no matter how much he begs, no matter what he offers, he *will* die."

I felt proud of her, of how well she was doing. At the same time, sadness shot through my thoughts. *She still carries such a burden.* I held her hand and looked her in the eye. "I'm ready, have no doubt. As soon as I find him his life ends. His words mean nothing to me. Any offer made is hollow, meaningless. Eirickson will die," I promised.

She nodded and started crying. I hugged her, holding on until she stopped shivering.

After letting go of me, she stood, and I followed her outside.

The only people waiting were Crum and Tindra. They stood near the corner of the building.

Crum came running when he saw me.

"You win," he said, hugging me. "You have to win, and you have to live. If you fail, Satra will destroy Croy after they conquer Varia. Our survival depends on your victory."

"I know," I said. "Maybe don't get married until after I'm victorious."

"Win, and come back to attend the wedding," he said, letting me go. "Go get some sleep, the day starts early for you. Travel safe, strike swift and true."

I walked to Tindra and asked, "Where's everyone else?"

She turned to me. She'd been crying.

"What's wrong?" I asked.

"Nothing's wrong," she said, wiping her eyes and looking at the tears on her fingers. "Crum told me I was the only one on the mission he trusted to watch out for you. He said he trusts me with your life. He made me swear, not only on my life, but on my family's, I would give my life to save yours. I gave him my word without a second thought. I'd already made the decision on my own, but it made me happy to hear him say he trusted me with your life."

I've always valued Crum's opinion, but does he know Ander would sacrifice me for Varia's future? Tindra swore she'd never lie to me...is this the first test? I nodded. "He's changing. Where did the rest of the team go?"

"They left to get the horses and secure them at the tower."

"And so, we get to walk," I said, grinning.

"Do you trust me to watch your back?" she asked, as we walked toward the tower.

"The six of us should look out for each other. Out of the group, I think you have the most to gain by keeping me alive."

"Not the same as saying you trust me," she said, frowning.

I sighed. "Crum doesn't always think ahead. He's worried about me, rightfully so, and doing what he thinks will help. I doubt he's considered the truth I face. I'm about to go to battle leading a team of criminals and mercenaries. I trust each of you to do what you think is in your best interest. That's a long way from actual trust, but it's what I'm willing to give."

Sparks crossed her eyes and her cheeks reddened. "You'll see who's trustworthy."

I decided to keep my mouth shut.

Lightning flashed in the distance as we reached the tower.

"Sleep well," Tindra said, walking past my room.

Chapter 51

Someone had put my saddlebags on the table. I stripped out of my armor and changed clothes before lying down. The weight of the coming mission should have made it hard to get to sleep, but a stomach full of pork and wine changed the tide of battle in my favor.

A clap of thunder woke me. Out of habit, I rolled out of bed, changed clothes, and pulled my armor on in the dark. By now, the weight was a comfort instead of a burden. I lit a candle before walking to the door and looked into the hall. It was empty. Closing the door, I returned to the table and took inventory of my bags.

The young workers gave us extra rations, taking up space needed for clothing and other necessities. I ate a big breakfast to make space. Satisfied with my repacking job, I threw the bags over my shoulder and headed to Tindra's room.

I raised my hand to knock.

She opened the door and gasped.

"You're up," I said.

"Thunder. I spent some time getting ready and decided to get you up."

I chuckled. "Same."

"Plus, I wanted you to carry my saddlebags," she said, winking at me. "Can you take them out while I wake everyone else?"

"Be glad to."

She headed for the stairs. I grabbed her bags and walked through the rain to the horses. With everything secured, I mounted and waited for the rest of the team. Sitting in the downpour made the wait seem longer. Everyone finally exited the tower and mounted while grumbling about the miserable weather.

I led the team at a brisk pace to the market area. Flashes of lightning gave glimpses of the activity around us. We reached the caravan before most of the volunteer guards.

"We're supposed to report to Sergeant Elias," I said, to the first person we found. "He here yet?"

"Last I saw, he's in front, discussing the route with the lead driver."

I thanked him and motioned for everyone to follow me.

We found a stocky, barrel-chested, bald man gesturing to two men seated on a wagon. After he seemed finished with them, I cleared my throat. "Sergeant Elias?"

"Who wants to know?" he growled.

"Fitzeirick. Reporting for duty with Tindra, Sabast, Albin, Anifas, and Halmar. Sir!"

"Ah," he replied. "Nice to meet you. Your equipment forced us to bring an extra wagon."

"Our equipment, sir?" Tindra asked.

"Someone named Kurt had it delivered to the armory late yesterday."

I turned to my team. "Do any of you know what the sergeant is talking about?"

Everyone shook their heads.

"Where's the equipment?" I asked.

Elias glared at me. "I don't have time to lead you around." He pointed down the line of wagons. "Third from the end. You're assigned to guard it. Go."

We saluted and rode back to the wagon. I looked in the back but couldn't see anything. "I need a lantern."

Halmar got a lantern and held it so it lit the inside of the wagon. There were six suits of dull black leather armor hanging from the walls and a large chest sat near the front.

"Tindra, Sabast, see what the council gave us," I said.

They slid down from their horses and climbed into the wagon. Tindra lifted one of the shirts. "This is awfully heavy for leather."

Sabast lifted another and shook it. "Lamellar plates between leather. The sleeves are only leatherm, but the chest and back have plates. Same with the legs; around the knee is leather, but the rest is stiff. Much quieter than this stuff we're wearing."

"And it's the perfect shade for sneaking around at night," Anifas noted.

"What's in the chest?" I asked.

Tindra lifted the lid and reached inside. "Cloth. Feels like wool." She held some out to look at it in the light. "Dark cloth."

"Pull some more out," Albin said. Tindra hefted some more out and held it higher. "Looks like woodsmen's cloaks," Albin said. "What else is in there?"

Sabast dug deeper into the chest while Tindra tried to get untangled from the cloak. "I feel a wooden handle," he said, and he pulled out an ax.

"Why'd the council give us cloaks and axes?" I asked.

"Disguises," Halmar said.

I looked at him.

Albin chuckled. "We're going into the Croian capital posing as woodsmen."

"Secure it all for now," I said, nodding. "We need to be ready to leave. Halmar, give me the lantern. I'll put it back."

I rode to the front of the wagon and secured the lantern.

"Find what you were looking for?" the driver asked.

"You know what's back there?"

"Of course," he said. "I helped pack it."

"We'll keep it safe," I said, with a nod.

"I doubt anyone will mess with it anyway, but it's nice having dedicated guards," he said, and cackled.

The sound of cracking whips filled the air. Soon neighs, creaking wagons, and drivers yelling joined. The caravan was underway. We took a direct route to the trade gate. Moving at a steady pace, we left the city before sunlight lit the thick clouds overhead. As the darkness gave way to dim daylight the rain turned into a heavy mist. The wet ground slowed the wagons and the damp air made everyone uncomfortable.

Tindra rode beside me. "This is going to be one miserable trip if it's wet the entire time."

"We'll just have to make the best of it."

I heard her mutter something about optimists as she rode away.

I wasn't expecting Halmar to ride next to me. "A word?"

"What's on your mind?"

"Tindra."

"What about her?"

"Her safety."

"She can take care of herself. She's a good fighter. You know this."

He shook his head. "At night," he said. "Sleeping."

"Are you saying someone might attack her while we sleep?"

"Suspect it," he said.

"Who?" I asked. "Not one of us."

"Guards."

Can I trust anyone on this trip? "Every guard?"

He shook his head again. "A few."

"Why?"

"Don't like a woman in their armor."

"Let me talk to the sergeant."

He shook his head. "Might be one of them."

She swore to have my back. I have to take care of her. I nodded. "Tell Sabast to come to me, please."

"He sent me."

"You talked to him about this first?"

He nodded.

"I'll talk to him," I said. "Tell the brothers to keep an eye on her."

"Anifas will be happy," he said, chuckling, before riding away.

I got close to Sabast. "Talked to Halmar. You have a plan?"

"Not a good one."

"Maybe I can make some improvements."

He shrugged. "She sleeps in the back of our wagon with the driver. We sleep nearby, so no one can get in without one of us knowing."

"Sounds like a pretty good plan. What's wrong with it?"

"The guardsmen will sleep on the ground. If they find out the lone female's allowed to sleep in the wagon, there will be more ill will. Plus, there's the driver."

"I see your point," I agreed, "but why be concerned about the driver?"

"He's one of ours, but I'm sure he has a price."

"Not a loyal mercenary?" I asked, smiling.

"Nils is loyal...until someone pays more."

"What about Halmar? Is he loyal?"

"Of course," he answered. "No question."

I shrugged. "So, he sleeps in the wagon with them."

"What about Anifas?" he asked, smiling. "He'd be sure to stay right on top of her."

"I'm pretty sure it wouldn't turn out in his favor." I chuckled. "I think Halmar's the best choice. Talk it over with him. I'll talk to her."

Sabast laughed and rode off.

I found Tindra riding close to the front of the caravan. "What are you doing here?" I asked.

"Trying to figure out how long this trip's going to take," she answered, frowning.

"You think it'll take longer than our trip here?"

She nodded. "At least a day longer, most likely two. Caravan's moving slower and stopping before moonrise to set camp."

"True," I said. "Come back to our wagon. We need to talk." She gave me a questioning look, but followed. "There's some concern for your safety while we sleep," I said, once we were alone.

"Why?"

"Some guards may be insulted by a woman wearing guardsman armor."

"They should say something. I'm sure I can help them understand," she said, smiling.

"We're supposed to blend in. Sabast and I have a plan. You sleep in the wagon with Nils and Halmar. The rest of us sleep nearby."

"Any particular reason it's Halmar and not you?" she asked, smile growing wider.

"Sabast suggested Anifas would be the most interested in keeping you safe."

"But who'd keep him from doing something stupid?" she scoffed. "You didn't answer my question."

"Principles," I said, returning her smile.

"That's what I thought."

"Either way...do you have a problem with this arrangement?"

"You're right to suspect something. And it's what is best for the team, for you," she said.

"One more thing. Try to stick close to the brothers. Halmar told them to keep an eye on you."

She snorted and rode back toward the front.

I reached into a saddlebag to get something to eat as rain fell again. The downpour became blinding, slowing the caravan to a crawl.

After a while, Sabast came to me again. "Everything in place?"

"As far as I know. Don't think she's happy with the situation, but she'll do what's necessary."

"It's what she does best," he said.

"Appreciate you bringing your concerns to my attention." I looked around. "You know, I traveled this way coming to the capitol and never ran into weather like this."

"Some years are worse than others. With any luck, the other side of the mountains will be better."

"At this pace, it'll be two days before we make it through the pass."

"Nothing we can do about it. I'm sure Croy will still be there when we arrive."

"Right now, I'm more worried about when Satra starts invading Varia," I noted.

"The war council is free to make moves now. Preparations are underway," he said, "just in case."

I nodded and took a drink from my waterskin. He headed toward the back of the caravan, leaving me alone again. Putting my heels to Andale, I looked for Tindra and found her riding near the lead wagon next to Sergeant Elias.

"Anything I should know?" I asked, as I got close.

"I'm helping the sergeant navigate. He isn't familiar with the route."

"No disrespect meant Sergeant, but why did the crown send an officer who didn't know how to get where we need to go?" I asked.

He grinned. "The whole detail's volunteer. I've never been outside the walls of the capital. Seemed like a great opportunity to travel, see my country."

"I can't see much past Andale's nose," I said.

He nodded. "Didn't consider weather when I agreed to lead."

"As soon as I found out, I offered my services as a guide," Tindra said. "I know the route well enough."

"Yes, you do," I agreed. "Think we'll make it to the camp we used when we came from Swinter?"

She shook her head. "Unless this storm lightens, I don't expect to get there until tomorrow evening. One thing's for certain, we won't try going through the pass in the dark."

"I'll let everyone know. See you this evening?"

"Tindra offered to stick with me until we reach Nikulas' town," Sergeant Elias said. "Starting to think she's bucking for a promotion."

"I see." Clenching my jaw, I turned to find the other four. *What is she doing? Guess I should spread the word.*

I found the brothers first, not far behind. "Albin, Anifas...seems Tindra has her own plans for security on this trip." I shook my head and sighed heavily.

"What do you mean?" Anifas asked.

"She's made herself indispensable to our untraveled sergeant. No matter, you two stay close to her. Keep an eye on her, but don't get in the way and don't anger Elias."

"Understood," they said, together, and moved to get closer to Tindra.

It took me some time to find Halmar. I was beginning to think he'd abandoned the mission, but found him riding close to the side of a wagon, trying to avoid the brunt of the driving rain. After filling him in, he grunted and shook his head. "Can I still sleep in our wagon?"

I laughed. "Doubt any one person here could stop you."

He grunted again and I turned to find Sabast.

"Has she lost her mind?" he asked, when I told him what was going on.

I shook my head. "She seemed sane enough to me."

"I expected her to turn on us at some point, but not this soon."

"What do you mean?" I asked, shielding my eyes against a sudden, hard downpour.

"Kurt told me *all* about her," he said, pointing toward the front of the caravan. "She isn't much more loyal than Nils, just demands a higher price. He suspects King Ander paid her to take Croy for him. He told me to watch out for the council's interests, look out for our people. You'd better watch your back."

"Everyone I trust is either dead, missing, or no longer traveling with me," I said, glaring at him. I smashed my fist into my leg. My heart sped up, blood roared in my ears. "The only person on this trip I've come close to trusting is Halmar because he hasn't said enough for me to make an informed decision."

"It's just his way. He knows his place."

I shrugged. "Still, I doubt Tindra's betraying anyone. I think she's making sure she has the sergeant on her side. Some of the guardsmen may not like she's here, but they're still well disciplined. They won't cross their commanding officer. And why would your king want her to take Croy?"

"He has some odd ways about him, likes using people to do his dirty work. Tindra's his favorite because she enjoys dirty work. The dirtier the better."

"Ander's backing this caravan to get *me* in place to kill Eirickson," I reminded him. "You weren't at the meeting. Tindra wasn't part of this mission at first. She insisted on coming."

"Why insist on coming unless someone made it worth her effort?" he asked, raising his eyebrows.

I didn't let him know that I knew why. "I'm sure she has her reasons. She likes a good fight, that much I know."

He chuckled. "She can find good fights without leaving the capital. What she can't get there is the opportunity to seize control of an entire country."

"What about Albin and Anifas?" I asked. "You trust them?"

"Why question loyalties now?"

I pointed at him. "You're the one who brought up the subject. Either way, you didn't answer my question."

"They'll follow orders. You can rely on them"

"Told them to keep an eye on her. If they don't see any betrayal, would you feel better?"

"It'd be a start," he said, "but I still don't like the whole situation."

"Me either. Maybe you should watch her yourself."

"I'll consider it," he said, and headed toward the front of the long line of wagons.

I rode alone for a while, just keeping pace with the caravan. Eventually, the weather broke. It was hard to feel happy when you're sopping wet, but a sense of relief flowed through me when the torture of pelting drops of falling water stopped.

Soon I heard shouts in the distance, coming closer and the line of wagons curved away from the mountain range. I pushed Andale to walk faster and heard one of the driver's yell, "Circle the wagons for the night." Everyone on horseback moved into the center of the rough circle.

"I need everyone's attention!" Sergeant Elias yelled. "Push the wagons together once the drivers unharness their teams. Corral all horses inside the circle. Cook outside the circle. I want to be clear: there will be no fire inside the circle. We do not need injured animals. Anyone not moving wagons should build fires and prepare food. Once everyone has eaten, I recommend you find a wagon to sleep in or you can sleep on the wet ground if you want. Regardless, I expect everyone to be well rested and ready to move early. Get to work. No one eats until we secure the horses. That is all."

The wet ground made for slippery footing and muddy work, but we got the wagons pushed into a makeshift corral. Halmar and I found our team sitting around a fire while Nils cooked. We had a clear view of Tindra sitting at the sergeant's fire. *What are you thinking? You insist I can trust you, only you, then abandon me at the first hint of danger. Maybe Sabast is telling the truth. Maybe her knife slips between my ribs as Eirickson dies.*

"You want me to move to their fire?" Anifas asked, as I sat.

"Don't bother," I spat, looking away from her. "She's a grown woman. She knows what she's doing and what's at stake. Plus, it'd be a little obvious if you're the one to go over there."

"Fitzeirick's right," Halmar said. "Leave her."

Sabast nodded.

Anifas sighed.

"What's for dinner?" I asked.

"Dried meat stew," Nils said. "I recommend crumbling a hard roll or two into your bowl to thicken it."

"I'm sure I've had worse," I said, staring into the fire while the water worked its way to a boil.

"Dinner's just about ready," Nils said. "Who's the first victim?"

Albin lifted his bowl.

While taking my first bite, Anifas said, "I have to know. What's the story behind your scar?"

After chewing the tough meat, I swallowed. "At least you'll know why we're making this trip."

"Sounds fair," Albin said.

I looked at Sabast and Halmar. "Any objections?"

Neither man responded, so I gave a summary of what happened and how I came to be in Varia. Both of the brothers looked terrified while I talked about the branding and living in the tunnels. I thought Anifas was going to throw up when I explained how we survived on raw rats and snakes. Neither of them asked any questions, but both gave their thanks and turned to watch Tindra.

Sabast cleared his throat. "How do you know your mother's dead?"

"I got word from a trustworthy source."

"But they couldn't find your fiancée?" he asked.

"Nothing definite," I said, shaking my head.

"Better for her to be dead. Does Kurt know this?"

I nodded. "He knows enough. He didn't tell you?"

"I didn't ask."

"So why make the trip?" I asked.

"If we win, I'm in charge of operations in the new territory."

I looked at Halmar. "Why did you come?"

"Sabast."

"He asked you?"

"Not exactly," Sabast replied for him. "Offered him a promotion. He'll be my second in command."

I nodded. "Brothers, why'd you two come?"

"The adventure," Albin said.

"Chance to meet women," Anifas chimed in.

I laughed. "Anifas, when you get back to the Varian capital when this is over, be sure to go to the castle and spend some time with Crum...tell him I sent you. I have a feeling you two have much in common."

"I just might," he replied.

"Albin, it seems you haven't learned something about adventures," I said.

"What?"

"Adventures are fun to talk about when they're over, but no fun at all when you're having one," I told him, smiling.

He wrung water from his hair. "I'll have to think about that."

Everyone else laughed.

I finished the meal, thankful it was warm at least, and yawned. "I'm heading to the wagon."

"I'll go with you," Nils said.

For the first time in a while, I had to sleep sitting up. I found a corner and grinned, thinking about Mam sleeping in corners whenever possible.

Chapter 52

During all of the hours of Varian guard training, no one mentioned they use a horn to wake everyone when deployed outside the city. We almost destroyed the wagon trying to exit at the same time.

Everything outside was damp and a cool, fine mist hung in the air.

"Get fires going to cook breakfast!" the sergeant yelled, from the center of the corral. "Once everyone has eaten, move the wagons apart, so the drivers can hitch their teams! After the wagons are ready, everyone else mount up and move out!"

"I'll take care of the fire," Sabast said. "Albin and Anifas, get the grains and a waterskin."

"I'll get my team and gather everyone's horses," Nils said. "Save some food for me."

Sabast and the brothers filled their bowls first. Halmar and I split the majority of what they left, making sure to leave some for our driver. Much like last night, the main redeeming factor for the meal was its warmth.

"Time to move the wagon," I said, to Halmar, after Nils finished eating. He grunted and immediately pulled strength from the ground. Between the two of us, we pushed the wagon out about five paces, leaving plenty of room to hitch the team.

Light rain fell as I mounted Andale and the warm meal became a faint memory. I sighed and settled into the saddle for another day of uncomfortable riding. We didn't move until the irregular circle of wagons uncoiled into a long line. With Tindra staying near the sergeant and others keeping an eye on her, I rode close to our wagon.

The solitary riding combined with sporadic, heavy rain made it seem like the day would never end. Well before twilight, I heard yells and the wagons circled again. Everyone did their jobs and we were eating in no time.

In the middle of my meal I looked around the fire and realized, for the first time in a long time, I wasn't in contact with anyone I'd consider a friendly. *Out here, Tindra's the closest thing I have to a friend.* She had planted herself at the commanding officer's right hand. Sabast seemed friendly enough, but I suspected he didn't have my best interests at heart. The other three took their orders from him. I shivered thinking about how alone I felt in this crowd. Those thoughts weighed on my mind as I choked down the chewy meat and watery broth before crawling into the wagon to go to sleep.

A clap of thunder replaced the horn for waking me. Sabast mumbled something before stirring. I stretched and tried to get the kinks and knots out of my muscles, but my body let me know it was all in vain. We woke the others and hit the ground ready to work. Sabast had the fire going before Sergeant Elias started yelling orders.

"Think it's going to rain all day?" I asked, filling my bowl.

"If it rains much more, we'll have to turn the wagons into barges," Albin said.

Everyone chuckled.

Sabast said, "I think we're getting close to the pass. Weather should break on the other side."

"We aren't too close yet," I said.

"How do you know?" Anifas asked.

"I haven't seen the stone corral I made when I came this way from Swinter."

"You made a stone corral? Why?" Albin asked.

"We had five horses between us. The forest was too dense to use for cover, so I sythed a wall to keep the horses safe."

"You're strong enough to do that?" Sabast asked.

"He is," Halmar said, before I could answer.

Sabast smiled at the big man. "I'll take your word for it."

"Assuming we're not blinded by the rain, it should be easy to see when we get closer to the pass," I said.

"I'll try to keep an eye out for your handy work," Sabast said.

"I'm not saying it's anything to brag about. A quick and dirty effort. I even forgot to make a door."

"How'd you get them in and out?" Anifas asked.

"Sythed a jagged hole in the wall."

"Effective," Halmar said, and chuckled.

I nodded. "Pretty much sums up the entire thing...effective."

"Still," Sabast said, "I'd like to see it."

"Hope you do," I said. "Because it would mean this storm has slacked up."

Everyone chuckled. We finished eating and prepared to move. The continuing downpour again overshadowed the comfortable feeling of a warm meal in my stomach. I frowned at the prospect of another lonely, miserable ride. The rain didn't let up and the wagons turned into the pass without me seeing the corral. I couldn't help but think it seemed almost as dark as the night Crum and I drove through there. At least the sound of rain covered all the noises made by the wagons. I considered pushing Andale into a trot to see if better weather waited on the other side.

After making the turn out of the pass, I almost stopped moving because it was still raining. The only reason I didn't was Andale kept pace with the caravan. Familiar yells letting everyone know it was time to stop for the night brought me a strange sense of relief. Another circle, more work, and another bland meal before I settled in to sleep.

The blaring horn disturbed everyone's slumber. We all grumbled and groaned as we got out of the wagon. There was a pleasant surprise waiting for us; it wasn't raining. The chill in the air and damp smell couldn't wipe the smile from my face. Not a single drop of rain fell as we set about our morning tasks.

"I need to speak with the sergeant before we get to Swinter," I mentioned, while we ate.

"Why?" Sabast asked.

"It's not a good idea for me to get near Stone Roof."

"Heard it's a nice place," he replied. "What have you got against it?"

"Nothing against it as such," I said. "To be honest, I enjoyed my stay there. Question is, how long does Jahon gold a grudge?"

"Jahon's not a bad guy," Halmar said.

"You know him?" I asked.

"Deals with Arne a lot," Halmar said. "Been assigned to him before. Excellent pay."

"Bodyguard?" I asked.

Halmar nodded.

"How recently have you worked with him?" I asked.

"About a year ago," Halmar answered.

"Guess you haven't heard about the fight."

"You got in a fight with Jahon?" Sabast asked.

"No. I got into a fight in Stone Roof. I think several people got hurt. Killed the guy I was fighting."

"You killed a Varian in Stone Roof?" Albin asked.

"No. A Croian named Olver."

"And you left without talking to Jahon?" Sabast asked.

"Wasn't my idea," I said. "Tindra made me leave."

"Hard to believe she made you do anything," Albin said.

"She could make me do —" Anifas began.

I didn't want him to complete his thought. "She's extremely persuasive when she feels the need."

"I think I'd like to see that side of her," Anifas said.

Everyone laughed at him and I said, "Trust me, it's no fun at all."

He frowned.

"Soon as I finish eating, I'll talk to the sergeant. We need everything to keep going smoothly."

"Do what you have to do," Sabast said. "Elias can work something out."

"Any of you have a problem if I suggest we skirt Swinter and meet with the caravan on the other side?" I asked.

Sabast shrugged. "Your call. The council sent us to support you."

"Thanks," I said, and finished the bland meal, before walking toward the sergeant's fire. I stopped outside the ring of guards sitting with him. "Sergeant, a word, sir."

He nodded. "Sit."

"I'd prefer it in private, sir."

He glanced at Tindra and she nodded.

"I need to check out my saddle anyway. Walk with me." We were a few paces away when he said, "What's on your mind?"

"I should stay out of Swinter or at least avoid Stone Roof."

"I know," he said. "I had no intention of trying to wind the line of wagons through there anyway."

"Tindra told you?"

"She did."

"With all due respect, sir, what else has she told you?"

"Nothing you need concern yourself with."

"You didn't answer my question, Sergeant."

"I know, but it's the answer you're going to accept."

"Understood, sir," I said.

"If that's all, you're dismissed."

I nodded and walked back to my team. "Sergeant's already planning to avoid Swinter."

"You don't sound happy. Figured you'd take it as good news," Sabast said.

"He made those plans because Tindra's been talking."

"What?" Sabast exclaimed.

"What else has she told him?" Albin asked.

"He wouldn't say."

"No problem," Halmar said.

"What do you mean?" Sabast asked. "Given what she knows, she could cause all kinds of problems."

"She's good," Halmar said. "Won't cause trouble."

"Maybe I should talk to her," Anifas suggested.

"Leave her alone," Halmar said.

I looked at him. "As much as I want to disagree with you, you're right."

"I don't like this," Sabast said.

"Me either, but we need to get moving before the caravan leaves us behind," I said.

The wagons moved faster on the drier ground. Near midday, the clouds opened again. Everyone got another drenching before we stopped for the night.

I fought back the urge to attack the hornblower after another rude awakening. Looking at the men around me, I wasn't the only one entertaining the thought. At least we were dry, but thunder boomed not far away.

One thing broke the monotony of breakfast. A guardsman walked from fire to fire. He seemed to be delivering orders.

"Hey!" I yelled. "Why'd you pass us by?"

"Sarge said this doesn't concern any of you."

"What? Come here!" I yelled.

He glanced at me before looking toward the next fire. For a moment, I thought he was going to ignore me, but he shrugged and came back.

"What doesn't concern us?" I asked.

"We're getting close to where Satran incursions have happened in the past few months. Elias wants night-watch volunteers, said none of you are eligible."

"Oh," I said. "Sorry to bother you."

He nodded and went on his way.

"Satra this far north?" Sabast asked.

"I thought we were still a ways from Croy," Albin chimed in.

"We are," I said.

"So why are we hearing about Satra here?" Sabast asked.

"Maybe they're getting bored or maybe Eirickson's feeling bold."

"No matter," Halmar mumbled. "Stay on mission."

"He's right. Satran presence or not, if we finish the mission, we change everything," Sabast said.

"True," the brothers said together.

"I need to talk to Tindra," I said. "After dinner, we head for the capital."

"You know how to get there from here?" Sabast asked.

"I do," I said. "Just need to decide which way's faster."

"What options do we have?" Albin asked.

"Either we take the Carved Scar or go in through the mountains."

"The Carved Scar? Sounds like a tavern." Sabast said.

I shook my head. "Man-made pass, the shortest route between this side of the mountains and the Croian capital. But to avoid anyone seeing us we'd have to travel at night."

"And the mountain option?" Sabast asked.

"How Jesca and I got away from the capital. We go further south, turn southwest, and work our way through the mountains. That route puts us on the east side of the capital."

"You did it on foot?" Sabast asked.

I nodded. "Not sure we can do it on horseback,"

"Any other options?" Albin asked.

"We go even farther south and hope the southern pass is open. If the ocean's too high, we can't get through there."

"Then this scar is the only reasonable option," Sabast said.

I clapped my hands together. "Finish eating and get mounted. Unless I say otherwise, plan to ride on tonight."

Everyone nodded and focused on eating.

I waited until we had been underway for a while before riding to the front. "Tindra. A word in private, please."

"Of course, what's on your mind?"

I slowed, waiting until the sergeant was out of earshot. "You made yourself liaison, so tell Elias we're leaving the caravan tonight. If Satran soldiers are this far north, it's best for us to get away from the group and avoid getting caught."

She glared at me. "I didn't make myself anything. I took steps to keep myself safe."

"Doesn't matter, we're leaving. I'm assuming you still plan to go with us."

"I told you I'd watch your back."

"And yet you spent this whole trip ahead of me. Make sure the sergeant knows."

"Of course," she said. "I'll meet everyone at the dinner fire."

I nodded and rode back to pass along the news.

Albin and Anifas seemed relieved Tindra would rejoin us. Albin offered to go find Halmar. Anifas was more interested in keeping his eyes on Tindra. I laughed and told him to enjoy the view while he could, before riding off to find Sabast.

"She didn't argue with the decision?" Sabast asked.

"Not at all."

"Did she explain why she felt the need to get so friendly with the sergeant?"

"She did it to keep herself safe," I said.

"We had a plan to take care of her."

"Exactly what I told her," I said. "After dinner, we change armor and leave."

"And if Elias doesn't let us go?"

"We'll burn that bridge when we get to it," I said, smiling.

Sabast smiled back, nodded, and turned to ride off somewhere.

The sky was still cloudy, but the storms stayed on the other side of the mountains. Despite the better weather, we moved slower than I expected. I think the mention of Satra made everyone a little more cautious. Still, we made good progress and stopped for the night in sight of Nikulas' town. Sergeant Elias accompanied Tindra as we got ready to eat. "Mind if I join you?"

We all stood. "Of course not, sir."

"At ease. I know you six aren't guardsmen; Captain Torsten and Lieutenant Aerison both made it clear to me when I volunteered. Still, I appreciate the way you conducted yourselves and the work you did to make this trip go smoothly. Tindra made sure I knew where to go and kept me informed of any issues that might arise. Fitzeirick, I wish you success in the rest of your journey. I almost regret not being able to go with you the entire way."

"Thank you for the praise and understanding, sir," I said. "I do have a favor to ask."

"What can I do for you?"

"This evening we'll leave this armor behind. Can you return it to the armory?"

"I'd be unfit to command if I were to let such valuable items leave the custody of the Varian guard," he said.

"Thank you again, sir."

I had a mouthful of watery stew when the sergeant asked, "What do you usually talk about?"

"Nothing, in particular, to be honest, sir," Sabast said. "By the end of the day, we're all too tired to do much talking."

"What do you talk about over your meals, sir?" Anifas asked.

"Depends on who I'm eating with," he said. "Lately it's travel plans and potential issues to watch out for."

"Considering the source, I'd guess most of those issues centered on me," I said.

"Not all," Tindra said.

Elias chuckled.

"Good to know," I replied.

"Should I leave you to your meal?" the sergeant asked.

"You're welcome to stay," Sabast replied. "Something on your mind, sir?"

"Is it as bad as she says?"

"From what we know?" I said. "Yes."

"Why not attack Croy in force?" he asked.

"We aren't ready," Sabast said.

"And King Ander wouldn't allow it," Tindra added.

"If we don't stop Eirickson now and instead attack Croy, what happens if we fail? We'll have an even smaller force to face the coming Satran onslaught," Sabast said.

"As much as I hate to admit it, you're right," Sergeant Elias said. "Are you sure the six of you can get to Eirickson? I can send men with you."

"If we can't, Croian forces will come to you sooner or later," I said.

He shook his head. "What can I do to help?"

I looked around the fire. "Wait in town for a week. If we haven't found Eirickson by then, we'll send word. If we find him and kill him, we'll send for your men because we'll need help. If you haven't heard anything in a week, return to Varia and tell everyone who will listen to get ready for war."

"Tindra," the sergeant turned to her, "do you agree with him?"

"Every word."

"The rest of you? You agree?" he asked.

Sabast nodded. "If we don't kill Eirickson, war will come...maybe sooner instead of later. A failed assassination attempt is sure to spur him into action. If he doesn't strike back the Satran leaders might see it as weakness or fear and turn on him."

"They will," Halmar muttered.

"Do what you have to do to win," the sergeant said.

"My plan all along," I replied.

"I'll leave you to your mission. Travel swiftly and, when you get there, strike hard and true. Do your commanders proud," Sergeant Elias said, and walked to the next fire.

Tindra shook her head. "Poor man had no idea what he volunteered for. He has the potential to be a great man, but he isn't ready to lead anyone into battle. If not for my help, this caravan wouldn't have made it."

"Because you're the wise, well-traveled, royal spion," Sabast said.

"I am well-traveled, true, and that's what we needed to get here. Elias didn't think to make sure he had anyone with him who knew the land. He knew, in general, where the caravan needed to arrive, but didn't think to ask if there were any concerns. If I hadn't advised him otherwise, he'd have taken us right through the middle of Swinter. Can you imagine the uproar having this many guardsmen there would cause?"

"Could've been unpleasant," Sabast commented.

"At least the caravan would've been safe," Albin said. "No one there would've dared try stealing anything."

Sabast shook his head. "Word wasn't sent ahead. No one in Swinter expected us."

"Oh," Albin said.

"What's done is done. We need to eat, change, and get on our way," I said.

Tindra nodded.

After our meal, everyone focused on what we had to do. I made sure no one else got in the wagon while Tindra changed.

"What took so long?" I asked, after she climbed back out.

"Had to find the right cloak."

"I'd have helped," Anifas said.

She raised her eyebrows. "I'm certain I'd hurt you more than you'd help me."

Everyone, but Anifas, laughed.

"Albin, Anifas, you two next," I said.

"What do you think of this armor?" I asked her.

"It's stiff. We should have worn it earlier to break it in a little."

The wagon shook back and forth while the brothers changed. They both had bows in their hands when they got out. "We found knives and a large maul under the cloaks and axes," Anifas said.

"Maul's for me," Halmar said.

I looked sideways at him. "I thought you used a sword."

"Prefer the maul," he said, shrugging. "Wasn't worth arguing."

"Suit up," I said. "You three gather the horses. We need to secure everything before we leave."

Halmar made an impression when he climbed out. A large, black figure with a massive, wedge-shaped hammer over his shoulder. He'd frighten anyone who didn't know him.

Sabast was the next to change. He looked more comfortable in the armor than anyone else.

"I take it you've worn this before," I said.

He nodded.

"Any tips?"

"It's like thick leather, takes time to loosen."

I climbed into the wagon and stripped out of my guardsmen armor and still damp clothes. Tindra was right. The layered armor was stiff and hard to get into. It took a while before I had my hammer's harness in place. For the first time since Per gave me the weapon, I couldn't feel it resting against my back. I grabbed the last cloak and made my way out of the wagon.

"What took so long?" Tindra asked, mocking me.

"I had trouble getting my hammer situated," I said.

She smiled and stuck her tongue out at me.

"Albin, Anifas, hand out the rest of the stuff from the chest," Sabast said.

They went to work and soon we had knives inside our boots and axes secured across the back of our saddles.

"Fitzeirick, where are we going?" Sabast asked.

"South until we come to a bridge. Cross it and head west. Probably best we avoid people and taverns."

He nodded. "Sounds good. I have some instructions for Nils. Go ahead and I'll catch up."

Halmar and I pushed the wagon out of the way long enough for Nils to lead the horses out. We put it back before mounting and heading away from the caravan. We could still see the glow from the fires when Sabast caught us.

"Everything's set," he said, as he rode next to me.

"Anything I need to know?" I asked.

"No. It's something Kurt wanted taken care of."

"Where will we bed down?" Albin asked, after we'd been riding for a while.

"After we cross the bridge, we'll find someplace to sleep in the foothills before we reach the Scar," I said.

"Sounds good to me," Albin said.

We rode west of Nikulas' town and followed the river to the bridge. This late at night the path was deserted so we kept moving. We found a well-hidden place to make camp before sunrise. Albin and Anifas sythed a workable corral out of some young trees, while Halmar and I made a shelter inside a hill. If it started raining, we'd stay dry. We decided to go without a fire. The meal of hard rolls, dried meat, and water was no worse than the thin stews we'd eaten before. Going to sleep mostly clean and with a full stomach was a welcome improvement from the hunger and filth I'd dealt with last time I'd been in these hills.

Chapter 53

The sun flew high in the sky when my eyes opened. Tindra and Sabast were gone.

Doing my best to not disturb anyone, I made my way outside, pushed my talent into the ground, and found the two early risers near the horses.

"You're telling me in all your travels you haven't been to the Croian capital?" Sabast asked her.

"For the fourth time, no," Tindra said, aggravation clear in her voice. "I don't know how many other ways to say I've never been here. All my work's been in Varia."

"You mean he's the only one who knows how to get where we need to go?"

"Without attracting unwanted attention, yes."

"I don't like it," he said.

"Why not?" she asked. "What makes you think he isn't going to do right by us?"

"Because he's not Varian *and* this mission is personal for him. Do you think he won't sacrifice the five of us to kill his brother?"

"His half-brother," she corrected.

"Half-brother, brother...doesn't matter. Do you really believe he'll put *any* effort into keeping us safe?"

"I trust him," she said, and paused before adding, "Yes, even with my life."

"And where does your loyalty lie?" Sabast asked.

"With King Ander and Varia," she said. "Didn't Kurt make it clear to you?"

"Wanted to hear you say it."

Ander's more than willing to let me die for the cause. Sabast is right, I'll sacrifice them all, if that's what it takes. What I don't know is who Tindra's trying to convince...Sabast or herself.

I slipped away and stomped back, making more noise than necessary.

"Who's there?" Sabast called out.

"Fitzeirick."

"Anyone else awake yet?" Tindra asked.

"Not as far as I know. What are you two doing?"

"Looking over the horses. Making sure they're sound and the gear's all in good condition," she said.

"Need some help?" I asked.

"No," Sabast answered. "We're nearly finished. Figured everyone would get up and eat soon. What about the rest of the day?"

Scratching my chin, I looked around. "There are usually some good-sized goats around here. We could send the brothers out hunting. It'd be nice to have some fresh meat before we start riding again."

"Is it smart to send out two of us? What if they're spotted or get hurt?" Tindra asked.

"It's common enough for people to hunt these hills," I said, sweeping my arm toward the rises around us. "Chances are nobody would even look twice at them. I'll make the suggestion. If they want to go, they can."

"Do we chance a fire?" Sabast asked, leaving the corral.

"Should be safe enough during the day," I said.

We returned to the shelter and found the other three men awake and eating.

"Albin, Anifas, interested in going hunting?" I asked. "There are usually some nice, fat goats in these mountains. I think we'd all appreciate some fresh meat."

"What's Tindra think?" Anifas asked.

Albin sighed. "She thinks you should think for yourself." He looked at me. "Hunting sounds like fun, when do we go?"

"Head out after you finish eating. I'd recommend heading northwest. If you run across someone, tell them you're out hunting. Don't get hurt," I said.

"I'll go," Halmar said.

"Good," Albin said, smiling. "We'll need you to carry the goat." He slapped his brother on the back. "Choke that down, I'm ready to shoot something." He put their bows together while waiting.

Finished with their meager meal, the three men each took a waterskin and left camp.

"Use your head and be safe!" Sabast yelled, as they left.

"Think they'll be successful?" Tindra asked.

"They're excellent archers," Sabast said. "If they find something, one of them will put it down."

"They'll find something," I said.

"Too early to talk strategy?" Tindra asked.

"If you ask me, we don't know enough about where we're going to enter to get into specifics," Sabast said.

"I agree. Everything I know about the capital is at least a year old. Once we have a look at the area, we can talk strategy. I mean, we have to get inside the wall before we can locate Eirickson," I said.

"So that's the extent of our strategy for now," Sabast said.

"Any ideas for how we'll locate him?" Tindra asked.

"During the day, he'll be at the council hall. After sunset..." I shrugged. "Could be anywhere. Maybe prowl around taverns, listening for gossip."

"Most of us can mingle and not get noticed," Tindra said, "but what do we do about your brand?"

I touched the scar. "I don't know...cover it somehow?" I had nothing to hide, but the mission was more important than my pride.

"A mask would attract attention, cause people to ask questions," Sabast noted.

"True," Tindra agreed. "How about a bandage?"

"No way to bandage over it without covering my left eye."

"Not a problem until fighting starts," Sabast said, shrugging. "Then you pull it off."

I took a moment to think about it. "Sounds like the best solution. Do we have enough cloth?"

"I packed as much bandage cloth as I could," Tindra said.

"Good thinking," I said. "Those porters seemed more interested in keeping us fed than anything else."

"With the scare you put into them, I think they were in a hurry to get us to leave," Sabast said, and laughed.

I smiled. "Did what I had to do."

"Not saying what you did was wrong. Can't argue with the result."

I nodded and laughed.

Tindra sighed and walked back toward the corral.

"Anything else we need to discuss?" I asked Sabast.

He shook his head. "Nothing strikes me as important right now."

"Sometimes the unimportant details turn out to be important."

"Nothing strikes me as unimportant either," he said, grinning.

"Glad we got that settled," I said, and walked to the corral.

"Sabast not being much of a conversationalist?" Tindra asked, as I climbed over the improvised fence.

"Didn't seem like he wanted to talk to me. Just as well, I wanted to check Andale myself."

"No need," she said. "I checked him. Everything's fine."

I debated mentioning overhearing the conversation between her and Sabast when Albin and Anifas ran to the corral. "Decide where you want to cook this thing. We'll eat well this evening," Albin said.

"Go see Sabast," I said. "Where's Halmar?"

"Not far behind."

"He's way too happy about this," I said.

Tindra chuckled. "I have to admit I'm looking forward to some fresh meat myself."

"Guess we'll help get everything ready," I said.

By the time Halmar, dead goat draped over his shoulder, made it back to camp, we had a fire going in a pit. I sythed some supports for the long spit Albin made.

"Who's cleaning this?" Halmar asked.

"I will," Tindra said, pulling a knife from her boot. "Get an axe to cut the head off."

The big man dropped the fat goat in front of Tindra and walked to the corral.

"Fitzeirick, roll this thing over on its back and hold it still," she said.

I did as she asked and she split the belly in one smooth slice before peeling the skin away from the meat.

"Ready when you are," Halmar said, when he returned.

"Hold a moment," Tindra said, while pulling and slicing until most of the skin was free from the body. "Take the head off at the base of the neck and chop all four legs at the knees."

"Move," Halmar said.

I felt energy move through the ground toward him.

Releasing my hold on the goat, I stepped away before he took his swing. The placement wasn't perfect, but he chopped the head and most of the neck off the body. Four chops later and the legs were done too.

"Thank you," Tindra said. "Fitzeirick, I need you to hold it off the ground so I can get the skin off the back."

I did as she asked, but found it hard to hang onto the now slippery carcass. With a few tugs, she had the entire skin lying on the ground.

"After I gut it, one of you take the skin and innards away from camp. We don't need scavengers around the horses."

"I'll do it," Anifas said, with a sly grin.

She looked at him, smiled, and batted her eyes. "I appreciate you volunteering your services."

He smiled so wide I thought he was going to swallow his ears.

"Halmar, do you think you can chop open the rib cage and keep it clean?" she asked.

"I can try," he said, lining up his swing. He pulled in more energy and the axe passed through the goat's rib cage, slightly off center.

"Good enough," she said, continuing the cut with her knife and removing the goat's insides. "My work's done. Get it on the spit and over the fire. Anifas, take this and get rid of it."

He jumped up, grabbed the skin like a sack, and headed away with a spring in his step.

Albin tried to shove the spit stick through the carcass, but wasn't making much progress.

"Let me," Halmar said.

Albin stepped aside and the large man pushed the stick straight through. He looked at me. "Little help."

I nodded, lifted the bloody end of the spit, and we placed it over the fire.

"Now, we wait," Sabast said.

Tindra stared at the fire, keeping track of something. A couple of times she asked us to place more wood in a specific area. More than once she took a long stick and moved the coals around. Soon the smell of cooking goat hung thick in the air. Without warning, Tindra plunged her knife into the side of the goat and cut out a small hunk. Juices flowed from the wound, as she tasted the rosy-pink meat. She smiled and extinguished the fire. "Eat your fill."

It'd been too long since I'd enjoyed wild goat. It tasted bland, but the meat was tender and juicy. Compared to the meager meals we'd had on this trip, it was a king's feast. The way the other five tore into it, I guessed they felt the same way.

"My compliments to the chef," Anifas said, after swallowing his last bite.

Albin looked at his brother and shook his head. "You'd compliment her even if it tasted horrible."

He shrugged.

Sabast chuckled for a moment. "Everyone can rest, I'll get rid of the bones. Where did you throw the guts?"

"Small ravine to the north, not far from here."

"The sooner we get inside the wall, the sooner we get to work," he said, lifting the spit. "Tindra, start working on the cover for Fitzeirick. I want to get on the move when I get back."

"Is this really going to work?" Anifas asked.

"It should," Halmar mumbled.

"What do you think?" Anifas asked, looking at me.

"As long as no one recognizes me, we'll be safe enough," I said.

"Good enough for me," Anifas said, turning to Tindra. "Need any help?"

She smiled at him. "You've done your good deed for the day."

Albin watched her until she made it to the corral and then turned to Anifas. "Brother, give up. She isn't interested in you no matter how hard you try."

"A river will wear down a boulder if it flows long enough," he said.

I couldn't keep from laughing.

"Laugh all you want. You'll see I'm right. It takes time."

"I can't say anything against a man with a lofty goal," I said, still smiling. "Look at me, I plan to overthrow the ruler of an entire country and claim it for myself."

"It's not much different than your father conquering south Varia," Tindra said, appearing next to me with a roll of white cloth in her hand. "Sit still and let me get this disguise in place. Everyone else get ready to go."

Sabast returned as Tindra finished wrapping the bandage. I could see out of my right eye, but she covered the left side of my face along with the top of my head. I couldn't move my mouth much. Keeping the cover in place while talking would be difficult, eating impossible.

"Did he tell you where we are going before you wrapped him up?" Sabast asked.

"No," she said. "But he can point."

I nodded, mounted, and put my heels to Andale. It didn't take long to get to the entrance for the Scar. We found a surprising amount of people still entering the pass this close to sunset.

"Is it always this busy?" Sabast asked.

I shook my head.

He turned and waved our fellow travelers forward. "Tindra, brothers, mingle a little. See if you can find out why everyone's going into the pass so close to moonrise."

We were about halfway through the Scar when Albin made his way back to us. "There's supposed to be a celebration in the capital tomorrow evening."

"Any reason you can think of for a celebration?" Sabast asked.

I shook my head.

Tindra came back with an annoyed look on her face. Anifas trailed behind her.

"Eirickson's wedding is tomorrow," she said. "Big celebration in the middle of the capital tomorrow evening."

I almost fell off Andale when she said 'wedding.' If I could've talked, I would've yelled loud enough to shake the walls of the cavern. Instead, I stared at her in wide-eyed surprise.

"Sounds like we'll have something to talk about over dinner," Sabast said.

We all took the hint and kept our thoughts to ourselves until we found a good place to bed down. Once Albin and Anifas had the horses secured, Sabast made a small fire.

"Why no word from our people around Nikulas?" Sabast asked.

"Maybe it came after we left," Albin said.

"Without a messenger passing us?" Sabast asked.

"We took the most direct route," Tindra said, "but not the only route."

"Maybe your people didn't even know. Nikulas could've held off deciding to attend the celebration until today. He could leave in the morning and still make it," I said, after unrolling the bandage from my head.

"Doesn't matter," Sabast said. "This makes it easier to get into the city and to find Eirickson."

"More guards," Halmar noted.

"He's right," Anifas chimed in. "There could be an army around our target."

Sabast shrugged. "Maybe, maybe not. Fitzeirick, any idea where the ceremony will be?"

"I'd expect it to happen in the council chamber. The eldest Thane will oversee the oaths. The rest of the council will witness."

"Any Croian tradition dictating the correct time for the ceremony?" Albin asked.

"No," I said. "Some weddings happen at sunrise, so the beginning of a new day symbolizes the beginning of the union. Others choose a time they feel holds some significance."

"Does the celebration being in the evening mean anything?" Sabast asked.

"It's tradition to have the celebration right after the conclusion of the ceremony itself, but I don't expect Eirickson to honor any tradition."

Tindra laughed.

"What?" I snapped.

"Do you not see the irony? Your half-brother encouraged the invasion which cost you everything, including your marriage plans. We're about to invade his wedding, intent on taking everything from him."

"Sounds like something Crum would call poetic justice." I chuckled. "He'd probably want to set the story to music." *Too bad he's not here to see it for himself.*

"One thing's certain, Fitzeirick," Sabast said. "Win or lose, a lot of people are going to know something happened. Word will travel fast. Are you ready?"

Attacking a wedding...what if the bride's innocent? A shiver ran down my back and my chest tightened. "Tindra, when the fighting starts keep the bride safe."

"The bride's not important," Sabast argued.

"She may be innocent," I countered. "I don't want innocent blood spilled, if we can avoid it."

"Fitzeirick is right," Tindra said. "I'll do my best to protect her."

"Fine, you do what you want with the bride. *We* need to focus on Eirickson," Sabast urged. "How do we get to him?"

I raised a small copy of the council building from the ground. "The only way I know, for certain, to get in is through the front. Even if there are no guards outside, there will be guards stationed inside. From there it isn't far to the council chamber door. Expect more guards stationed there. I found out the hard way stonesything doesn't work inside the council chamber. I have no idea if it affects wood or fire talents, but I suspect it does."

"How does that work?" Anifas asked, handing me a full skin.

I shrugged. "All I know is I couldn't pull strength from the stone there. The tunnels were the same way, but if we end up there, we have lost."

"How many guards?" Sabast asked.

"Last time I was there, four. Tomorrow, who knows how many will be there."

"Easy to get inside the city walls in the morning. Easy to make our way to the building. Hard to get in," Sabast said, rubbing his chin. "I'm open to suggestions."

Tindra cleared her throat. "If it's easy to get into the city, we should leave the horses before we get near the council building. Easier to move through the crowds on foot and we'll attract less attention. From there, we get as close to the building as possible before charging the door." She stopped talking for a moment and focused on me. "How do you feel about killing Croian guards?"

"Anyone who stands against me can die," I said.

She nodded. "We cut down everyone in front of us as fast as possible. What do you know about the doors?"

"Heavy wood, open inward. I suspect they're barred, but didn't notice last time I was there."

"We'll assume they're barred," she said. "Either the brothers syth them or you and Halmar knock them down. Any guards inside stand aside or die. Once inside the chamber itself, it's all skill and determination. Assuming the bride's innocent, I'll do my best to keep her safe. Everyone else goes for Eirickson."

"The councilmen die after him," I said. "They allowed his treachery. It should go without saying, but kill any Satran you see, too."

"Only inside the building, don't spend time fighting outside," Sabast said.

I nodded. "I want to be the one who kills Eirickson, but if, for any reason, I'm not able, make sure he's dead. Don't let him get away and keep him out of his private chamber."

"That's where the hole is, right?" Tindra asked.

"Yes. I don't know if he can open the floor in the council chamber. I'm sure I can't so I doubt anyone can."

"Eat and get some sleep," Sabast said. "We need to be ready to go at sunrise."

Chapter 54

We all woke when the rain started. It wasn't like the storms we rode through on the way here, just enough to get everything wet. As the clouds broke, we saw the moon near the horizon.

We ate in silence. It felt like knowing it might be our last meal weighed on everyone's mind. I know it was at the forefront of my thoughts, as Tindra reapplied my disguise.

When we heard the sounds of people moving close by, we mounted and worked our way into the crowd. The gate in the southern wall stood wide open without a guard in sight and we entered the city without anyone giving us a second look. Inside the walls, the shouts of men and women hawking their wares filled the air. The smell of breads and meats assaulted my nose. We worked our way through the thick crowd and got off the main street as soon as we could.

We rode past several rows of houses before dismounting our horses. I patted Andale on the neck and felt sad, thinking I may never see him again. He snorted at me and lowered his head to eat grass from someone's lawn as I walked away.

I led us, as best I could, around the growing crowds to the center of the capital. When the council hall was in sight, I noticed a chest high wall around the courtyard. *That's new.* It kept people from approaching the building.

It took a lot effort, and no small amount of rude behavior, but we reached the barrier. Only two guards stood at the door.

"This is too easy," Sabast whispered.

"We aren't inside yet," I mumbled.

"And we're not going to make it to the door without attracting attention," Tindra added.

"Albin, Anifas," Sabast said. "Once we're over the wall, can you drop the two guards before we reach the door?"

"Not from behind you," Anifas replied.

"Either we go over first and you wait, or we move away from you," Albin added.

"Move to get a clear shot. We'll go over the wall when the arrows hit," Tindra said.

The brothers left in opposite directions.

Soon I heard the twang of bowstrings.

The guards at the door slumped over, arrows in their necks.

I helped Tindra get on the wall before clambering over myself. When my feet hit the ground, I glanced left and right.

Albin and Anifas fought people in the crowd to get loose.

I made about three steps before men appeared from underground. Sabast paused and dodged an awkward sword swing from a man rushing toward him. I stopped and checked the ground around us. The well-groomed grass hid four holes giving access to the courtyard from beneath. After a deep breath, I forced the holes closed, crushing two men.

I took a moment and looked back for the brothers. They were finally over the wall, running with their daggers drawn.

Tindra and Sabast fought three guards. Halmar smashed a fourth to the ground with his maul.

Ignoring my disguise, I yelled, "Get to the door, we have to get inside!" and drew my hammer. It was difficult to keep from getting it tangled in my cloak.

Albin raced past my left and sliced across the nearest guard's leg. That gave Tindra enough of an opening to cut the man down while Sabast and Halmar dropped the other two.

Anifas reached the door and called out, "Barred from the inside. Three big timbers."

I glanced over my shoulder before running to the door. Some of the crowd recovered from the initial shock of our attack and clambered over the wall. The ground trembled as the guards trapped underground worked to open the holes.

"We don't have time for anything fancy!" Sabast yelled. "If you two can't syth it open, we knock it down!"

As we reached Anifas, he sagged a little and shook his head.

"Halmar and Fitzeirick, get this door open or this attack is over," Sabast ordered. "Everyone else, keep the crowd back."

I felt Halmar pulling in strength at the same time I did. He swung his maul as I sythed a spike on one face of my hammer. His blow cracked the door. Mine knocked a small hole near the split. We swung again, opening a hole big enough for both my fists to fit through.

"Move," Halmar bellowed.

I turned away and moved between Tindra and Sabast to face down the advancing crowd.

Energy rushed beneath my feet and Halmar roared. "Down."

We dropped to the ground and the heavy door flew into the growing crowd.

Jumping to our feet, we made short work of the guards gawking at the hole where the door used to be.

"How do you plan to keep people out?" Sabast asked, as we hurried past Halmar

"Go," the big man said.

I didn't look back, but I felt the building tremble before stone ground against stone.

We ran into four more guards at the council chamber door. They weren't used to fighting together; we were, and it showed. The last body hit the floor as Halmar bellowed, "Coming through."

Thundering footsteps echoed as he ran down the hallway. Twisting his body, He drove his shoulder into the door. It gave way with almost no resistance and he stumbled into the council room off balance.

I heard yelling and a loud crash.

We ran into the room, ready to rescue our teammate.

Three Thanes stood near their smashed table, watching Halmar push himself up. The oldest Thane stood behind Eirickson and his veiled bride.

"What is the meaning of this?" Eirickson spat. "Who dares disrupt my wedding? Guards!"

I ripped the bandage off and smiled. "Call for guards all you want. You'll be dead before they get here. Tindra, see to the bride."

Eirickson's laugh echoed through the chamber. "Should have known *you* would pick today to attempt vengeance."

Before I could say anything, the bride screamed, "Get away from me. You ruin everything."

I recognized the voice. "It can't be." I froze, not wanting to believe my ears.

Tindra glanced at me, concern etched on her face, before ripping away the cloth covering the bride's face and her mouth dropped open.

Stina.

"I knew I should've had you killed when you brought *her* back home," she yelled. Stina pulled a dagger from somewhere and attacked. Without my armor, she would have gutted me. Her blade opened the first layer of leather and skipped across the metal plates covering my chest.

Tindra reacted before I could and stabbed Stina in the side.

The Varian princess' eyes opened wide. She grabbed Tindra's wrist and tried to speak. Instead, she coughed, spraying small drops of blood on Tindra's face before slumping over.

"Traitor!" Sabast yelled. "I knew you'd betray us. How could you kill the princess?"

He charged and swung his sword at Tindra. She moved, but not fast enough. His strike severed her right hand from her arm. She screamed, grabbed at her arm, and fell to the floor.

Eirickson laughed again and drew his sword.

Through my shock, I noticed something around Stina's neck; the necklace I'd given Aesa, when she became my promised. A fire started in my gut and spread through my body.

Anifas tackling Sabast before he could kill Tindra prompted me to action.

I spun to face Eirickson and locked eyes with him. This time, I wanted him to see what I felt.

"Albin," I shouted, "keep your brother and Sabast apart! Halmar, stop anyone from coming in!"

I channeled all my feelings: anger, despair, doubt...everything and roared before charging my half-brother.

His smile never wavered as he held his blade at the ready.

I knocked it aside with practiced ease and brought the handle of my hammer across my chest before driving him into the wall. He hit hard enough to knock the air out of his lungs.

If nothing else, he wasn't laughing any more.

"Where's Aesa?" I barked. "How did you get her necklace?"

He coughed a couple of times, dropped the sword, and pushed against the handle trying to free himself. "Seems you have excellent taste in women and jewelry, even if you can't pick allies. It was a gift from the Satran general who took your beloved. He kept her for a while. When he grew bored of his new toy, he sold her to a brothel specializing in entertaining soldiers. The way he tells it, she tore her wrists open with her own teeth and bled to death. It only seemed fitting her necklace go to our next Brunor of Croy and soon-to-be Queen of Varia. Alas, she'll never sit on the throne. I wonder what Varia will do to pick their next ruler."

Fury made my blood burn hotter. His ribs cracked as I pushed into him harder.

He wheezed.

"Not that you care, but Jesca's doing well. She'll take the throne when Ander passes," I informed him.

"How do you think Stina disappeared? I've placed people to kill Ander, Ines, and Jesca before sundown. My marriage would have joined Croy and Varia. Now, that country will fall into chaos and be ripe for the picking."

That's not possible. He's lying...trying to distract me.

"People running this way," Halmar bellowed.

I brought the hammer up and across, striking the side of Eirickson's head. His eyes rolled back and I let him slump to the floor.

I turned and found Anifas and Sabast circling Tindra with Albin struggling to keep them apart. *I'm too close to winning. I won't lose because a firesyth can't control his emotions.*

"Sabast," I yelled. "I need you at the door with Halmar. Keep the hole closed."

"No. She killed Stina. She has to die," Sabast spat, without taking his eyes off Anifas.

"Enough," I bellowed. "Stop being stone-headed and think. If warriors get in the door, you won't live long enough to see her die."

He glared, flicked his sword at me, and ran across the room.

Now to save Tindra...if she's still alive. "Anifas, get the bandages and see to her arm. I don't want her to die on the floor here. She deserves better."

Tears streaming from his eyes, he scrambled for the cloth I'd thrown to the floor.

Tindra screamed, voice going hoarse, as he wrapped her bleeding arm.

My heart hurt to hear her pain, but it meant she was still with us.

"Albin, grab the Thanes, and come with me," I said, heading for Eirickson's private chamber.

"Are we going to kill them in here?" he asked, as we entered the dark room.

The four men gasped.

"They may yet live," I said.

"You said they die along with Eirickson," Albin argued.

"You heard what he said about your king's family. I need answers. Keep them in here, out of the way. Can you start a fire?"

"Not without tools," he said.

This is all going to the fire...quickly. I ground my teeth and pointed out of the room. "Go help Halmar secure the door. If your brother's done with Tindra, have him help too. Send Sabast in here."

"What are you going to do with us?" a voice in the dark asked.

I slammed my hammer into the floor. "Anyone who can give me answers, I have a use for. Anyone who can't...I'll rid myself of a burden."

"We all know a lot. We'll tell you everything," an old voice said.

"You may see another day."

"What do you want?" Sabast growled, from outside the door.

"I need a fire," I said. "Fireplace's in the corner of the room."

"We will have words later," he said, through clenched teeth.

"You took it upon yourself to strike down our other firesyth and," I thrust my finger toward the fireplace, "I need a fire *now*."

The air went cold before the fire roared to life, lighting the room.

Memories of the last time I saw this office flooded my thoughts. The waterfall, the pool, and the stone chair, everything looked the same. I glared at the chair, sent my will through the floor, and turned it to dust.

"Watch them," I ordered, placing two branding irons in the fire and walking back to the door to make sure my half-brother was still unconscious.

"What are you going to do?" he asked.

"What I have to," I replied and turned to the Thanes. "If any of you leave this room without my permission, you give up your life."

They all nodded and sat huddled on the floor while I walked back to the fireplace.

After removing my cloak and placing my hammer on my back, I took the irons from the fire. I held a glowing, red T and a bright-red X. A smile crossed my face all on its own.

Sabast's eyes shifted from the irons to my scar. He nodded when I held them out for him to take.

"Keep these hot and follow me."

I dragged Eirickson, by the legs, to the middle of the room before grabbing his neck and pulling him to his knees.

People banged on the blockaded door. The brothers were sweating from holding the opening closed against other woodsyths.

"Albin. Anifas," I called. "I need you."

"But the door," Albin protested.

"I want witnesses anyway," I said. "Take his arms, keep him from falling over."

As soon as their hands left the wood, holes opened in the door. They ran to hold Eirickson where I had him kneeling on the floor.

"Sabast hand me the T, grab his hair, and hold his head up."

Halmar bellowed at the effort from keeping the door closed.

I looked at him. "Step away. Let everyone see."

The opening jammed with people trying to enter the room.

"Everyone here witness the downfall of Eirickson, traitor to Croy!" I yelled, before pressing the glowing letter into his right cheek.

He screamed as he woke. The smell of burning flesh filled my nose carrying memories I'd rather forget. "Hold him fast!" I yelled, dropped the iron, and continued my speech. "He allowed the invasion of our country, allowed savages to kill our people! I declare Eirickson an exile for his betrayal!"

I held my hand out and Sabast handed me the second iron. *He deserves this and more.*

Eirickson screamed before I pressed it into his left cheek.

"No exile has standing in Croy. I, Fitzeirick the last of Eirick's blood, declare myself the new Jarl of Croy. If anyone hearing my voice would speak against my claim, say so now."

I waited, chest heaving from breathing so hard. Looking from one person to the next, pausing at every eye, I dared anyone to dissent.

No one said a word.

"Clear the door!" I shouted. *Time to end Eirickson's reign.*

People pushed back from the opening, yelling for others to clear the way.

I walked behind my half-brother, grabbed him by the neck, and lifted him to his feet. When Albin and Anifas released his arms, he struggled, but I clamped down tighter and pushed him toward the door.

"Halmar, are you hurt?" I asked, as I passed.

"I'll live," he mumbled.

"You and Sabast watch the Thanes while I finish this. Keep Sabast away from Tindra. Albin, Anifas, I place her in your care. It's important to me she doesn't die."

Once I stepped into the hallway, I pulled enough strength to lift Eirickson's feet off the floor.

"Clear the courtyard!" I yelled.

People rushed out, pushing and yelling, as I walked a slow and steady pace and me. Eirickson wailed, as I carried him through the rubble where the entrance to the council building once stood.

"Are you going to beg me for mercy? Ask me to spare your life?"

I felt him try to shake his head.

"Good, saves time."

A chorus of gasps and shrieks filled the trampled courtyard.

I waited until everyone was quiet to start my speech.

"Look upon Eirickson, your disgraced tyrant. He abused his title and committed the worst treason possible. He not only allowed Satra to invade our country and kill our people, he encouraged it. Satra conquered *my* skati by *his* order. He allowed them to savage and kill fellow Croians. When I demanded he defend his country, he branded me, his own blood, a traitor and sentenced me to a hidden prison. I escaped, found out about his treason, and swore my vengeance. Not for myself, but for *my* people and *my* country. Upon Eirickson's death, I declare my right, as the last of Eirick's blood, to lead Croy. Does anyone here dispute my claim?"

The crowd remained silent.

I softened the ground in front of me, buried Eirickson to the middle of his thighs, and hardened the dirt to hold him fast. He fought as soon as I released his neck, but couldn't break my hold.

I reached for my hammer and moved the ground, turning him to face me. "Look at the ruins of the building you used to betray your country and your people. It will be the last thing you see," I said, and raised my hammer.

A spike grew from its face as I smashed the weapon into the top of his head.

The crowd cried out when it struck. The force of the blow split him to the center of his chest.

It felt like I could float, with so much weight lifted from my shoulders. I wanted to scream my joy. Instead, looking at the stunned crowd reminded me there was still much work to be done. I shook some blood off my hammer, placed it on my back, and turned to a nearby guard. "You. Tell me who's in charge here."

"Y...you," he stammered.

I chuckled. "Good answer, but not what I meant. Who is your commanding officer?"

A well-muscled man with a groomed, graying beard stepped forward. He knelt and bowed his head. "Agrim, at your service, Jarl Fitzeirick."

"I still have business inside. Keep this building secure — much more than it was a short while ago. Have every man you can spare working to keep the peace while spreading the word of what happened here. I will not allow this city or this country to fall to chaos."

"As you wish, sir," he said, standing.

"I need escorts for my friends. They will have safe passage wherever they need to go, and any assistance requested to carry out their assignments."

He nodded. "I will assign my best men to them."

The ground pushed my dead half-brother free and I grabbed one of his legs. "Agrim, one other thing."

"Of course."

"If there are any Satran inside our borders, I want them dead. Make it clear to your men. Anyone who looks Satran or sounds Satran — if they even smell Satran — they die. Understand?" I saw Tudal in my mind for a moment. *Good thing he's not in Croy.*

"Your word is law."

"See to it," I said.

"With all speed, Jarl."

I dragged the mangled corpse into the council chamber.

"Sabast, outside is a man named Agrim. Ask him for a horse and a guide. Tell Sergeant Elias I am victorious and need his men. Once you've done that, stay away from the capital. I'll send for you when I'm willing to let you come back."

"Tindra —"

I raised my hand. "I respect your passion, but this is more important. You have my word; we will talk when the time is right."

"Albin, tell Agrim you also need a horse, a fast one. Ride back to King Ander and make sure he and his family still live. When you return with news, find a Croian named Roi living in Swinter. Tell him I need him here."

"With all possible haste," Albin said.

"Anifas, take Tindra. Tell Agrim we need the best herbalist and men to get her to aid."

"Of course. I'll see she's well cared for."

I pulled Eirickson's body inside his office and looked at Halmar. "Has everyone behaved?"

"Haven't moved," he mumbled.

"Please wrap Princess Stina's body with my cloak. See she gets a proper burial."

"The necklace?" he asked.

A tightness gripped my chest. "It's too tainted to keep."

He nodded. "Sorry."

"Thank you."

I swung my half-brother's body over my shoulder, slamming it between me and the Thanes.

Blood splattered on the ceiling, down the wall, and on the councilmen. "That's the blood of your countrymen. Blood you spilled through complacent inaction. I will *not* allow this to continue."

Dragging the body to the waterfall, I looked at the men, opened the hole, and dropped Eirickson. I didn't bother to close the hole. "That is where you four allowed him to put me. What I did was more merciful than what he did to me, what *you* allowed him to do."

One of the Thanes stood and fixed me with a defiant stare. "Now, you see here!"

I grabbed the handle of my hammer, whipped it over my shoulder, and let it fly.

It struck him in the chest, crushing him against the wall.

"I will not be questioned by toothless, lap dogs unable to do their duty!" I shouted.

They scooted away from their dead colleague. The fear on their faces was easy to see as I retrieved my hammer and disposed another body down the hole.

"We could not control Eirickson and knew better than to oppose him," the eldest Thane said.

"What is your name?"

"Roald."

"How long have you sat on the council?"

"I served under your father."

"Then you *knew* it was *your* job to rule. Jarls aren't meant to be dictators."

"Crossing Eirickson would cost our lives," another Thane protested.

I turned to him. "Name?"

"Porsey."

"How long?"

"Handpicked by Eirickson."

"And you?" I asked, pointing at the last, living member of the Council of Thanes.

"Boril, also handpicked by Eirickson."

"Roald," I said. "Was the fourth also Eirickson's?"

"Yes. I did not dare work against them," the old man said.

I nodded and looked at each of the men. "Which of you wants to live under my rule? Before you answer, listen carefully to what I say. My rule will not include a Council of

Thanes. Instead, Croy will have an honest king, not a corrupt coward hiding behind a table of gutless bootlickers. Do any of you care to live in those conditions? Knowing you and your families will live in disgrace and shame?"

"I may be of some use to you," Roald replied, voice still shaky. "I know things, many things the younger members never had a chance to know."

"Tell me one thing you are certain I do not already know," I said.

"I know why Jesca was cast to the vil'fangi."

"You knew she was down there?" I asked, raising my eyebrows as a shiver shook through me. "Did Eirickson?"

"Of course," he said. "He watched your father cast her into the hole."

"Why put her in those tunnels? Surely she would have been useful as leverage on King Ander."

"Stina was not the first attempt at marrying a Varian princess to Eirickson. When Eirick found out the Varian royal family was fleeing his invasion, he had Jesca captured. He brought her here to wed Eirickson and link the families together. She proved unwilling, eventually turning violent. Eirick cast her out of the world after she tried to cut Eirickson's throat."

The room spun around me. I stumbled before smashing my hammer to the floor to steady myself. After several, deep breaths, the dizziness cleared, but I still felt sick to my stomach. "Swear on your life you'll serve me, as you served my father — without question."

He dropped to his knees. "Until I die, my loyalty to you will not falter."

"You two," I said, turning to Porsey and Boril. "Why should I allow you to live?"

Porsey looked at Boril. Boril nodded. "It doesn't matter what you do to us, you've doomed the whole country."

I glared at him. "What do you mean?"

"Roald wasn't privy to Jarl Eirickson's dealings with Satra." Porsey answered.

I tapped my hammer on the floor. "That's not a useful answer."

He cowered. "Eirickson sacrificed your skati to save the country. He wanted to marry Stina to join the two nations against Satra, stop them from taking over everything."

"I don't believe you," I said, resting my hammer on my shoulder. "Crum saw him planning with Satran generals. A Satran general gave him Aesa's necklace."

"I have nothing to gain by lying to you," he said, hands raised. "Eirickson was lulling Satra into a false sense of security."

"Why not approach King Ander, propose an alliance?"

"And openly betray the agreement which saved most of Croy from Satra?" Boril noted.

Is it possible Eirickson was telling the truth? Are Ander and his family in danger? "Can either of you prove this?" I demanded.

Both shook their head.

I raised my hammer. "Then you are of no use to me."

"If you kill them, you're no better than your half-brother," Roald interjected.

"Why do you care?" I asked, glancing toward him.

"If you're no better than the evil you're replacing, why bother? Let the country fall to Satra." he replied and sat next to Porsey and Boril.

I took a deep breath and turned toward the door. "Halmar!"

The big man appeared in the doorway.

I pointed to the younger councilmen. "Take these men outside. Find Agrim. Tell him I said they are under house arrest. They die if they attempt to leave their homes."

He stomped over, tossed one over each shoulder, and left the room.

"You can't lock them in their homes forever," Roald said, once we were alone.

"I know."

"What will you do with them?"

"It's not important right now," I said, shaking my head. "I do need something, though."

"What?"

"A safe, comfortable place to stay for the night, a meal, and a good night's sleep to be ready for the morning," I said.

"May I ask what happens in the morning?"

"I start rebuilding my country and putting plans in motion."

"Plans?" he asked.

"Yes, plans. First, to take back my homeland. Then, I will eliminate the nation of Satra."

To the reader:

Thank you for reading this novel. I encourage you to leave a review at your preferred book retailer. If you enjoyed my story, please recommend it to your friends.

You are welcome to follow me on social media at:
www.facebook.com/JAGuynnAuthor
www.twitter.com/JAGuynnAuthor

Also follow my publisher at:
www.facebook.com/3220Group

Other titles by J.A. Guynn

Branded Book 2: King
Branded Book 3: Conqueror
Water Princess: Through the Storm

www.ingramcontent.com/pod-product-compliance
Lightning Source LLC
Chambersburg PA
CBHW020839020726
47497CB00005B/1176